Stunt Road

A novel by

Gregory Mose

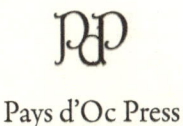

Pays d'Oc Press

*In memory of my father, who taught
me the value of going it alone.*

ISBN: 978-0-615-30663-6

3

I have seen wicked men and fools, a great many of both; and I believe they both get paid in the end; but the fools first.

– R. L. Stevenson

Praise for Stunt Road

"clever, witty, and at times laugh out loud humor"

"perfectly captures the essence of LA culture"

"current and captivating"

"Strong writing, heady moralistic battles laced with sharp wit, and a cinematic feel make this a very enjoyable read."

"an engaging combination of humor and drama"

"a novel of ideas wrapped up in the guise of a thrilling read"

"mystery, suspense, conspiracies, corporate intrigue,...new age mysticism, for-profit religions..., and a little bit of a love story... very funny pop culture references, and a potential new self-help meme (What Would Jim Rockford Do?)"

"compelling, original and consistently surprising"

About the Author

Gregory Mose is a lecturer in law, politics and creative writing in Aix-en-Provence, France. *Stunt Road* is his first novel.

PART ONE

1

I should have trusted my instincts.

Earthsong. It sounded like a progressive music camp where hippie parents send their kids to learn to meditate and play the bongos. The way I was feeling, I had no business coming anywhere near a restaurant called Earthsong. But it was Diego's party. He was my best friend.

"Come on, you can put up with vegan finger foods and movie industry people talking about karma for a couple of hours, can't you? Emily's coming. And it's open bar." Diego can be very persuasive.

Just ten minutes from Malibu, tucked away in a quiet fold of Topanga Canyon, Earthsong billed itself as a spiritually-minded retreat from the crass commercialism of LA. As if to keep the material world at bay, a large statue of Kali guarded the entrance, waving swords and severed heads at me as I parked at the end of a row of Mercedes and BMWs. Edging past the god of death I descended a set of stairs and joined a well-dressed crowd scattered in groups on the restaurant's creekside patio among gnarled oak trees, fountains and oversized pottery. A faint smell of incense drifted through the warm June air. It was like arriving at the country estate of a wealthy Hobbit. A Hindu Hobbit. It could only mean trouble.

I felt the urge to sneak away again – I just wasn't in the mood for a party full of flaky strangers – but I shook it off and went in search of a drink. Two waitresses were carrying trays of wine glasses, but they both seemed determined to avoid me. One of them had just hurriedly shot the gap between a hyperactive scriptwriter and a large plant when I spotted Diego whispering into the ear of a pretty blonde. I hesitated, not wanting to butt in, but he waved me over.

"Hey Pete, how's it going?" Diego's smile was almost broad enough to eclipse his bald spot. I glanced at the girl. Clearly he expected to score.

"Fine, just fine. Nice party. The studio's really paying for all this?"

"Of course. Got to show some appreciation to the cast and crew. And to friends of the director of course... Speaking of which, let me introduce you, this is Stacie."

"Stacie Sullivan. Technical consultant," she emitted in a sharp, strong, controlled voice. "Good to know you," she added, as if as an afterthought, and held out a lean hand to shake.

"Peter McFadden," I replied, taking her hand and shaking it as firmly as it seemed to invite. "Party crasher."

A faint smile lingered on her face as my attempt at humor bounced off her and clattered to the floor. Diego maintained a patriarchal silence for a second or two before he intervened.

"Pete's an old friend of mine. Computer animation geek, nothing to do with the film. Pete, you drinking the chardonnay or the pinot grigio?"

As if on cue a waitress appeared out of nowhere and handed Diego a glass of pale white wine, which he passed on to me like an aid worker handing out food rations. I couldn't help but smile. To me Diego would always be the sloppy twisted film student I'd shared a room with at UCLA, and this annoyingly smooth young Hollywood director he had become seemed like an imposter. Stacie was clearly taken in by it.

"Cheers then," said Stacie, holding up her glass. "Nice to actually talk to someone who doesn't work in Hollywood."

"Well, I have to admit, I did spend a couple of years in the business, sort of."

"But you're sort of out it now?"

"I'm sort of out of a job now." I did my best to smile and glance around casually, hoping to avoid the look. I would usually get one of two looks: either the smeary greeting card "I'm so sorry" look, or that tightening of the lower lip and quick nodding of the head which said "I feel your pain, but we've all got to hang in there sport." They both sucked. What I got instead was worse: an unobstructed view of Daniel, miserable evil you-got-Emily-and-I-didn't-you-bastard Daniel, giving the love of my life's perfect backside a lingering squeeze. I quickly looked back at Stacie.

"Oh, sorry to hear it," she said gently. "But you did something with computers?"

I glanced at Diego, who was elbowing me in an almost subtle and mildly painful way while waving over another woman. "I was doing CGI work for a cybergnat in Pasadena."

She stiffened slightly. "I'm afraid I don't know what that is." Something in her voice made me feel that this was my fault.

"Computer generated imagery, special effects kind of stuff," I answered, perking up at the opportunity to explain possibly the only thing I'd ever been passionate about. I'd been proud of my job at Alcantrix, and not too bad at it either. Making monsters, building spaceships, designing planets to help fill the sitcom-bleached void that used to be the territory of children's imaginations – it was every boy's dream. Well, it was mine, at least, and it had come true. Until I screwed it up. That's an ugly story, best forgotten. It turned out that my boss didn't have quite the same sense of humor as I did, especially when it came to prank video clips involving him and several barnyard animals that a thoughtful colleague of mine accidentally forwarded to him. Not my proudest moment. Six months had passed, but the blood still rushed to my face whenever I thought of it.

Stacie encouraged me to get back into the saddle and wondered aloud if low self-esteem might be holding me back. This happened to me from time to time, I'd meet sensitive people who wanted to help me. Not that they wanted to give me a job – no one wanted to do that. They just wanted to talk to me, get to the root of my problems, help me think through my situation and visualize a positive outcome. It drove me nuts.

"I'm not worried," I insisted. "There are a lot of options out there." This was my standard line. Vague and positive. People love that.

"Excuse me," Diego interrupted as a tall, striking Chinese woman, 40-ish I'd guess, arrived in answer to his slightly manic hand gestures. "Lin, this is my best friend Pete McFadden. Pete, this is Lin."

We shook hands. "A pleasure," she said in a crisp, almost melodic English accent, eyeing me skeptically and waiting for Diego to explain his oddly placed enthusiasm. But Stacie was not so easily derailed.

"Peter here is unemployed," she remarked, as if this were good news. "I was just about to ask him his sign. If it's not too personal a question," she added, turning to me.

I gave her a blank look.

"You know, your star sign, in astrology."

"Oh, Leo."

"Thought so," she said, with a smug smile creeping over her face. "You're obviously really intense, energetic, assertive. Classic Leo. I wouldn't worry – you won't give up until you achieve your inner goals. Do you know your ascendant?"

I'd gotten used to this, too. Most people on the planet are content to read a horoscope, accept it if it's good, laugh at it if it's bad, like you do with fortune cookies or those eight-ball shaped fortune tellers you get in magic shops. But in California you inevitably get stuck talking to someone who takes astrology seriously and wants to discuss its finer points as a doctor might talk about the latest advances in gene therapy. And there's no arguing with them either. Point out that the system depends on a pre-Copernican view of the universe with the earth at the center, they will tell you "oh, they've adjusted it for that," as if it's a minor point that can be fixed with a little adjusting. Ask them how a random pattern of stars could affect our characters, they'll make vague references to the moon and the tide. Any excuse to convince themselves that they have access to answers that you don't, that they can know your weaknesses even if you are oblivious to them. Any excuse to be able to judge you. I was not in the mood to be judged that evening.

"Sorry, but I don't buy into astrology. Too medieval a worldview for my taste, destiny and fate and life being ruled by the stars."

She flashed a knowing look at Lin. "That's a common misconception. Astrology is not medieval. It's been practiced since ancient Sumerian times. In any case its ancient origin doesn't make it outdated, any more than it makes agriculture outdated."

It was my turn to glance at Lin. No response but a funny, concerned sort of expression on her face. Diego looked panicked. I realized that I was probably embarrassing his girl, maybe blowing his chance at scoring, but somehow I couldn't hold back. I was already in a bad mood, and "serious" astrology pissed me off. I'd made a living indulging people's fantasies just like astrologers do, but I never stood around at parties trying to make evolutionary arguments for the existence of three-headed dragons. I'd always found much simpler ways of embarrassing myself.

"Okay, but the constellations have changed since then. We've discovered new planets. The sun and stars don't revolve around the earth anymore, last I checked."

"That's been adjusted for." Her smug smile remained, but she was beginning to sound weary, like a mother telling her kid to brush his teeth.

A good-looking guy – late 50's, wearing a blazer and that classic Yankees baseball cap people wear when they're too old to be wearing baseball caps – drifted up next to Lin and took her hand. Diego narrowed his eyes at me and his head trembled a little. Stacie smiled at the newcomer but continued her argument with me.

"You see astrology, Peter, is actually very scientific."

"Can we change the subject..." Diego began.

"But science is about observation and experiment and all that."

"And three thousand years of observation isn't enough for you?"

"People see what they want to see. They just want a little reassurance that they're not messing things up. I even saw something in the paper the other day on consulting the stars when deciding where to go on vacation, like Jupiter cares whether I go to Tahoe or Tijuana. Trust me, astrology's a con."

Stacie looked pleased, and just a little bit vicious, answering "I teach astrology, both western and Vedic. I also work as a consultant on mind, body and spirit issues generally."

"Oh." Shit.

"If the article you read was the one in the LA Times in April, I wrote it." She stared right through me as she might the remains of a bug on her windshield. Pathetic. I'd had months to cultivate an air of bitter middle class disillusionment, and it turned out I wasn't even good at that.

"Of course there's a big difference between the rubbish horoscopes you get in the Sunday paper and the experience of consulting a talented practitioner like Stacie." Lin's soothing voice, each of its elegant English syllables gently foreshortened by a hint of no-nonsense Chinese, seemed immediately to dampen any hostility that had crept into the conversation, but its contrast with my own made me feel all the more ridiculous for not knowing when to shut up. "I used to be very skeptical as well – of course in Hong Kong I grew up with Chinese astrology, but I never thought much of it – but then I met Stacie. I can't claim to understand why it works, but in her hands, astrology works. Even Vasili can't argue his way round that."

She pulled her partner's hand closer and gave it a brisk rub between her own, a sort of consolation for his inability to argue away her belief in astrology, or maybe a gentle warning not to try.

"The thing is," I answered, determined not to give up, "of course it seems to work. It's really not that hard to make a bunch of generalized observations and have a few of them turn out to be right."

"But so many seem to be right, and so few wrong," Lin objected.

"That's because we remember the right ones and forget the wrong ones. It's just a question of understanding human nature."

"The best psychologist in the world couldn't get the results I do." Stacie was getting mad. Diego tried to interrupt again but I wouldn't let him.

"He could if he dressed it up with some New Agey terminology, based it on something a little spooky. You don't have to be the Bagwan Sri Rajneesh. Given a little time, I think I could do it myself.

Stacie scoffed. "Not a chance."

"Can I, um, break in here for just a second." Diego sounded stressed and irritated. "I just wanted to introduce you two..."

At this point Lin's partner, who so far had listened silently to our discussion with a bemused look on his face, held out his hand to me. "Vasili Papayannis." My hand shook his up and down, mechanically, but every other biological process in my body had frozen. Vas Papayannis. Damn.

The world of computer-generated imagery is a constantly changing one, but there are a few names that have stuck around right from the beginning. Everyone knows ILM and Pixar and those guys. But one layer down on the food chain there were a handful of animation studios doing amazing

CGI work. And Vas Papayannis' company IMaginInc was one of the best. The guy was a legend, and I'd have killed to work for him. Shit, I'd have killed to work as assistant to his PA's secretary. Getting this bastard his coffee in the morning would have been a good career move for me even when I had a job. I'd sent his company my resume three times. And each time it had bounced back off his human resources department like a rubber ball. "Thank you for your interest in IMaginInc. Your credentials are impressive, but unfortunately do not suit our immediate requirements. Best of luck in your future endeavors." Yeah, fuck you too.

"Er, Peter McFadden, nice to meet you, although I feel like I already know you. I mean, not, you know, know you, but, well..." Duh.

"Pete here is in your line of work," Diego explained, smiling furiously at me and digging his heel quickly into the top of my foot.

"Really? Who you working for?" He was that type of overachiever who could act like your best friend in the way you might pet someone else's dog.

"Well, I was an animator with a company called Alcantrix, but I..."

"Pete's taking some time off to think about what direction he wants his career to take." Good old Diego.

"Alcantrix, I know them. That's Dave Abramovitch's outfit, isn't it? Hey, you ever see that barnyard video clip of him that was floating around the internet last year?"

I smiled weakly.

"So where you looking to go now?"

"I'm hoping for a bigger studio job. I, um, I'd like to work for you, to tell you the truth."

This is where I expected the guy to look nervous, but he didn't even blink.

"Never know," he said casually, "when we get to a point where we're hiring again... But listen, about what you were saying, how would you do it, make up your own system of astrology?"

That had to be one of the most pathetic changes of subject to avoid an awkward conversation I'd ever heard. Whatever, this guy would never give me an interview, much less a job.

"Well, first of all I'd decide on a handful of personality types, make them as broad and vague as possible, and then tack them onto something else instead of the positions of the stars. Come up with some kind of formula where you would plug in people's birthdays, or the number of freckles on their noses, anything. Any excuse to assign them to one of the personality types."

"And then?" Lin and Vas both watched me intently, as if something monumental depended on my answer. Stacie had turned her back to me and was involved in a whispering argument with Diego.

"I'd have to think about it a little more," I said, becoming flustered. "You'd need some kind of spiritual-sounding pretext, I think, some reason why it was all supposed to work. Something to do with Mayan pyramids, maybe."

"But what you're saying is that there'd be no real connection, nothing genuinely causal. And then you'd just tell people what you think they want to hear?"

"Exactly! If you played it right, I think it could be just as convincing as astrology or tarot cards or whatever."

Vas turned to Lin and raised an eyebrow.

"I've got to admit," she said thoughtfully, "if someone could show me that that worked as well as astrology, it would be food for thought."

"I think it would be a little more than that, Lin." This was too good to be true. Vas was on my side.

"It wouldn't actually prove anything, though..."

"So Pete," Vas turned back to me, "is this something you're actually working on, or is it just casual party bullshit?"

"Well..."

"Because I'd be really interested to see how it works. It's kind of a running argument between me and Lin, this whole astrology business. I'd be pretty excited if someone could come up with proof like that. Lin's very open-minded about it all."

"It's kind of a work in progress." Yes, inspired. Brilliant. Completely nuts, but anything, anything to get this guy on my side, was worth a try.

"Great. Listen, here's my card. When you've really got it polished, give me a call. Great stuff."

Vas and Lin were dragged off by a few of the other guests – employed-looking sort of people – and Stacie broke off from arguing with Diego and rushed to join them. Diego just glared at me for a minute before administering a not-too-gentle smack on the side of the head.

"Nice people," I offered.

"Well done, dickhead. Can you not possibly spend five minutes, just five minutes of your pathetic failure of a life, without opening your mouth and pouring out a bucketful of idiotic bullshit?"

"I think we hit it off. He found me interesting."

"Sea urchins are interesting. They still don't get jobs. Hopeless."

"Yeah, well while you were battling it out with Mystic Martha, Vas gave me his card. Said to give him a call." Diego's eyes grew very wide, and then contracted again right down into two skeptical little pinpricks.

"Why?"

"He asked me to do him a little favor, and he made it sound like maybe if I succeeded he might do me a little favor in return."

Diego shifted gears from scowling to beaming in 0.6 seconds. After a few Yes's and high fives – he'd really been trying his best for me – he asked me what the favor was.

"Well, he was just hoping, um, all I have to do is disprove astrology."

Diego stared blankly at me. "Oh, is that it?"

"Yep."

"Disprove a system of thought that is more widely believed than Christianity? Sure that's all?"

"That's all."

He nodded his head slowly and, with less conviction this time, hit me in the head again. "Sorry, man."

He was being called away by some of the other guests and slowly turned to go.

"Hey Diego?" I called after him.

"Hmm?"

I just stared stupidly back at him, the words not coming.

"Don't mention it," he muttered, and left me alone in the hum of the crowd.

2

"Would you get me the Parmesan cheese? Oh, no, sorry, I keep it in there now." It was a few days later, and I was hiding in my mother's kitchen.

My parents lived in a Spanish style four-bedroom house with pool, nestled in a Spanish style four-bedroom sort of cul de sac in Woodland Hills. I spent my childhood in that same quiet landscape of stucco walls, dark brown window frames and undulating S-bend tiles that rolled across the roof like a terracotta ocean, and my parents were spending their semi-retirement there. Most of my friends had endured childhood dramas of divorce, a parent dying, being abandoned on a mountain to be suckled by wolves, stuff that had made them happy to grow up and move on. But my folks, they never moved, never divorced, never even seemed to fight much. I'd had an idyllic American middle class sort of childhood, and part of me had never really left it behind. That house was still home, still the place I grew up in, and still the emotional low ground I inevitably slid back to like the smog that collects on the Valley floor.

I found my mother's Parmesan for her – not the real stuff, but the long lasting powdery version in the green can – and she kept on cooking while we talked about nothing. Then I noticed her starting to fidget, and the pauses between sentences growing longer. That warned me that something was coming.

"I had lunch with Sue the other day," she said in her typical way of launching into a story entirely out of context.

"How's she doing?" I asked, glancing out the kitchen windows at the juniper hedge, which was desperately in need of trimming.

"Really well. She just had some dental work done, and she looks so much better. It used to be so embarrassing, trying not to stare at that gap while she talked. Well, Dr. Kim did a really nice bridge and she looks wonderful."

"Hmm, that's great."

"Well," she continued after a pause, "now, Peter, I hope you don't mind, but I mentioned to her a little while ago that you were still having some trouble finding a job..."

I rolled my eyes and puffed a little, as my teenage self had done a thousand times. Mom glanced away as if she smelled something burning, then continued "... and she spoke to her husband Phil about it. You remember Phil, don't you? We ran into him that one evening at Puccini's, around Christmas I think."

I remembered Phil. He was bald.

"Phil's the manager of the San Fernando Savings branch down on Fallbrook, and he said that they're always looking for good tellers. He said he'd have to check with his personnel people, but he seemed pretty sure that..."

"Mom."

"Well honey, it is a job, after all."

"I'm not a bank teller. I have no interest in being a bank teller."

"Sometimes you have to start small and work your way up. You would learn all about banking and then, who knows? You could do all sorts of things with a background in banking."

"Mom, I'm not a kid just out of high school looking for a job. For Christ's sake I've got a degree from UCLA and six years of work experience."

"Please don't swear. I'm only trying to help."

"I know, I'm sorry."

"I understand that you're looking for a better position than that, but maybe, just in the meantime, you should be willing to consider something that isn't quite so ambitious. There must be so many jobs out there that you could do really well if you put your mind to it. But you're not going to find them if you refuse to look at anything less than perfect. Your brother even worked for free for a while, remember?"

Yeah, I remembered. That unpaid internship at the State Department before he went off to Harvard. Poor guy. I tried not to let all this get to me, but when your own mother tells you to set your sights lower, it's kind of hard. After a few more helpful suggestions, such as "maybe you should write a résumé," and "aren't there people who specialize in finding other people jobs?" I managed to turn the conversation in a less painful direction. Dad came home, we had a nice dinner with minimal controversy, and then I drove back to Tanya's.

Tanya was a relatively new addition to my life, although it didn't feel that way. She was an okay girlfriend: pretty without being unobtainable, neither fat nor thin, smarter than average but not overly ambitious. Kind of like a peace lily: decent looking, unexceptional but easy to maintain. I wouldn't have put it that way when a mutual friend introduced us at a party almost two years ago. She was a junior associate at a law firm in Studio City doing real estate law, and she had seemed sexy, intelligent, upwardly mobile. We had a great few months together when we first started dating. We both had a taste for long lazy weekends, getting up late and spending the day watching crap movies on cable and eating popcorn. We didn't challenge each other, but we also didn't judge each other, and, thinking back on it, we were happy. Up until meeting Tanya I'd nursed my old unspoken crush on Emily, one of my college friends, and used it as a sort of excuse to avoid serious relationships. But when Tanya came along, I guess I was ready to grow up a little. I accepted that my idealized longing for Emily was becoming silly, and for the first time I was with someone I really cared about.

But things changed when I lost my job and moved in with her. It had seemed like a good idea at the time. Things were going well between us, what could go wrong? I'd have a new job soon and life would be better than ever. But it didn't work out that way. The new job didn't happen, so I played video games and moped. Tanya got herself a new job with a bigger firm and a paycheck to match. I grew bitter, she grew resentful. After just a month of sharing a bathroom seven days a week, the stress of familiarity started to take its toll. She nagged me about cleaning the apartment. I nagged about her nagging. And somewhere in the middle, the spark died.

By the time I reached her apartment that evening I wasn't in the greatest of moods, having spent my trip across the Valley with "Welcome to San Fernando Savings, how can I help you?" echoing in my head. Tanya was there, decked out in her standard ratty old college sweatshirt and pajama bottoms, puffing distractedly on a cigarette, watching a game show on TV. She glanced in my direction as I came through the door, but her attention quickly returned to glowing screen in front of her. The cold remains of a pack of instant noodles sat on the coffee table, along with a half-finished two-liter bottle of Diet Coke and the Calendar Section of yesterday's LA Times.

"Hey, you still up?" I asked absent-mindedly as I closed the door behind me and turned the bolt. A moment of silence followed.

"It's 10:30," she responded. The look in her cavernous eyes as they peered at me from under a tired tangle of hair seemed to tack a silent "you dimwit" on the end. Her attention was drawn back to the television. I knew better than to interrupt again, so I kicked off my shoes in silence, pulled a beer out of the fridge, and joined her.

"Mom and Dad say hi," I ventured during the commercials. They hadn't really. They never did. My parents didn't particularly like Tanya, and she knew it.

"That's nice," she replied mechanically. "How are they?"

"Fine. Dad scored two birdies yesterday."

"Go Dad," she muttered.

"How was your day?"

"Fine. Don was being an asshole again. He keeps hinting that times are tough and they might have to let someone go, and then dumps more work on me. If there is that much work around then times can't be that tough, can they?"

"He knows you won't quit."

"Whatever. It's just a job."

"Speaking of which, Mom wants to get me a job as a bank teller," I added dryly, assuming the irony spoke for itself.

"Hmm, where?"

"Well, the offer was for San Fernando Savings, but I think I should hold out for Wells Fargo, don't you?" Maybe she was right, maybe the best I could hope for was a career in customer service, but I wasn't about to admit it.

She just stared, and I thought for a second that she didn't get it.

"Tanya?"

"You don't need to be stupid about it," she said after giving me a brief contemptuous look. "It wouldn't be that bad."

"Bank teller," I repeated, clearly, just to be sure we were talking about the same thing.

Tanya blew out a puff of smoke and shrugged. "Better job than you have now."

"It's one step up from pizza delivery."

"Since when are you such a snob, anyway? I've worked some shitty jobs before. I even spent a summer working at the Gap."

"Tanya, it's not that being a bank teller is the worst thing in the world, it's just that I'm not one. I need to get my career back on track, and I'm not going to be able to do that standing behind a counter helping people fill out deposit slips." As if my career had ever been on track. As if I even had a track. I was as trackless as a fucking pachinko ball.

"Fine, whatever." Tanya's attention returned to the TV screen, which had started counting down the best music videos of the 1980s without the slightest doubt that we cared. We sat in silence, listening to Madonna and Culture Club squeak and croon with all the neatly packaged sterility of a children's breakfast cereal. Eventually Robert Palmer showed up with his leggy, humorless guitar girls pretending to play in the background. "I always hated this one," Tanya murmured. Me too, I agreed dutifully, although I remember having been pretty beguiled by all that red lipstick when I was younger. Tanya smiled at me in a moment of false complicity, then turned her head again to watch the video that she thought we had managed to share a dislike for.

Duran Duran finally spelled the end for me – I took my laptop into the small spare room and surfed the net for what seemed like an hour. By the time I emerged into the living room, it was past one. I hadn't noticed the TV being turned off, but Tanya was already sound asleep.

3

Even the laziest of cynics can reduce the ancient arts of divination to a series of bumper stickers.

"Astrologers do it with stars."

"Numerologists do it with numbers."

"Ceromancers do it with molten wax."

"Geomancers do it with marks in the sand."

And Pete McFadden? What was he going to do it with? Vas Papayannis had thrown down the gauntlet and, to my credit, I'd taken it up without a moment's hesitation. Nearly. Okay, there were a few days in between which I'd spent playing video games, maintaining a steady beer buzz and feeling sorry for myself for having screwed up my chances by not knowing when to shut up.

But then I'd pulled myself up by the bootstraps. The following Friday night Diego and I had met up at Pickwick's, a slightly grungy English pub on Ventura where we hung out. It's not that it was such a great bar or anything, but it was more or less middle ground for our small group of friends, and it had the advantage – rare for an LA bar – of not being filled with hormone-enhanced jocks in tank-tops trying to score with silicone-boobed office girls. Diego and I were standing at the bar, enjoying the fact that the particularly bad band that were being passed off as "live music" that night were taking a break, when suddenly I felt a hand on my shoulder, and there was Emily.

Emily and I had met during our first week at UCLA and somehow had stuck together ever since. I liked her from day one, and continued to like her even when it became clear that she wasn't going to sleep with me. She was a little off-beat, quirky but self-assured in that vaguely disturbing way of only children. Her parents had both been college professors in some scary place out in Montana, before her mom died and Emily moved to LA with her dad, so her oddness could be explained by a bizarre childhood filled with books, squirrels, intelligent conversations and no TV at dinner. Now she'd become a math teacher at a small Catholic school in the north Valley, the sort of teacher you inevitably have a crush on. Cute face, small slender body, perfect ass, and the amazing ability to laugh at most of my jokes. The perfect woman, and, like all perfect women, taken.

I offered to get her a drink, but then Daniel appeared next to her. Asshole. I never understood why she was with him in the first place. They'd met at some fundraising event – saving Amazonian tree slugs, or something causey like that – and she'd fallen for his passionate convictions and supposed good looks. He turned out to be one of these brash go-getters who talk politics and drop references to articles in the New Yorker and depend on mothering girlfriends to keep them from having nervous breakdowns. Yes he seems arrogant, but that's just a front, she'd say. He's fragile, he needs me. Yeah, bullshit. Almost four years of fights, separations, and my persistent and totally un-self-interested advice to dump him hadn't convinced her. She was far too forgiving, which is also, I suppose, the reason she was still my friend.

Daniel got himself and Emily a drink and started talking to Diego. He liked Diego – Diego was successful, Diego was vaguely political, and Diego wasn't Emily's best friend from college who was so clearly in love with her. Good old Diego – it gave me and Em a chance to talk. I told her about the party and my lost chance to impress Vas.

She looked at me like I was nuts. "I don't get it," she said flatly. "You guys were agreeing on something, he thought what you were saying was interesting, and he gave you his card. So what's the problem, that's great, right? Call him."

"But I just insulted his girlfriend by talking crap."

"So what? You talk crap all the time, why should that stop you now?"

"Thanks for the encouragement. Anyway, you know I can't disprove astrology any more than she could prove it."

"Listen, you don't have to disprove astrology. What you said – correct me if I'm wrong – was that you could fabricate a system that worked just as well, or at least that seemed just as convincing. Right?"

"Yeah."

"Then do it." That simple. Do it. Emily's no nonsense approach to things sometimes drove me nuts. Obviously I couldn't just do it.

"But I wouldn't even know where to begin."

"Well, tell me, what would Jim Rockford have done?" It's a hard life lesson to learn, but an important one: even to your closest friend, never ever admit that your source of inspiration in childhood was the Rockford Files. I shrugged, but I knew what he'd have done. He'd have gotten off his ass and done a little digging around.

"So get off your ass and think the thing through," she urged me. "What do you need as a start?"

"To get a grip," Daniel interjected. He and Diego had tuned into our conversation and I guess Diego had filled him in on what had happened at Earthsong. "Pete, no offense, but astrology dates back to the ancient Babylonians. Not that I buy into it, but I think you'd have a hard time matching thousands of years of hard work overnight."

Sumerians, you condescending fuck, but Emily intervened before I had a chance to say anything.

"Don't be so negative, Daniel. I think he's got something here. So come on," she persisted, bright eyed and defiant of any sense of realism that might get in her way, "what would you need?"

"Um, well, first I'd need a premise for it all. Astrology has stars. Tarot has cards. I'd need something like that. Problem is that it's all been done. Palms, bumps on the head, coffee grounds, tea leaves – they're all taken."

"Dice?" Diego suggested.

"That's boring."

"You guys are messed up," said Daniel, obviously regretting that he'd encouraged this topic of conversation.

"Seriously," I continued, "you just need some kind of a platform; you know, something that you can base your guesses on."

"The ancient Romans used to kill sheep and read the future in their entrails," Emily offered. I ignored her and continued.

"Of course you'd need something you could link to a specific individual. Astrologers use birthdays. I guess you could use any sort of data, though, as long as it's personal. Like the exact ratio of their height to the length of their thumbs, or how they score on some test. Something unique."

"And presumably something not dependent on subjective human measurements. You couldn't convincingly use inches or centimeters or anything like that, since they are random quantities. You'd need something occurring in nature. A ratio of numbers." Emily was getting enthusiastic. She raised her beer glass to her lips but found it already empty.

"But numbers aren't very interesting. No offense to the math geek," Diego added quickly, shooting an ironic look at Emily.

"No, you're right," I agreed. "What you need is a picture, like a map. Astrologers, tarot card readers, palm readers – they're all doing the same thing, in a way. They interpret a picture that somehow belongs to the person they're doing the reading for, like the stars at the minute he was born, or the pictures on the cards that happened to come up when he was sitting in front of them. So whatever data you'd get from people needs to be turned into a picture, but ideally it should be something spacey, or pretty, or witchy. Something that seems spiritual.

"Oh that's easy," chimed in Emily, her voice calm and matter of fact, but her eyes shining with excitement. "You could use fractals."

In return, she got a blank stare.

"Fractals are just sets of numbers generated by equations, specifically the domain of convergence of a series based on complex numbers, so you can already imagine the sort of kooky mysticism that sometimes surrounds them..."

I gulped my beer and shook my head. To me numbers were tools I could use when doing programming, or obstacles between me and the successful filing of my tax returns, but to Emily they were beautiful in themselves, and that scared me.

"Spin-off science of one of the government's secret weapons programs," Diego remarked casually. Diego had a conspiracy theory for everything, although we were never quite sure how many of them he actually believed. I think he just enjoyed the effect of tossing them into a conversation at random.

"Sorry Em, thumbs down. Vas and his girlfriend are smart and all, but we need something in English..."

She scowled at me. "Do you actually want something that'll work, or not?"

"Well, yeah, but..."

"Then shut up." She stared into the middle distance for a moment and then looked up at me.

"Okay, this isn't exactly right, but start with a simple triangle. You can cope with that, can't you?" she began, animating her explanation with her hands, her sarcasm poorly masking her excitement. "Now, stick a smaller triangle in the middle of each of the three sides, so you have a six-pointed star. Each of the points is basically a triangle, right? So on each side you keep sticking a new triangle in the middle, each time the triangles getting smaller and smaller. What you get looks like a big snowflake, right?"

I said yes, that I imagined it would, and waited for her to make her point.

"The thing is, you've got this finite snowflake in front of you – it fits on the piece of paper you drew the original triangle on, and even though you go on adding to it, it doesn't get bigger spatially. But if you keep adding on triangles into infinity, and then follow the edge of it all the way around, you find that it's infinitely long. You've made your snowflake infinitely complex by adding an infinite number of smaller and smaller triangles. It's called a Koch curve."

"Uh huh..."

"Think about it. Infinite length, infinite complexity. Pete, you've just created an entire two-dimensional universe on a single piece of paper – you can't tell me that isn't cool."

She looked as if she wanted to shake me. I had to admit, it was kind of cool. I didn't see how it could help me, though.

"So Benoit Mandelbrot came along and started explaining this, and some similar but more complex shapes he computer-generated, in terms of fractional dimensions, which he called fractals. He argued that the snowflake we were just talking about is neither a one-dimensional line nor a two-dimensional plane, but a 1.26 dimensional object. It turns out that the patterns can get infinitely complicated, chaotic but not entirely random, and the geometry of these fractals explains all sorts of stuff in the real world, like the distribution of earthquakes and fluctuations in the economy."

I think I'd started to giggle at that point, realizing that I was being led hopelessly out of my element.

"It's part of chaos theory," she continued, ignoring the smile on my face.

I did my best to try and focus. "That thing about a butterfly in Africa causing a hurricane in Cuba?"

"Exactly, chaos theory is built upon Mandelbrot's work with fractals. Clouds are fractal, and so is the way smoke rises and the way water flows. It's all random, but at the same time it's like clumps of recurring patterns that work from a microscopic scale to a huge scale. So by understanding how small air currents move you learn about how hurricanes work, to a point, anyway.

"Mandelbrot's fractals are like little maps revealing the secret order behind a chaotic universe. The micro becomes a symbol for the macro. You can imagine that a lot of people see this as meaningful. God's blueprints. The universe in a grain of sand, that sort of thing."

"Okay, but how does this relate to astrology again?"

"You wanted to be able to take a number and turn it into a picture, didn't you? Well, this will do it, and in a pretty spectacular way that has all sorts of mystical implications. You want to convincingly pretend to tell the future and all that? The Mandelbrot Set is perfect. Trust me."

I trusted Emily, and the next day I got an email from her, nestled among the usual assortment offering videos of sex crazed lesbian midgets and advice to buy shares in obscure technology companies.

"Hey P, c attchd. This is what I was tlking abt last nite. Totally fckd off today, tell u ltr. LE." From the bottom of the message a deep blue hyperlink had stared back at me. Any irritation I felt at her vowel-impaired cybertalk was blurred to insignificance by the warm familiarity of being just "P." I was her best friend. Her buddy, her pal. Better than nothing. Better than anything else in my life, actually. Certainly better than my slowly-dying relationship with Tanya.

But that lazy Saturday afternoon the little hyperlink was as much a connection to Emily as I was going to get, so I clicked on www.ntua.gr/mandel/mandel.html.

"The Mandelbrot Explorer."

She had promised me funky shapes, and she had delivered, but it was the colors that surprised me the most. Bright and varied, they raged viciously across the screen in what looked vaguely like patterns, or bits of patterns, of jagged pink teeth and sickly green spirals. In image after image, the colors would burst from bizarre patterns of black, emerging bright and concentrated, and then radiating outwards like heat, progressively darkening and changing as they distanced themselves from the black web-like structures which formed the core of the set. It reminded me of pictures of stellar nebulae, or of colored high-resolution topo maps of the ocean floor. I saw canyons, tree roots, coral. Things at once familiar and unearthly. It was like arriving in a city for the first time and finding that you instinctively, inexplicably know your way around.

And that's when it struck me. This wasn't just some interesting gimmick. Okay, it might be complete science fiction for all I knew, but that didn't matter. What mattered was the semblance of truth. These shapes all seemed like they meant something, like they contained a message from the deep forces of nature. God speaking in semaphore. They offered a glimpse of a secret world veiled behind frosted glass, a reality all the more powerful for being so vague, the way a monster is always more frightening while it stays off-camera. I stared and clicked for another hour, searching through other fractal websites, but that only confirmed my first impression. This might not quite work, but it was too cool not to try

So that same night, after Tanya had fallen asleep, I returned to my laptop. I could talk a good story, but I didn't actually know much about the occult, and I needed to understand how others convinced people that they could tell the future in order to do it myself. I wanted to get ideas, do a survey of what was out there, and I was blown away by how much I found. I took notes on just about every system of divination and personality typing known to man, and found them as idiosyncratic, and nearly as monotonous, as I had expected them to be. It was amazing just how many astrology sites alone were on the web, and that's not counting the other stuff like Tarot, numerology, psychics or angels. The market in vague, feel-good garbage never seems to slump. It kept me up for hours.

The next morning Tanya stared at me over a plate of toast with a bemused look on her face.

"You were up late last night."

"Um, yeah, I guess so. I kind of got involved in something.

"Not online gaming again?"

"No, nothing like that, just a little project I'm working on." I wasn't ready to tell Tanya what I was up to. Not yet. I'd hammer out some details, I figured, and then surprise her. It would be fun.

She flashed a mischievous grin. "Sure you're not battling wizards and trolls again?"

"Honestly, no trolls."

"I hate those trolls."

"It's going to be a surprise. Trust me."

I worked on my "surprise" for days, trying my best to understand why millions of people are convinced that they have so much to learn about themselves and their destinies by doing a bit of math or disemboweling a chicken. What I figured out is that fortune tellers these days count on the rest of us to accept just a few basic propositions.

First, that there is something out there guiding our fate. It may be just the Universe, or it may be that there is a supreme being, but something out there is in charge, something bigger and fuzzier than mere science.

Second, whatever force is out there shaping our destinies, apparently it can do practical stuff, like make you miss a flight, fry your computer or kill your cat. Medieval astrologers believed that the positions of the stars and planets could affect us because of the movement of the spheres that were nested in each other and wrapped around the Earth like babushka dolls. Copernicus and modern rocketry have blown that theory out of the water, so now astrologers talk about some kind of "energy" that is all around us. This energy has really strong opinions about who you sleep with and what lottery numbers you pick.

Finally, whatever the system of divination, its purpose is to read that energy – which tends to speak in funny languages like star and planet, medieval playing card, or palm line – and translate it into English. And, lucky us, there are always a few people out there who have some sort of gift, a priestly class who can mediate between us and the big energy beast up in the sky.

For better or worse, I'd set myself on the path to becoming a member of that priestly class, and by the end of the week I had a reasonably good grip on how I could pull it off. In fractal geometry I had the perfect explanation of what energy was out there and how it could affect our futures and our personalities. I had a scientific claim to understanding mathematical patterns woven into the fabric of the universe – there was no need to rely on abstract energy to somehow guide us, since the patterns were integral to physics itself, to the blueprint of the universe. With a little work, a computer, and a decent imagination, I could really do this. I could convince Lin and win Vas's gratitude. Peter McFadden was going to tell the future.

4

It took me three weeks and two days.

I didn't do it all alone. Emily's enthusiasm backfired on her, and before she knew it I'd roped her in as my unpaid technical consultant. But that was fine with her. It was August – summer school was over but the new school year hadn't yet begun, so she had time to hang out with me and help me figure things out. We met almost every day for a week. I'd call her up and ask "your place or mine?" We both knew the answer. Her place was her own – her sense of independence and her often stormy relationship with Daniel had kept them from moving in together. My place was Tanya's place, and Tanya was irritated both by the idea of what we were doing ("The guy's not going to give you a job for inventing some stupid gimmick") and by my spending too much time with Emily. So I'd drop by Emily's, and we'd talk about the site, about programming problems, about fractals, Chaos theory, food, movies, mutual friends... pretty much anything I could think up to put off having to leave. We'd never spent so much time together before, not even in college. I was beginning to remember how much I liked it.

Emily provided the science background for our system and helped me make it sound both convincing and mystical. We called it Horokinetics, the science of studying the fractal patterns that characterize our movement through time. Our theory was that the fractal patterns embodied in the Mandelbrot Set, which govern natural phenomena such as weather patterns and the movement of smoke, also influence people. They structure the way a person's life unfolds just as they determine how the water in a stream will flow. To look at it another way, we compared Horokinetics to figuring out what a building was going to look like by sneaking a peak at the blueprints. It all sounded far too true to have come from us.

But mastering the physics and the metaphysics was only half the battle. While brushing up on the history of divination I had noticed that the systems that had really prospered – the ones that world leaders and talk show hosts took seriously – were the ones which incorporated a psychological profile. It was all well and good for someone to throw a few knuckle bones in the sand and advise you not to hunt mammoth that week, but these days people first want to hear something more about themselves. Tell me about me, modern seekers insist, and if you get that right you can tell me about the future. That bit was going to be tricky. I needed professional advice. Luckily I had Susan.

Susan was my oldest friend, and one of my closest. She didn't start out that way; as an eight-year-old I couldn't find it in my heart to befriend a classmate who was so clearly a girl, but within a few years I had managed to forgive her and decided that I liked her enough to talk to her at lunchtimes. We grew older and went off to different high schools, and that, I had thought, was the end of that.

Our mothers, however, had different ideas – they had kept in touch, so we hadn't needed any luck to run into each other when we both arrived as freshmen at UCLA. And it was only then that we grew close, if you could call it that. Susan was a little complicated, and friendship with her wasn't quite the warm fuzzy phenomenon that it tends to be with most other women. She could be almost as stiff as her intimidating parents, and even if she was feeling genuine affection, she wasn't always that talented at expressing it. But Susan would never betray you, or talk behind your back, or embarrass you, or otherwise remind you of the disappointment that can seep through the gaps between friendship and human nature. For that I could put up with a little stiffness now and then.

Given Susan's personality, I was never convinced that psychology was the ideal field for her. She did a lot of marriage counseling, which, considering her inability to have a serious relationship, was pretty funny. But she was driven, and I guess brains, education and hard work must count for something. At 29 she already had her own practice and was doing very well at it. She might not be super-intuitive, but she was technically brilliant, and that's what I needed. So I'd given her a call and arranged to drop by her office one afternoon between clients.

It had only taken a few minutes for me to start feeling a little stupid. Susan listened patiently, as I knew she would, but I couldn't help feeling embarrassed as I saw her eyes narrow, premature laugh-lines gathering at the edges. In her sharp suit, with her short shock of blond hair and thin-framed glasses, she seemed way too professional and mature to have to spend time listening to this crap.

But I kept going. I told her about the conversation at Earthsong and about Emily's idea of using fractals as a pretext for telling the future. And then I got to the point.

"But if I'm going to do this right, I'm going to need a psychologist."

"No kidding," she smiled sarcastically. "Actually you might be a case for serious meds..."

"Look, would you just suspend your professional skepticism for five minutes? And your sense of humor, such as it is."

Susan smiled again and waited for me to continue.

"Okay, here's the thing. Emily and I are managing to figure out how we can convince people we're telling the future. But we've still got to deal with the other part of the equation, the 'what's your sign' part that explains to you what your personality is supposed to be like. And in a way, that's the important part, isn't it? I mean, that's the part that a lot of otherwise sane people buy into."

"Well, you don't have to be insane to buy into any of it. A good astrologer can be pretty astute when it comes to character typing. In fact I know a few therapists who use astrology. You remember Maria? She swears by it."

"You mean use it to treat patients?"

"Use it to help *clients*," she quickly corrected me. "Don't look so surprised – you're the one who just said that people take it seriously. Say what you like about it, personality typing can be very valuable in helping people understand themselves. I've used the Enneagram with a couple of clients. There are lots of systems, some are a bit better than others, but.... "

"So even psychologists would say that there's more than one way to personality type people?"

"Well, yes. I mean, you can't say just anything, but for us the point isn't to say 'you are a Gemini, so you are like X.' It's more about working with people's potentials. Typing can make people aware of forces within themselves that may help them accept what they are feeling or understand why they are behaving in a certain way."

"Yeah, fine, but how? I mean how does astrology do that – come up with all these personality traits?" This was exciting. Not only had Susan studied the background of all this, she'd actually done it.

Susan shrugged. "I thought you were the one who had that figured out."

"What I... well, what I think I've got figured out is that you can describe a hypothetical person in vague terms and then convince actual people that you are describing them. I guess I just need some help to figure out some convincing stock personality types. As an amateur I could just think up various character traits and then mix and match, but if I want to do it well, I need a professional to help me mix and match them convincingly."

"So you want to create your own signs and have pre-fab personalities to attach to them?"

"Yeah. In astrology I'm a Leo. Apparently that means that I'm intense, sincere, and extraverted, that I'm a born leader, and that I'm prone to back problems."

"Back problems?"

"Better than being a Scorpio – they get venereal disease. Really, I looked it up. Anyway, that's what I want to do for my fractals."

"You have to realize that psychology is a little more complex than that," she said, finally realizing that I wasn't kidding.

"I know, I know. But this isn't therapy. It's just entertainment. I need something a little simplistic.

"I've got some books you could look at, I suppose..."

That was fine for a start, but I managed to drag her in more directly than that. Books led to questions, and the answers to those questions led to further questions, so by the end of week two we were camped together on Emily's sofa sketching out Horokinetics' unique system of personality typing.

And by the end of week three, Susan, Emily and I had managed to blend mathematics, psychology, and hocus-pocus almost seamlessly. I rigged up a computer program that would take your basic information – your name, place of birth, the phase of the moon on the day were born – and turn it all into numbers that, once plugged into an equation, gave you a unique set of coordinates on the Mandelbrot Set. The picture that would fill the computer screen once this tiny square was magnified 4000 times its original size was called your "fractal." It was perfect.

Having your own fractal was like knowing your exact DNA sequence. It would be the key to all that you were, and hold clues to all that you could be – if you knew how to read it. I spent hours and hours staring at fractals until I finally came up with seven basic recurring shapes: circles, twiggy treelike things, V-shapes, etc. We called them Ideomorphs, and linked each of them to one of our seven personality types. Your fractal would inevitably contain a few of the seven Ideomorphs, so we would take whichever Ideomorph seemed to predominate and assign you the corresponding personality type. That was the first step, the equivalent of telling you that you are a Capricorn or a Taurus, and pretty much as vague. But instead of being branded as some generic goat or bull from the zodiac, you were assigned a colorful, one-of-a-kind spiky swirly picture. It was very 21st century. But then came the cool part.

We had a picture, but we needed more. The picture itself was too static; it didn't have the advantage of the stars, which move in a calculable pattern and so allow astrologists to predict the future. But Emily had the answer to that.

"It's all about infinite self-similarity," she said proudly when I made the objection. "You could in theory zoom in a different section of a person's fractal for every day of her life. You don't need it to move or change, you've got infinity right here." For such a beautiful girl, she could be a serious geek.

But she was right, and that became our version of a horoscope. Your fractal was your own piece of infinity, your roadmap to the universe. For any particular day we would simply take the date and plug it back into the equation to choose one section of your fractal to enlarge, giving you a whole new picture to interpret. We practiced a little on each other, and it started sounding pretty good.

"*Ideomorph alpha* seems to predominate in today's reading. *I-alpha* is associated with ambition, aggression, and intellect. Most occurrences of *I-alpha* point downwards, however, and there is also a strong *I-gamma* in the corner which, taken together, indicates using some caution in proceeding with any plans which involve risk. Patience, though difficult, will pay off." It sounded pretty convincing to me.

Susan explained that as long as I kept the predictions vague enough to allow a number of different interpretations it would be convincing. "It's called 'confirmation bias,'" she explained to me one afternoon. "The mind tends to interpret information in a way that confirms its pre-existing biases. People focus on what they expect or hope to hear, and they forget the rest." It seemed like a pretty blunt instrument for clubbing into submission the vast and subtle panorama of human experience, but I tested it on a couple of unsuspecting friends, and it worked. This Lin chick would have no idea what hit her – all I needed was her subconscious willingness to ignore any bits I got wrong, and I'd be on my way to a brilliant career with ImaginInc.

It was Tuesday, less than a month after the party at Earthsong, when I got up the courage to call ImaginInc and ask to speak to Vas.

"I'm sorry, he's in a meeting right now. Can I take a message?" Sure. A couple of days passed, but he didn't call back. So I tried again.

"I'm sorry, he's not available right now."

"I'm sorry, what was your name again?"

"I'm afraid he's out of the office. What was it regarding?"

"Oh, hello Mr. McFadden, no I'm afraid not."

Another couple of weeks went by. The receptionist got to know me. She hated me. There was some kind of subtle hint in all of this that I was refusing to get. But I persisted. Emails disappeared into cyberspace. I even got drastic and sent a letter snail-mail. No response. It was like trying to negotiate with Santa Claus.

On the morning I finally accepted that there was no point to calling ImaginInc anymore, I headed for the canyons. That's where I'd go when I needed to think. Sometimes I'd drive for hours, stopping here and there to walk up the fire trails, chase rabbits, and breathe in the smell of sage and dust and ozone that seems to cling to every rock and half dead bush. They're like another world, the canyons, and a pretty effective antidote to the colossal marketing gimmick that in LA passes for reality.

Most importantly, they were mine. Over the years I had made the canyons my own by entrusting them with childhood secrets – the crumbling hillside where the dinosaur bones are buried, the hidden path to the Indian burial ground, the scrub oak forest inhabited by dragons – personal fantasies into which I invested so much time and attention that they had taken on a life of their own. They were the sort of memories that color a place and give it meaning. Memories of family car trips to the beach, laughing at the billboards warning drivers "Danger, Death Lurks Ahead," and the tunnels through which we would hold our breath, pressing our hands flat against the roof of the car and making wishes. The wishes never came true and as I grew older I stopped catching glimpses of dragons in the trees. We were even wrong about the billboards: turns out that a lot of people do lose control around those curves and crash over the railings into the canyon below.

I drove for an hour or so, along Mulholland Highway, through Las Virgenes, up the coast, back through Kanan Road, up and down all those winding channels cutting through the mountains, connecting valley to sea, filling every last crevice of them with angst and nostalgia. Eventually I got fed up with moping, tired of cruising the low roads, and decided to get a little altitude.

I rolled through a sun-scorched landscape dotted with oak trees and new housing developments, doubling back along Mulholland as it sliced through small hills too steep to pave over until I came to an unremarkable little turnoff on the right. There I started to climb.

Stunt Road picks its way up through the hills rather than following the creek beds down to sea level. It flies between the canyons, inking a squirming line on the blank stretch of map between Topanga and Las Virgenes Road, and you fly with it, watching the hills change, from the strange crumbling black rock at Mulholland, up through the splintered jumble of pinkish limestone and into the layers of beige strata near the top. The rocks themselves seem like they're trying to escape the earth as they jut their ragged edges through the sparse foliage, flat layers of sediment pushed almost vertical when the mountains were formed. This was still a place of my childhood, still dragon country, but it was something else too. A heroic and unshackled place where I could see things clearly, where maybe I could re-acquire a grip on reality and figure out what the hell to do.

My car engine groaned as I wound steadily upwards to a long ridge, a saddle between two peaks, where the road reaches an abrupt end and, as a parting gift, unveils the massive expanse of the Pacific far ahead and below. The sky opens out so suddenly it's like reaching the end of a ramp, as if with enough speed you could just keep going and launch yourself out to sea. But right before it would otherwise carry you over the cliff, Stunt Road splits in two, each fork taking its own name as it descends toward the ocean.

There, where the road stops short and two new ones begin, up at the top of things, I parked the car. On one side I could see the Valley, on the other I looked out over the ocean, with sailboats, tankers and Catalina Island all floating in the distance, nestling in the broad arc of Santa Monica Bay. As good a place to think as any.

So I got out of the car, and stared, and thought. An avalanche of images roared through my head. They were random, chaotic thoughts – fractals, Tanya, Emily, my old job, video games – but they carried a perverse logic along with them. Chaotic as they were, they led someplace, and I let myself follow along.

I'd fucked up. An obvious point, but one that I had yet to really accept. Fate hadn't done me a raw deal. Society had not betrayed me. My parents hadn't failed me, the system hadn't screwed me, luck hadn't run out. I had purely, simply gotten lost and ended up sabotaging my life. What was done could not be undone. It was time to seize control and find my way out of the wreckage.

I picked up a decent sized flat rock and launched it from the edge of the road, a good healthy sidearm throw giving it some loft before it arched sharply to the left and into the gully below. A couple of birds fluttered away nervously.

First of all, I needed a job. Unemployment had made me not only poor, but depressed and fairly useless as well. It was like a drug – the longer I was inactive, the less inclined I was to find work. My brains and ambition, such as they were, were getting me nowhere if all they were good for was dreaming up phony metaphysics that no one cared about. I was getting gloomier and more unbearable by the day, and the longer I had to live off my girlfriend and parents, the more I began to resent them and dislike myself. I had to break the cycle. I had to get a job, any job, and start making a little money again. Even if it meant being a bank teller.

From there, I could keep looking for something better. Maybe I wouldn't find the ideal CGI job again. Maybe I'd have to do something a little less flashy for a while, work my way back up, just so long as I didn't lose track of what I was doing and why. Stay determined, stay focused. Eye of the tiger. Fuck. I was doomed. If I could just have gotten Horokinetics in front of Vas…

I suppose I had become so absorbed in my own thoughts that I hadn't heard anyone approaching, but suddenly I felt vulnerable standing there at the edge of that steep rocky hillside, one push away from a nasty tumble through jagged shale and dry brush. Instinctively I turned, and felt my pulse surge on coming face to face with a horse just a couple of feet behind me. It was surreal. If my momentary sense of panic showed, neither the horse nor the man riding it seemed to notice. I looked up at the rider, but he just sat there, serene as the Buddha, taking me in with eyes so blue that they seemed more like holes looking directly out onto a vivid clear sky floating within his skull. I suppressed a nervous shiver and opened my mouth to speak, but somehow nothing came out. I was more than surprised – I was spooked.

"Hey, sorry," came a clear, mellow voice, presumably from the rider, although I hadn't noticed his lips move. He slid effortlessly from the saddle and stood facing me, gripping the reins loosely in his right hand. "Didn't mean to startle you. You just looked... are you okay?"

The first thing I remember thinking as he stood there was how tall he was. Tall and perfectly straight, almost like a soldier, except that his straightness lacked the forced, rigid look taught in basic training. There was a sense of command and power about him, but unlike that of a general, it was relaxed, natural, resulting from energy rather than discipline. Turns out that he was only six feet tall, just an inch taller than me, but you'd never know it unless you stood us back to back.

His hair was straight too. Very blond and very straight, the kind of hair girls dream of. Healthy hair, sheared off in a straight line half way down to his shoulders, framing a thin but strong face, with angled features softened by a hint of golden stubble. He looked in his mid-thirties, but it was hard to tell. It was hard to tell much of anything about him, but something about that straight cut-off hair, or maybe the serene expression on his face, made him look like a monk.

"Um, yeah," I stammered. "Fine, thanks. Just, you know, thinking." There was something creepy about being sneaked up on out here, in the hills, alone, yet as soon as the initial shock faded I didn't feel frightened. I probably should have, but there was something in this guy that seemed to make me want to trust him. His short, quiet laugh, however out of place, inspired confidence.

"I thought for a minute you were going to jump," he remarked, glancing down the slope behind me.

I followed his look down the tangled but relatively gentle slope beneath me and suddenly understood why he was laughing. "I like to think that when the time comes I'd pick a better spot than this."

"'When?' Not 'if'?" His smile lingered, but his voiced dropped, as if the thought genuinely worried him. "Okay, if" I conceded quickly. I hadn't noticed that I'd said "when." It was a little disturbing, but I kept talking, hoping, I suppose, to avoid giving the impression that I was some fragile soul in need of help.

"Look, thanks for being concerned, but I'm fine. I'm just, um, thinking."

"Mind if I ask what about?"

I was about to make some excuse and leave, but something stopped me. Sometimes the best kind of solitude is that found in the company of a total stranger. So I told him I was unemployed, that I'd just blown my big chance at a dream job, that I'd been so desperate for this job that I'd spent several weeks of my life working on a phony system of divination just to impress some computer animation geek and then couldn't even get the guy to return my phone calls. Put like that, it was actually kind of funny. The guy on the horse just listened patiently, seeming to be genuinely interested. When I'd finished my story, he stared at me for a minute.

"So, how did this system work?"

"Okay, let me first ask you a question," I began, quickly trying to collect my thoughts. "Do you believe in astrology?"

As a reply I got a thin smile and a dramatic pause, until at last he said, hesitantly, "Well, that depends on what you mean. Do I believe that there is an objective body of information that can be read from relative positions of the planets and stars at any given time? No, I don't."

"But do you believe that some people can tell the future?"

Again he paused, weighing his answer carefully.

"We can all tell the future, to some extent, with some degree of precision. I'm pretty certain that tomorrow I'll wake up, some time between 6:00 and 7:00. I usually do.

That's not magic, it's just a prediction based on previous experience. Now, I haven't been in LA for that long, and I only have one real friend here. She runs some stables not too far from here, actually. I can't say for certain that Jericho will call me tomorrow, but I can say that there is at least a decent chance of it, and certainly the odds that she'll call me are better than that she'll call you, for example. Which is your loss," he added, whether ironically or not I couldn't say. "Now that's predicting the future, in a sense, it's just not doing it based on something like the movements of stars, which, let's be honest, have nothing to do with me."

It was a thoughtful answer. I wasn't prepared for thoughtful answers, so it confused me for a minute. But I pressed on.

"So would you be prepared to buy into an astrology-like system that claimed to make predictions about you and about the future based on something scientific?"

Another pause, then a smile. "Such as...?"

So I started selling it to him, just as I'd planned on doing to Vas. I had had an entire conversation worked up in my head for a guy who wouldn't return my phone calls. So I explained it all. Horokinetics, a system of creating horoscopes based on the patterns found in the Mandelbrot Set. You provide the numbers and my computer would plug them into an equation and produce your fractal. And that fractal, I explained, with all those funky seahorses and waves and valleys and splatters, would contain messages about you. Messages not from the stars or from playing cards or tea leaves, but messages derived from the patterns of the universe uncovered by cutting edge chaos theorists. I hate to think how stupid I must have looked standing there, probably nodding my head like some teenager showing off his knowledge of Led Zeppelin trivia, waiting for his response. But to his credit, he remained polite.

"So the idea is to repackage New Age mysticism as a science," he stated calmly, turning over the implications in his mind like some fossil or artifact he'd just picked up on an archeological dig. It sounded a little stupid, put that way. And a little creepy. "You know," he began again thoughtfully, "what's your name?"

"Pete."

"Pete, I'm Jake." We shook hands. "Now let me ask you something," he went on, his eyes lighting up. "Do you believe in all of this?"

"No, of course not," I answered, almost offended at the thought.

"So tell me, why should I believe it?"

"Well, you shouldn't. I made it up. It's pure bullshit."

"Come on, imagine I'm this woman you were trying to convince. Why should I believe it?"

I sighed audibly with impatience. "Because it's based on chaos theory, and it's supposedly scientific."

"Fine, but evolution is scientific, yet more Americans believe in UFOs than believe in evolution. Ever wonder why?"

"Because they're freaks."

Jake shook his head. "Because they don't want to be alone. Because they find it more beautiful to believe in a universe peopled by many advanced civilizations than it is to believe that we are descended from apes. People want to believe in something beautiful."

"And aliens are beautiful? Green-skinned kidnappers who get their kicks using us humans as guinea pigs."

"I didn't say pretty. I said beautiful. The Romantic poets would have said sublime – that's the word they used for something that is at once beautiful and frightening, something big enough that it makes you reflect on your own mortality."

"That's kind of a lot to ask of something that's basically a fraud, don't you think?"

"No, it isn't." Jake was shaking his head emphatically, his straight blond hair waving behind him. "You have to be bold with this kind of thing or no one is going to buy it. As long as you try to play it safe, it's going to come out wishy washy and no one will feel compelled to believe it.

"You play baseball?" he asked suddenly, a sense of urgency in his voice.

"Um, yeah, I did little league."

"Remember stealing second? You had to totally abandon first base or you were lost. And at least once we all tried to have both ways, didn't we? You'd start for second, but hold back a little, in case you had to return to first. And you'd get thrown out, every time."

I laughed. "You're not one of these motivational speakers, are you?"

"Let's just say I take an interest in how people come to believe what they believe."

"Psychologist?"

"No," he answered, almost dismissively. "Philosopher, maybe. I don't know. At the moment I'd have to just say I'm like you, between jobs."

"Listen," he said, now balancing carefully on a rock a few feet away from me. The sun was at his back, and I had to squint as I looked up at him. "Truth is about more than science or facts. It requires belief, which unless you're doing primary research yourself, requires faith. And if you want to inspire faith, you're going to need more than a theory and some technical jargon. You need beauty. If you stop short of that, no one's going to listen."

No one was listening anyway, I reminded him. This was a story written for two people, Vas and Lin, and I couldn't get through to them. Jake smiled, looking almost bewildered by my stupidity.

"But it's obvious, isn't it? You get their attention by really doing this. Get it out there in the real world. Then it's not a matter of trying to call them – they'll hear about it and call you. You send them a link to your website, or a few magazine clippings about the new form of divination that everyone is raving about. Simple."

Yeah, simple. This guy was a little twisted. "How am I supposed to do that, exactly?"

"Your system, does it work? I mean, is it as convincing as Tarot or numerology or crystal healing?"

"Yeah, I think so."

"Then do it."

"Do what?

"Make it a business. Start with a website, go to New Age fairs, train a few people to go out there and spread the word."

"That kind of thing takes cash, man, and I don't have any. Besides, I'm not a business guy, I'm an animation geek."

"There will always be obstacles if you choose to dream them up. A website costs next to nothing. Training you'd do yourself. People would probably even pay to get training if it were well known, but you'd start out doing it for free. Invest a little time and you could even make money doing this – lots of people do it. And for what it's worth, I think the premise sounds great. You've got a winner here, if you can find the guts to pursue it."

He pulled a crumpled piece of paper out of his pocket, jotted something down, then handed it to me. "That's my number. I can help you with it. Find you people, help you with a website, anything. I've got time on my hands, it'd be interesting. Call me."

He turned to go, but then stopped and turned to face me again.

"Build this thing," he said softly, confidently. "Make it beautiful, then you'll make it true, and they will believe."

With that, he swung himself back into the saddle and began making his way down the winding path toward the coast, leaving me there to think, alone, my head boiling in the late summer sun.

5

Las Virgenes Road is one of LA's great drives, leading you uphill through state parkland and then down in a slow, winding descent to the coast between wild, jagged cliffs, always keeping the deep blue sea in view. But the Pacific hid behind a thin layer of fog as we came over the canyon that morning. There was something spooky about it, as if we'd get to Pacific Coast Highway and the ocean might not be there anymore. As if we who claimed to see into the future were being mocked by a world in which even the present was opaque.

We followed Malibu's gloomy strip of shoebox beach houses until it was time for another left, following a side road as it pointlessly climbed back towards the Santa Monica Mountains, a crumbling wall of rock and dirt and federal land it had no hope of crossing. In less than a minute we saw the Malibu Dunes open-air shopping center and, stretched bikini-tight over the entrance to the parking lot behind it, a large red banner with gold lettering. Welcome to the Soulcraft Festival.

September mornings on the coast can be cold, but luckily our neighbor. Kim, of Kim's CrystalCraft, had brought a large thermos of coffee, and had even had the generosity of spirit to bring extra cups for the occasional fellow traveler. It was pretty awful – one of those flavored coffees over which wise, special women in comfortable sweaters share their secrets on TV commercials – but it kept our hands warm as we set up our equipment.

"Stay centered, okay?" she advised us quietly, and then returned to arranging the huge assortment of crystals, stones, and pamphlets on her table. Jake and I shared a smile and nodded, sitting down to finish our coffee and wait for the fair to open.

As the morning crept by, it became harder and harder not to agree with the Angel lady across from us who kept complaining that we were giving off bad energy. I wasn't really sure what I was doing there in the first place. In a moment of foolish and fateful politeness a few days earlier I had called up Jake to tell him why there was no way in hell I was going to go any further with my ridiculous idea, and by the time I had hung up, maybe ten minutes later, he had convinced me to come with him and try the system out at a sort of psychic fair in Malibu. He knew one of the organizers, he said, and could secure us a last-minute place.

"One day of your life, Pete. If you're not convinced, I'll respect your decision."

The crisp fog that coated the Malibu coastline like foam on the ridge of a coffee cup slowly burned away. It turned into a clear cool morning, a gentle drift of crisp sea air mixing lazily with the smell of incense, tiger balm and curry rising from the three dozen or so tents and tables around us, and the good weather rivaled the promise of enlightenment in its ability to draw the crowds.

By lunchtime the place was packed. It occurred to me that the new age crowd aren't always what you'd think. I had expected a stereotypical group of spacey young white girls with dreadlocks and dirty fingernails, hippies hung with beads and crystals and hemp necklaces, fat women dressed in purple tunics and middle aged men with long white hair and papery fair skin suggesting hormone imbalances. And there were plenty of all of the above. Witches and shamans and Jerry Garcia look-alikes who all seemed to order their clothes from the same shop in Middle Earth drifted back and forth past our table, munching on veggie burritos and pappadums and connecting with the cosmos. But despite a shitload of silver and amethyst jewelry, the majority looked surprisingly normal. These were bank tellers, bank managers, accountants. I'm pretty certain that I caught sight of my ninth grade Spanish teacher getting a tarot card reading. It wasn't much different from Venice Beach on a warm day: a scattering of freaks mixed in with the steady mainstream of humanity who buy their clothes at Marshall's, work nine to five and drive SUVs. It was just what they were all carrying around inside their sane-looking, well-groomed heads that set them apart. These were people seeking something different, rebelling against the backward politics that had tainted Christianity and the sense of irrelevance they felt in the face of science. Refugees from the spiritual dead-ends of western culture.

Jake and I had plenty of time to watch and to comment. Our table was set up in a good spot, half way down the row that led from the food stalls at one end of the parking lot to the port-a-potties at the other, and I think the ayurvedic chakra bhaji stand provided us with a lot of extra traffic in both directions. Hungry faces, urgent faces, enlightened faces, questing faces, they all passed by, but they didn't seem inclined to turn our way. Kim didn't have any problem, and neither did the Angels Around Us lady, with her pastel butterflies and winged fat children leering at each other in sympathetic holiness. By mid-morning I was starting to get nervous. All around us were tables covered with pretty things. Purple crystals, funky jewelry, unicorns, dolphins, ankhs and Buddhas and miniature feathery pool-skimmers meant to be able catch your dreams for you. All ancient and powerful and mysterious, but also by some happy cosmic coincidence all wonderfully decorative. I began to understand why telling the future with bird entrails or dog shit hadn't been embraced by modernity the way crystal healing and tarot had. And I began to look at our jumble of wires and stacks of high quality computer printing paper in a new light. People are less interested in enlightenment if it doesn't involve fuzzy animals or sparkly things.

But finally, just before lunch, we had a taker. Eryka, a chubby forty-something with spiky hair, dreamcatcher earrings and a suspect y in her name, one of those y's meant to let you know that this isn't some boring western name – not Erika or Erica – but something deeper, more ancient, maybe Celtic or Ashanti or Lemurian.

"I think I read about this," she said cheerfully as she sat down in a chipped folding metal chair across the table from us and nibbled delicately on the organic churro clutched in her left hand. Jake smiled at her, and she smiled back, hoping maybe that this attractive blond young man would be part of the future we were about to divine for her. I silently added shamelessness to the list of surprising qualities that I had discovered in Jake over the past couple of hours and launched into my routine.

Yes, I had a routine. During my research I had come across a book about cold-reading, the art practiced by psychics, diviners, salesmen, and other assorted con men to make themselves seem supernaturally convincing. Oversimplified, it works like this: you make a vague statement, pay attention to your listener's response, and continuously adjust your message. If done well, the person listening not only gives you all the information you need, but does so without even realizing it. You ask him if a relative has recently died, he tells you his uncle died last year, and by the end of the conversation you have him believing that you "saw" the death of his uncle in the tea leaves and he's forgotten that he told you. I doubted until I tried it on a few friends. If done well, it works. Usually.

"Now Eryka," I explained with all the condescending patience of a dental hygienist, "before we begin, I should explain that what we do is not divination in the classic sense of the word. Horokinetics is a scientific process that involves calculating your location on the fractal continuum – that's the mathematical pattern that underlies everything in the universe – and then trying to draw some conclusions about you and your life based on your fractal."

"Um hmm, okay," she nodded her head with a businesslike pinch in her lips to let me know that she was digesting all of this just fine. I talked to her for a few minutes and had her fill out a form, and then entered her data into the computer and brought her fractal up on screen, a multicolored swirl of whirlpools lined up in two branching rows to form a large skewed V shape. I stared at the shapes for a few seconds, repressing my sudden sense of fear at doing this live. Taking a deep breath, I looked my subject in the eyes and started talking.

"This is an interesting reading," I began, injecting my words with as much gravitas as I thought Eryka could bear. "You see this large round shape, it's like a beach ball that all the other shapes cling to the sides of. That's a strong Epsilon – Epsilon is one of what are called Ideomorphs. They're the basic shapes that recur in fractals." I paused for effect. People generally love lingo, the more obscure the better. Eryka stared at the computer screen, nodding her head but looking as if she was trying to break wind.

"Studies have shown that a strong Epsilon in a fractal tends to coincide with people who have strong personalities, either in the sense of heightened aggressiveness or more often in the sense of being of patient or enduring."

"I'm not too patient," she answered loudly, whether or not with a hint of menace I couldn't say.

"Well, um, especially since the Epsilon is pointed downwards rather than upwards, I would say this one implies more of a "go get 'em" type personality." I waited for a hint whether or not I was headed in the right direction, but got your classic blank stare in return.

"Now, branching off from the edges of the Epsilon, you've got a repeated series of Ideomorph Gamma. Those are the little trees." I pointed at the series of spiky claws, starting small at one end and growing slowly bigger towards the other, as a doctor might point out a shadow on a lung x-ray. Eryka took it in about the same spirit.

"Uh huh," she mumbled, deep in the back of her fleshy throat.

"I love to see Gammas." Always stay upbeat. Divination isn't just about facts, it's about spiritual growth. Help your client grow. "The appearance of Gammas on your identity fractal tends to signify intuitiveness, both intellectual and emotional. I bet you often find you suspect things will happen before they actually do, don't you?"

"Well, yes, I imagine so. I suspected I was coming here this morning, and here I am." She said it so deadpan that I didn't realize she was joking until she exploded with a laugh that made the Angel lady jump off her chair.

"Now, I see an upward trend to these Gammas, so I'm going to go out on a limb here and guess that you're a people person, life of the party. People like you, and that's a skill that has helped you in your career."

"Well that's not so hard to spot, sweetheart." She took another bite of churro and looked over at Kim's crystals. I was losing her.

"Now Eryka, this is your first encounter with Horokinetics, isn't it?"

"You should be telling me," she snorted, clearly skeptical but not in an unfriendly way.

"Good. Since you're obviously someone who's already very in touch with herself, let's skip over some of the fractal analysis and move directly to a reading." I began typing some numbers into the computer and then hit enter. A new fractal image lit up my screen. "You can't be so intuitive that we shouldn't be able to tell you a thing or two you don't already know." I braced for that percussive laugh again, but it didn't come.

"Okay," I continued, "what do we have here? Well, more Gammas, as you can see, and the introduction of some Zetas."

"Gammas and Zetas, sounds more like Star Trek than astrology." Her voice carried an edge, a hint of accusation that I had somehow broken the rules by drifting into another genre.

"Horokinetics uses Greek letters to indicate the various Ideomorphs. Greek is the language of science, after all."

"That's fair enough. So what does science have to tell me about my future? Are Zetas good?"

Something held me back from delivering the party line that the Ideomorphs were neither good nor bad, but simply reflected tendencies induced by the structure of the fractal pattern underlying her life path. A keen sense of self-preservation, I guess.

"I see this as a very positive reading. Zeta structures indicate change, and I think given the context of their appearance here that it will be positive change. Their positioning suggests something involving your career. Are you thinking of changing jobs, or are you maybe in line for a promotion?"

Eryka licked a bit of sugar off her upper lip and rolled her eyes down towards the oil stained asphalt as if to avoid seeing something shameful. But whatever she saw down there seemed to lighten her mood; she let out a laugh, quiet this time, that involved only one side of her mouth, and her eyes snapped up again to meet mine.

"Listen, sweetheart, I've got to get going. You're trying hard, and I think that's great. Thanks. Really."

I asked her if she wanted a printout of her fractal, but after glancing at an imaginary watch on her left wrist she crinkled her nose and shook her head. No thanks, she mouthed silently, and crossed over to the "Healing Hands" Reiki tent across the way.

I looked at Jake for a reaction. The food-poisoning grimace was not encouraging.

We had a few more people try out Horokinetics that day, and to be fair the readings weren't all as bad as Eryka's. No one else laughed and, more importantly, no one else called me sweetheart. But as the light faded and the crowd thinned, it became harder and harder to remain upbeat. Jake kept me company and did his best to keep my spirits up, so to speak, but apart from a pleasant ten minutes flirting with a crystal healer and learning that I have an unusually strong aura, I had to conclude that this was a wasted Saturday. Except that I'd learned one thing: Horokinetics done badly was pretty awful.

We packed all the equipment into the car without speaking, each of us I suppose lost in his own dismal thoughts as the events of the day played themselves over and over in our heads.

"Listen, Pete," Jake said once my car was packed, emphasizing my name as if he had individually crafted the word for me alone, "don't take it so bad. You live, you learn and you move on. Tomorrow will go better. Tell you what, why don't you follow me over to my place and have a beer?"

I agreed. The guy was nuts, but didn't seem dangerous, and to be honest I was kind of growing to like his offbeat, no-nonsense brand of spookiness. So I climbed into my blue Fiesta and followed his battered-looking old motorcycle back up Topanga Canyon, along Saticoy and through a maze of side streets to his peeling stucco apartment building. It was dark, but garden lamps illuminated two skeletal palm trees flanking the entrance like burned-out tank carcasses, and sad yellowing wall lights freckled with dead moths lead us up the concrete stairs to number seven.

"I've got a frozen pizza I can put in the oven, if you're hungry." He emerged from behind the fridge door with a couple of Sierra Nevadas, setting them on the breakfast counter of his small open plan kitchen while he fished through a drawer for a bottle opener.

"Yeah, thanks," I answered, hunger gripping my stomach at the mere mention of food. I walked over to the counter as

Jake popped off the bottle caps and turned to fish our dinner out of the freezer.

I took a long sip of much needed beer and glanced around. It was a small apartment, sparsely furnished and unusually ascetic in a town so thickly and famously scattered with movie stars and breast implants. None of the glossy posters from headline museum exhibitions that were normally used to hide the bare walls of pseudo-intellectuals. None of the Japanese teapots, collections of beach pebbles or other badges of purity that clutter the houses of the spiritual-minded. None of the multi-volume biographies of Freud or French editions of Sartre that tend to be displayed a little too prominently on the shelves of armchair philosophers. It was just simple – a sofa, an easy chair, a small desk, an Ikea bookcase with a dozen paperbacks and a CD player. No TV. No photos. No souvenirs from backpacking through Thailand. Just a clean, ordered quiet place in which to live and to think. Confident, disciplined, unpretentious. It was a little disappointing. I was expecting some bric-a-brac to give me some insight into Jake's character or clues about his past. But I had arrived at Jake's apartment to find all these things infuriatingly absent.

"It'll take about 15 minutes," he warned, emerging from the kitchen and dropping himself almost weightlessly into the sofa.

"Nice place," I said, awkwardly.

"Thanks." He seemed unphased by the absurdity of the comment. Then he laughed, "Can't say I've done much with it, but I'm moving into a new place in a couple of weeks anyway. You live somewhere around here, don't you?"

"Not that far – right now I'm staying with my girlfriend Tanya, at least for the time being. She's got an apartment up on White Oak, that big complex by the freeway."

"Tanya. She's the one who came up with the idea to use fractals?"

"No, god no. She thinks that Horokinetics is a stupid waste of time."

"She thinks it's a bad idea? Or is it that she doesn't like the competition?"

"Little of both, maybe." Jake said nothing, but somehow the depth of his silence carried an implicit invitation to fill it, so I kept talking. I told him about my old job, even the true story of how I lost it. I told him about the long, deadening days of unemployment, about Tanya's disenchantment with me, about her frustration with what she saw as my failure to take responsibility for myself. I told him that I thought she might be right.

I probably would have continued, but Jake began shaking his head slowly. Responding to a burning smell, he disappeared into the kitchen and returned a few minutes later with our pizza – salvaged just in time – and a couple of plates. Once he settled back in, he spoke again.

"Pete, why do you think I've taken such an interest in this creation of yours?"

I shrugged and admitted that I had been wondering that myself.

"I told you that I was taking time off from getting my Ph.D. in philosophy at Boulder. I never told you what I'd done before that." As he spoke, his pale blue eyes remained fixed on a point somewhere in the distance, somewhere obviously well beyond the walls of his apartment. His voice grew even more mellow than usual, and he trudged resolutely, word by word, through his memories. His story was clearly precious to him, almost as if he were recounting his last conversation with a dying parent.

"You might not believe this, but I used to work as a geological engineer. I was a graduate of the Colorado School of Mines, specialized in geohydrology. Don't ask me how I got into that – it's another long story, but a less interesting one. Anyway, I ended up working for a group called EDDA. 'Engineers for Development and Disaster Assistance.' We worked with international charities in the Third World, helping build bridges and roads, dig wells, that sort of thing. I spent nearly four years of my life digging boreholes for villages and refugee camps in the Sahel and southern Sahara. Spent a lot of that time in Mali and Burkina Faso.

"I had a serious girlfriend back home in Colorado. You can imagine what that was like. I was in some pretty rough places sometimes – Chad, Sudan – and even where I was based in Bamako it wasn't very easy to communicate. She was worried. Worried that I'd never come home, either because I got myself killed or because I just wouldn't be able to settle down into a normal life in the Western world again. You see that a lot – people get so used to life out in the field that they can't adjust back to being home anymore. I told her it would be two years, and that after that I'd come back to the States and get a normal job.

"Well, it's a long story, but she broke it off, and I kept extending my contract." He drifted off for a moment, as if waiting for a response from me. I hardly knew what to say: it wasn't how I imagined Jake's past, but only because I hadn't been able to clearly imagine any past for him at all. I could have pictured him doing anything, but I had a hard time pinning him down to anything in particular. Engineer? Aid worker? Astronaut would have been just as conceivable, if only a little less likely.

"But you did go home in the end," I ventured. He smiled.

""I think this is where I'm supposed to say that you can't go home again. But yes, in the end, I did leave Africa."

"And decided to study philosophy?"

"And needed to study philosophy."

I didn't say anything to that, but he could see my skepticism. I mean, come on, nobody needs to study philosophy. People need to eat, need to find a job, need a coffee to wake up in the morning. But philosophy? This was sounding too much like bullshit. Jake paused for a long time, staring at his beer bottle until I started to wonder if he was going to say anything else. But at last he answered.

"Once you set foot outside of suburban America, you find out that the world can be a scary place. I saw terrible things out there. I learned things... things I didn't really want to know, that none of us want to know if we can help it."

I nodded my head, even though I had no idea what he was talking about. I'd seen almost nothing of the world beyond our borders, apart from Mexico and the handful of European capitals that so many middle class college students visit for a day each while strapped to oversized backpacks. So my experience of Third World suffering was limited to a bit of food poisoning at a restaurant in Tijuana, and I had to delve into the archive of images I'd gathered from television to picture crowds of starving black children and merciless dictators.

"It can't be easy, seeing so much poverty so close and not being able to help."

"Oh, you get used to the poverty after a while," he said, almost dismissively. "You have to, or you have to leave. And it's by staying, by pushing the horror of all that poverty well toward the back of your consciousness so that you can get on with your work, that you are able to do something about it. We gave thousands of people access to clean water; in Africa a lot more people die every year from dirty water than from AIDS.

"No," he went on, his blue eyes seeming to fade to a vague gray, "I left because one day I woke up and realized that I wasn't there for Africa. Not that many people are, but I had really thought I was there because my sense of morality had told me that I needed to help people. But one day, just walking past a mechanic's shop in Bamako, I took in a deep breath of engine grease, and it hit me. I suddenly saw myself on the motorbike I had as a kid, doing the most dangerous stuff I could, all because I had this dream of living on the edge. And I realized I was still doing it. I wasn't in Africa to help anyone, I was there because it matched this idea I had built up of the kind of person I wanted to be. It fit a picture of my life I had drawn as a kid on a motorbike. That was it. I'd spent thirty years on this planet before I understood that what I had always taken for a sense of morality was nothing more than an overdeveloped sense of aesthetics."

Jake paused for a minute to let all of this sink in. This is important, his silence whispered. It is crucial. I took another sip of beer. This was becoming personal and awkward.

"Aesthetics," he repeated. "I had built my own personal mythology when I was young, and everything I did mattered only to the extent that it fulfilled one of the roles I had assigned myself in that mythology. It was all about tapping into my past, into the little moments that remained filled with meaning for me, so that I could draw out some of that meaning to apply to the present. That was how I built my world. Do you see what I mean? I was in Africa to relive my own childhood fantasies and construct my world in the image I wanted. I wasn't seeing Africa, I was seeing a world in my head built of ideas I had of Africa and of myself. At the time, I felt like I was looking at nothing but a world built of my own lies."

"We all have our own little delusions, I suppose," I answered, figuring I had a rough idea of what he was talking about and assuming that now was when I was supposed to tell him that there was nothing wrong with it. "The point is, you did help people."

"I did more than that," he said, an odd grin appearing on his face and seeming to banish the shadows that had gathered there. "That was the first moment when I started to understand."

"Understand?"

"How we build the universe. How each of us, in his own little way, is his own god."

I guess my skepticism was showing again because he grabbed the bottle of beer out of my hand and set it down on the table in front of me. "Listen," he said, growing excited, "I want you to play a little game with me for a minute. Now concentrate. Think of your favorite book from when you were really young. I'm talking picture books. Now, you don't have to tell me what it was, but you had a favorite page, didn't you?" I did. The book was a big picture book of dinosaurs, and the best page was the one with a brontosaurus chewing leaves in a strange tropical landscape, the sun setting behind its droopy phallic head. Something about that scene, the weirdness of the landscape and the light, had always intrigued me. I'd spent hours looking at all the funny little details of the swampy forest the illustrator had so patiently rendered just to house this ridiculous animal. I nodded to Jake.

"Okay, now, this is tricky, but work with me. Keep that page in your mind, deep in the back of your mind. Just soak up the feeling that that page evokes." I did as he asked. There was definitely a feeling that went with the page. Not really an emotion, I guess, but a feeling, the syrupy psychological goo in which old memories are preserved like the specimens used in science classes. "Now," he whispered, maybe hoping not to disturb me from some trancelike state I was supposed to be in, "where are you?"

I opened my eyes, only in doing so realizing that they had been shut. "I'm in your apartment, Jake," I said lightly, but I knew what he meant. In those few seconds my mind had taken me to a few places at once. Places in my memory. I had seen the forest where, as a kid, I had imagined that dragons lived, up in the hills along Stunt Road. I had felt the heat of a certain afternoon in my early childhood and experienced the smell of the chicken Dad was burning on the barbeque. I had revisited the unaccountable fear and fascination I'd felt for a certain corner of our school playground, and the flutter in my stomach as I entered my first class at college. But it was more than that. I hadn't just seen those places, I'd felt them, moments crystallized in emotion like flies in amber. I told

Jake none of this. These memories and the emotions that came with them were a bit too personal.

Jake smiled at my remark, but then continued to speak, quietly, more like a priest than a friend or colleague. He was no longer telling a story, he was trying to help me live through something. And he had succeeded in sending me on errands in my own head, to places I hadn't visited in years. It freaked me out.

"It takes practice, but what you just felt is what I started to understand that day in Africa. We lose so many fragments of conscious memory that are meaningful for no logical reason, but meaningful because they're the building blocks of our characters and our visions of the world.

"Those moments and the feelings they bring are personal mythologies, tools for constructing the unfolding stories of our lives. They are keys to a palace in the subconscious in which dwells all that is truly unique in each of us. Everything else – every idea, every thought, every emotion – we share with others. Those are things that are given to us by society, family and genetics. But the weird, quirky associations we draw between the outside world and the inner mythologies we've developed as children... those are our own, and they are how each of us constructs his own universe. It's like biology. Think about the evolution of a species. People will tell you that it's about the perfecting of certain traits over time, but that's wrong. It's error that drives evolution; individual quirks that deviate from what has gone before, accidents, mutations. Well, deep memories are like little flaws in your emotional DNA. They make you different, and can make you strong, if you learn how to use them. With a little practice you'll start getting to the really powerful ones, memories that are maybe one static image, but mostly pure emotion. Whatever anyone tells you about God or karma or Tao, it's those emotions that are the real fabric and meaning of the universe. The meaning you give the world around you, like a fossil that shapes the soil and stone surrounding it.

"That's why Horokinetics has so much potential."

"Huh?" I had been more or less following him until he said that.

"Pete, look at the occult. Ever asked yourself what's really wrong with it?"

"It's silly."

"Why is it silly? It wasn't always. Spiritualism, mysticism, even the simpler stuff like tarot started out with some clear, desirable goals in mind. You see the same pattern again and again through history, across cultures. The dominant way of thinking, mainstream religion and science, succeed in packaging up the world in neat, sterile boxes, and some people feel the need to reach farther out into the world, to blur its edges and reclaim a sense of its mystery. It's a form of poetry. But the occult eventually begins to crystallize into just another search for some meaning out there in the world, and by doing so it loses its soul. It gets hijacked by teleology. That's what has happened in the western world. People started believing in spiritualism, rather than practicing it, and so it evolved from poetry to pseudo-science. The spirit forces of the ancients – wonderful images of how myth and memory and emotion color our world – were cheapened into telepathic powers and poltergeists. Wise women were degraded into psychics and spirit mediums. It all became cheap.

"But with Horokinetics you've depicted a universe that can be expanded infinitely inward as well as outward. Don't you get it? It's just an image, but it's a fantastic image of the infinite complexity of the human mind. What interests me is that inward journey through memory and association and all those vague feelings we don't have names for, the secrets held in that place in the mind where no one else can come. As a society we accept the idea that psychologists can dig into the negative feelings and memories created by trauma. But the ability to harness the positive ones is, to me, the most important of all creative processes, the only one that gives us any real power over ourselves that can't be broken by mass culture. It points to the one fundamental spiritual truth: that meaning is not to be found, but to be created."

I was going to have to take that home and chew on it. I tried not to let on how much my own inner tranquility had been disturbed by our brief little mind trip, or how little I'd understood of what he was talking about. "So, sorry, that's why you left Africa?"

He paused again. The silence was stifling, seeming to muffle even the street noise outside. And then the cloud lifted, as if the film we had been watching had come to an end and someone had turned the lights back on. He smiled, his eyes brightened, and his voice resumed its calm, matter-of-fact quality.

"That's what convinced me I had to study philosophy. I wanted to do some serious thinking. I needed to figure out what I believe, and why I believe it. To try to deconstruct our ideas of the origins of truth, the nature of reality and how it relates to all this stuff in here." His long forefinger tapped the side of his head.

"And now here I am," he added, grinning and taking another swig of beer, "assistant fortune teller."

The spell was broken. We both burst out laughing, and as beer succeeded beer the conversation moved rapidly away from philosophy and onto baseball. Jake more or less convinced me that my indifferent support of the Dodgers was nothing short of immoral, and after a half hour of the kind of mindless debate over Cal Ripken's legacy that boys indulge in after too many beers, we concluded that I was in no fit state to drive home. I crashed on Jake's couch – I just had to hope that this was all harmless metaphysical bullshit and that I wasn't going to wake up with my head shaved and some Hindu prayer tattooed on my chest.

Sunday at the fair was calmer than Saturday, and a little weirder. Maybe all the more straight-laced New Agers were in church, but the crowd that turned up for day two of the

Soulcraft Festival were pretty hard core, and sunk any hopes I had of improving on the previous day's performance. If relatively mainstream people weren't inclined to give "scientific" divination a try, what hope did I have with a bunch of telepaths, druids and militant Wiccans?

"Don't worry so much," Jake reassured me as we unpacked our gear. "I think we'll nail it today." I wasn't quite sure what that meant, but it was vaguely comforting.

The morning got off to a very slow start, but as I returned to our table after having wandered off to buy my third gluten-free biodynamic fudge brownie, I saw that we had a customer. I had been doing the readings so far, determined to see if I could get it right before sharing all the fun, but now it was Jake's turn. Across from him sat a girl, maybe 19 or 20, with a pink tuft in her otherwise black hair and wearing an enormous twiggy roughspun cotton sweater over tight ripped jeans. I guess she had just filled out her form, because Jake was still calling up her fractal on screen. I sat down beside him, introduced myself to our client, and watched.

Jake ignored me. He seemed totally absorbed in the girl and in the fractal image meant to be the mathematical mapping of her soul. He stared at the screen for nearly a minute, muttering to himself, before speaking.

"Katie," he said in a voice like dryer fluff, "you're a dreamer. I'm right, aren't I?"

The girl bit her lower lip and nodded solemnly.

"Yes," he continued, smiling like a stoned televangelist, "a dreamer, but I see something more rare than that. So many dreamers aren't doers, but you're different, aren't you? You have a great capacity for action." A pause, a look of recognition from Katie, and he kept going. "You aren't content to let your dreams rest. They lie there patiently, but they direct everything you do. They're your inspiration, deep inside you, the still point of the turning world, and they direct your actions in ways that other people just don't seem to understand."

Katie began nodding urgently, but she didn't say a thing. Her eyes grew wide, dreamy, and were fixed on Jake.

"But there's a problem, isn't there? Something is blocking you. You know..." Here he leaned towards her confidentially, crossing his arms and resting his elbows on the table. "The beauty of Horokinetics is that it's not time bound. It reaches infinitely into the past and future, unpicking the fabric of time itself, so it can find answers and ask questions that have existed for millennia and will exist for millennia. Yours is an ancient problem. You are Odysseus. You are Electra. Joan of Arc, Dido. You have everything you need to go forward, and yet there seems to be something in between you and your Ithaka. Katie?"

Her eyes grew bigger and she inhaled, waiting for his question as if she'd been waiting for it all her life.

"What's your favorite book?"

Her mouth fell open and stayed there for a moment before her tiny voice managed "The Catcher in the Rye."

Jake nodded. "I thought it might be. You see those fields in front of you, don't you. And you walk, and walk, but you can't seem to get to the other side." Katie started nodding back at him and never really stopped until the reading was over, slouching through her back rather than bending her neck, a slow rhythmic body nod.

"But you need to stop worrying. Horokinetics is about more than technology. We all rely so much on technology for results, don't we? Quick results. We live in a microwave oven culture. But it leaves us empty. Why? Because there's more, Katie. More to the pulsing glacial flow of time than results. There are voices inside you, Katie, voices heard, half-heard, in the stillness between two waves of the sea. Listen to them. What they'll tell you is to forget about what's on the other side of that field. Keep living your dreams, and trust them to take you where you need to go. Life is a road. Hope it's a long one, full of adventure, full of discovery. Okay?"

And that's when, swear to God, the girl started crying. No sobs or nose blowing or anything like that, but just a couple of tears, a quivering lower lip, and that idiotic nodding. "No one knows that," she whispered. "But you're right. Thank you."

Jake smiled gently at her and said he hoped that their little talk had helped. She whispered thank you again, smiling weakly and brushing the final tear from her cheek, and then walked, seemingly dazed, in the direction of the organic juice bar.

Jake turned to me and smiled. "Like I said, we all build our own private universes." He spoke quietly, as always, and without a hint of the smugness I might have felt in his position. "Luckily they all look more or less alike. What I just did, Horokinetics can do, if you let it. Let me help you make this big, and even your friend Vas will have to listen."

My eyes grew wide and I just nodded, a slow rhythmic body nod. "Damn," I muttered, and swallowed another bite of brownie.

6

I don't know if Katie ran around telling everyone at the Soulcraft festival about her experience or not, but shortly after she had drifted off like a puff of smoke from an incense stick, Jake began to attract a crowd. He performed another dozen readings, each of them as magical as the first. Not everyone cried, but everyone was moved in one way or another, and they all wanted more. No website, no leaflets, no phone number? Enlightenment by Horokinetics was a one-shot deal, and our growing flock were panicking at the thought of being left shepherd-less, as if they could already hear the wolves howling in the distance.

"Give us two weeks," said Jake confidently, out of nowhere, "then do an internet search for Horokinetics. We'll be there." First time he said it I looked at him in panic, second time in mere alarm. By the fourth or fifth I managed complicity, which was quickly replaced by excitement and determination. Horokinetics worked. This was going to be big.

Our self-imposed timeline involved several days in which we seemed to do nothing but talk. Emily and Susan got dragged back in for what started out as an evening of brainstorming and ended up with Jake and Susan talking excitedly about Jung and Joseph Campbell in one corner while Em and I drank coffee and talked about her problems with Daniel and whether or not she should move to San Francisco to accept a teaching job there. Over the next few days Jake would call me or Emily now and then with questions, and when Susan did it once as well it suddenly occurred to me that they were working together on something. I started to feel like I was losing control of my own creation. But that Saturday Jake unveiled to me what they had been up to, and any resentment I had felt was blown into some far distant corner of the fractal continuum.

Jake had taken Susan's psychological insights, Emily's science and my inspired bullshit and interwoven it with myth, history, poetry and spirituality to create a philosophical/metaphysical/divinatory system that was at once majestic and still clearly my own. The basics of Horokinetics remained intact, but richer, deeper, suddenly as intricate and bewildering as the fractals themselves. And to my surprise Horokinetics now had a thousand year history, dating back to the Greek Byzantine heretic monk Theogenes of Athos, who had been nourished by Heraclitus and Pythagoras and had in turn inspired Martin Luther, William Blake and even Albert Einstein.

"There's not much scholarly work on him," Jake had explained when I had objected that an internet search on the name yielded absolutely nothing, "and what little exists is mostly in Greek or Russian. The only existing copy of the Book of Apeiron was found in 1993 in a street market in Thessaloniki. A German tourist picked it up from one of the Black Sea Greeks selling bric-a-brac there. Not a bad find - I think it's still at the University of Heidelberg."

Jake proudly showed me his copy of the Book of Apeiron, a photocopy of a sad, tattered typewritten manuscript, with notes in the margins in German, presumably by whoever had translated it from the Heidelberg manuscript. He explained that Theogenes was born some time near the end of the 10th century in Trebizond, in what is now northern Turkey. Apparently there was little or nothing known of his childhood, since his next appearance in the historical record is in the year 1025 when he is being kicked out of the monastery of Megisti Lavra on Mount Athos after he pissed off the head monk in some complicated theological debate. Most scholars agree that Theogenes traveled widely throughout the empire during this period and spent considerable time in Egypt before returning to Athos in 1037, only to be branded a heretic and flee for his life in the following year. What became of him after that is pure conjecture, but he was rumored to have fled to live among the Seljuk Turks or back to Fatamid Cairo. Apart from such speculation, all that is left to history of Theogenes is the Book of Apeiron. "The Book of Infinity." Perfect.

"I'm not so sure about Blake, though," I objected. I'd had an English professor in college who was obsessed with Blake. It had made my first semester of sophomore year hell. It had almost kept me from majoring in English.

"Blake is worth the trouble. It's dense stuff, but if you're willing to do a little digging, and spend some time with it, you come up with some amazing passages straight out of Horokinetics. Lines so riddled with potential meanings that you could spend forever mining them. Stories within stories, ideas within ideas."

I nodded, paused, and then admitted that I found Blake pretty obscure.

"Exactly!" He pronounced the word triumphantly, as if Blake's obscurity clarified everything.

Nor think thou seest a wild Disorder here;
Thro' this illustrious Chaos, to the Sight,
Arrangement neat, and Chastest order reign...
Confusion unconfus'd! Nor less admire
This Tumult untumultuous.

"Everyone finds this kind of thing confusing. That's why it works. It's like the doctrine of trans-substantiation. Ever try to wrap your head around that? It works because ultimately people want an excuse to hand over the thinking to someone else. In a logical world, the risk is that people have to take responsibility for themselves. There are facts they need to learn and judgments they need to make on their own. But if

66

the world is run by mystical forces that are beyond their comprehension... well, then all we can do is have faith and trust in the Lord, right? Or trust in those few people who can understand and interpret the Lord's desires for us. We can't be blamed if we get it wrong. Makes life a lot simpler...

"We need to learn from Blake. He has a way of triggering dormant memories in his readers. He hints at half-remembered myths and legends and images that make his poetry eerie but somehow familiar, like he's speaking of far off worlds that you secretly visited in childhood. It's all vague associations and unintelligible promises. When he's not tapping into myth and history, he's inventing his own, and the combination gives you the feeling that he must know a lot more than you do, and that you had better trust him."

Jake's long blond hair swayed back and forth as his head moved in rhythm with his thoughts. I could suddenly imagine him as a very popular professor, one who filled lecture halls teaching subjects no one would otherwise ever want to touch. Spiritual guru never popped into my head, although it should have.

"Look, you've got to start appreciating what you've done here. Horokinetics is based on one fundamental and beautiful idea, that infinity can stretch inward as well as outward, that each of us contains within him an infinity at once ordered and chaotic. It's the stuff of gods, yet we have these psychedelic computer generated pictures that encapsulate it, help explain it just enough to put it almost within reach. It helps people open up a small window on the universe within them, and once they've seen what's in there, once they've realized that infinity is within them, part of them, then they're empowered. Then they can take control of their own lives and remake them, remake themselves. It's like having the Cliff's Notes to heaven. That's the idea, isn't it? Patterns of conscious thought behind the structure of the universe? Order behind the disorder?

"We now just need to do what the Nikes of this world do. We need to convince people that Horokinetics is truly a part of who and what they are, that it's part of their past and their identity in a way too profound to consciously understand.

"So I've tried to do that by enriching it, mixing metaphysical and scientific vocabularies and linking it all conceptually to great thinkers, poets and mystics. Add a little more complexity."

Horokinetics was already asking people to think about math, computers, the future, human nature, chaos theory and a non-Euclidean drawing of infinity, and here was Jake telling me that it needed to be more complex. If it had been anyone else I might have hit him.

But it worked. Looking at his writings, Theogenes of Athos really was an 11th century Horokineticist. Blake really was writing about fractals. Lao Tzu had the Mandelbrot Set in mind when he wrote the Tao Te Ching, and Dharma was nothing other than the bewildering cosmic unity of the fractal continuum. In Jake's hands the entire world seemed to wrap itself around the idea of Horokinetics and make it more real than science itself. And it was magic.

The hard part was getting all this magic out into the big wide world. Building the website was pretty easy, but we would need people to churn out our customers' fractal readings. If there was going to be a Horokinetics stand at every New Age event, fractal readings once a week in your local occult bookstore, then we needed to train people. But again, Jake had the answer.

"You don't have to hire anyone. You've got the website covered, so what we need to do now is give a training workshop. I already know a few people who'd be interested. They get free training so they can set themselves up as Horokineticists, and as a fee they pay you a percentage of their own profits. Part of their training is to work on the website, producing the fractal readings. I've got a lawyer friend who could help us incorporate as a company and deal with the trademark and copyright issues. You could probably even get college kids to volunteer as interns for 'work experience.' And if we need an office... yes, we need an office. I know someone who can help with that too. He's got an office up in Northridge on a long lease that's standing empty until next year. I'll talk to him."

Friends, friends of friends, and a handful of bored weirdos looking for something to do – that was the beginning of Horokinetics as a business.

Diego was baffled. He'd been convinced that I was joking when I first told him about it, and he still wasn't quite able to accept that I was actually gathering a team together and putting Horokinetics out there in the real world.

"Stacie would go apeshit if you really did this. She still hasn't forgiven you for the party."

"She's just going to have to deal, Diego. It's really happening. I figure I'll have the new site up live in another few days."

"And have a room full of teenagers giving people their horoscopes? Come on..."

"Not horoscopes, fractal readings. And they aren't teenagers. Except a couple."

Diego rolled his eyes and laughed.

"Well, it's your ballgame. Tell me when it's up and running."

We started with the website, figuring that if we had something solid we could point to, it would make us that much more convincing. The idea was to offer a free fractal analysis and sample reading to people logging on for the first time. After that, if a client were silly enough to want regular readings, he would have to pay a small fee. But to do all that, we needed some bodies to churn out the readings while we organized the training seminars for the live readers.

Emily's contribution was a couple of her more esoteric-minded high school students who were thrilled at the idea of getting involved in the genesis of this supposedly ancient metaphysical tradition. Jake produced Alana, whose part-time boyfriend lived in his apartment building. The others were a quiet girl named Sylvia who never talked and a couple of guys, Dave and Ed, chubby sorts of guys who drank two Cokes an hour and you can bet had their own blogs where they posted lists of their all time top ten classic rock albums or their strategies for playing World of Warcraft. Nice guys, and fairly smart, but when we started practicing giving fractal readings it became clear that smart wasn't enough.

Jake had proven at the Soulcraft Festival that reading a fractal, like casting a horoscope or reading tarot cards, was a subtle business. You've got to sound convincing, and that means learning to speak in a language that people want to hear. It's not just knowing the story, but knowing how to tell it. We needed expertise. And in the end, we found Magda.

Magda was the Hinks Memorial Professor of Tarot at the Thoth Institute of Higher Science in Santa Monica, and I had managed to persuade her to give a few of us a three day condensed version of her "Tarot: Introduction to Principles and Practice" course. The idea was Emily's, and was one of the few points on which she and Jake agreed. All we needed was a quick course in how to give tarot readings, and it would be easy to transfer those skills to Horokinetics by simply changing the lingo a bit. Magda didn't seem too interested in why we wanted the course, so I hadn't offered any explanations.

"Good morning," her heavy but clear accent rang majestically on the first day of class once everyone was seated. She then hesitated as if she expected applause, her wrinkled, sun blotched hands weighed down by at least a dozen rings and clasped in front of her as if in prayer. She was everything she was supposed to be: middle aged, Eastern European, a little stern and completely convinced of herself as a serious academic. "Before we begin, I would like to explain a little about my teaching style. I have been doing this for many years. My lectures are highly structured and finely tuned.

There will be time for interaction on the second and third day of the course, but for now I ask that you remain seated and silent. You may take notes, and at the end of each module I will answer questions. Now, as I explained to Mr. McFadden, we will be using the Thoth deck, which may be unfamiliar to some of you ..."

We held the class in the nearly empty office of Jake's friend, setting up three long tables to form a triangle. Four of us sat behind one table, four behind the second, and Magda sat enthroned behind the third. I looked around at my newly recruited "Horokineticists" and let out a soft little groan. Ed looked baffled. Tom, the shy high school kid who was in love with Emily, looked frightened. Big Dave chewed gum. Alana had a smirk on her face, but she always did. Todd and Catherine managed to take the thing seriously, already taking notes, but that almost worried me more than the blank expressions I was getting from the others. My future depended on this bunch of losers. I wasn't encouraged.

"Now I would like to say something about caring for your cards." She reached abruptly along the table and pulled a small wooden box towards her, the movement making her jewelry clink like windchimes and her wispy blouse balloon up and flutter in the air, as if she was giving off little puffs of smoke. She opened the box to reveal a greasy, tired-looking deck of cards.

"The cards must be allowed to do their work in dignity. They are not toys. Treat them with respect, and they will serve you well. They must be stored in a wooden box – it is very important that it be wood. I prefer cedar, but on no account must you use young pine. The wood is important because once you have seasoned the cards with your own vibrations, you must not allow it to be contaminated with other vibrations which may adversely affect your readings."

Alana glanced at me and pursed her lips together conspiratorially. Ed picked up his cards, sniffed them carefully, and set them down on the table again, looking more confused than ever. Magda continued,

"Many people will tell you that you must wrap the cards in purple or gold silk. It is an acceptable practice but, in my view, an unnecessary one. There is no evidence that cloth adds any protection for the cards. In my experience, it's only superstitious nonsense." Raking a batch of fingers and rings through her thick graying hair, she gave the closest thing to a chuckle that we ever got out of her and then went on to discuss the Major and Minor Arcana and the traits of individual cards. Todd took notes furiously. Alana kept pulling faces. Ed went into some kind of low blood sugar trance. It was a long, long day.

But by the end, I have to admit, it had become interesting. Day three was mostly taken up with practice readings, and it all sounded pretty convincing. Magda handed out our little diplomas, along with leaflets about her upcoming intermediate and advanced topics classes, and then left us with one last bit of advice.

"Remember," she said, standing, gripping the edge of the table with both hands, "the Tarot is an ancient and sacred art. To take it upon yourself to advise others is a heavy responsibility, and even though your advice is guided by the cards, you must dispense it carefully. Whatever the cards say, your message must be positive. You must encourage. You must show people the way forward to a better future, not condemn them to a grim and unalterable fate. Tarot is a gift. Give of it generously, but wisely. And congratulations."

Once it was over, we could forget about 80% of the information she gave us. The details of Tarot were irrelevant. But the process, the system of weaving someone's life out of nothing, was exactly what we needed. Magda had taught us how to breathe life into the skeleton of Horokinetics. All I could do now was hope that it would work.

7

"Accident at work? You might have long-term injuries you don't yet know about. Even if the accident was your own fault, you still might be entitled to compensation..."

"Sure you don't want another cup, Pete? Should be just a few minutes." Emily poured herself a coffee and settled back onto the couch next to me as the speakers hopped from commercial to commercial.

It was November, and pissing down rain, but I was happy. For a start, I like rain. Maybe you have to be from a desert climate to understand that, but when growing up, rain was an event. We'd even make popcorn. It was like a favorite old movie that comes on TV once every couple of years, that you'd probably never bother to rent on video, and that you would definitely get sick of if you saw it more often, but which, because it was both rare and somehow familiar, you'd get excited to see again. I was excited to see it again, because I knew it wouldn't last.

The couple of months that had passed since the party at Earthsong had been like one long freak rainstorm. Like Jack, I had planted a tiny bean that had come to me through my own stupidity. Rain had fallen and nourished the thing until it had grown into something big, something bizarre, leading into the threatening promise of the clouds. So there I was, busy climbing my own beanstalk, wondering if the goose that laid the golden egg was at the other end of it.

And then Jimmy called.

Well, okay, it wasn't Jimmy, it was his assistant, but it's the same principle. Jimmy Freewinder, the most popular, most controversial and most idiotic radio personality in Southern

California, wanted an interview. Jimmy was famous simply for being annoying and proud of it. But he reached millions, and people listened to him. Even if he said that Horokinetics was stupid, even if he said it was dangerous, a health hazard, guaranteed to shorten the penis of any man trying it, a huge percentage of his listeners would immediately want their fractals read.

"Yeah, listen, we checked out the site and everything, and we think homokonetics looks like just what we're after. Jimmy wants to make the show a little deeper. We'd be looking for the 'new path to enlightenment' angle on it, you know, something cutting edge for people who already have stone Buddhas in their backyards but are still searching. Wisdom for our age – you guys sound like the perfect fit."

You can bet your ass we were a perfect fit. We didn't need Buddha – we had Jake. The guy was brilliant, but just as important, he had something else I didn't – an unmatchable flair for dealing with people. He spent most of his time organizing our training program, which meant finding people who were interested in becoming licensed Horokineticists, training the trainers and overseeing the sessions. People raved about the training – he made Magda look like an incompetent amateur – and quickly we were building a small army of Horokineticists. Jake also took care of public relations; his Horokinetics blog and insightful Twitter feed helped keep us high in the search engines and drove traffic to our main website, but it was Jake's personal magic that generated the kind of word-of-mouth publicity we needed. He created a buzz that spread beyond the hardcore mind/body/spirit community and started reaching everyday, mainstream meat-eating sort of people. A hundred website hits became a hundred weekly and soon swelled to a hundred daily. One fractal reader in Northridge taught five readers in greater Los Angeles who taught twenty five from all over Southern California.

It's all teamwork, he'd insist. It was true to a point. His flair was nothing without all my work on the website. It would have gotten nowhere without Susan's insights and Emily's flash of genius. Even Diego had played his part. He agreed to spread the word among his more gullible associates, but on the condition that I never mention it to Stacie – ever since Earthsong she had referred to me darkly as "the con-man." He had gotten a few relatively influential people in Hollywood to take an interest – not big stars or anything, but we had a producer, a handful of casting agents and a couple of medium-timer actresses. By November Jake had compiled a small list of VIP clients whose readings he did himself. Among a still small but very cool set of people, we were beginning to matter.

And now Freewinder. It was too good to be true. I called Jake. I called Emily. I called my parents, Diego, Susan, anyone I could think of. Even Tanya was thrilled, and only Jake was not surprised. Steady growth was one thing, but this was immediate and spectacular. It felt great.

And then I panicked. Shit, what was I thinking? I couldn't give a radio interview. I'd sound like an idiot. I was an idiot. Freewinder would make a fool of me on live radio. My parents would hang their heads in shame, my friends drift away in embarrassment. I would die poor and alone, forgotten in some weed-infested unmarked grave. Clearly Jake needed to do the interview. However the interview went, I could count on Jake not to come away from it sounding stupid.

So the day came, and it was Jake in the studio. My family and friends were a bit less excited, but for me it was the best of both worlds. Horokinetics was still getting the publicity, but I could hide in the background. Or, more precisely, at Emily's apartment.

Out of the radio tumbled a jarring nanosecond of silence announcing the end of the commercial break. It was time.

"You are on the air with Jimmy Freewinder at KNAF Los Angeles. It's 5:00 and we've got a great show coming at you this afternoon. With us today is Jacob Simms. He's the leading expert in what they call Horokinetics, and he is here to tell the future. But first things first: let's take a look at the present with our 5:00 news summary. Over to you Bill."

"Thanks Jimmy. In a press conference held yesterday Russian President ..."

"Is it recording? Fuck, it's not recording."

"It's recording fine, Pete, relax."

"I don't think it is. Are you sure it is?" Emily was recording it all on her laptop, but she couldn't always be trusted with consumer electronics.

The radio droned on for a few more minutes of doom and gloom, and then Jimmy's sporty ironic sing song was back.

"Okay, today we're getting into some pretty heavy stuff, so I'm going to start off by asking Jamila a question. Jamila, are you with me?"

"I'm your sound technician, Jimmy. I'm paid to be with you."

"That's my girl. Now listen, and you've got to tell me honest, do you read your horoscope?"

"Every Sunday, and once a month in Cosmo."

"And you follow its advice?"

"When it makes sense, I guess I do. I swear by my lucky numbers."

"Use that for your lottery tickets?"

"That's right Jimmy."

"And do you win?"

"Sweetheart, if I won, would I be here?"

"Alright, well, we've got Jacob Simms here in the studio, and maybe he can help you out. He says he's found a scientific way to tell the future, and it's called – how do you say this Jake? – Horokinetics. Now Jake, why don't you tell me a little about it: what does that mean, Horokinetics?"

"The name comes from the Greek words for time and motion, but the essence of it is that we analyze the patterns, in both space and time, that structure infinity." Jake's voice was cool and professional, as if he'd given dozens of radio interviews before.

"So Horokinetics tells the future by studying infinity? Sounds like that could take a while."

"Put that way, it does sound like a big job. No, what we're doing is a little more manageable. We use computers to analyze the fundamental patterns that underlie everything and that, ultimately, weave infinity into a coherent whole. But it's about more than telling the future – these patterns are everywhere, and can help us explain our world and ourselves as well as predict where things are headed."

"Still sounds pretty heavy Jake. How'd you find these patterns?"

"That's been the work of poets, philosophers and scientists for millennia, and probably will be for millennia to come. But recent scientific advances – mainly in the realms of chaos theory and something called fractal geometry, which form the technical basis for how Horokinetics works – well, these advances have put us in a whole new league. With these tools at hand, we're progressing in leaps and bounds."

"Towards what?"

"Towards answering the big questions."

"What, you mean life, the universe and everything?"

"If you like."

"It's 42 man. Douglas Adams already answered it in the Hitchhikers Guide, it's 42."

Anyone else would have groaned, or more likely left an awkward silence not knowing quite how to respond to a comment that stupid. Not Jake – he had this funny aversion to other people looking stupid, even if their own genuine stupidity was the cause, and matched it with an ability to inject life into even the deadest joke.

"Okay, let's say it's 42. What happens when we try to live our lives by 42? We don't get very far. It doesn't tell us why we're here, or where we're going. With Horokinetics we're trying to take your 42 – what we know about our world and what it means to us – and reverse engineer it. We're trying to figure out how we get to 42. Once we understand that, we can start putting together a roadmap to the universe."

"Cool. Now you told me this morning that you think astrology is, in your words, a 'dangerous fraud.' Why is that?"

"All systems of divination are looking for the roadmap I was just talking about. Most of them don't spend much time speculating on the origins of that roadmap; they just try to read it with cards or tea leaves or whatever. But astrology is different because it claims to understand the causes. It doesn't just say that the position of Saturn is an indication of what may happen – it claims that the position of Saturn is the cause of what happens. Astrology is a jealous god. It's incompatible with other systems that look at causes. That includes most religions, unless you do some serious theological gymnastics."

"But Horokinetics does basically the same thing, right?"

"No, not at all. To keep with the map analogy, Horokinetics is a system to help people understand the lay of the land, to show them the topography so they can pick their path. Astrology, like most religions, supposes some kind of cosmic bus driver and tries to second guess what route he's going to take you on. Ultimately astrology is a teleological worldview. And teleology is slavery."

"Cool. Well, I was hoping we could talk about my – what do you call it? My fractal – so I went to your website, but... hate to tell you this, Jake, I went through the motions but never got it."

Jake didn't miss a beat. "We're a victim of our success these days – we've got a 48 hour time lag in producing readings, but we're hoping to cut that back down to just a few hours once we've trained more staff. But don't worry, I've got my laptop here, software's loaded, so we can do it live..."

"Nice save." Jake was magic. At least I thought so, and so did Jimmy Freewinder.

Emily and I listened to the rest of the interview in silence. When it was over, I took another sip of coffee and asked Emily what she thought. She shifted uncomfortably in her seat.

"I have to admit, he's pretty good. I still don't understand why you didn't do the interview yourself."

"Because I'd screw it up, Em, you know I would. Jake's too good at this not to let him do it. He's far more convincing as the public face of Horokinetics than I am." He was. In fact, the guy was brilliant. That calm voice, that tone of thoughtful confidence: he could have been selling vacations on Mars, and people would have bought them. And if it hurt a little to find that my own creation was coming to be associated with someone other than me, well... making the thing a success would be worth it, after all. Whoever's voice came over the radio, it was still my ball game. I kept telling myself that.

"You wouldn't screw it up, and please drop the low self-esteem crap. No, you are not your corporate-world high-flying brother. To be your high-flying brother you would also have to be a jerk. You are a jerk, of course," she added with a tolerant sort of smile, "just not that sort of jerk."

"That sort of jerk is coming back into town for Christmas, you know. I'm going to have to sit there over dinner in front of my parents and explain how I still don't have what my family would consider a real job and how I earn my living reading fortunes."

"I know." She took a breath and her voice softened. "I know. And I know how much it upsets you. You just seem to be taking all your cues from Jake these days, and I wish you'd start trusting your own judgment a little more."

"Look, let's agree to disagree about my ability to do a radio interview. Whatever you think of Jake, in just a couple of months he's turned Horokinetics from a failed science project into a successful business."

"I'm sure you'd have customers even if it weren't for..."

"Clients, Emily, clients. And those clients talk about Horokinetics like it's the next Botox. Jake did that. He's the ultimate guerrilla marketer. It's all about marketing, Em."

"Really, I thought it was all about getting a job with that CGI company. Have you ever called that guy, what was his name? Spaz something?"

"Vas. He didn't return my phone calls, remember."

"Sorry. Listen, I'm excited for you, you know that. I just worry that you've lost track of why you were doing this in the first place. Horokinetics is becoming more about what Jake wants rather than what you want. And to be honest, the guy gives me the creeps."

The guy was a little weird, no question. Anyone who'd choose to get a PhD in philosophy would have to be. And anyone who'd feel the need to take a break from it to give himself "the time to reflect on it all" had to be even weirder. Yet I wasn't the only one who found something valuable behind all the weirdness. We had all gotten to know Jake better after Soulcraft when we were busy reshaping Horokinetics to match his vision of what it could be, but Susan in particular had spent a lot of time with him. I hadn't given it too much thought, beyond being slightly annoyed at the knowing looks they gave each other when I admitted that I didn't know the difference between Jung and Freud. But clearly they had, and by the time Horokinetics.com had gone public, so had Susan and Jake. My jaw nearly hit the ground when they told me, but the fact that Susan approved of Jake enough to date him simply confirmed for me that he was brilliantly eccentric rather than dangerously twisted. The fact that Susan had a long track record of dating losers somehow didn't enter my head. Even if it had, one thing was certain about Jake – he was not a loser. The success of Horokinetics was proof enough of that.

"Don't worry, Em, there's plenty of time to track down Vas Papayannis and restart my CGI career. But right now… to be honest, I'm having too much fun. This is exciting, Em, I'm basically running my own business."

"Yeah, but is this really the kind of business you want to be in? Fortune telling?"

"Astrologers do all right."

"You hate astrologers."

"Listen, I'm just going to take it a little farther and then move on."

Emily looked at me for a minute. "Okay," she said quietly, obviously not entirely happy. "I'm sure you know what you're doing."

Victory Boulevard gleamed dismally as I drove back from Emily's that evening. Headlights twinkled in the damp, but nothing seemed able to light the vast oily puddle that was slowly filling the San Fernando Valley. The few cars that had ventured out raced to get wherever they were going in that typically fearful LA way of dealing with extreme weather: either don't drive, or drive like hell. As if by driving faster you might outrun the slippery road beneath your wheels.

It seemed to take forever to get back to Tanya's. I'd gotten trapped in sequence with the red lights; once you hit one, you hit all the others, and only a block of dangerous driving, either way too slow or way too fast, could enable you to squeeze through a yellow and get back in synch with the greens. Block by block I sped up, slowed down, stopped, sped up, slowed down, stopped, working my way painfully westward across the Valley, counting the taco stands and listening to the tinny music coming from my car's crappy stereo system. Finally I tiptoed into the apartment, checking my watch as I came through the front door. 10:27. It had seemed so late on the road, late in a guilty teenager sort of way.

Tanya was on the couch, watching an old rerun of Frasier. Normally I could expect only a brief distracted "hey" under such circumstances, but tonight Tanya's "hey" was much more animated, and was even accompanied by an almost unheard of gesture: she turned off the TV. She didn't just turn down the volume, or put it on mute. She turned it off. Blank screen. Silence. It was strange. But then Tanya had been behaving strangely recently. She'd stopped badgering me all the time. She had grown more lively, more demanding, more interested. More time consuming and less unpleasant. I wasn't really sure of what to make of it, but then I hadn't been able to give it much thought. For the first time since Alcantrix, I was a busy man, "trying to run my own business" as I would constantly remind her, my parents, and anyone else who might listen. My mind just wasn't on her, and I guess she'd noticed, and started to think that maybe it mattered.

"I tried to call you at the office," she said, twisting her body to face me and draping her arms over the back of the couch. "They said you weren't there. Did you hear the interview?"

"Yeah, it went great. Emily taped it, so you can listen if you like. Jake was fantastic." I handed her the CD, but I knew she wouldn't bother.

"So you listened to it at Emily's?"

Lie, don't lie? Lie, don't lie?

"Um, yeah. And I had to talk to Emily about a few things anyway. Weren't you going out with Jennifer and Pete tonight?"

"I cancelled. Jennifer's been getting on my nerves. Anyway, an evening in sounded nice for a change. I made some extra pasta in case you came home for dinner."

"I've eaten, thanks though." I peeled off my jacket and hung it in the hall closet. Tanya remained draped over the back of the couch, her eyes following me as I drifted into the open plan kitchen to get a beer from the fridge.

"I guess you and Emily got something to eat?"

"Uh, yeah." That seemed to answer her question, and she stayed quiet for a few minutes as I poured my beer into a glass and came over to sit on the small futon, a remnant from her college days that she still used as an easy chair. I started flipping through a magazine, as I'd normally do, expecting Tanya to turn the TV on again. But she didn't.

"Well," she said, lifting herself up and walking over to me, "I'm glad the interview went well. I'm happy for you." I looked up at her standing over me, smiling, and she promptly crouched down and kissed my forehead.

That's where I was supposed to drop the magazine and kiss her on the lips. I didn't though. I just smiled and looked back down at my magazine, so I didn't see the look of affection wither from her face. She sighed too loudly for any semi-intelligent man to ignore and disappeared into the bedroom, returning a few minutes later with a blanket and a pillow. With surprising accuracy from about ten feet she tossed them into my lap. I looked up and could see that she had been crying, but the look on her face was one of resentment, not sadness.

"You like the futon so much, you can sleep on it, dickhead." And with that she returned to the bedroom, slamming the door behind her.

I had hoped that the next morning things would be better.

"Hey, sorry about last night," I offered, a bit sheepishly, when she wandered into the kitchen and started making coffee.

"Mmm," was her reply, which was actually pretty normal for Tanya on a Sunday morning.

"I was a little distracted."

"No kidding."

Assuming that this was about as close to forgiveness that I was going to get, I joined her in the kitchen and gave her a quick hug from behind. She patted my hand, disengaged herself from me, and went over to the fridge for some milk.

"So are you fucking her?" she asked, her eyes elsewhere, maintaining a calm, detached tone in her voice.

"What?" I snapped, hoping to convey with that one word the right balance of shock, hurt and incomprehension. Of course I knew what she meant. Emily and I had been spending a lot of time together, and it didn't take any great understanding of women in general or of Tanya in particular to realize that she might become jealous. That was the one reaction I was prepared for, and had almost hoped for. I was very guilty of neglect and I knew it. Infidelity, however, was not my thing, so with this false accusation I was effectively absolved from feeling bad about having been a jerk. All I needed now was a little display of injury and forgiveness on my part, just to reassure her, and all would be well.

"Well, are you?" she repeated, this time with a bit more of a tremor in her voice.

"Who, Emily? Of course not – you should know better than that. We're just friends, and have been for a long time."

"And what about us?"

"What about us?" I hated it when she was vague.

"You and Emily are 'just friends'. So what are we?"

"What are you talking about Tanya, you're my girlfriend."

"You could try acting like it."

Shit. There was nothing I could say to that. No, I hadn't been acting like it, but to be fair, I never really had. Neither had she. But obviously I couldn't say that. So I tried being indignant.

"Damn it, Tanya, you know how hard I'm working these days." Jesus, I was starting to sound like Ralph Kramden. "Six months ago you were criticizing me for being unemployed, like I was some lazy pothead. Now that I've managed to get a job – start my own business, in fact – all you can do is complain that I don't spend all my time with you. I could use a little more support and a little less selfish bullshit."

As I spoke I could see her face growing redder and redder, but there wasn't much I could do about it. The indignant strategy wasn't working. The best I could do was to try softening it with a little more indignation, suitably redirected.

"You *know* that I care about you." It sounded lame. Tanya just shook her head in frustration, or disgust, or maybe despair. I was never good at reading her.

"If you're going to be stupid, then just shut up, okay? Go play with your precious computer and do whatever the fuck it is you do with your psychic friends all day."

"Fine," I shouted back at her. "If you're going to be like that, then..."

Then what? I'd started the sentence, but I had no idea how to finish it. I think the idea was that I would storm out of the apartment. But I was standing there in my underwear, smelly, unshaven and looking pretty ineffectual. So instead I stormed into the bathroom, took a quick shower, and emerged to find that Tanya had closed herself up in the bedroom again. In I went, trying to keep my dignity as I grabbed some clean underwear and got dressed while she sat on the bed, gulping coffee and breathing loudly. I paused in the doorway to announce, for no apparent reason, that I would be at the office, and only as I was half way out the door did Tanya speak.

"Pete?" she said. Had I imagined a tremble in her voice?

"What?" I replied, as surly as I could find the energy for.

"It's a stupid name." I looked at her blankly. "Horokinetics. It's a stupid name."

"Thanks," I muttered, and slammed the door behind me.

8

Our office was nothing special – basically it was a large cardboard box nestled among a dozen or so other cardboard boxes that housed other sad little companies people had started for reasons just as obscure as mine. But it had two advantages. First was that it was a place of my own. Home was, for the time being, Tanya's apartment, and I needed someplace to escape to. Escaping to my parents' house was a bit humiliating. Escaping to Emily's was comforting but also a constant reminder of what I wanted and didn't have. Escaping to "my office," such as it was, at least gave me some hope.

Its second advantage was that Jake's friend let us use it for nearly free. For a guy who hadn't lived in LA for that long, he seemed to have a lot of friends. He'd found us our trademark lawyer. A couple of our trainers were friends of his. I couldn't help wondering who all these people were, why they were so willing to help me as a favor to Jake, but I didn't question it too closely. When the goose lays a golden egg, you don't ask it awkward questions. They all seemed normal enough.

More normal than the sorry crowd who haunted the office, churning out responses to the many requests for fractal readings we were getting via the website. I drifted in, late as usual, and saw that everyone who should be there was there. Ed and Spencer were talking about football, Alana was chewing gum as absentmindedly as she was typing, and Todd was working steadily over in the corner as I slipped into the main office. The Vortex, Alana had called it, and the name had stuck. It was a dead room with stale air, no color but the brownish purple of the carpet tiles designed not to show stains, and full of people who really should have been doing something more productive with their lives.

"Hey Pete, what's up?" Apart from being the only one apart from Jake with a sense of humor, Alana was also the only one other than Jake who managed more than a grunt in the mornings. I don't know where she got the energy; by most standards her life story was even more uninspiring than mine. She was an actress – "whatever that means" she had added, in parentheses, on the sad little resume she handed me when I was interviewing applicants. Whatever it meant, it didn't mean anything she was paid for. Drama queen might have been a better description, but you can't write that on a resume.

I smiled and patiently asked her how she was doing.

"Oh I'm okay. Except Sydney dumped me again."

"Really?" Damn, had to stop. Turn. "I'm sorry to hear that." I didn't know what else to say. Sydney was a pool cleaner she'd been dating, and just about every day we got a detailed account of how the relationship was going. This was the second time he'd dumped her in a month.

"Oh, don't worry. He'll be back. My fractal said so." She flashed me her silly trademark grin, smiling while biting the end of her tongue, and sat down again at her computer. "Coffee's almost fresh," she added, and then returned to whatever she'd been doing when I came in. Nutcase, I thought, almost happily, as I passed into my own private office and closed the door behind me. The girl was too untalented to do what she was qualified for, and too underqualified to do anything else. We understood each other.

I spent the next half hour or so going through my inbox. One of the stranger results of the media attention was that we had started to get a lot of hate mail. Some of it was hilarious.

"To: Senator William Theodore Dobbs III

CC: Horokinetics Inc.
Subject: Save our Children!!!!!
Dear Senator Dobbs,

I'm just writing to ask you why in our great Nation under God (although we're not allowed to say it these days) where we are supposedly free our children are left to the Mercy of atheist cult leaders and God-haters. This new website called Horokinetics is obviously yet another liberal indoctrination scam to lure our children away from our traditional American Values. Why is our Government not acting? I am a taxpayer, therefore I pay your salary and I am YOUR BOSS. The time to act is NOW."

By linking the system to world religions and literature, we managed to offend a pretty broad spectrum of born-again Christians, high-strung intellectuals and humorless New Age mystics. And they all loved to send emails. Apart from the run-of-the-mill accusations of atheism and Satan-worship, I was accused of sullying the name of Lao Tzu, radically misinterpreting Blake, and even underestimating the role of Vishnu in the construction of a post-fractal cosmology. Not bad, for someone who a few months ago didn't know how to pronounce Lao Tzu and thought Vishnu was a type of curry.

Somehow I couldn't help reading them all. The fundamentalist Christian ones were the most common and the most boring, but I still enjoyed them. They were flattering. They told me that I mattered, that with Horokinetics I had done something significant enough for people to waste their time writing to me.

I was deeply involved in one of these emails when I looked up and found Jake standing in front of my desk, a funny sort smile on his face as if he'd heard me talking in my sleep.

"Jake!" I blurted out in surprise, my voice hitting an unintended high note.

"Hey Pete, sorry I startled you."

"No worries. Welcome back. How was your trip?" Jake had taken a long weekend "to sort some things out," as he'd put it.

He nodded. "Just what I needed. Went out to Joshua Tree, camped in the desert."

"Didn't you freeze your ass off out there?"

He laughed. "Listen, I'm from Colorado. A little cold is good for the soul. Anyway, the desert has its own seasons, and a desert winter has something... something pure about it. There's a silence you won't come across anywhere else. It frees you up to listen."

He slid the grubby blue backpack off his shoulder, setting it down on the chair in front of him and rummaging through it as he spoke. Pulling out a tattered black notebook and tucking it under his arm, he dug his hand in deeper for a moment and retrieved a small, clumsily gift-wrapped package.

"I picked this up on my trip," he said, handing the gift to me. "Just to say thanks for all you've done for me." I looked at the present, and then back at Jake again, not quite knowing what to say. "It's nothing big," he added, as if to mask my awkwardness from me.

"Thanks. You shouldn't have. Should I open it now?"

He smiled and nodded, so I ran my finger under a fold of the wrapping paper, popping open its scotch tape seal, and drew out a small box. Pulling the lid off, I stared for a minute, trying not to let confusion show on my face. The box contained a small brownish spiral shell, less than an inch in diameter, attached to a thin leather cord. A fossilized shell. It was heavy for its size, hard and cool, and on turning it over I saw that it had been sliced lengthwise down the middle and polished to reveal a series of chambers within. Each chamber was smaller than the next as they spiraled inwards into oblivion and each was filled with a subtly different colored blend of mineral that had seeped in and hardened over millions of years. The back was pretty but plain – the polished inside was dazzling.

"Thanks, man." As a kid I had been obsessed with fossils – part of my typical little boy's dinosaur fixation, I suppose, but it was more than that. I had always loved the feel of the things, the satisfying weight that such once-fragile beings had gathered over millennia as they lay buried, just waiting for a kid like me to dig them up one afternoon after school. There were hundreds of fossils to be found up in the canyons, if you knew where to look. Mostly clams, but that was exciting enough back then. I had a lot of fond memories of the hours I spent digging through the dirt along Old Topanga Canyon or Stunt Road, waiting to make my big find. The dry chalkiness of the dirt, the feeling of anticipation when you'd come across a good, large flat rock that would split easily, and the anticlimax when it turned out to contain nothing more than the tiny delicate brown marking of the roots of some long-dead plant, or a few round rusty splotches that could have been anything and were almost certainly nothing. The thrill of unearthing one of those corkscrew shaped shells, or a perfect undamaged clam shell. Happy times. Standing there with Jake in that bleak office, fluorescent lights buzzing overhead, I could almost smell the herbal tang of the bushes and feel the itchiness of the dust in my nose. And now I held in my hand what then would have been the find of my dreams, courtesy of Jake Simms. It seemed almost as if he must have known.

I rubbed the shell gently between my thumb and index finger, enjoying the contrast between the rough outside and the polished smoothness of the side that had been cut away to reveal its perfect spiral. With my thumb I could just feel the faint ripples in the stone where each chamber ended and the next began. Examining it in the light for another minute, I slipped the leather cord over my head and thanked Jake again. He replied with a faint, almost bashful smile.

"I got the other half as well," he continued suddenly, pulling an identical necklace out from under his shirt and taking it off so he could look at it better. "Don't worry," he continued, laughing, "it doesn't make us blood brothers sworn to defend each other's teepees or anything. I just liked it, and I thought you might too."

I thanked him, but awkwardly. Straight guys don't make thoughtful gestures to their male friends. It's somewhere towards the front of the Straight Guy Code of Conduct. Rule 5: No SG shall demonstrate affection, sensitivity, or thoughtfulness towards another SG except in cases of death, dismemberment (genitalia excepted – see Rule 17 regarding non-derisive genital commentary) or defeat of professional sports team in major competition. I was pretty sure that Jake wasn't gay. Rules just didn't seem to apply to him.

"It's not as random as it may seem. Mathematically it has the same property as fractals do, that it doesn't fundamentally change as a result of changes in scale – it's a logarithmic spiral, so however big it grows it never changes shape. It's been a sacred infinity symbol since ancient times in cultures all over the world, from the Celts to the Maori. An infinity you can hold in your hand, that rather than expanding outwards, spirals inward, diving forever towards the still point of a turning world. If there was ever a perfect symbol for Horokinetics, well... I've always been a sucker for symbolism," he laughed.

"Anyway, you've introduced me to a new phase in my life, so I just wanted to say thanks."

That was a constant fiction he kept up, that I was the one helping him, that letting him find me offices and lawyers, transforming my simple idea into something complex and even marketable was all some kind of big favor I was doing for him. This time, when I tried dismissing it, he had a different response than his usual cryptic comments.

"Pete, trust me, you've done more for me than you realize. I'm developing some great ideas for my dissertation from all this. Usually epistemology is something you have to sort of reverse engineer, but now I'm able to observe the development of a belief system from the ground up. Listen, why don't you come over to my new place tonight and have dinner. I've got some friends coming over, and you can get a little taste of where all this is going."

I accepted gladly. An evening at home would mean either another fight with Tanya or lots of tiptoeing around to avoid one, neither of which sounded like much fun. Besides, I was curious. Jake had left his little Valley apartment about a month earlier to move into a house, a big house from the sound of it, but he was so reluctant to give any more details about the place that we all found it a little mysterious. Even Susan had only seen it once.

"It's pretty," she'd said when the subject came up. "But it's way out in Agoura, up there in the canyons where everyone has horses." She said that Jake preferred to stay at her place anyway, and that she was only too happy. The one night she'd stayed with him and tried the commute out to her office had been hell.

So right after work I found myself once again following Jake on his old Suzuki as we raced up Las Virgenes Road, turned onto a forgotten little side road and left the civilized world behind. Our cars wound along a tiny, one-lane road until we swerved around a huge oak tree and, almost without realizing it, entered the driveway. My heart leapt into my throat as the nose of the car plunged downwards onto a packed earth road which, after about fifty feet, doglegged right into a large, roughly circular and very shady cul de sac. Three motorcycles and a couple of other cars – an old model Mercedes and a baby blue Nissan – were already parked there, but what I noticed first was the shade. The place seemed to be all trees and shade, as if the house, the canyon, and even the outside world were merely afterthoughts. No breeze blew, yet the dense pack of oak, sycamore trees and one huge incongruous magnolia all seemed to rustle in the suddenly cool air.

"Come on in," Jake invited me almost shyly.

As we first passed through the large, almost monastic front door, the place seemed surprisingly small. There was an open plan living room on the right, the sort of overly clean and well-decorated space that ends up being used only for special occasions. On the left, a door led into the kitchen, and I could see a short hall leading to a room at the back, and that seemed to be it. Susan's comment that it was "way too big for him" seemed bizarre.

But as with everything else about Jake, I simply hadn't noticed what really mattered. The house was built on a steep incline, a slope leading down to a small creek, so the spread of the place was vertical rather than horizontal. We were at the very top of a house which was built downwards, a series of landings, balconies, and floors consisting of only one or two rooms each, all branching off a central staircase like some crazy wood and shingle double helix pasted to the side of the canyon. Half the rooms were nearly empty, one housing an old futon, another a gigantic mahogany wardrobe, and the few that Jake occupied were almost as spare. Only the library, as he called it, was full, stacked floor to ceiling with books he must have had shipped out from Colorado since the evening I had visited his old apartment.

But most of his living, Jake explained, was done outdoors, and when we reached a level maybe two floors down from the entrance I saw why. Here the house seemed to jut out farther from the hillside, as if the bottom half had been pushed outward by some huge geological shift, leaving the top of the house where it had been. Where the two halves overlapped, a sliding glass door led out onto the roof of the bottom half, which formed a large half-covered terrace looking out onto a jumble of trees, gigantic boulders, and the creek a good 80 feet below.

Jake left me there to admire the view while he disappeared to get us a couple of Sierra Nevadas. I could see the roof of one other house poking out from the trees maybe a hundred yards away, but otherwise the impression was of total seclusion. We were wedged down in a creek bed among the trees, like moss growing between stones, protected from the harsh realities of the outside world, and even had there been a lot of other houses in that little canyon, we would hardly have noticed. The whinny of a horse somewhere in the distance told me that there were stables, or maybe just a riding trail, but the only other sounds were the chirping of birds, the rustle of leaves, and the faint trickle of the nearly empty creek below. And yet as soon as I began to actively listen and admire the silence, it was broken. There were people here. I could hear voices, faint voices, that seemed to come from the creek itself. I listened more closely: there were two voices, one distinctly male, the other uncertain, that seemed to be arguing in hushed tones from somewhere below me. Of course, the cars, I reminded myself. There were obviously more floors below this one that I hadn't seen yet, and Jake must have guests staying down there. He had said nothing about the others yet, but that was typical Jake.

"So how'd you come across this place?" I asked him when he had returned with our beers and a bowl of chips. At the back of the terrace, under the overhang, was a long wooden table flanked by benches, but he led me over to a small café table in the corner farthest from the glass doors under the fading light of the early evening sky. He looked unhappy with the question, but given how evasive he'd been about this house all along, I wasn't surprised.

"It's a long story," he said, popping a potato chip in his mouth as if to impede his own ability to tell it.

"I mean, I love it, don't get me wrong, but it's kind of overkill for a guy living alone, isn't it?"

"It wasn't entirely my own choice," he answered slowly. Visions of a secret life suddenly popped into my head: an insane wife he kept locked away in this sprawling house, a flock of illegitimate children he had fathered and now supported, a half-way house for refugees. But he was quick to burst the bubble.

"It belongs to an old friend of the family," he explained, his eyes uncharacteristically avoiding my own. "He's declared bankruptcy and, well, he's hiding assets. He pretends to live here, but instead he's renting it out cheap, for cash, to someone he trusts not to blow his cover. So that ended up being me."

"Damn. Not a bad deal."

"No," he agreed, but quietly, as if not entirely sure. He was uncomfortable with dishonesty, and it reminded me how happy I was not to be philosophical. Too many principles, I reflected, just make life difficult. "No, it's a beautiful place," he continued, perking up a little when realizing that I didn't think less of him for it. "It suits me, and it's allowed me to start my discussion groups – it was impossible to get a good group of people together in that little place in Northridge.

"I can imagine. So do you do a lot of these things?"

Jake smiled. "More than Susan would like, but no, not a lot. Once or twice a week I get a few people over and we talk, that's all. Something I'd missed from my Boulder days I guess."

"So, what? You sit around and talk about Plato? I can imagine that getting on Susan's nerves."

Jake glanced over the railing as the sound of voices again floated past before being reabsorbed by the conspiratorial bulk of the house and the trees around us.

"We talk about all sorts of things. Lately we talk a lot about Horokinetics, actually. I've got them all reading the Book of Apeiron, and I use quotes from it to get people talking about abstract ideas. It gets people thinking. You should come, we're having one tonight if you want to stick around."

I was just curious enough to say yes. I was even less inclined than Susan to sit around for hours trying to sound deep so as not to be embarrassed in front of Jake, but this was a chance to see Jake in his own element and perhaps to figure out a side of him that I'd never quite understood. So we sat and talked in the free and easy way we always did, and as usual the time went by more quickly than I could account for. Was it an hour later? Maybe only 15 minutes. Soon, in any case, the doorbell rang, but Jake didn't move.

"A few of the group are already here," Jake responded to my quizzical look. "One of them will get it. Relax, finish your beer. They'll all drift up here in a few minutes." I listened for and soon heard the quiet shuffle of footsteps coming from downstairs. Two women and two men filed out onto the terrace, and the steps of at least one other person continued upwards to open the front door. Jake took one more quick sip of beer and stood up as the group made their way around the long table and towards us.

A tall, lean but muscular woman in her early 40s walked at the head of the group, the others trailing behind her like attendants or bodyguards, and stopped a few feet from me and Jake.

"We're still missing Kyla, Avatar, and Fabien," she announced, eyes locked on Jake, as if delivering an expected report to her commanding officer. "Oh, and of course Daniel."

"Okay, well, I think we should probably start getting dinner together. They'll turn up soon enough."

She seemed to smile more with her eyes than her lips as she said "Arthur's brought his pesto sauce again. Kyla'll bring her own macrobiotic mung beans or whatever she eats." At a nod of approval from Jake, she turned, her sandy brown hair seeming to give off the smell of straw as it swung around, and spoke to a preppy-looking black man in round wire frame glasses standing a few feet behind her. Out of context, it had taken me a minute to recognize him as our trademark lawyer.

"Arthur, sweetie, you mind getting the pasta going?" Arthur smiled affectionately at her and then looked over at Jake.

"About twenty minutes Jake?"

"Sounds great."

"Tara, you mind helping me with the salad?" Next to him, an attractive and unhappy-looking woman in her mid-thirties frowned briefly, glanced at Jake and the other woman, and then agreed. "Okay, but if Kyla complains about how I chop tomatoes again I can't be held responsible for any casualties." Tara and Arthur turned and vanished into the house, and only when they were gone did the woman look at me. Her hazel eyes matched her hair and the freckles on her sun-leathered face almost perfectly, and this accidental coordination helped accentuate her look of perfect composure. She was beautiful in a stern, almost majestic way, like a Roman statue or an old ship.

She said nothing for a second or two, sizing me up, until Jake spoke. "This is Peter McFadden, the founder of Horokinetics. I thought it was about time he came to one of our little get-togethers." I smiled weakly and put out a hand.

"I'm Jericho," came her low, sensuous, gravelly voice as she took my hand firmly and gave it a shake. "How do you do," she added, with the formality and inflection of someone speaking a foreign language. She smiled briefly, as if at her own joke, and then turned back to Jake before I could reply.

"Anything else we need to get done beforehand?" she asked.

"No, I don't think so," Jake replied casually. "I'm not sure what wine I have left, but I'll take a look."

"I can do that Jake," rang an eager voice from the direction of the house. I turned and saw Emily's boyfriend standing at the door next to a short stocky man who looked like he could be a bouncer at a nightclub. Daniel noticed me standing there and for a second something like panic spread over his face, but he quickly regained control and nodded in my direction. The bouncer emerged from the semi-darkness and onto the terrace, revealing a young but hard face, which only the skull earring he had dangling from one ear could make look sympathetic. Daniel turned to go, but a word from Jericho stopped him.

"Not necessary Daniel. Arthur and I brought some Chianti." Daniel froze, turned back to face us and walked dejectedly out onto the terrace. He cast a resentful, defeated look at Jericho, but when the doorbell rang again a moment later, he was permitted to answer it, and seemed pleased.

"Weasel," the bouncer muttered audibly as he was leaving.

"Toby!"

Everyone froze: the bouncer, Daniel, the silent middle aged man who had come in with Jericho, even Jericho herself seemed to tense her lithe body. The voice was Jake's, and for the first time in my experience, it was angry.

"Sorry Daniel," Toby muttered, ungraciously. "Bad day."

"Daniel can take care of himself," Jake went on, his eyes never leaving Toby. "It's to me that you owe an apology. When you offend my guests you cheapen my hospitality."

Toby shrunk two sizes. All the power drained from his muscular arms, all the ferocity from his snarling face. Even his spiky peroxide hair seemed to wilt at the sound of Jake's voice. Stripped of his arrogance, I saw that Toby could not be much older than twenty.

Taking a second to collect himself, he breathed deeply, straightened his shoulders and answered.

"You're right Jake. I'm sorry. It won't happen again. You have my word."

"Now why don't you help Daniel carry stuff in and set the table. I'll get the door."

They all went their separate ways, leaving me alone with Jericho and the quiet man, who finally broke his silence and introduced himself, in a soft, vaguely European-sounding voice, as Mathias. He was the owner, he explained, of Mathias' Books in Pasadena, the kind of small new-and-used bookstore that Emily tended to haunt.

"I'm sorry I don't have a card," he said, smiling affably, "but it's not hard to find. Do you read German? We have much in German, one of the largest selections of German literature in Los Angeles. But of course English also." His face betrayed his concern – justified, in fact – that my lack of German might discourage me from visiting, so I told him I'd drop by some time and quickly changed the subject.

Jericho stood by watching us talk but made no effort to join in until Mathias excused himself and walked out to the far corner of the terrace. "You must pardon me," he explained, looking a little sheepish, "but I must have a cigarette before the others arrive. Otherwise I get a girl younger than my own daughter telling me that I am killing myself. Not good."

I glanced awkwardly at Jericho, searching quickly for something to say that wouldn't sound stupid.

"So what's your sign?" she asked me, deciding that I wasn't likely to break the silence any time soon.

"My...? Oh, Leo" I stuttered.

She smiled and leaned her head towards me confidentially.

"That was a joke," she explained, enunciating the words carefully in what I took to be friendly mockery. I nodded and chuckled, relieved that the ice seemed to have been broken between us.

"Well, the famous fortune teller. The man who started it all – Jake's told me a lot about you."

"Anything good?" When she showed no sign of enlightening me, I continued, "So how do you know Jake?"

"Old friend," she answered vaguely, glancing over at Mathias. "I have a riding school a little farther up the canyon, so we're almost neighbors."

"Really? My mother always wanted me to learn to ride."

"You should," she answered, but I was sure she didn't mean it. Something in this woman made me feel conspicuously unworthy of horses, and it was pretty obvious that it was only out of respect for Jake that she bothered talking to me at all. She was one of those people who belong to a sort of natural aristocracy, born with an ability to be condescending to seemingly anyone without needing to justify it based on wealth or status.

"Must be great, riding up in the canyons all day," I said just to have something to say. "I learned a little when I was a kid, but I never was very good at it. Horses didn't really seem to like me."

Her gaze shifted from me to the dark canopy of trees surrounding us.

"Horses aren't like people," she murmured, half to herself. "You can't bullshit them. If you respect them, then they listen, and it's like you become one with them. There's no horse or rider, because together you've become something new and different. And if you can do that – if you can recreate yourself and the horse into one being – then there's no need for persuasion, because what you want and what the horse wants is the same. It's a very Zen, very creative process. You have to experience it to understand." She fell silent, watching the trees, and clearly had no more use for me.

The others returned in a few minutes, thankfully, and before long we were sitting around the table working our way through Arthur's spaghetti and Jericho's wine as the darkness and the mosquitoes collected around us. A line of citronella candles running down the center of the table kept both at a distance, and gave the whole proceeding the feel of a medieval banquet. Jake sat like a patriarch at the head of the table, with Jericho immediately to his right. Between me and Jericho sat a very tall, lanky guy with long jet black hair who called himself Avatar and obviously enjoyed trying to shock me with his tales of seducing naïve young Scandinavian men on a recent vacation in Spain. To my right sat Daniel, who seemed relaxed and cheerful after having had his cause defended by Jake, then Fabien, a French philosophy student who spent much of the evening nodding and muttering to himself. Across from me was a tedious twenty-something new age traveler named Kyla, complete with beads and dreads and a chemically-induced hazy stare. Toby sat between her and Tara, and on her left were Mathias and Arthur. The far end of the table was flanked by two awestruck girls whose names I never caught.

Once we were all about half way through our first glass of wine Jake started to speak. His voice, unannounced and quiet though it was, fell like a damp towel on the four or five different conversations going on around the table, bringing an instant hush. Even the crickets seemed to grow quiet.

"Thanks everyone for turning up tonight. I think it's great that you're willing to give up a Friday night to come over and bullshit, and I hope we can get a really good discussion going and make it worth everyone's while. And hopefully no injuries this week..." A few chuckles acknowledged Jake's in-joke and marked the true regulars from the newbies.

"As most of you know, tonight we've got Pete McFadden with us, the man who married the timeless wisdom of Theogenes with computer technology to give us Horokinetics. Our discussions would be much poorer if it weren't for Pete's courage and vision."

I got a brief round of applause, and there was some excited whispering at the far end of the table before Jake resumed his monologue.

"For the past few weeks we've been talking about man's role in relation to society and the various strands of fatalism and conformism which bind individuals to the community. We've also been looking at the work of Theogenes of Athos, one of Western culture's most daring, if little known, intellectual non-conformists. The two strands of thought have been pretty harmonious so far, but I think we should start exploring some of the complexities." Jake paused for effect, his eyes capturing and holding those of each member of his audience in turn.

"Tonight," he continued, "I want to talk a little about what I believe to be one of the central passages in the Book of Apeiron, as well as being one of the shortest. It's Verse 14, and runs simply 'Death is a page with no margins.'"

There was a rustling noise and, looking around, I saw that the majority of people there were quickly thumbing through identical small white books, almost like little address books but thicker.

"Now, let me contrast that with Verse 34: 'In Thessaloniki there stands a plane tree on each of whose leaves is written the end of the world.' Or verse 27: 'In the beginning God brought forth order from chaos. Weather is the sand he sprinkles over his tracks.' Now it seems that there are two conflicting strains of thought here. The last two verses are both about control, aren't they? They show us a world where there's a pattern, a map already laid out for us. Horokinetics has always been about finding the pattern underlying the chaos. That tells us that things are fixed: past, present and future are already written, at least to some extent, because the pattern was laid out at creation. Or to put it in mathematical terms, the equation has been written.

"And yet, we have to ask ourselves, what was Theogenes thinking when he described death as a page without margins? You have to bear in mind that in the Middle Ages the margins of a book were very explicitly seen as a space for the reader to write his own thoughts. But if all is already written, what does Theogenes want margins for? So my question is, have we found a internal contradiction in the Book of Apeiron, or is there a way of reconciling the idea of an ordered, patterned universe with free will?"

Jake looked around the table calmly, then sat back in his chair awaiting a response. A few minutes of silence followed, broken only by the sound of leaves rustling in the cool breeze coming down the canyon and the occasional clink of cutlery. I began to wonder what I was doing there.

"Let me add to the confusion," offered Jericho with a mildly sadistic smile. "There's a passage in Heraclitus that reads 'Whoever cannot seek the unforeseen sees nothing, for the known way is an impasse.' This from the man who inspired Theogenes' vision of the oneness and infinity of the universe. So if the world is one unified being, what does he mean by the unforeseen?" Awkward silence. Jake took another sip from the small glass of iced water next to his untouched wine glass.

"I'd say we don't have free will," came Kyla's misty voice after a minute or two. "I mean, free will, you know, isn't it just this western concept imposed on us by governments and corporations to convince us to work harder for them? If you're really at one with the Gaia, then she embraces you and you don't need free will. Look at nature – it doesn't go on about free will. It just does what it does, at least until we come along and destroy it." I looked around the table and caught a number of winks and giggles.

"Yeah," Avatar added testily, "is free will something anyone takes seriously anymore?"

Jake smiled, and his calm reply made Avatar and Kyla sound harsh and aggressive.

"Well, free will certainly has it critics, but most of that criticism stems from the idea that we cannot claim freedom from our own past. People will argue that you can't talk about freedom to choose if your choices are dictated by your upbringing, environment, or genetic heritage. But in the Book of Apeiron we're faced with a whole different animal: here's a claim that the future is determined not by the past, but by a background pattern or formula that underlies our actions rather than preceding them. And yet the same man who makes that claim is here emphasizing the need for freedom, for creative space. But are these two ideas compatible? And if they are, what can that tell us about how we live our lives?" Again there was a silence and the sound of eating.

"But that's not what Theogenes is saying," Toby blurted out a little more loudly than he seemed to intend. All heads turned, and a few people glanced over at Jake nervously. But Jake smiled.

"Okay, good. Why not? What do you think he's getting at here?"

"Well," he replied, nerves adding a slight tremor to his voice, "I guess I'm thinking of chaos theory. This whole idea that there's order behind the chaos: well, the flip side to that is that there's chaos behind the order. Maybe there's this pattern or equation, but that doesn't mean that every little detail's already been decided." He looked around defiantly, then back to Jake.

"Alright. But then what does Theogenes mean when he writes of a tree in Thessaloniki where the end of the world is written on every leaf?"

"I don't know. It's like, okay, there can be a pattern, but that doesn't mean that everything's decided. Maybe the broad outlines are decided, but we still have some effect on what goes on there. That we have a duty to change what's out there, to do whatever it takes. I mean, you're the one always going on about taking responsibility for things and the power of the individual, right?"

Jake nodded, chuckling, but Jericho interceded before he could respond.

"Toby's made an important point. Theogenes may talk about the future being written on a leaf, but if you go with that analogy, you could picture the fabric of the universe as the veins of the leaf. They give it structure, but there's still all that space in between left open for creativity and free will. And if you think more broadly, the structure of the leaf can only partly determine how it will blow in the wind, or what an insect might do to it. That may be beginning to sound silly, but what I'm getting at is that even if the equation determines the structure, our lives and how we live them are still subject to chance and other influences. Including our

104

own choices. That limited space for individual action is what Theogenes is talking about when he talks about the margins on a page."

There was more whispering at the back, like students comparing notes. Some of these people, like me, were struggling to follow.

"But where would we find that space in our daily lives? I mean, in a literal, practical way, what would that mean?"

"Well..." Tara's quiet, didactic voice was almost lost in the intervening space, "a postmodernist might claim that it is in our ability to interpret our environment. Rorty would refer to it as the vocabularies we employ to describe, and therefore to create, reality." Her eyes were on Jake, sad, shy, and very obviously in love.

"You've talked about that before," burst in Daniel proudly. "The dignity of interpretation. You were saying last week that human dignity rests on our ability to be creative and to reconstitute our own realities." Seeing that all eyes had returned to Jake, Daniel looked around at me and sneered.

Toby took in a breath, but Jake's voice cut in before he could speak.

"Exactly. Thanks Daniel," he added, quickly glancing around the table as if someone might challenge his kindness. I had learned over the past months that Jake was a sucker for lost causes, and always took it upon himself to protect the weak from the strong. Like anyone else who's spent a part of his life as a nerdy bookish 14-year-old, I couldn't help but admire him for it.

"The dignity of interpretation: the first freedom we demand as children, and I would argue the most important. Think for a second about the universe that Theogenes proposes in the Book of Apeiron, and more specifically about the universe as elaborated by the modern fractal theory of Horokinetics. The Mandelbrot Set doesn't chart a predetermined universe – it charts the entire universe, a universe of infinite possibilities.

"So we come full circle to last week's discussion, when we concluded that all of art, all of culture, religion, science – everything we value – comes down to the attempt by man, not to understand his world, but to create it."

"And of course," Jericho added quietly, "deep memory forms the building blocks we can use to create context, to give structure to the emptiness of infinity. It's no coincidence that the margins of a page mark its borders. Creativity coincides with the limits of the text rather than the text itself."

All this meant very little to me, but the wide eyes and reverent stares surrounding me suggested that the others were taking in what Jake was saying like gospel. Only Jericho looked above it all, and seemed more interested in the reactions of the group than in the content of Jake's words. After glancing at me, her eyes fixed themselves on Toby, whose fervently nodding head seemed strangely at odds with the way he was rolling his eyes and pouting. It was the look of a frustrated, self-proclaimed misunderstood genius. But Jericho's regal gaze silenced whatever dissident response was boiling up in him.

"Perhaps," said Mathias, more assertively than I might have expected, "it would be interesting to hear from Mr. McFadden on this point. You have discussed this before with reference to the newly emerging world of corporate controlled mass communication – the branded world that Naomi Klein famously described – and I am curious to know what problems and prospects our esteemed friend foresees in the commercialization of Horokinetics, particularly in the 'post-human' environment of the internet." Mathias sat back in his chair, a polite inquisitive look on his face, and all eyes turned in my direction. All I could think at that moment was that I suddenly liked Mathias a lot less than I had a half hour previous. Damn, what had ever happened to that confident bullshit artist I'd been in college?

"Um," I muttered, or something else equally brilliant. "I'm, uh, not really sure I understand the question exactly. But the Horokinetics website has been a big success so far. It lacks a little of the human element, but people don't seem to mind." Frowns everywhere, except from Mathias, who looked as patient as a priest.

"I am more concerned with the tension between what I would call creative irony, that is, our ability to construct our world by defining our own descriptive vocabularies, and the need for global capital to harmonize vocabularies in order to increase the appeal of brand images."

"He's talking about commercial bullshit," Toby interjected with a scathing look in my direction. "Companies need to sell us crap, and selling crap means getting us to buy into an image, the same image, all of us. If we start questioning the system and stop letting big companies co-opt everything from alternative music to black history to poetry into one big white middle class ad campaign, then the whole economy could collapse. They need to keep us stupid, 'cause it's easier to sell things to stupid people. So if Horokinetics becomes just another way to sell us crap, how do you keep it from betraying its message of the need for creative irony?

"Or do you?" he added, the challenge clear in his voice.

"Pete's not like that, Toby," Jake mercifully interceded. "The website's become a business, but all he's selling is a tool. People can do with that tool what they like – they can comfort themselves and stay mindless, or they can use it to explore their creative abilities. He's not selling you Nikes. He's selling you yourself."

"I hope so," Toby muttered, "but I don't see how you can avoid eventually having to sell us some kind of prepackaged 'Horokinetics experience' to keep your advertisers happy."

"Have a little faith Toby."

"But Pete," began Tara, hoping maybe to ease the tension by changing the subject, "we all think what you've done to bring the concepts of Horokinetics into the 21st century is amazing, so I hope you don't mind if we're curious about your views on some of these issues. But – and this is related to Toby's concerns – do you worry that Horokinetics' historicity might, for some people, transform it into a narrative of legitimation for a sort of philosophical or even religious metanarrative that can be used to dampen ironic inquiry rather than promote it? I'm thinking specifically of Lyotard's Report on Knowledge..."

"Especially since by using the internet you are, on a certain level, participating in Žižek's 'digital heresy.'" Fabien joined in suddenly as if he had just become aware of the rest of us. "Don't you think that the internet and its neo-Gnostic faith in a disembodied, post-human mode of being is the ultimate decontextualization and therefore represents the obliteration of the individual?"

Jake didn't let this go on for very long. He knew perfectly well that I had no idea what these people were talking about, and was quick to divert the conversation so that this fact would not become more obvious to the others than it already had. Anyone else in his position would have quietly made it known among his philosophy-geek friends that it had been he who was the brains behind all of Horokinetics' mumbo jumbo. But not Jake – it was pretty clear that no one in that room, with the exception of Toby, and maybe Jericho, suspected that I had only built the skeleton of Horokinetics, and that it had been Jake who had put all the flesh on it. After the meeting broke up, most people drove off, but a few headed downstairs to crash in one of Jake's spare rooms for the night. I quietly thanked Jake for trying to keep me from embarrassing myself.

"No worries man," he whispered cheerfully, slapping me on the back just like my little league baseball coach used to do when I had screwed something up. "I'm really glad you came." He walked me to my car, quietly evaluating whether or not I was okay to drive.

I was okay – my sense of the surreal was more of a danger to me at that point than the small percentage of alcohol that was left in my bloodstream. Who on earth were these people? Jake was constantly forcing me to revise my opinion of him, constantly challenging me with strange new facts every time I got comfortable with the idea that I understood him. Tonight had been another layer added to the bizarre pastiche of information that made up what I knew of Jake Simms. These people looked up to him as lowly undergraduates might revere a famous professor. I couldn't help thinking, and not for the last time, that there was more to Jake than I was able to appreciate.

"Hey listen, one more thing," he said suddenly. "If it's all the same to you, I wouldn't mention to Emily that Daniel was here."

I hesitated, not quite sure what to make of this.

"It's just..." he looked sheepish for a moment, "well, I feel bad for Daniel. Behind all that cocky bullshit he's pretty fragile, and I think coming to these talks is good for him. He needs something like this, something that isn't subject to her approval or disapproval. If she knew about it, I suspect he'd stop coming. You'd be doing them both a favor to keep it quiet. You'd be doing me a favor as well."

"Um, sure, if you want, I won't tell her."

"Thanks, I owe you one. Now get yourself home safe."

I turned around in the driveway, accelerated nervously up the steep path to the road and cleared the shoulder with a slight scraping sound against the undercarriage of my car. Turning right, brights on, radio blaring, I set off towards the freeway for the long drive back to Tanya's, to the relatively sane and thoughtless world I had found myself longing for all evening.

9

That weekend Tanya and I finally sat down and had the talk we both knew had to come sooner or later. Our relationship wasn't working, and neither of us had enough energy or desire to fix it. We managed to break up without spending too much time trying to decide which of us was the evil one responsible for everything that had gone wrong. There was no need to kick a dead horse, we agreed, and I think we were both kind of proud of ourselves for being so adult about it. I wouldn't say we parted friends, but there was no burning of clothing or gutting of stuffed animals, so I guess that's something. It was at once a little sad and euphoric. A new beginning, I told myself as I shuffled around Tanya's apartment, tossing tee-shirt after tee-shirt into a duffel bag. Hopefully a good one.

I'd had a couple offers from friends to help me out and let me crash at their places for a while, but Diego's had been the only sincere one. Diego would have been hard to refuse even if the whole world had offered to put me up: he had a spare room in his place down in Santa Monica, an apartment so unrealistically large and improbably located – on Nielsen, right across from the beach – that it could have been the setting for an LA version of Friends.

"Perfect situation Pete," he'd told me, as if I needed convincing. "On the one side you've got LA, and on the other you've got 5000 miles of deep cold Pacific. You're totally buffered from reality." It was true. I'd always wanted to live in Santa Monica partly because it seemed like it was its own little kingdom. You've got the beach, Main Street and Cha Cha Chicken all within walking distance, so you feel as if you hardly need to leave. In the Valley you're always driving, always trying to escape and finding that there's no real end to the place. In Santa Monica you can actually walk places. And the ocean provides it with a little geography, a natural boundary to give it shape and limits. Knowing that the ocean is there, and that you don't have the option of just driving across it into the next shapeless suburb, is somehow comforting.

Diego was a good roommate, at least he had been in college, and I was looking forward to spending a little more time with him. He was between films now, just tinkering on some smaller projects, so we would hopefully have plenty of time to lie around on his balcony drinking beers and watching the waves roll in. He would keep me distracted with his endless supply of stories and conspiracies, and maybe take me along to some of the Hollywood parties he was constantly getting invited to. In return I'd pay him rent – not much, but as much as I could afford – and provide him with the full-time audience for his bullshit that he so desperately needed. It didn't sound all bad. For me the only downside was Stacie. She had her own place but she spent most weekends at Diego's, so for two days a week I was going to have to endure her disapproving looks and condescending remarks. I just brought out the worst in her, Diego explained. She was sugar and spice when I wasn't around. That was almost consoling.

Ridding Tanya's apartment of all evidence of my existence took a depressingly short amount of time, much of which involved sorting through stuff in search of things that could be thrown away. When I'd moved in with Tanya, most of what I'd accumulated since high school had gone into boxes in my parents' garage, so everything I had to shift to Diego's place fit in the trunk of my car, with the exception of the battered old easy chair that I decided I could leave behind. It suited Tanya – had even grown to look like her, in the way pets start to look like their owners. I piled the rest in, wrapping my computer in a protective wad of underwear and bath towels, locked Tanya's door behind me and headed south, toward the freeway, towards the 405 that would take me over the hill and into a new phase of my life.

It took only a few days for me to feel more at home in Diego's apartment than I ever had in Tanya's. I suppose moving out of my girlfriend's apartment into my friend's spare room could hardly be seen as that great a step up in the world, but I was happy. If you carry a load for long enough, you stop realizing how heavy it is until you put it down. Tanya had been a burden, even when things had been good between us. I didn't need my fractal to tell me that leaving her behind would open up a whole new world for me. Okay, maybe it wouldn't immediately bring me financial success and make Emily declare her love for me, but it couldn't hurt. The idea of becoming a responsible, independent adult again was a little daunting, but I could at least pat myself on the back for taking a step in that direction.

And as the weeks passed and Christmas approached, life was looking pretty good. Horokinetics was a bigger success than I had ever imagined it could be. The people we trained gave us very positive feedback, and business from the website kept growing fast. We had gotten sophisticated enough that we had regular clients who subscribed for weekly readings so they would never need to be without the advice and emotional support and whatever the hell else they found in all those squishy color graphics and spooky talk of Betas and Gammas. Before Freewinder we'd been pretty excited about the positive review we got in *Wicked Womyn*, a sort of feminist hippie witch "mag" with a circulation somewhere in line with that of Lama Ranchers Quarterly. Now we'd had some attention from the mainstream press – and a handful of article and reviews had appeared in newspapers and "women's" websites – and would soon be appearing in a national magazine. The reviews were almost all good, with such brilliant commentary as "It was really good – I'd say about half of my fractal was wrong, but what was right was exactly right, especially the part about me having the courage to live up to my potential." Beautiful.

One of the other things that took me by surprise was the popularity of Jake's blog and his weekly feature "Our Nation's Fractal" on our website. Jake wasn't content just doing individual readings and training, so to spice things up he had started to produce a weekly forecast for the world at large, vaguely analyzing tendencies in anything from weather to politics to spiritual energy, but always steering clear of predicting anything that could later be proven wrong. He was brilliant, if at times a little deeper than I would have liked – preaching cultural awareness and environmental consciousness and denouncing materialism as disruptive of the fractal continuum was, I thought, unnecessarily antagonistic – but it attracted publicity.

And publicity helped to bring in advertising. A few more small fish had signed on in November after the Freewinder interview, and we had just landed our first big advertising contract. Riodelibros.com, one of the biggest online bookstores, wanted to place an ad, a full banner ad across the top of every page, as well as links to their website scattered throughout our site, wherever there was a sensible tie-in to a book they had for sale. It was big money, at least by our standards, and the legitimacy it conferred to our site would almost certainly attract other advertisers as well as customers. Even my brother Michael would have to be impressed.

I told myself that it didn't matter what Michael thought. Without being too judgmental, my brother was a selfish, aggressive, arrogant abusive asshole. A pure Ideomorph zeta if ever I'd met one. I had grown up in his shadow, and it had always been very clear that the only purposes he served on earth were to make money and make me feel inadequate. Now that I was an adult with my own life and career, I didn't need to worry what he thought. Except, of course, on the rare occasions he returned to LA. Then I'd have to see him face to face. I'd have to talk to him and listen to his snide comments. Then, of course, it mattered. A lot. And for the first time in years, Michael came home for Christmas.

Michael had already arrived at Mom and Dad's house when I turned up on Christmas day, and he looked like hell. I found him in the kitchen, wrapped in an old bathrobe, his damp hair sticking in all directions from having been towel-dried but not brushed. He had worked through most of the night and had slept for maybe an hour or two before heading for the airport. He had been working like crazy for months now, giving companies advice on how to survive a slump in the economy – he forbade us to use the word "recession" – and had just put the finishing touches on a project before coming to LA for his first vacation for over a year. I almost felt sorry for him.

"A lot of people may disagree," he was saying, pointing at our mother as he talked with one of the Santa-and-his-reindeer coffee mugs she'd taken down from the attic right after Halloween. He paused a moment when I came into the kitchen interrupting himself with a smile and an affectionate "Hey squirt, Merry Christmas," before returning to his lecture.

"A lot of people disagree, including some of my own colleagues, but I think the occasional economic downturn is a good thing. When you get a lot of people buying houses they can't afford or putting money into companies that aren't up to scratch, they need to get stung for it. A bull market always gets inefficient, prices start to creep up out of proportion with true value. No way that can last forever. So then the market buckles, the losers get weeded out, and the survivors can get down to business."

"I do feel bad for all those people who lost everything, though," my mother answered, predictably. She's such a persistently good person – it drives me nuts.

"I don't," Michael shot back in his clipped nasal voice, a voice that when I was a kid made my braces hum like high voltage wires. "I mean, you know, don't get me wrong, it's sad, but if you look at it objectively, they got what they asked for. People were spending money they didn't have on things they didn't need. And the banks were just spinning off derivative after derivative on the blind assumption that it would all go on forever. That's just wrong, so the market corrected itself. The economy will be better for it in the long run."

"Well, I suppose so, but all those poor people losing their jobs..."

"The good people will find new jobs, and the bad ones didn't deserve them in the first place. If they can't run with the big dogs, that's their problem. And anyway, for those good ones who survive, it creates some really interesting opportunities. I'm getting some of my best work out of mopping up what the losers can't manage anymore. It's exciting stuff."

While all this was going on I had poured myself a coffee and migrated toward the fridge, hoping to find some milk and possibly a bit of cyanide. I am nearly thirty, I reminded myself. It would not be mature to lash out. It would not be mature to start humming the theme from Star Wars. The mature thing is to drink your coffee. Just drink your coffee. It didn't bother Michael that we hadn't said much to each other; at this point, it was enough to have been in each other's presence, to sniff around each other like dogs, just looking for humanly acceptable ways of marking our territory. He belted down the rest of his coffee and then ventured one last comment before he disappeared upstairs to get dressed and unpack.

"Mom tells me you've got your own business started. How's it going?"

"Fine."

"Good. Good. Let's sit down and talk about it later. I'm curious."

That was it. Welcome home bro. It's been a long time.

Christmas dinner was, as it had always been, just another episode of the Michael McFadden show. For years, ever since Michael took freshman economics at Penn, he and Dad had enjoyed talking about business while Mom and I stood on the sidelines, either looking baffled or trying to have our own conversation over the noise of theirs. They had their own language, full of words that sounded familiar but had been given their own specialized meanings – why call debt debt when you can call it leverage? – and we mere English speakers could only listen quietly as they discussed what the great and the wise should be doing to make the world safe for capitalism. But something had changed. I still didn't know all the terminology, but somehow their conversation didn't sound like some long verbal Masonic handshake anymore. It hovered on the edge of sense, and I suddenly realized somewhere over dessert that I was one of them now. I got it. Not on any really deep level, I suppose, and certainly not all of it, but running my own business had given relevance to all the vague concepts they were discussing. I still didn't really understand what the Fed does, but at least now I could think clearly about interest rates and what they mean for businesses and investors. I could read a balance sheet. Capitalization was no longer something you did to letters. I still didn't feel the urge to talk, but at least I was managing to listen.

Eventually Michael ran out of things to brag about, and things to eat, so Mom started clearing up. Dad and I both made our habitual and insincere offer to help with dishes, and Mom responded with her enduring and patient refusal. The three men migrated into the living room, where the bottle of Scotch finally put in its appearance, together with more self-important talk about business. Except this time it was my business.

"So how is your little project going?" Michael had asked as we sat down. "Dad started trying to tell me about it," he continued, unperturbed. "Something about astrology?"

I had been determined to avoid this conversation. I had thought and thought about it, and had promised myself that under no circumstances would I stoop to trying to justify Horokinetics to Michael. There was no way he would get it. He'd always thought my career choice was idiotic to begin with, and I could easily guess how this new venture would seem to him. Justifying it would make me seem weak. Whatever I said would sound stupid. And yet all he had to do was say "little project" and I started to justify. I went on about Jake's brilliance at injecting the required soul into the body of Horokinetics. I bragged about the tech wizardry of Emily's friend Cal who had us up at the top of the search engines in a matter of days. And I patted myself on the back for managing to drum up enough advertising to be more or less covering costs.

And then a funny thing happened. I had expected some ribbing, maybe a snide comment or two before he changed the subject, but Michael blind-sided me with something so outrageous that I hardly knew how to react, something that sounded suspiciously like encouragement. "What can I say little brother?" he said to me with what I think was meant to be a smirk, "It's not exactly what I would have done, but I've got to hand it to you, it sounds like you're really taking your best shot at it. Good for you."

I think I just stared at him for a minute, waiting for whatever cutting remark was sure to follow. But it didn't come. There was just an awkward moment of silence before I was finally able to manage, "Thanks Mike."

"I mean, don't get me wrong," he continued, "I think the concept sounds idiotic. But I like the fact that you also seem to realize that it's idiotic, and that you're focusing on the right things for a change. However dumb it is, you've identified something that people want and you've figured out how to package it and sell it to them. That's just basic business, and I think it takes guts to have gone out and tried it." My mother drifted back into the room and sat down, happy to have the men of her life all in one room and apparently getting along.

"Uh, yeah, I guess so," I answered awkwardly. This was new territory for me; I don't think I'd ever been praised by my brother before, so I didn't quite know how to react. My father didn't seem convinced.

"You really think this can grow into something bigger, Michael?" he asked. Dad had never said much about Horokinetics, but it had been obvious from the start that he wasn't crazy about the idea. Dad tended not to be crazy about my ideas, but anyone could guess that after taking one look at him. His unfashionably close-cropped hair, fixed on his large head like the charred remnants of some mysterious edifice that had once towered above his bushy eyebrows, marked him as one of the many small time cold warriors that still populate Southern California and the pension funds of its aerospace industry. He had been a vice president at Lockheed, which when I was little always seemed pretty impressive, until someone told me that there were lots of "vice presidents" at Lockheed, and that it didn't mean he was second in command. I grew to accept that, but it did quell my interest in Dad's career, so as I got older I never bothered to figure out what exactly he did over there. Make airplanes, I guess. Stealth bombers, for all I knew. Whatever it was, it was practical. It was real world. It wasn't running a new age lemonade stand along the path to enlightenment.

"Sure, I think so, up to a point. It's all just a question of marketing. I mean, there's someone dumb enough to buy anything, and if someone's sad and desperate and thinks he can find out what the future has in store for him, then he might even buy this. For what it's worth, Pete, I'd keep it simple. Your friend can be as smart as he likes, but remember that your audience isn't. They just want to be told what to do, and I doubt they care why."

I thought back to Jake for a second, with all his enthusiasm and creativity and his obvious obsession with using the website to help people in spite of themselves. At that point I was clear in my head whose approach I preferred. Michael was a reptile, and the more he talked about bottom lines, the more I took Jake's side and started getting excited about Horokinetics as a positive influence on people's lives. I guess at times we're all suckers for that whole good and evil thing.

"The big challenge is picking the right time to sell." Michael was on his third glass of scotch, and I was most of the way through my second, so I had to ask him to repeat this. Even then, I wasn't sure I was understanding him right.

"Sell?"

Michael rolled his eyes. "Of course you sell, you dumb ass. Listen, I don't want to belittle what you've managed to do with this. It's a clever idea, and I'm really impressed that you're making such headway with advertisers. But what you've got to realize is that even if you're seeing some success now, it's not likely to last. To maintain your edge you'd have to keep innovating and reinvesting in order to keep people's interest, and even then it'd be a hard sell. You've developed a buzz with all these articles and interviews, but a buzz in that sort of business doesn't last long, and there are plenty of other tech wizards out there who sooner or later will leapfrog over you on the search engines. When you're not news anymore, the free publicity will stop and your customers will move on to the next fad. It's great what you've done, but I'd say ride the wave for a little while, and then sell quickly before it crashes. That's where the real money is, if you don't fuck it up. Sorry Mom."

Real money sounded nice, I had to admit.

"Actually," Michael continued, "most of my work involves advising companies on their M&A strategy. With the securities markets being as dead as they are, a lot of companies that would have been in a great position to go public are now stuck in limbo, just waiting to be snatched up by conglomerates and arbitrageurs. But a lot of our clients are focusing on smaller companies as well, little startups that might have really been something if it weren't for the slowdown, and still could be once the recovery is in full swing. Last year it was all about IPOs. This year, my clients are all on a spending spree. The big boys are buying up garbage like yours like they're at a flea market. The venture capital market may have dropped out, but the solid companies are cleaning up."

"They buy little companies like mine?" I asked again, incredulous. "You mean, with money?" Since I hadn't gone into Horokinetics as a business, I had never really thought through all its business implications. All I figured it needed to do is pay for itself and hopefully give me a little spending money before it earned me a job at ImaginInc. Then I vaguely supposed I'd hand the thing over to Jake.

"Yes, real money. You know, that green stuff you buy beer with?" Fucker. "Don't get me wrong, small fry like this isn't likely to make you a millionaire. But if you really manage to take this thing mainstream, I'd say the intellectual property alone could earn you a digit or two more than you might think."

"Someone might buy Horokinetics?"

"Listen, squirt, I don't know the ins and outs of the spiritual bullshit market, but what you've got doesn't sound any more stupid than anything else out there. My old secretary believed in tree spirits. I got rid of her, but half of them believe in something like that. As long as you have an audience, you have a market that some company may want access to. Stranger things have happened. We had a deal come through a few months ago..."

I had stopped listening, but two things stuck in my mind that evening. First was the idea of getting rich from Horokinetics. Second was the look on my parents face when they listened to Michael telling stories about his work. I guess you never stop wanting that look, and it never really stops bothering you if you never get it yourself. I don't know that I thought much about it at the time – it had been just another slightly annoying holiday made very annoying by the presence of my brother. But the look and the talk of making Horokinetics into a business success story combined in some chemical reaction in my head. It paved the way.

I crashed that night on the sofa bed in my parents' guest room – my own room not all that long ago. I slept badly, spending most of the night tossing and turning, and once asleep I was tormented by repetitive, unsettling dreams that were all emotion and no tangible details. There was no sign of Dad when I crawled out of bed and downstairs late that morning, but I could hear Michael taking a shower. Mom was in the kitchen and, still thrilled with the idea of having both her little boys under one roof, made us bacon and eggs and sat smiling at me and Michael as we did our best to make small talk. I got out of there as soon as I could without hurting mom's feelings, making some excuse about having to get to the office to check on something urgent.

"Good catching up with you, Swami" Michael said as I got up to go. He'd been calling me Swami all through breakfast, as if it stayed funny. "I head back to New York on Sunday, but I'm sure I'll see you before then."

I took De Soto on a whim, just to drive down a different road for a change, searching for memories and associations that could give meaning to the apparently meaningless scenery appearing in my windshield and shrinking again to nothing in my rearview mirror. Jake kept telling me to search for deep memories and emotions that could enrich my understanding of myself and the world around me, and generally it seemed to work. But pulling into the parking lot of a strip mall, just like any other strip mall in the Valley, it seemed like there wasn't much point. Across the street stood an office building, its reflector glass widows mirroring back at me the strip mall with its convenience store, donut shop and copy center. Next to it, a vacant lot, a Spanish style building housing a carpet store, and then a strip of one-story ranch houses baring their patchy brown lawns obscenely at passers-by. Just like anywhere else in the Valley, incoherent and characterless. I stocked up on snacks and headed north.

When I got to the office I made myself a cup of coffee, took a bite of greasy chocolate sprinkled donut, and logged onto our website. Michael had shaken me up. I needed to look at this through his eyes, through the sort of asshole eyes that might want to pay me lots of money for the rights to Horokinetics.

Welcome

Who are we?

A simple question, but the answers are as infinite as the stars. A simple question which, amid the culture wars between stifling religious dogma and limitless corporate-controlled mass media, is all too often answered for us. We are what we wear. We are what we buy. We are what we watch, listen to, read. We are what we are told to be. There must be more than this.

The science of Horokinetics suggests that there is. Horokinetics is the study of time in motion, but above all it is a science of the self. Employing a unique combination of computer technology, cutting edge mathematical theory and accumulated wisdom of our cultural heritage, our purpose is to examine the structure found within the chaos of our universe, a chaos laced with patterns which are themselves laced with their own quirks and flaws. By understanding the chaos within the patterns within the chaos, we find that the universe is embedded with clues about ourselves – our personalities, our memories, our hopes – that we ignore at our peril.

Horokinetics is a marriage of science and spirit, history and mathematics, philosophy and biology, culture and chaos. It is the study of the infinite made whole. Made accessible. And most importantly, made human.

I sat back and took another sip of coffee. I'd looked at this crap a hundred times. It was weird. Maybe I'd been hanging out with Jake too much, but I had started finding some comfort in all these empty words we had dreamed up to sell a lie. They seemed such an antidote to the world around me, the world shaped and ruled by men like Michael. I couldn't be sure whether it was the words themselves, or simply the comforting knowledge that they were part of my own creation, that I found so soothing. Jake would argue that that was one and the same thing. I thought back to that evening at his house, the serious discussions of memory and emotion and the creation of meaning. All these strange but clearly intelligent people believed that there was something of value in Horokinetics, that it really was a profound elaboration on the work of Theogenes of Athos. Shit, they all seemed to take for granted that Theogenes existed. I still wasn't so sure. It seemed just a little too convenient to have stumbled across an obscure medieval heretic whose aphorisms read like the result of staring at fractals on acid.

Looking again at the site that afternoon, thinking about Michael's advice, I realized that he was right. Horokinetics was great, but I needed to get out while the getting was good. Emily had been saying for a while now that I was losing perspective on why I had done this in the first place, and I was beginning to see her point. I'd never set out to become an entrepreneur or a cult leader or anything else even remotely stressful. I just wanted a steady job designing computer-generated monsters. Nine to five, with a paycheck. So the following Monday, the day after Michael said his goodbyes and headed back to NY, I tried calling Vas again.

This time I got him.

"Hi, Mr. Papayannis, I'm not sure if you remember me..."

"Yeah McFadden, I remember you. Very well. Earthsong, last summer."

"Well, we'd been talking then..."

"You've got some nerve calling me, pal, I'll give you that."

"Sorry?"

"You know, you really had me going. You and your bullshit about disproving all this spiritualist crap. I really believed it, I thought here's a guy on my side, someone who'll help me convince Lin to be a little more sensible, down to earth."

"So, she hasn't stopped believing in astrology?" I didn't know what to say. Vas was pissed off, but I just didn't get it. It's not like I promised him anything.

"She stopped believing in astrology alright. Now it's nothing but fucking Horokinetics. She swears by her stupid fractal reading. She would hardly leave the goddamned house unless this Simms asshole said it was okay. It wrecked our relationship."

"Well, the idea was that...."

"Yeah, whatever, just stay the fuck out of my way." Click.

I guess certainty in life is a good thing. I now had certainty about one thing, at least. There was no going back.

10

I dreamed of sugar, blowing like atoms into the heart of you. Night, blackness, a void of never ending possibilities, swirling in aromatic abandon under a scudding, moon-tinged blanket of cloud. That foamy firmament kissed the face of you, posing the unanswerable questions of love. Mocha? The electric pulse of caffeine? Sailor from the Indies, pilgrim from across the ancient Ethiopian deserts? What news do you bring? HOPE.

Bullshit, I murmured, plunging my tongue through several feet of milk foam in search of the espresso shot lurking somewhere at the bottom. The Starbucks poet should be boiled alive in decaf Sumatran. He talks to you from everywhere in that clean, smooth non-fat voice. The design of the cups, the pale wood of the chairs, the cleanliness of the sofas are all him. Even the music is his. I don't care what it says on the CD cover, whatever cool jazz or soulful blues is playing, once it's playing at Starbucks it becomes his. The Starbucks poet turns everything he touches into Starbucks, like some birchwood laminate King Midas. Even you, when you walk through that door, become part of his perfect, sterile universe. Walk into a Starbucks sometime and try to have an original thought. Go ahead, try. Speak it out loud. It will resonate with his voice, insipid as a skinny decaf latte.

Luckily Susan didn't keep me waiting too long.

"Sorry I'm late," she said, giving me a quick kiss on the cheek and sliding her slender body into the chair across from me. There was no question about it – she had lost weight since I'd last seen her a couple of weeks before Christmas. She had always been thin, but now she had that twiggy look, all pointy elbows and cheekbones. If I had been a girl I might also have noticed a redness in the eyes or a lack of luster in the skin. But as a guy, my observations of women, even my friends, were confined to two: cute, or not cute. Susan was becoming thin enough to border on not cute.

"You look great," I told her, getting a smile in response.

"Thanks. Can't stay too long, I've a got a client at three. But it's good to see you. How've you been?"

The look on my face must have given away at least something of my foul mood, because she quickly took it upon herself to answer her own question.

"Well, Jake's kept me up to date on how you've been. Poor guy. Is there anyone left who doesn't think you're the incarnation of evil?"

"You, I guess."

"Don't be so sure." There was a hard edge to that smirk on her face.

"What's the matter, is Horokinetics turning your clients into Satanists?" She laughed, shaking her head in what I supposed was some kind of grudging sympathy.

The hate mail had been growing worse ever since the Freewinder interview, and it seemed that hundreds of people had made it their new years' resolution to spread the word about the inherent evil of Horokinetics and, by extension, me and Jake. That past couple of weeks had been hell.

I had managed to trace a lot of the trouble back to the Society of Christians Against Terrorism, SCAT, a grim group of born-agains who had set Horokinetics in their crosshairs and started a mass mailing campaign against us. Chief Vice Reverend and Holy Designate of Christ Dave Tinglehoffer had sent a personal message out to all his brethren asking them to take urgent action to combat the proliferation of what he called "a new and dangerous weapon of moral mass destruction." So we got letters and emails by the dozen, most of them using almost the exact same wording, warning us that our satanic witch cult was doomed to failure, and that we had best stop now and embrace Christ while there was still time, before the Rapture left us behind and we were condemned to eternal damnation. One nutcase had taken it upon himself to call us every day and chirp down the phone "Why be a sinner, when you can be a winner?" Compelling stuff.

As stupid as it was, I was worried. For a start, the efficiency of their mailing campaign put the Publishers Clearinghouse Sweepstakes to shame. Various versions of their letters and emails were sent everywhere, many of them dangerously sensible-sounding and well tailored to their audience. Newspapers were receiving them and, judging from the CCs on some of the letters, congressmen, senators, the White House, even Oprah's mailbox was overflowing with complaints about our anti-American activities. It wasn't quite on the level of the Divest in South Africa campaign, but after a while it began to seem almost that organized and well-funded. They had even managed to convince *Cult Report* to post a bulletin on its website listing Horokinetics as "a quasi-religious organization with a number of distinctly cult-like features, including the use of various mind control techniques on its inner circle of initiates." They claimed to have received complaints about aggressive recruitment tactics and the psychological abuse of "initiates" by "this quasi-cult's shadowy, charismatic leader who goes by the name Jacob Simms," and promised to continue to investigate. The attack on Horokinetics was threatening to become credible to people who were not keeping bottled water in their cellars in anticipation of Armageddon. We started getting complaints from sane people. We had even lost an advertiser over it.

"Anyway," I continued, "Jake is the great Satan these days. I'm nothing but his henchman."

"Well, he seems to keep his poor little henchman pretty busy these days – I haven't seen you in ages."

"I'm not the only one he's keeping busy."

Susan smiled broadly, looking almost sheepish.

"You're the one who introduced me to Jake in the first place."

"Yeah, well I didn't know you'd get all disgusting with him."

"You're deeply repressed, Pete." Whatever. It was their business. More power to them. But I guess it had ticked me off that I just hadn't seen it coming. Childish, maybe, but in protest I had simply been refusing to take them seriously.

"And you can joke all you want about it," she continued, ignoring the face I made at her, "but the hate mail is really upsetting to him. He's been so moody recently. All this hostility, it's so unfair. It's so... not what Jake's about."

"It's not a barrel of laughs for me either. Neither of us had any idea that a bunch of religious freaks would go postal on us."

I didn't say it to Susan at the time, but sometimes I wondered how well she really knew her own boyfriend. Jake wasn't at all upset about SCAT's hostility. Jake and I had just had a long talk about it the other day. I was the one upset by it. Jake, in his peculiar way, managed to see SCAT as an asset.

"Being attacked by nutcases just gives us more credibility with our mainstream audience," he had insisted. "Horokinetics will weather the storm and come out even stronger."

"You think so?"

"Pete, sometimes I don't think you appreciate what it is that you've created here, what we've created. Horokinetics has become its own world, with its own rules, in which it can be all things to all people. It's a mythology. A philosophy. A religion. It's self help, science, art all rolled into one. And all tailor made for each individual by the fusion of computer technology and a little human creativity. We've built a starter pack for people to build their own vision of the universe, and people are beginning to catch on. One day this is going to be bigger than you or me or anything we've yet had the balls to imagine. It's like the gift of fire – even the gods themselves didn't manage to snuff that out once mankind had got a hold of it." His excitement vibrated behind the weird calm in his voice.

"Maybe. But I've got to admit, these guys freak me out."

"You know what it says about that in the Book of Apeiron, don't you?"

I had shrugged, and Jake laughed.

"Absolutely nothing. Maybe we need to add a line or two. How about, 'Stop being such a chicken shit and have a little faith in yourself.'

"I don't think old Theogenes would be too happy. Anyway, faith in myself doesn't seem to be my strong point these days. Where the hell do you get yours?"

"Nescafé," he said, looking serious and swirling his coffee mug a few times as if to revive the greasy brown sludge at the bottom. I peered down into the cup and groaned.

"Is it worth it?"

"It's not so bad," he answered, taking a sip and running his tongue over his front teeth. "With milk and a little sugar, at least. Drink this shit black and it'll rip your intestines out.

"Seriously, though, you must have wondered why I drink it at all."

"I just figured you were a psycho."

"Well, there is that, but there's more to it."

I rolled my eyes. "Isn't there always?" That got a laugh out of him.

"Nescafé is all there was in West Africa. They drink it like fish there. You get used to it after a while, and somehow I grew to like it. It got wrapped up in memories of cool village mornings when we'd stop in the market and get breakfast, omelets stuffed in French bread and chipped dirty mugs of Nescafé sweetened with condensed milk. The taste always takes me back to those mornings. It's just another part of all that memory bullshit I keep going on about. Sometimes things become symbolic, they carry with them moments that give you inner strength because they're part of your inner knowledge of who you are and what you can be. That's what's behind the symbolism of the fossil shell I gave you; for me, it's like each chamber is a new phase in your life, and the strength to solve the problems you encounter in the chamber you're in can always be found in one of the previous chambers."

I guess I looked skeptical, because Jake shrugged and looked away for a minute. "It's a silly way of looking at it, maybe, but symbols are important. They're the only way we can really keep hold of abstract meanings. I once heard someone say that symbols are the handholds we cling to on the cliff face of selfhood."

I kind of knew what he meant. The fossil had become a symbol for me, too. Nothing so thought-out as for Jake, maybe, but it had acquired its own associations: associations with childhood fossil-hunting, with Horokinetics, with Jake himself and the success he'd helped make possible. It was a reminder of all I had done in the past half a year, and of the simple fact that one day last summer I had managed to get off my ass and start something.

But this was a whole side of Jake that Susan didn't seem to understand, and which I somehow didn't want to try to explain to her. Maybe that just wasn't a part of himself he wanted so share with her. Whatever. I told Susan that I'd stand by Jake however I could, that I wouldn't abandon him to the born-agains, and that she should try to find a little more time to spend with her friends. She smiled, finished her coffee and headed back to work. I ordered another, stared into space for a while, and slowly made my way back to the office.

It was maybe a week later, a hung over Monday morning, and I got to the office late. I'd been answering emails for a few minutes when Ed walked into my office, looking as dazed and vacant as always, and greeted me with his usual "Hey Pete."

"Hey," I answered, trying my best to speak his language. "What's up?"

He seemed to seriously consider the question for a few seconds.

"There was, um…. A guy called. He left a number."

"What'd he want?"

"Dunno." It had been one of my many unrealized projects to try to teach our staff the basics of taking phone messages. I bit my lip, answering,

"Great. You get a name?"

"Uh, yeah, it was Bob something." He started flipping through a spiral notebook until he found the right page, tearing off the relevant corner and handing it to me.

"david garcia patching intentional." An LA phone number. Nothing else.

"What the hell does this mean?" I asked, managing to scrape together just enough energy to sound irritated.

"Dunno. He said that was the name of his company. Something about buying investments or something. Maybe it will make more sense once you call him."

I grumbled "Thanks" and tossed the scrap of paper onto a pile on my desk.

"Oh, there was something else," he added, half way out the door. "We're almost out of toilet paper again."

This kind of crap drove me nuts. I glanced at the scrap of paper again, crumpled it slowly, and tossed it into the garbage can.

The next morning the phone rang and this time I answered it. A woman briskly asked me to stay on the line. Then came a male voice, abrupt, confident, and a little too loud.

"Mr. McFadden, I'm David Garcia calling from Apatchi International…"

"Sorry, David, listen, I don't need any shares advice. I don't have any money to play the stock market anyway."

"But Mr. McFadden..." Click. You let these guys talk and they'll never shut up. A minute later and the phone rang again.

"Mr. McFadden, please don't hang up. I don't want to sell you shares."

"Well, whatever you want to sell me..."

"Please hear me out. I'm buying, not selling. I represent one of the largest multinational corporations in the world, Apatchi International. I assume you've heard of Apatchi?"

Sure, I'd heard of them. They owned pretty much everything on the planet. Except for Horokinetics. That's why he was calling.

11

Monday morning found me in my best suit – my only suit – slipping into the obsessively marbled lobby of Apatchi's office building downtown. Ashton, the overpriced junior partner at Arthur's firm Jake had convinced me I needed to take along, kept telling me to relax. It was well meant, but as we ascended to the 15th floor reception and were led into the sleek, pale wood paneled conference room, I began to feel that relaxing was about as much an option as simply vanishing into thin air. And less preferable. The far wall was all window, offering a dizzying view of Los Angeles and Santa Monica Bay through the slats of the floor to ceiling vertical blinds. Between us and infinity ran a long narrow table, almost the entire length of the room, punctuated at arm's-length intervals with bottles of mineral water and obscure-looking teleconferencing equipment.

"Can I get you a coffee? Tea? Soft drink?" asked the crisp, clean, blonde receptionist with all the seamless hospitality of an airline hostess.

"Coffee, thanks," I replied, not because I wanted one, but just because it seemed like the right answer.

"Look," said Ashton after she had left, "you have to remember, they're not here to do you any favors. The fact that you're here means that they're already interested in acquiring Horokinetics. The question is simply on what terms. You don't have to be eager to please – they're not going to be offended if we play hardball. Want to know what I tell myself every time I walk into a negotiation?" he asked, a paternal smile creeping across his face.

"Hmm?"

"'They don't like me anyway.' The worst thing you can do is want them to like you, so just keep saying to yourself, 'they don't like me anyway.'" I smiled, remembering why I had never been tempted to go to law school.

Our coffees arrived. About five minutes later the door opened again and three men and one woman filed into the conference room. The last of the four closed the door behind him and, as we all started handing business cards back and forth, made the introductions.

"Peter, glad to meet you in person," he said, a little too friendly and a little too loud. "I'm David Garcia, VP Operations. Let me introduce you around. This is Axel Lindbergh, our Head of Consumer Technologies. Andy Chang is head of our in-house IP management program, and Fiona Glass is from legal."

I shook hands and, managing to tear my gaze from Fiona's perfect breasts, I introduced Ashton. We all took our seats and David kicked off the meeting.

"We all know why we're here, but I'd like to set the framework for today's discussion by talking briefly about why we believe your product is a good fit for Apatchi and, Peter, why we think that a business relationship with Apatchi is a good move for you."

David picked up a small remote control and, pushing a few buttons, dimmed the lights and illuminated an overhead projector. I looked around. Only Axel seemed to make an effort to follow David's slide show on Apatchi's recent restructuring and how Horokinetics would play a role in Apatchi's marketing strategy. At the same time I had the bizarre impression that he was watching me. A faint smile illuminated his thin rugged face and, in collaboration with his spiky, prematurely gray hair, made him seem both intense and passive, like a live electrical wire sticking innocuously out of a wall. It made me nervous.

Courage, I kept telling myself. You're the mastermind behind Horokinetics. They need you as much as you need them. I did my best to focus, and when that didn't work, I took Jake's persistent advice and just let go. I unfocussed my eyes and let my mind drift for a minute or two, searching for the memory that I knew would calm me down, the image of a much younger Pete McFadden digging in the crumbly soil by Old Topanga Canyon Road in search of fossils, keeping a sharp eye out for the dragons whose nest only I knew was in the trees just up the hill.

"Just take your dragons with you," Jake had said to me before I left for the meeting. It was our little joke, but he was right: the happiness of the memory, the feeling that it was mine and mine alone, something that these slick bastards could never quite understand, was comforting. I felt my breathing slow and my shoulders relax as my mind felt its way along the edges of the moment. Just another chamber of the shell, Jake would have said. A chamber that's all your own, that contains your individuality and strength and power to shape your world on your terms. Stupid bullshit, I would have thought if I'd heard myself say it out loud. But when you are silent and frightened and alone, a little corny-sounding bullshit isn't such a bad thing.

After the slide show was over, we started getting into details. We talked price for a while, but soon the conversation descended into depths of legal and business jargon that made Theogenes of Athos seem straightforward by comparison. Ashton seemed outgunned, somehow, as he followed Fiona point by point through a draft contract. When we had more or less hammered out a deal the following week, it all seemed impossibly complicated, but Ashton was happy. He should have been, the bastard, given what he was charging me.

"Look," Ashton assured me as we went through the draft term sheet, "at the end of the day, what you've got is pretty straightforward. One of their subs called DTITech buys the rights to Horokinetics and then leases them back to you. Then, through a separate contract, they hire you to engage in the various promotional activities we talked about the other day. Basically they'll give you a good salary plus bonuses to keep doing what you're doing, and keep earning most of the profits from it, subject to their little marketing whims. It's like going from being an independent race car driver to being a sponsored race car driver. They'll own your car, but you'll still get to drive it. Good?"

It was good. Very good. Okay, it wasn't millions, but it added two digits to my bank account and left me with my business more or less intact. Too good to pass up, in any case. Too good, it seemed, to be true.

That was the problem. Sitting on Diego's balcony staring out across the grimy blue expanse of Santa Monica Bay, I couldn't shake the persistent feeling of vertigo. Those waves were calling me, as if already lapping at my shins, tempting me out with the maternal hushing of the sea even as it threatened to suck me straight down into the toxic ooze that lay below. It all just had to go wrong. I had to be missing something. Ashton thought it was fantastic. My accountant said it was a dream come true. Diego suggested that I just go with flow, relax, and drink all weekend. Susan kept repeating "stay calm" until I got so wound up I hung up on her. Here I was being threatened with success, and for some reason it made my stomach churn.

It didn't help that the two people I trusted most, Jake and Emily, were the least enthusiastic. Jake was unusually quiet about it all, as if he had some compelling reason not to interfere. "Do you think this is a good thing?" was his annoying response when I asked him what he thought. I told him yes. He'd nodded, a faintly sad look on his face, and said simply, "Okay, then I'm with you." As for Emily, she was at least a bit clearer. Apatchi was a despicable company. If I sold out, I would be giving control of Horokinetics to a corporation that had a nightmarish environmental record, invested heavily in the arms trade, ran sweat shops in the Third World, and was ruthless in its determination to shut down smaller businesses so that it could grow its empire.

The weekend before we were set to sign the final agreements, she came over to have a drink and keep me company. I was nervous, more so than I wanted to admit.

"I wish you had as much faith in yourself as I have in you," she said quietly. I smiled.

"Me too." We were out on Diego's balcony watching the sunset while Diego was mixing margaritas to go with our takeout Mexican food. I was silent for a minute, listening to the waves, the traffic and the sound of Diego's blender humming in the background.

"Pete," came her hesitant voice, "If you think this is for the best, then that's what you have to do. But I'm worried about you. How are you going to feel when your creation isn't your own anymore? What happens to you? What will they do with Horokinetics?"

"I don't know."

"Just... try to keep some control over what they do with it. I don't understand what they could want with Horokinetics, but it seems weird to me. I'd hate to see them take what you've built and do anything..." She trailed off and shrugged, as if she herself was not quite sure what she meant.

"Em," I ventured, "you've never really liked the idea of Horokinetics, have you?" She sighed audibly, thought for a moment, then replied,

"I don't know. You feed people the lies they want to hear, and maybe that's not even so bad. Maybe it's art, I really don't know. I don't know where creativity ends and fraud begins, but wherever that line is, I feel like you're on the wrong side of it.

"You're tinkering with people's beliefs," she continued, "with their values, their sense of themselves. Even though it's only in a small way, you're still changing people's worlds. And that's got to have consequences. It makes me nervous."

"So how come you helped me?" I asked, trying to keep the hurt out of my voice, but probably failing. She looked up at me and frowned, her forehead crinkling. "I mean, you put a lot of work into this thing. You kept saying it was a bad idea, but you kept helping me anyway. Why?"

She continued to frown. "Are you really asking me that?"

I hesitated, knowing that I was supposed to say no.

Emily shook her head and smiled weakly. "Sometimes you really are dumb Peter McFadden."

Monday came, and I signed Horokinetics over to its new owners. I still think of that day as a high point in my life, in spite of how it all turned out. My parents were ecstatic, and I finally experienced, for the first and almost certainly for the last time, what it felt like to be the successful child. My dad gave me the kind of over-firm handshake and slap on the shoulder that he usually reserved for his golf buddies and told me he'd never been more proud. My mother glowed, as only mothers can, and kept saying "oh honey" until I almost wished she'd stop.

Even Michael was happy, and didn't seem to mind having his golden pedestal usurped for a day, probably because he was confident that my success couldn't last. He was the first to admit that he was shocked that the deal went through, but the fact that he had bothered to pick up the phone and congratulate me told me that he was not only shocked, but actually happy for me. That would take some getting used to.

"I never thought you had it in you, squirt," he teased down the telephone line a couple days after we had signed the deal.

"Neither did I," I had admitted.

"I guess a little advice from your big brother isn't such a bad thing every once in a while. But seriously, Apatchi's a good company – if they decide they want Horokinetics to really be something, then believe me, it will be. These people decide what we read, what we watch, what we eat and what color we shit it out. You're finally running with the big dogs, little bro."

Some part of me still wasn't so sure. I had thought that the only reason I really cared what happened to the company was my ambition to get a good CGI job, but it had all become a bit more complicated. I suppose, like parents with their children, it's the nature of a creator to worry about his creation. Now that I no longer owned the copyright and trademark rights, now that I legally could not do fractal readings without the permission of Apatchi, Horokinetics started to seem all the more strange and fragile.

But now was the time to celebrate, not to worry, and that Friday night Susan helped me arrange a small victory party at her pristine apartment in Brentwood. She seemed almost as pleased with me as I was as we stood there in her brushed steel and granite designer kitchen, drinking champagne. "Do you realize what you've done?" she kept asking me, each time shaking me by the shoulders as if I were a Coke machine that had swallowed her quarter. I kept insisting that I did, but she seemed unconvinced. After roughing me up a little more, she broke off for a second to refill her champagne glass, and started tapping it with a spoon to get everyone's attention. It was a small group: me, Susan, Emily, a few of the Vortex guys who'd been there since the beginning, Diego. Everyone except Jake, who had cancelled last minute.

We all went quiet.

"When Pete first came to us with his idea," she began, each word pronounced hard and crisp as if it were in itself something important, "I don't think any of us imagined that we'd see a day like today. Horokinetics started small, and in just six months has worked itself up to becoming affiliated with one of the world's most prestigious and diverse multinational corporations." It was typical Susan – well intentioned and all just slightly wrong – but we all lapped it up that night.

"Each of us," she continued, "contributed in his or her own way, but today's success all comes down to the dedication, hard work, and vision of one man. Pete..."

(Cheers from Ed, who had asked for beer instead of champagne and had already downed a couple). "Pete has never been the kind of guy any of us would have imagined having become a successful entrepreneur at 29. So I'd like to propose a toast to the new Pete." We all clinked glasses, grateful that the speech was over, and drank. I was still trying to make out whether or not I should be flattered when Susan swooped over to shake me again.

She smiled a lot and chatted nervously with me for a few minutes, talking as if her life depended on it, and that's when I first started to suspect that something was wrong. I've never been the kind of guy given to great bursts of intuition but somehow, at that moment, I realized that Susan was babbling like an idiot, and that it must have something to do with Jake. We were all disappointed that Jake wasn't there that night, but I don't think any of us were surprised. It seemed like he always found excuses to be elsewhere whenever our group of friends were getting together, like a bigamist who has to avoid parties to which both his wives have been invited. And it didn't take a very sensitive soul to understand that for Susan it was awkward, and that she might be hurt by his habitual absence. But I was just perceptive enough to see that there was something more going on, and just drunk enough to have no inhibitions about asking her.

She was quiet for a moment, staring with inexplicable interest at her cappuccino maker, obviously having hoped to avoid this conversation.

"It's not that there's anything... anything wrong between us," she started. She had always been bad at confiding things. "It's just that, well... he's funny."

"I thought that's what you liked about him," I answered, a little too carelessly. Susan continued.

"Well, it is," she conceded, smiling weakly, "but it's also..." She again consulted her cappuccino maker for moral support. "Don't you find it weird that he isn't here tonight?

I mean, don't you sometimes find him just, I don't know, just a little more than eccentric?"

"Meaning?"

Susan's silence echoed with disappointment.

I was supposed to understand, and deep down, I suppose I did. He was more than just a little eccentric – along with his intelligence and charm came a whole raft of strange habits and inexplicable behavior, from his dislike for group socializing to his recently acquired habit of vanishing for hours or even a day or two at a time without any explanation. And with this more-than-eccentricity came a knack for dismissing it; whatever he said, you took it at face value, and if later – it was always later – it occurred to you that something he had said or done was odd, you found yourself making excuses for it, or finding it amiable, or questioning your own ideas of what is and isn't normal. He inevitably made people question things – everything, that is, except himself.

"I'm not hurt by his not being here, if that's what you're worried about," I added. I started feeling defensive, although whether it was on my own behalf of on Jake's I wasn't really sure.

Susan glanced up and flashed me a grim, almost menacing look. I was missing her point, and we both knew it.

"You know that he drinks?" Her voice had grown flat and bitter.

"I assume you're not talking about the ten cups of Nescafe a day, are you?"

She just frowned at me, so I continued.

"I have a beer with him sometimes. I've never seen him go overboard, if that's what you mean."

"I'm talking vodka, Pete. Lots of it. He tries to hide it sometimes, but I know."

"That's crazy. I mean, he drinks, but I've never seem him wasted."

"He doesn't get drunk. That's what so scary. I once found that he'd emptied a new bottle of Stoli one night without my even realizing it."

"Look, I know you're upset with him, but you're not making sense."

"You don't understand. He's a different person with me than he is with you. You think you know him, but you don't, not all of him. He only shows you as much of himself as he thinks you can handle, but there's so much more to him than that.

"Look," she continued after a pause for air. "I'm not telling you this because I'm angry at him – I'm telling you because I'm worried. There are things about Jake that I don't understand. I think I love him, but he's so different from anyone else I've ever known that sometimes... sometimes I wonder if I know him at all. It's hard..."

"I'm sure it is, but..."

"Just... just keep an eye out, would you? For anything weird, okay? Will you do that for me?"

I said yes. I kind of had to. But I didn't mean it. Jake and Susan were both friends, and I wasn't stupid enough to try to insert myself into their relationship. So I drifted over to Emily and clinked her glass with mine.

"You okay?" The question seemed intended to sound casual. I told her I was.

"Why?" I asked.

"Dunno. You look a little shaky."

"Nervous, I guess. Monday morning I have a meeting with this Axel Lindbergh guy. I'm going back to Apatchi to be told what to do with my own invention. I'm going to have to hold my own with these big corporate types. It's just a little..."

"Unfamiliar? Unexpected?"

I nodded. Emily leaned over and gave me a kiss on the cheek.

"Relax," she said confidently, smiling, as if just a few days ago she hadn't been all doom and gloom. "You'll be great."

"We'll see."

Axel Lindbergh's office seemed to contain almost everything except Axel Lindbergh. His tattered-looking, beech wood desk was spread corner to corner with papers, folders, two laptops, ball point pens in various colors and at least a dozen yellow sticky notepads. Along the walls to either side of me were bookcases neatly lined with labeled binders, but once they passed the leading edge of his desk, they became home to an odd assortment of books, photos of children – presumably his – and variously shaped Lucite blocks given as souvenirs of some of his bigger deals. On the floor, a framed Harvard diploma leaned unobtrusively against the full-length window behind his desk, next to a viciously spiky potted plant. A small round conference table had been crowded in by the door, but shoved into the corner so that it could only accommodate two chairs. I sat in one of them – the other waited for Axel.

"I'm sorry, I'm sure he'll be right back. Cream or sugar?" asked his secretary as she disappeared to get me a coffee. I watched her go through the glass partition that formed the fourth wall of the office. Apatchi was all about transparency, she had told me as she led me from the elevator down the row which divided open plan secretarial pools from the row of glass walls and open doors which housed the businessmen, accountants and lawyers busy sustaining one of the largest conglomerates on earth. Open doors, open minds. Or something like that, she'd giggled, rolling her eyes in conspiratorial exasperation. Only the doors, the desks and the royal blue carpet tiles seemed to have any substance to them. It was like walking on scaffolding.

After a few minutes Axel turned up, his coffee cup entering the office well before he did as he paused to ask a question of someone standing in the hallway.

"Two thirty? Can we make it three? Okay, thanks, see you then. Peter, how are you?" he asked as his colorful tie and crisp smile crossed into the office. We shook hands, he closed the door behind him and sat down next to me at the table. This was, he had said, to be our first strategy meeting, and as such he had asked if I wouldn't mind coming to his office alone.

"Nothing against Jake, you understand," he'd quickly added in anticipation of my question, "but I think it would be best for the two of us to talk before we start widening the discussion. I like doing things one on one when I can."

I had no idea what to expect.

"You know," he said once he had sat down, sipping his cappuccino with that same economy of motion that made everything he did seem effortless, "when I first got here, I put a big map of the world up on that glass partition. Within an hour I was asked to remove it." He chuckled quietly. "When I complained that everyone looked in as they went by, I was told that that was the point. I still find it distracting."

I glanced through the partition and my eyes met those of a woman in a tight turtleneck who was passing by. "I can imagine."

Looking wistfully across the hall for a second, he put down his coffee and turned to face me squarely.

"Anyway, I guess we'd better get down to business." From a folder lying on the table he pulled a piece of paper and handed it to me. "That's an organigram of the Apatchi group, just so you can get an idea of the structure." He walked me through the various branches of the Apatchi family tree, each branch punctuated by little rectangles filled with the names of all the company's various subdivisions. Somewhere towards the bottom, an inch or so right of center, was DTITech Innovations, the new owners of the Horokinetics trademark. I had become a business partner of a subsidiary in a subdivision of a division of a subsidiary of a holding company. It was a little disheartening. Axel calmly fondled the tip of his tie as I read through it, his eyes fixed on me but betraying nothing.

"All these companies form a family," he continued once I had looked up, his smile seeming to mock his words even as he spoke them. That was the weird thing about Axel: you always got the impression that he had just told a joke that you hadn't quite picked up on. "I know that sounds like corny corporate bullshit, but it's true in a very real way. Apatchi hasn't grown at random. As it has expanded over the years, it has picked only companies and assets that could benefit the entire family of companies. It's a funny mix of horizontal and vertical integration. It's all about synergy." I nodded knowingly, hoping that I didn't look too stupid. He smiled again.

"You've done something wonderful with Horokinetics, Peter. It's different, it's creative. I've looked at some weird stuff, but I don't think I've ever seen anything quite like it. It's very convincing for anyone into that sort of thing." I smiled proudly. And then the axe fell. For the next few minutes – it seemed like hours at the time – Axel explained to me everything that was wrong with Horokinetics as a business. Horokinetics may have been a clever idea, it may have been deep, beautiful, complex, subtle, all of the things that Susan, Emily and most of all Jake had helped me to make it, but it was a lousy business, which I had run poorly, and which, on its current course, would never have any hope of being profitable.

"But we're going to change all that, Peter," he added calmly after taking a minute to savor the look of horror on my face. "You and I." That's how he talked. It was always "we," as if we were joint coaches of a team that we both passionately cared about and wanted to succeed. Ideas were "our" ideas, and "we" were going to implement them. He made me feel like Horokinetics was still my baby, as if he were simply some strange millionaire who had decided to drop in and help me out. And I gladly fell for it.

"It's all about cross promotion," he explained, his cool liquid voice making it sound like he was simply repeating the obvious. Apatchi companies worked together to help each other down the long, perilous road to financial success, and now that Horokinetics was part of the Apatchi empire, doors would open that I had never even realized existed. DTITech Innovations had access to know-how and to public relations resources that Horokinetics Inc. could only have dreamed of. Apatchi's PR machine would be put to work promoting the concept of Horokinetics. The buzz Jake and I had managed to create would become a roar. Newspapers and magazines would fall over each other to write about us. Talk shows would fight to get Jake to do readings on national television.

Axle's confidence would have seemed surreal without the organigram of the Apatchi Group. I ended up keeping a copy of it pinned to the wall in my office – it seemed like every newspaper, magazine and radio station I'd ever heard of was owned by one of those little rectangles.

Axel then started to fill in the details of what would be required of us. Apatchi would promote Horokinetics and help to make me rich, he explained, but we at Horokinetics Inc. had our own work to do. He outlined a vision of the website in which commercial links and pop up widows spread like bacteria. Horokinetics.com was to become a sort of marketing machine for various Apatchi-owned companies. Their products would help promote ours, and our product would be used to promote theirs.

"Okay, Pete, here's a simple example. We've recently acquired a major line of health food products, supplements, that sort of thing. We want to keep people interested in that market sector, right, so what do we do? Well, that's where you come in. Horokinetics.com adds a Mind and Body section. You talk about the spiritual benefits of healthy living. Maybe this Theogenes guy was a vegan? Whatever, we work on it. The point is that it creates new opportunities for promotional tie-ins. Our businesses build on each other.

Horokinetics gets excited about health food, and health foodies get excited about Horokinetics.

"The real beauty of it, of course, is your customer list. You have created the perfect pretext for gathering detailed and very personal customer information. Your questionnaires – it's pure genius Pete, I don't think you realize just how useful it is. Your customers are paying you for the chance of telling you all about themselves so that you can market Apatchi products and services more effectively back to them. By helping them, you're helping us. It's a win-win situation. Get it?"

I got it. It all seemed kind of petty and stupid to me, but Axel insisted that it all played into a long-term strategy. Whatever. In any case, it was pretty clear to me why he wanted to talk all this over with me first before breaking the news to Jake. He and Jake had circled around each other like hawks when they met, each taking good measure of the other, and neither seeming to like what he saw. Axel was a good enough judge of character to see that his proposals were not going to sit well with Horokinetics' high priest. He would need my help if he hoped to convince Jake of the necessity of bringing Horokinetics into the corporate fold.

"Peter, you and I are businessmen" he said just as we were finishing up, "and we both know that Jake is a huge part of what sells Horokinetics.com. Now, you know him better than I do, but my reading of him tells me that he might have a problem with some of this. Jake is the public face of Horokinetics. If he doesn't believe in what we're doing, no one else will either, and you and I both know what that means. It all depends on you being able to keep him involved in a way that won't create problems. Can you?"

I said I thought I could. Did I believe it? Did I believe the line I used to sell it all to Jake, that this contract would keep Horokinetics alive and that together we could preserve its strange beauty and integrity? Kind of, I suppose. I know I believed in Jake's friendship. I believed in my own common sense. I believed that we both were well-intentioned.

And, say what you like, I genuinely believed that all of that mattered.

PART TWO

12

"Okay guys, listen up."

The room fell silent. Even the air conditioning seemed to hum more quietly as Jake took his place at the front of the room and began to talk. I had seen Jake the philosopher, Jake the guru, Jake the regular guy, but now I was seeing something different. Jake the NBA coach. Jake the general. His voice and his presence filled the Vortex, and even the least intuitive of my sad little team had the sense not to interrupt.

"The conference begins tomorrow, so we really need to stay focused. Alana, I need you to keep tabs on the out-of-town participants. They'll be trickling in today, so just be sure they've settled into the hotel and know where they're supposed to be tomorrow.

"Dave, I've already talked to the hotel about the lunch menu, but please double check it, and be sure that on both days there's a genuine vegetarian option. No tofu lasagna, got it? Now, between the last session on Friday and the keynote dinner we're going to need..."

The upcoming conference was to be the first of what we had hoped would become an annual event, and we were all feeling the strain. Horokineticists from all over the country, our entire network of trainers and many of the practitioners they had trained, were converging on LA for two days of refresher training, comparing notes, troubleshooting and basking in the warm fractal glow of the legendary Jake Simms. Just the idea of it was nauseating, but I knew that this was an important part of our business, and I was grateful to

Jake for having managed it so well. Without the trainers and the live practitioners, we would have been nothing more than a website. As it was, in the four months since we'd signed with Apatchi Horokinetics had become a national obsession.

"Have you fucking seen this?" Diego would shout at me from the sofa every once in a while, the same incredulous high-decibel shout whether I was in another room or sitting right next to him. He would inevitably be looking at some showbiz magazine, and would have found another reference to Horokinetics. "They're calling your buddy Jake 'super-guru to the stars.' That's seriously fucked up."

"Damn, Lindsay Blackstone is checking into rehab, and says her fractal reading helped her accept that she had a problem. No shit she has a problem, she should be checking into acting classes..."

"Hey Pete, did you hear that Dan Cruz and Penelope Highwater are naming their son Theogenes Jacob Cruz? That's your fault, you owe that kid an apology."

Hollywood was hooked, and the rest of America had obediently followed. We were part of the country's common vocabulary now. Everyone was getting their fractals read, just as once everyone was driving around with "Shit Happens" on their car bumpers.

My friends and family watched the shit happen with varying degrees of awe and concern, but what they had in common was that they all watched at a distance. It was a lonely time. I spent long days and far too many weekends either at my office or at Apatchi's, and in my absence the people in my life went on quietly with theirs. My parents left proud or worried messages on our answering machine a couple of times a week, but I think they were disappointed that my success didn't involve lots of long dinners where they could ask me questions or show me off to friends. Susan I hardly saw or heard from at all for a few months. Even Emily I saw only now and then. It wasn't for lack of trying, but inevitably whenever I had the time and energy to get together she was with Daniel. It seemed to me like he was tightening his grip on her, not letting her spend time with anyone else, and it was pissing me off. But finally one evening we both found the time to get away and have dinner together, and Em explained.

"He's not doing well. Emotionally, I mean. A few months ago he joined a self-help group, but if anything, that's just made it worse. When he's not being really arrogant to me and saying he needs his space, he's crying in my arms telling me he's worthless and can't live without me."

"I don't know, Em. I feel bad for the guy, but you've got to think of yourself. Maybe you just need to spend some time apart."

"That's what he says. But then a few days later he's on my doorstep again. I just don't know where it's going. He keeps telling me that I don't understand. He won't confide in me. He won't even tell me what his self-help group is all about apart from helping people to 'regain a sense of control in their lives,' whatever that means. He says they're not supposed to share details outside the group, something about the confidentiality of the other members."

"Needs more than a self-help group, if you ask me." Let him talk to Susan. Let him consult his fractal, for fuck's sake. I had other things on my mind that Daniel's emotional crises; with Axel's help we'd just signed a contract with a major newspaper and were discussing a book deal with a publishing company. Her struggles with him went on and the months went by, and I sympathized, but at a distance. For now, that needed to be enough. I had other shit to deal with.

"Don't let this conference worry you, Pete, it's going to be fantastic" Jake reassured me, I guess in response to the frazzled look on my face after we'd wrapped up our staff meeting. "I know you've got a lot to deal with on your end. Just make notes for what you're going to say at the dinner on Friday, okay?"

"Don't worry, I'll think of something. Is Susan coming?"

"To the dinner? Yeah, she's coming. She can't work all the time."

"Had me fooled."

"What about you, you going to bring one of your Facebook groupies?"

"Shut up man."

"There were some cute ones."

"Okay, I was a little naïve to start accepting random friend requests. I've stopped. And I'm taking Emily, to get back to the subject. She and Daniel are spending some time apart again, whatever that means."

"Great. Listen, I've got to keep going, but I'll catch up with you later. And really, don't stress, I've got it all under control."

I believed him. He'd proven over the past five months that he could mobilize people and resources like he'd done it all his life. From the self-assured way he could run a simple office meeting to his uncanny knack for coordinating what had quickly become a national network of Horokinetics practitioners and trainers, Jake made everything he did seem effortless. After that first strange conversation with Axel, I had wondered what exactly Jake's role in the new Horokinetics would be, but Jake had found his niche very quickly. Apart from being the public face of Horokinetics and continuing to produce his weekly "Our Nation's Fractal," Jake made a point of having as little contact with the website – and with Axel – as possible. When not organizing training courses, he kept busy traveling to seminars, conducting personal fractal readings for the Hollywood glitterati who raved about the benefits of Horokinetics in Diego's magazines, spouting timeless wisdom on his blog or seducing the media with his calm smile and enigmatic comments. Discussion groups had sprung up everywhere, like independent franchises under Jake's supervision, and Jake would occasionally go on a sort of road show to check that they weren't becoming too weird or culty or otherwise damaging to our interests. This was his favorite part of the whole business, and his face lit up whenever I would tease him about his "new age Tupperware parties."

"You're missing out, man," he'd answer, and we'd both laugh, but I had a suspicion that he meant it.

Meanwhile I dealt with the website, and with Axel. I still had my little office in Northridge, but almost overnight we had had to open a call center and upgrade our I.T. facilities to deal with the thousands of fractals being requested every day. We had to sacrifice on quality a little, but no one seemed to care. The pictures seemed to be almost more important than the reading itself, judging from the number of orders we received for personalized fractal coffee mugs, mouse pads, even jewelry. For about one customer in a hundred, Horokinetics was a complex and thought-provoking challenge to their long-held ideas about time, fate and human nature. For the other ninety-nine, it was just more crap to buy.

One of the things that surprised me most was how much crap there was to buy. And not just from us. Axel's promises to turn Horokinetics into an effective marketing tool hadn't been hollow. He'd talked about commercial tie-ins and massive publicity, about the wonders of deep-pocket corporate backing and its ability to shape the imagination of large groups of people, and he hadn't exaggerated. But the overt marketing had only been the tip of the iceberg. Horokinetics was the key to our clients' personalities and futures, and those futures became increasingly bound up in whatever product Apatchi wanted to push at that particular moment. Fractal readings would now encourage home improvement, or seeking sound financial advice, or taking a vacation somewhere warm. Of course the advice would be accompanied by banner ads on the website for products that just happened to fit the bill. Targeted ads would then follow them everywhere on the internet. Once you told

Horokinetics about yourself, Apatchi brands would stalk your every move and seem ready to fulfill any desire.

The funny thing was that having the website sell other stuff turned out to be a selling point for the website itself. I shouldn't have been surprised. Michael could have told me, if I'd bothered to ask. He probably knew some clever business school term for it. Call it the tee-shirt effect: no matter what you're selling, whether it be coffee, consumer electronics or even ideas, it will sell better if people can also buy the tee-shirt. Or the mug, or whatever. There is no experience on earth that cannot be made more popular and enjoyable by turning it into a shopping experience.

Now that logging on to Horokinetics.com inevitably ended up pointing you towards something nifty to buy, it resonated even more with people who had never heard of Blake or Lao Tzu. Axel's changes were the yin to Jake's yang, interweaving Jake's odd combination of philosophy, literature and the occult with opportunities, some more subtle than others, for commercial interaction. So now our clients could not only get a glimpse of the future on our website – they could do something small to change it. Tomorrow may or may not look bright, but you could make it brighter by treating yourself to a weekend trip to Santa Fe, or a new pair of running shoes. It was like alchemy - that one extra ingredient turned lead into gold overnight.

The fan mail, the encouraging emails, the party invitations, the glowing reviews – it felt great. But not everyone was so positive. Our popularity was making us enemies. SCAT was now being joined by other, bigger interest groups, churches and televangelists in warning their flock to avoid the temptations laid before it by the evil conspiracy of corporate greed and devil worship. Thanks to Apatchi's involvement, the anti-globalization activists joined in as well. And then there were the individual loonies, the ones who weren't calling or writing because some group they belonged to told them they should, but simply because they'd gotten it into their heads that Horokinetics was responsible for whatever ailed them. Over time I felt like I was getting to know some of them. Apart from the "Be a winner not a sinner" guy, the most entertaining one was Photis.

The first Photis email had appeared some time in May. "Peter McFadden, why did you sell out? stop making Jake Simms take the blame. it's you, we know its you. Stop the spiritual desecration of Horokinetics NOW. I am Photis."

I ignored it, despite its having been directed to the new email account I had set up when the religious fundamentalists had started overloading my inbox. Only Apatchi, business partners who bought advertising on our site, my friends and the better quality Mexican spammers knew that address, but it looked as if at least one of the various batches of lunatics who had become so hostile to Horokinetics had managed to find it. If it got worse, I might have to change my email account again.

Soon they started to trickle in pretty regularly, a few each week.

"Peter McFadden, judgment is nigh. Repent. I am Photis."

"Peter McFadden, Lucifer was cast from heaven. You will be, too. I am Photis."

I didn't mind too much. Photis at least had developed a signature style, and did his best not to repeat himself. I kind of appreciated the effort, given that so many of the other maniacs were clearly reading from a script.

But the biggest reason I didn't mind was the simplest. I was a success. I'd arrived. And anyone who didn't like it could go to hell.

13

Axel finally looked up from his desk. It was 5:30 Friday afternoon. I'd been waiting for him for almost half an hour. He looked almost surprised to see me still sitting there.

"Pete, great you could drop by today. Sorry about moving things around, but Monday's a non-starter. You alright?"

"Yeah, fine. It's been a crazy week getting geared up for this conference, but it's going well."

"Good, good, sorry I missed it. Wasn't invited, come to think of it." Axel gave me another of his looks, the sort of look you might get from a teacher who has caught you ditching class but hasn't yet decided whether or not to bust you for it.

"Well, Axel, I think Jake kind of figured, um..."

"No need to make excuses. Jake kind of figured that I'm the antithesis of everything he stands for and that I've got no business at his conference anyway."

"Well..."

"He's got a point." He was enjoying this.

I wasn't. I knew that Axel had no time for Jake's ethics and that Jake felt more and more pushed into a corner by Axel's aggressive use of Horokinetics in his various marketing schemes. He was still playing the game in the sense that he did just about anything I asked him to, but only because I made sure not to ask him anything too outrageous. He was the voice of Horokinetics, our spiritual guru, the one whose face and voice and ideas sold Horokinetics and all the stuff that went with it. But he was unhappy. Jake sold Horokinetics, but with a strange detachment, treating it with a sort of reverence in the face of indignity, as might a classics professor whose discourses about Homer were used as the introduction to a techno dance version of the Iliad. And Axel started to treat him as the producer of a techno dance version of the Iliad might treat an expert on Homer – an annoying necessity bordering on irrelevance. Horokinetics started to drift away from Jake, and he started to drift away from Horokinetics. And from me. I felt like I saw more of him on television or in newspaper articles than in person.

"Don't let it stress you, Pete," Axel continued after having watched me squirm for a second or two. "When Jake came onto the project, Horokinetics was in trouble. I know Jake worked hard but let's be honest Pete, a lot of what he did was irrelevant or even counterproductive. Hear me out..." I was shaking my head, trying to find the right words with which to object.

"Listen," he continued, not giving me the chance to interrupt, "I know he made Horokinetics seem deep, but that can scare off people as well as attract them. I applaud him for understanding the importance of addressing the needs of your core market. But do you really think the wider base of consumers we're now attracting care how some Byzantine monk's writings prefigure modern physics? I can tell you, Pete, they don't. What's made Horokinetics successful is its ties with Apatchi. You agree?"

I hated to agree. It killed me to agree – I felt as if I was betraying Jake if I agreed. But however brilliant Jake's work had been, it hadn't made us economically viable. It was Apatchi that made us famous and, more importantly, made us profitable. I shrugged my shoulders reluctantly.

"Well, Jake's not stupid, he knows it too. And if I were him, I'd be a little irritated by it. Give him some breathing space. He's still finding his new role in Horokinetics – let him. And in the meantime, you can get on with fulfilling your contractual obligations to Apatchi. Don't forget that you've got a year-end bonus coming to you if all goes as planned."

I did my best not to let him see how uncomfortable I felt with all this. Axel stared right through me for a minute, let a thin smile creep over his face, and continued.

"Now, I've just a few things I wanted to go over. First, have you gotten the new spyware program up and running yet?"

"Yeah, Dennis sorted out the kinks."

"Good. I don't have the full file yet for this week's pop-ups, but Liz'll get it to you over the weekend. Um..." Axel shuffled through some paper on his desk for a few seconds.

"Oh yeah, trademark issues. A new website has cropped up called FractalVisionQuest.com. They do more or less the same thing you do, but they're claiming that theirs is a rival system of Horokinetics developed in the 15th century under the guidance of the Patriarch of Antioch. They say it's the true Horokinetics, and that yours is heretical."

"Uh oh, competition," I laughed.

Every once in a while Axel and I managed to share a joke. Not this time. He ran his tongue along the front of his top teeth as if looking for something, making his upper lip bulge and giving him, just for a second, a mean and stupid look.

"Come on, Pete, we've been through this before. If we don't police our trademark, we could lose it."

"Our" trademark. Every once in a while Axel needed to remind me that Horokinetics Inc. no longer owned the rights to Horokinetics. Even our name wasn't our own – we were allowed to use it only under license, which meant that at any minute everything I'd created, from the system itself down to our office stationery, could be yanked out from under me.

"Yeah, but I still think it's a shame. I got a call the other day from a freelance journalist who wants to do an article on how to be sure that the people casting your fractal are genuine or not. He said he understood that Jake Simms was one of the most respected authorities in the country on the subject and that he'd like to interview him. These small timers are turning us into experts in our field – it's almost flattering."

"We don't need flattery, we need to protect our intellectual property. Anyway, I've already taken care of it. One of my colleagues had a word with the guy and made him see that his own fractal held a dismal future for him if he didn't stop."

I wanted to ask whether his colleague had a thick neck and large biceps, but I kept quiet. Axel would just have answered something vague and flashed me that smug smile again, and I didn't think I could bear it.

Axel and I went on for another half hour talking over various details of the site and the complex marketing agenda that he wanted woven into our fractal readings for that week. I kept glancing at my watch, but he didn't seem to get the message until well after 6:00.

"Hey listen, Pete, you've got this dinner to get to, you don't have time to sit here gabbing. Have fun, and we'll talk next week."

"Thanks Axel, have a good weekend."

"Yeah sure."

With only a little bit of reckless driving I managed to arrive at our table just ahead of the appetizers.

"We were getting worried." Susan gave me one of her chaste kisses on the cheek as she said it, but I could feel that she was annoyed. This is Jake's big night, that kiss told me, you could at least have been on time.

"My meeting with Axel dragged on a little. Everything alright?"

"No problems, today went off without a hitch." Jake was all smiles. Susan was right, this was his big night, and Jake's quietly dominating presence had expanded to fill it. We were surrounded by a dozen other tables, seating nearly a hundred Horokineticists from all over the country. We could hear them all discussing in animated voices what they had learned in today's sessions, but beneath the hum of their voices, or in tandem with it, we could sense that all eyes were on Jake. It was like sitting with royalty.

Susan sipped her wine and stared off into space for a second. Shrugging off whatever irritation she still felt for me, she suddenly smiled and started chattering about her work. We had hardly spoken over the past few months, and she seemed like she was trying to make up for lost time. After about five minutes of monologue about her expanding practice, her new colleague, the new offices she was moving into next month, and all the work that these changes involved, she took a breath and asked me how I was. But before I could answer I felt a hand rest on my shoulder and turned around.

"Hey you," Emily said brightly. I just stared for a minute. She looked gorgeous, and I managed to tell her so without sounding too much like an idiot. I'm not sure, but I think she even blushed.

Susan turned her attention to one of the Horokineticists at our table as Emily sat down beside me.

"Sorry I'm late."

"No problem, I've been having all sorts of fun." Emily enjoyed this sort of thing, milling around and talking with total strangers. You could drop her into a room full of alligator farmers and she'd come away having made a few friends. A Horokinetics conference was maybe an even tougher crowd – alligator farmers are less likely to give you unwanted hugs or try to engage you in discussions about the cosmos – but Em had made the best of it. "The guy over there, the one with the long gray ponytail, he claims he can see fractal patterns radiating off people. Like Kirilian photography."

It was great to have Emily there, but as the evening wore on, I could tell that something was wrong. She was too animated while talking, and too subdued while quiet.

During the next lull in the general conversation, while Jake had disappeared to talk to someone at another table, I asked her what was wrong.

She stayed quiet for a second.

"Daniel and I broke up yesterday. For real this time, for good." I did my best to sound sorry to hear it. "Well, it's been coming for a long time, I suppose. We've grown apart. I've done everything to try to keep us together, to try to understand him, but there's some weird stuff going on with him..."

The sound of a microphone interrupted her. Carlos, the nervous, lanky guy who had become Jake's assistant and had helped set up the conference, was asking everyone to be quiet. My time had come. Jake gave me an encouraging slap on the back.

"Just take your dragons up there with you," he said just loud enough that only I could hear it. I smiled, took a deep breath, and went up to the mike.

I said a few words of appreciation to all those who had done so much to make this first annual conference possible, especially Jake (applause), and to thank everyone for attending. It only took a minute, after which the real show was to begin. Jake took over and began his keynote speech. The whole room fell dead still. Jake's eyes scanned the crowd for a moment, letting the silence linger and the tension rise, and then he began.

"God, he is good, isn't he?" Emily whispered as Jake calmly conveyed his convictions about the importance of the work they had together undertaken. He was good. He spoke at once easily and passionately about our historic mission, the beauty of reconciling science and spirit, the importance of upholding values, as if he had never once questioned the truth behind this phony system we'd cobbled together from scratch. It was hard not to be taken in.

"Finally, we must all constantly remind ourselves that we are not simply a living link with an ancient wisdom. Yes, as you've often heard me say, we are the Bridge, but our task is much greater than that. Knowledge is a sacred trust, but an even heavier responsibility is that of power. Many of you will feel uncomfortable with that word. It's an ugly word, a word for something that has been abused for so long that we find it easy to condemn outright. But power is neither good nor evil. It is what you make of it. And the first step towards wielding it responsibly is to embrace it as your own.

"We, as the holders of an ancient wisdom, as counselors to others, as purveyors of knowledge at once impossibly vast and deeply intimate... we are powerful. Accept that power. If you recoil from it, if you reject the responsibility that it entails, then you abandon along with it the ability to help. And I would argue that we who know have a duty to help. Our eyes are open – it's too late to shut them now. As Theogenes wrote, "Let him who sees, speak, and him who speaks, act." That is our burden. Let's bear it together, and bear it well. Thank you."

Applause shattered the air around us. People were standing up, some were crying. One woman with little wooden animals matted into her dreadlocks was shaking her head dangerously from side to side shouting "yes yes yes." As the room surged with adoration for Jake, Emily's hand found its way to mine and gave it a squeeze. We looked at each other, unable to speak for the noise, but what she wanted to convey was clear enough. This is scary. This is not right.

I smiled reassuringly and took my hand back to applaud. Emily was wrong. This wasn't scary – it was success. And I owed it all to Jake.

14

Emily and I hadn't had a chance to finish our conversation that night, and for the next week or so we spoke very little. Every time I got her on the phone she was hesitant, awkwardly tiptoeing around the various topics of conversation that would really have mattered, like why she broke up with Daniel, what had happened to me and my company now that it was the faithful servant of a global corporate empire, or maybe the fact that for the first time since college we were both single and that it was finally time for me to admit I was crazy about her and for her to admit that she'd always known it and for us to kiss and fall in love and get married and have babies.

But then, out of the blue, she called and suggested that we get together that Saturday.

"I know some stables out in Agoura," she said, with something approaching her old enthusiasm. "We can rent horses and go for a ride on the fire trails."

"Um..." She might just as well have asked me if I wanted to go squirrel hunting so we could make a pie.

"Come on, you keep promising you'll come out and ride one of these days. Do it for me. We've got a lot to talk about."

So she picked me up that Saturday morning and we drove out into the canyons.

"So where did you learn to ride?" she asked me once we had left the stables and reached the top of a steep dirt path where it emerged from the shady lower canyon into the sun and joined a larger dirt road. It was a perfect day: the sun was already warm but would take a few hours to reach scorching, and the cold of night still lingered in the shady parts of the long narrow valley we were slowly working our way along. The air was still cool, and the silence unbroken except by the occasional bird, the soothing clip clop of our horses' hooves against the dusty packed earth, and the ever-present background hum of cars somewhere in the distance. I had tried to stay behind Emily, but my horse kept insisting on bringing me right up level with her so she could see how awkward I looked perched up in a saddle.

"Summer camp," I muttered, clutching at the saddle horn as we topped another short steep rise. Camp Bobcat was one of several day camps up in the canyons that exist to help parents convince their young children they don't really live in one of the largest crime-ridden and pollution-fouled urban sprawls on the planet. There I had been taught impractical skills such as archery, horseback riding and how to catch pollywogs, and learned for myself much more useful things, such as where to buy illegal fireworks and what secret messages Led Zeppelin songs revealed when played backwards. I had a lot of fond memories of those days at summer camp, but equestrian classes were not among them.

"You're doing well," she said cheerfully, obviously encouraged by my ability to stay in the saddle. "You may want to lean a little more forward on the uphill parts." I tried it: it helped, but it also reminded me why riding is more popular with women than men.

"We should have done this ages ago," I answered, through gritted teeth.

"Well it's not like I haven't asked you enough, I've been nagging you to come do this for years now. You should learn to trust me."

"Of course I trust you Em. It's the horses I don't trust." She laughed and then spurred her horse ahead of mine so that we could pass single file beside a couple of walkers coming the other direction. The path took a strong curve to the right, passing under a steep bank shaded by a thick tangle of bushes, chaparral and scrub oak. A dry creek bed passed under the road through a cement pipe and continued down the gully as we rode along the curve and back on to a shaded straight-away. The air was a lot cooler tucked back in this U-bend in the hillside, and the chill and shadow could almost give the impression of an entirely different climate, one that would not be leaving us sweaty and thirsty in an hour. Emily shivered. A couple of quail fluttered and disappeared into the brush ahead of us.

"In Montana we used to spend whole summers on horseback," she said dreamily once my horse had again come level with hers.

"With... with your family?" She smiled sadly and nodded. Emily hardly ever talked about the death of her mother, so it was a subject I tried to steer clear of. I told myself it was out of consideration. But dead parents have a way of filling a person's past, so whenever we'd talk about Emily's childhood, I'd usually bump into her mother somewhere along the line, like a fellow guest in a small hotel.

"We didn't have horses of our own, but there were plenty you could rent and some of my parents' friends had them. Sometimes the three of us would go camping up in the mountains for a few days or a week, just riding and fishing and at night we'd look at the stars through my dad's telescope that he'd always bring along. We got lost once."

She said it as if leading into a story, but her pause grew longer and longer and nothing followed but a heavy silence. After a few minutes she glanced over at me, as if expecting me to say something, but I had nothing to offer. So she spoke.

"Something weird has happened, Pete, that you need to know about," she said, her voice an emotional void that she seemed to be waiting for me to fill.

"Okay," I answered. I was searching for something encouraging to say, but didn't find anything. She took a deep breath and went on.

"It's a few things, really, but they're related. I mean, I think they are. I don't know anymore. It's..."

I'd never seen her this confused and inarticulate.

"I've lost my job at St. Cuthbert's" she managed after a few seconds of catching her breath. "They let me finish out the school year, but that's it. They don't want me back in fall." Her voice wavered a little. "I've taught there for five years."

"But... That's crazy. I mean, why? Why are they firing you?"

She stared at me for a moment.

"There have been complaints. Angry parents. Apparently... Sorry." She wiped her eyes and took another deep breath. "Remember the kids who were working for you last summer, doing the fractal readings? Well, some parents complained. The administration is saying that it was inappropriate for me to get them involved in a spiritual movement that wasn't sanctioned by the Catholic Church."

"Spiritual movement?"

"The parents are claiming that Horokinetics was being used to lure their kids away from the Church."

"That's fucking nuts."

"Well, that's what I thought." Emily looked away from me for a minute, watching the path in front of us as the horses kept on their steady pace. "But I got thinking. Pete, when Daniel and I broke up he was saying a lot of strange things. He said he was part of some religious order, something new and exciting, something I wouldn't be able to understand. He was talking about the unity of the cosmos, secret ancient writings that explained the nature of the infinite. Weird stuff, but familiar, don't you think?"

It was. Chillingly. I still felt guilty not telling Emily that Daniel had been going to Jake's discussion groups, but I'd promised Jake I wouldn't tell her, and I was determined to keep that promise. And yet, now... well, what difference would it make for Emily to know? She would just blame Jake, and me for not having told her. I trusted Jake not to let Daniel continue in the discussion group if he thought Daniel couldn't handle it. Anyway, Jake's vague spiritual bullshit had become so fashionable that everyone was talking about ancient wisdom and cosmic unity. That wasn't Jake's fault. Or mine.

"So you think Daniel has started taking Horokinetics too seriously?"

"I don't know. Nothing would surprise me with Daniel. But the complaints at school are something different. Todd and Catherine are good kids, and they've both told me that they have no idea why their parents have freaked out. I think they were getting warnings from some kind of Christian organization who think Horokinetics is satanic."

SCAT again. I knew it, the fuckers.

"These bible-thumping assholes can't even look at a little harmless entertainment without seeing the devil poking his horns out from behind it."

"Not completely harmless, Pete," Emily snapped. "Anyway, do you really think that's all there is to it? Entertainment?"

"Well, okay, it isn't just entertainment. Axel has pushed things to a point where I can imagine parents getting a little annoyed. It's pretty unscrupulously commercial, but...."

"They're not complaining that it's commercial, they're complaining that it's spiritually manipulative."

"That's just silly. Shit Em, I'm really sorry, I never meant to get you into trouble over this."

"It was my own choice, Pete, it's not your fault."

"I thought you always said that St. Cuthbert's was a pretty laid back place?"

"It is. I wouldn't have worked there if it were some kind of born-again Bible college. The headmaster told me that more than one set of parents complained – not just Todd's and Catherine's. Something bigger is going on here. Maybe someone else is using Horokinetics for reasons of his own."

"You mean Jake."

"Maybe. Maybe someone else. I don't know. You've said yourself that a lot of people get angry that Horokinetics has become so aggressively commercial. Maybe there are people out there taking it more seriously than you realize."

"Whatever. But listen, what are you going to do now?"

"Don't know. The Marin Academy job is still open. It's a great school. I'd be head of the science department – less money, but I'd have a real say in the curriculum. Ellen keeps asking me."

"Yeah, you've mentioned that."

"It would mean moving to San Francisco," she added, glancing at me. I stayed quiet for a minute. My stomach was doing little backflips. San Francisco. She had been tempted before, but her relationship with Daniel had kept her in LA. Shit.

"Um, yes, I guess it would. It's a nice town. A little cold." Em watched me for minute, as if gearing up to say something, or maybe just waiting to hear what else I might add to my dumbstruck travel and weather report.

Either way, neither of us got the chance, as we were distracted by the approach of a line of people on horseback. At their head was a tall, thin woman with long brown hair and a familiar look of quiet amusement on her face. I recognized her instantly.

"Well, well, if it isn't the fortune teller himself," came Jericho's gravelly voice as she pulled her horse to a halt directly facing my own. The four others in her group were still approaching, about 50 yards behind, chattering together and seeming not to notice us. "And on a horse?" She glanced down at mine as if to double check.

Emily came up alongside me and allowed her eyes to flit questioningly between me and the woman blocking our path.

"This is Jericho, a friend of Jake's. Jericho, this is Emily."

She nodded curtly at Emily before returning her attention to me. "Do the good people at Apatchi know you're out having fun while you should be making them money?" She smiled as she spoke, but there was no humor in her voice.

I remembered the feeling she had given me when we had spoken at Jake's, the feeling that she had access to some secret wisdom that she considered me unworthy of sharing. Emily watched her silently, but with a ferocity in her eyes, like an animal who smelled danger.

"They let me out occasionally."

"I'm surprised – sounds to me like Axel Lindbergh keeps you pretty busy. I'm glad you're getting a break. It's hard work convincing people that hamburgers and cell-phones bring them closer to God." I bit my lip but said nothing. It was hard to fight back against an accusation that my own conscience was whispering repeatedly in my head.

"Not everyone has the luxury of riding around on horses for a living," Emily snapped.

"No," answered Jericho, her eyes never leaving me. "Pete here is too busy playing around with people's lives." I reached over and placed my hand on Emily's, hoping to keep her from lashing out. I knew she could be fierce when she felt defensive, and I had no interest in provoking an argument with Jericho. It was hard to say whether that was because she was Jakes' friend, or out of some deeper instinct for self-preservation.

"I like to think I'm enriching people's lives," I said cheerfully, hoping to lighten the mood a little.

"You're enriching someone, no question about that." Jericho returned my smile, as if the whole conversation were one long clever joke.

"Well," she continued as the rest of her group caught up with her, "I'm glad to see you out here. It's always a good thing to conquer your fears."

I bristled at that. "I just said I wasn't very good at riding, not that I was afraid of it."

"No, there are so many other things to be afraid of." Her eyes fixed on mine again, steady and intense, as if she were using them to hold me in my saddle. "It's a big, scary world,

Mr. McFadden. But I'm sure your fractal has already told you that."

She clicked her tongue and her horse obediently sidestepped ours and continued around us, her fellow riders following behind and smiling stupidly at us as they passed.

Emily guided her horse forwards, easing ahead of mine and turning to face the line of riders disappearing down the trail behind us. She watched them silently until they disappeared around the bend, and then looked hard at me.

"What was all that about?" she asked quietly, fear and accusation mingled in her voice.

I shrugged nervously. "Dunno. She's weird, but harmless."

Her eyes narrowed. "Pete, you find everyone harmless. Jake twists you around his little finger and you call him harmless. Axel bullies you and you call him harmless."

"And you seem to think everyone's out to get me."

"No I don't, I just think you're too trusting. These people don't mean you well. Not Jake, not Axel, and certainly not that bitch..."

"Lighten up, for God's sake," I snapped, a little more harshly than I'd intended. "She was just joking."

"Fine," she muttered. "You're not going to listen anyway. Not as long as it's other people who are paying for it." She turned her horse around again and we continued up the trail, sullen and quiet, emerging some time later into the sunlight and finding that the heat of the day was already growing unpleasant. After another fifteen minutes we turned around and headed back to the stables. I got no more compliments on my riding that morning.

15

Emily's paranoia wasn't helped by the fact that the emails and phone calls, particularly from Photis, were becoming a daily event. And they were getting more hysterical.

"Peter McFadden, you are the problem. *Quit while you still can.* I am Photis."

"Peter McFadden, The wages of sin is death. I am Photis."

"Peter McFadden, Stop or we will stop you. I am Photis."

The messages didn't worry me too much, as they weren't very different from the other garbage I'd received since the beginnings of Horokinetics. The phone calls were even more stupid, the voice at the other end trying to mask itself like in a bad detective movie.

But it worried Emily. She forgave me quickly enough for our little scuffle that Saturday horseback riding, but she refused to stop playing mother hen and telling me to be careful all the time. It was annoying, but that fact that our conversations were becoming so frequent more than made up for it. We talked almost daily. Sometimes about nothing, sometimes about everything. And sometimes about Photis.

"Come on Em, look at them, they're too stupid to worry about." I read them out to her one evening at Diego's, laptop in one hand, a slice of pizza in the other.

"Peter McFadden, one life is a small price to pay for the souls of thousands. I am Photis."

But that just made her more nervous.

"He's threatening you," she argued, underlining her sense of urgency by digging her surprisingly strong fingers into my arm. "He or she," she added ominously. "You need to tell the police." I rolled my eyes. This was the third time we'd had this conversation, and every time it sounded more and more like an episode of a cheap detective novel. I told her that none of the emails had actually threatened me, and that even if one or two were a little suggestive, that still didn't give me a real reason to worry.

"Have you showed them to Jake?" she asked. "Or Susan?"

"No, why should I? Susan doesn't have the time – I hardly ever even talk to her these days – and it's not like Jake's opinion is going to convince you anyway."

"Well, sorry, but I think you need to be careful when the lunatic fringe start getting angry."

"I've got news for you Em, we are the lunatic fringe."

She gave up after a while, and I was finally able to change the subject.

What surprised me was that Diego also seemed to take the so-called threats seriously.

"Diego, I've gotten this kind of thing from day one, from all sorts of people. I'm still here, aren't I?"

"Yeah, but you were a nobody then. Now it matters. Do you realize that at the last three parties I went to I overheard people discussing their fractals? I know some really serious people in Hollywood who've stopped talking about Zen and started quoting Theogenes. Not just the stars, but the people who matter, the ones who make decisions about what America sees and hears."

I couldn't repress a self-satisfied smile.

"Hey, I get invited to the same parties these days. I hear it for myself. Excuse me while I wipe back the tears."

"Don't laugh," he went on. "One of these days you're going to piss off someone who can do you harm. Just watch your back, okay?"

"Relax, man. It's just a few puritans and anti-globalization nutcases who hate us. Everyone else thinks we're Viagra for the soul."

"I'm not so sure about that. I mean, I don't give a shit, but a lot of people are accusing you of being a sell-out. And you said yourself the other day that it was all becoming a little creepy."

"Diego, listen, every day parents sit by while companies like Apatchi convince their children that chocolate coated corn puffs count as a healthy breakfast. Some of them get mad, but you don't hear about breakfast cereal CEOs being attacked by angry mobs, do you? I don't think anyone's going to go postal just because a fortune-telling website subtly convinces people to spend their money."

"Stacey says it's all her friends talk about anymore."

"She hates me, doesn't she?"

"Well, she's not your biggest fan..."

"Man, I'm getting in the way here, I need to find my own place."

"Hey Pete, come on, don't be stupid. I like having you here. Stacey understands that you're my friend, and if she doesn't want to deal with you we can always go to her place. Seriously."

"Thanks Diego, but you've got to promise to tell me when it starts becoming..."

"Shut up."

"Okay, okay. Anyway, about Horokinetics, it's really nothing to stress about. Jake and I have told Axel that we need to tone down the commercialism a bit, and he agrees, so no worries."

He chilled out after that, and I made a point of not telling him or Emily about the dead rat I found nailed to the front door of the office one morning. It was local, small time juvenile stuff. If God or Mother Earth or the inhabitants of the slums of Sao Paulo were upset with what I was doing, they'd let me know. Until then, I wasn't going to worry about it.

What did worry me was Jake.

Jake hadn't been himself for the past few weeks. It was something I would have found hard to imagine without having seen it with my own eyes – he wasn't depressed, exactly, but somehow the spark that usually animated him was gone, or at least muffled under a vague sense of gloom. It was hard to define, and probably unnoticeable to anyone who didn't know him well. But it seemed clear to me. Going from occult genius to playing the red-nosed clown for McHorokinetics in just a few months could hardly have been uplifting for him. And being told to do it by someone he counted as his friend only made it worse. It was casting a shadow between us.

It was a few weeks after my ride with Emily that Jake went on vacation. I told myself that I was happy about it, that some time off would do him good. But I wasn't all that sure that it would do me much good; I hated to admit it, but I didn't like the idea of having to function on my own without having Jake around to bounce ideas off of. So I offered to drive him to the airport, both to help him on his way and so we'd have some time to talk before he vanished for two weeks.

I held my breath as my shiny new BMW convertible nose-dived into the gaping jaws of Jake's driveway, and found him already waiting for me outside. In his faded tee-shirt, khakis and well-seasoned hiking boots, he looked half way to Honduras already. We tossed his backpack into the back seat and set off down the canyon for the coast.

It was early enough that the beach traffic was still light, and we left behind the night-coolness of the shady canyon almost before I'd had time to notice. The ocean fanned out before us, a smooth deep blue, flecked with sailboats and a couple of tankers, stretching into oblivion as it was swallowed up by the pale haze hanging over Santa Monica Bay. In Malibu we stopped to pick up some coffee for the road and then headed down Pacific Coast Highway, Jake talking all the while about the two weeks ahead of him visiting a buddy in the Peace Corps who was living in a village a hundred miles down a shitty road from Tegucigalpa.

As if the answer wasn't obvious, he had asked me if I had ever been down to Central America.

I shook my head and laughed. "Not unless you count Cabo. I don't like taking vacations in places where they might shoot me."

"Hell, you're more likely to get shot in Northridge. My friend insists that Honduras is okay these days."

"Not too safe, I hope. I'm looking forward to some stories."

He laughed, "I'm looking forward to having some to tell."

"How's Susan taking it? I can't imagine Miss Prudence letting her man wander off into the jungle just like that without a fight."

Jake seemed to wince at the mention of Susan. He glanced out the window at the beach houses and surf shops racing past. "No," he muttered, "not without a fight."

"Ouch." I felt a tinge of guilt as I tried to commiserate with Jake, as if I was betraying Susan by being compassionate. "Well, I'm sure she'll get over it," I added, wishing I hadn't brought her up in the first place.

"Hmm. If that were the only problem, she might." We both fell silent, each uncertain what to say next or whether to say anything at all.

"Susan hasn't really been herself lately."

"Really? I've hardly talked to her recently."

"That doesn't surprise me. Her practice has been keeping her busy – she's taking on too much work, and it's starting to get to her. And trying to tell her to be a little less ambitious really doesn't help."

"I can imagine."

"And..." It was one of those rare moments when Jake couldn't quite hide his frustration. He shook his head helplessly. "She's just not making sense these days. I'm worried about her. It's like she's a little schizophrenic – she can sound perfectly fine, but the next minute she'll get paranoid and start accusing me of things. She's started getting very resentful of the time I spend working on Horokinetics. And the discussion groups aren't helping. She seems to see it all as competition. What can I do? I've tried my best."

"So have you...?"

"Listen, just keep an eye on her, will you?" he blurted out, obviously finding it difficult. "I'm worried about her. "

"Yeah, of course I will. I'll give her a call later."

"Good."

Jake watched the waves while I kept my eyes on the traffic as we raced up PCH. Soon we reached the Santa Monica Freeway and were heading inland towards the airport, and he started to talk again.

"Didn't you say you had something else we needed to talk about, for work?" There wasn't much to cover – we'd already gone over just about everything over the last day or two. That's no exaggeration: I still consulted Jake on everything, both because his advice was always sound and because, since Axel Lindbergh had embedded himself deep into the flesh of our business, I felt that I had to work at it to keep Jake involved. I needed him, not just as a friend and advisor, but also as a counterweight to Axel's relentlessly corporate approach to the website. Axel's strategic manipulative way of doing business was a little too slick, and I needed Jake's common sense and finely tuned moral compass to help me maneuver around having to do anything too sordid. If he started to drift away, as it seemed at times that he was doing, as I suspected Axel of hoping he would do, there would be nothing left to slow Horokinetics' downhill slide from an intelligent fraud into an insipid one. So I asked him for advice on everything, whether I needed to or not, and he patiently answered as best he could. But there was still one subject we had avoided, and it was one of the few that I couldn't take action on without him. And I had promised Axel that I would ask before he left for Honduras.

"Um, yeah. Listen," I began sheepishly, keeping my eyes meticulously fixed on the straight and relatively empty five lane freeway ahead of me, "Axel brought up his idea again, the one about doing a live TV reading." Jake watched me silently for a moment, then turned to stare straight ahead.

"I just don't understand what the guy hopes to gain," he said, doing a poor job of concealing his irritation. "I went along with him and did most of the talk shows and radio shows, and on every one of them I did a sample reading. And they all went pretty well, don't you think?"

"Yeah, I agree. Last week was fantastic. I'm almost getting used to seeing you on TV."

"So why does Axel want to risk us getting caught faking a spectacular reading when we've been having so much success giving decent, honest readings that don't pretend to be something they're not."

"I don't know, Jake," I said, feeling exasperated that we had to have this conversation at all. My gut instincts followed Jake's, that planting a fake audience member whose past Jake could read with astounding accuracy was not only a creepy thing to do, but was asking for trouble. But Axel kept insisting, and I was beginning to feel like a wishbone torn between the two of them. "He said we need something that isn't so vague."

"Then tell him to hire one of those guys who bend spoons with their minds. Or tell him to stand up there himself and commit a transparent fraud on national television."

"I don't know. After all, fraud is what we do."

He turned to answer, but stopped himself, as if to gather energy for what he had to say next. The irritation suddenly drained from his face, as it might from a well-meaning teacher who has to remind herself that the horrible little creature in front of her is, after all, just a child.

"Pete, come on," he said, managing a patient smile, "that's Axel talking. We've always stopped short of fraud. That's what's kept me here all this time. We're still on the right side of that line."

"Are we?" I asked, wanting to test him, hoping vaguely that he might convince me. "I mean, we've invented a system of divination out of the blue, told people that it has an ancient and distinguished history, told people that it's based on real science, told people that we can use it to tell their future and to tell them about themselves. We're deceiving people for money."

"Are we?" Jake asked, mimicking me without a hint of irony in his voice. I just shrugged and waited for him to continue.

"What are we really deceiving people about? We've never promised anyone that we can give detailed predictions about their future, or that we can replace their psychiatrists or grant them salvation. We just tell them that we can help them understand themselves and their place in the universe, and we offer them a mythology within which they can do that. That's a far cry from getting on TV, making wild claims that we're performing some kind of magic and then faking proof of it."

"Well," I conceded, still not entirely convinced, "I agree that the TV thing has an added yuck factor to it, but..."

"It's more than just a yuck factor, Pete. It crosses a line, and it's an even clearer line than Axel crosses by using the fractals to convince people how to spend their money. Faking a reading is clear, deliberate deception, and it deprives people of the ability to make informed choices. And that denies them their dignity, which is the one thing I've always promised myself I'd never get mixed up with.

"What we're doing," he said, seeming to anticipate the question that would have occurred to me a few seconds later, "is creating. It's not lying, to create a new truth. Horokinetics has become real – it's not just a system of divination any more. It's become a way of thinking.

"Think of it this way: if it could be proven that as a historical figure the Buddha didn't exist, would you turn around and say that Buddhism is nothing but lies? Of course not, because what's important to Buddhism is what it teaches people about life and about themselves. It's the same with us.

Horokinetics is a system of thought now. It adds beauty to people's lives and helps them make their own choices. We're teaching people to see this as a world of infinite possibilities, helping them draw their own map through the maze of marketing bullshit that our society has become.

"Everything else out there tries to teach people to stop thinking, and to convince them that life is about choosing between the two or three brands of useless stuff that are presented to them. Society exists to make people passive. Global mass culture has deprived people of the dignity of real choice, and we're helping to give it back to them. Every time you create something new, you give people a little bit of dignity by making their world that much bigger. You give them the freedom of interpretation."

"You don't think we've just added to the clutter of fake garbage out there?" I somehow felt compelled to challenge him, even though I knew it was pointless.

"Horokinetics is not fake just because we invented it, Pete. It is real because we invented it well. And that's something we should both be proud of. That's why we now and again have to draw a clear line and say 'This is not okay.'"

I shook my head and laughed, conceded defeat.

"Alright Jake," I muttered in mock exasperation, "no TV show. I'll tell Axel you won't do it." I held my breath and slowed down, the most dangerous thing you can do on an LA freeway, and tried to peer around the enormous SUV lumbering up the road ahead of us at 70 mph. Our off-ramp was coming up, so I quickly sped up again and managed to scoot off the freeway just in time. Swerving through the increasingly nervous traffic, past the landmark Nude Nudes strip bar, we finally found our way into the massive complex of LAX and rolled up to Jake's departure terminal.

Two enormous police officers eyed us as if we'd just pulled up in a windowless van with Saudi license plates while Jake calmly pulled his backpack out of the back seat and hitched it up onto his shoulders. Jake then leaned over, careful not to topple from the weight of his pack, and stuck his head through the passenger side window to say goodbye.

"Have a good time," I said, still cheerful at having got what I expected to be an unpleasant conversation out of the way. "Be careful – sorry, I'm starting to sound like my mother."

"Don't worry, I will be. But listen, you take care of yourself, okay? Something tells me you've got a lot more to worry about here than I do down there."

I paused, waiting for an ironic chuckle, but it didn't come.

"I mean it," he insisted, not a trace of humor on his face. "Don't trust anyone, especially not Axel. Not everyone around you has your best interests at heart. Watch your back."

I had been hearing a little too much of that for comfort. But before I could ask him what he meant, he had turned to go, and I watched silently as his well-worn backpack bobbed off through the crowd and out of sight.

16

Monday morning I found Axel in his office armored in a gray suit and a white shirt so heavily starched I thought it might crack if he made a sudden movement.

"Sit down Pete, I'll be right with you," he muttered, still absorbed in whatever he'd been reading. When he looked up a few minutes later, he seemed tired and exasperated. He seemed to already know the result of my conversation with Jake.

"So, what are we going to do about this talk show?" he asked abruptly, slowly rubbing the barest hint of iron gray bristles on his chin. I shrugged ineffectually.

"I think he'd do the show," I offered reluctantly, "it's just the fake audience member gimmick he doesn't like."

"Yes, I know. He's quite... moral, isn't he, your friend Jake." I twisted in my chair nervously at his reference to Jake as "my friend." I felt instinctively that Axel was disappointed, and that he somehow blamed me for it. I responded with a smile and a nod of the head, as if to say "yeah, not like us men of the world, eh?"

"That's a good thing," he said flatly, as you might if you were told what the government had done with your taxes. "Apatchi takes pride in its ethical approach to business. But there are times when individuals need to put aside their personal beliefs, aren't there? To do what's best for the company. Pity he doesn't know where to draw the line between being principled and being a pain in the ass."

"He said he thinks it's wrong to manipulate people by faking things like that..." I was trying to keep my cool. I needed to keep Axel happy, but I felt angry and defensive as soon as he criticized Jake. The best I could hope for was to play the man of reason, roll my eyes a bit at Jake's exaggerated moral sense and Axel's carnivorous instincts.

"I know what he thinks," he cut in, impatience sharpening his voice. "He thinks he's the only one out there with ideas, and he thinks it's his mission to use Horokinetics to spread those ideas."

"I don't think..."

"And we've let him do it, you and I." He went on, seemingly unstoppable, with resignation in his voice but no real anger that I could detect. "Haven't we? We've let him do it because he's good at it, and it all fits in with the brand image we're trying to convey. But he's starting to let the mystique of it go to his head."

"Oh, I don't know. I mean, he talks a little spooky sometimes, but he's pretty down to earth once you get to know him."

"Pete, you're loyal to your friend, and I admire that, but come on. You've noticed it as well as I have. This thing he does every week, "Our Nation's Fractal," it was a great idea, started out great, but it's become some kind of one-man anti-global capitalism show. His blog's even worse. He's making our Board nervous, and that makes me nervous. And it should make you nervous. If Horokinetics comes to be identified with some kind of left wing agenda, then you know as well as I do that we would have to reconsider our arrangement with you."

That was true enough – Jake did seem at times to wander off into his own brand of spirituality that wasn't exactly calculated to appeal to Wall Street, or even to Wal Mart. His discussions of how the world would be affected by the interplay of the four elements on the fractal continuum often drifted into moralizing about taking responsibility for the state of the planet and the obligations of individuals to transcend group thinking, to embrace radical solutions that focused on the well being of all. It could all be seen as kind of anti-corporate and peacenik.

"Maybe he takes it a little too far at times, but he has a point about the TV show."

"Quite frankly, we don't need him for the TV show. You could dredge up half a dozen guys who could do a convincing job of it. Our PR department uses an agency that can set it all up. I'll get them to give you a call."

"But..."

"I know what you're going to say, Pete, and you're right. The issue goes deeper than this talk show. I think you need to have a talk with Jake. Tell him we're all happy for him to do his thing as he sees fit, but that he needs to tone it down a little. Stop sounding like David Koresh. Stop going on about morality and fulfillment and independent thinking – I mean, for God's sake, kids can access this site." He downed the rest of his coffee like a cowboy would shoot bourbon.

"Okay, okay, I'll talk to him, see if he can't take the edge off a little."

"You know his girlfriend, don't you? Susie, or something like that?"

"Um... yeah. Why?"

"Then it's simple. Talk to her. Ten bucks says she'll help convince him." His smile was that of an awkward little boy who has managed to use just the right swear word on the playground.

"I'll, um, yeah okay, I'll give it a shot."

A sickly smile passed across his face and stuck there.

"No, don't give it a shot. Do it. Listen Pete, you don't seem to understand the importance of this. All these religious freaks and lefty protesters are getting worked up, and that's okay with me, but if you're not careful Jake's going to start upsetting decent, law-abiding consumers. Now maybe it's my own fault for giving you such a free hand, but you're allowing Horokinetics to become something irresponsible, and some might say un-American. If you're not willing to do something about it, there are people out there ready to convince you. Not nice people either. And I don't want to have to intervene, understand?"

His paternal hand on my shoulder sent a wave of cold down my arm. I said I understood.

"Great. In the meantime I'll get that agency to give you a call. Jake's a great guy, and I sympathize with your desire to keep him on board, but there's no harm in hedging our bets a little.

It had been a couple of weeks since I'd talked to Susan, and what Jake had said about her on the way to the airport was still weighing on my mind. I knew she could be a stress bunny at times, and I knew she was working like crazy, but Jake knew that too. If he was worried, then she must really not be doing well. I hated to add to her burden by asking her to talk to Jake, and I wasn't convinced that it would help, but Axel's request gave me added incentive to give her a call. I figured I could at least see how she was doing and, if she seemed okay, then I could feel her out about whether she thought Jake was straying a little too far from Planet Earth. I dialed the number and got the familiar sound of her stilted answering machine message. "You've reached the office of Susan Anson, MFCC. I'm sorry I can't take your call right now, but please leave your name, telephone number and a brief message after the beep. In case of an emergency, please call my pager at..." I left a message asking her to give me a call, and then returned to the pile of correspondence on my desk.

Susan never did call back, so I packed up and headed home around 6:00. I was tired, and it was all I could do to focus on the road in front of me. Too much on my plate, I thought to myself as I roared down the 405 past Sunset. I hope she's okay. It wasn't like her not to return a phone call, however busy she was. All I could do was try again tomorrow.

Finally, bleary eyed, I pulled up in front of Diego's apartment building and was half way to the elevator before realizing that I hadn't locked my car. I went back, found that I had locked it after all, and then climbed in the elevator. I heard voices through the door to Diego's apartment and winced at the thought that he might have some friends over tonight. I loved living with Diego – I kept putting off getting my own place because I enjoyed being here so much. But his friends could be annoying, and tonight I really wasn't in the mood. I put the key into the lock, braced myself, and opened the door.

There was a shuffling sound, and Diego suddenly appeared at the door, shifty and awkward.

"Finally," he said, as if he'd been waiting for me for hours. I could hear the fridge closing and a sort of hiss in the background, like someone was lighting a cigarette.

"What's up?" I asked,.

"Oh, nothing." He was about as convincing as an infomercial. At that moment a light appeared over his shoulder.

"Surprise!" It was a cake, covered with candles, and behind it, Emily. "Happy birthday!" She and Diego sang a round of Happy Birthday to You, after which I managed to blow out most of the thirty candles in one breath. Emily put down the cake, wrapped her arms around me, and gave me a lingering kiss on the cheek.

"Surprised?" She was beaming, obviously pleased that she had taken me by surprise. She had – after she had called that morning to wish me a happy 30th birthday I had forgotten all about it. My parents were going to take me out to dinner on Saturday, so I had put off any thoughts of turning thirty until then. There was so much else to think about.

Diego opened a bottle of champagne and brought out three glasses. Three. It hit me for a minute, the sadness of it. A year ago it would have been a lot more. I couldn't help running down a checklist of notable absences. Friends from work had evaporated when I became persona non grata at Alcantrix, but even the list of likely guests in my post-Alcantrix world was pretty poorly represented. The party of a few months ago would have included Jake, Susan, Tanya, Daniel, Stacie... The rate of attrition was pretty disturbing. Tanya was out of my life. Daniel was apparently insane and effectively out of Emily's life, except for the occasional weird phone call late at night. Stacie was coping with some mysterious emotional problems that Diego couldn't quite grasp and therefore temporarily out of commission. Susan was too busy. Jake was away. Well, those absences that weren't easily explained were actually pretty desirable. And these days I could have replaced them a hundred times over if I'd wanted. I could fill a hotel ballroom with people who wanted to be my friend. I didn't need a bunch of animation geeks to hang around with. I silently toasted the shedding of baggage, and we cut the cake.

"Shit, I almost forgot," Diego blurted out suddenly, putting down his cake and grabbing his champagne flute again. "We've got something else to toast. To the post-capitalist utopia." He raised his glass and gave me a smirk. I smiled sheepishly and we clinked glasses and drank. Emily looked puzzled.

"Dickhead here didn't tell you either, then? Here, have a look." Diego put down his glass and grabbed a magazine from the coffee table. He handed it to Emily.

"The Utne Reader? Pete, you and Jake are on the fucking cover!" She rolled up the magazine and smacked me on the head with it, then flipped through it to find the article. "'Selling the Faith: market-driven mystics are selling a post-capitalist utopia, but should we be buying?' I can't believe you didn't tell me."

"It's not a big deal. Who reads the Utne Reader except maybe a few college professors? Anyway, it's pretty critical."

Of course it was a big deal. But critical was an understatement. The article accused guys like me of hijacking the messages of visionaries like Jake and using them to promote a corporate agenda. Still, it was even more publicity for Horokinetics, and I should have been happy about it.

Emily skimmed through the article while Diego and I ate cake and speculated on whether or not there was any point to eating dinner. "Hmm," she started, her brow furrowing, once she had reached the end. "It's interesting, but I wonder..."

The phone rang and, assuming it was my mother, I picked it up.

"If you want more birthdays, the desecration must stop. I am Photis." Again that stupidly disguised voice. I told Photis to go fuck himself and slammed the phone down. Diego and Emily watched me silently.

"It's nothing," I snapped. I was almost more annoyed by the thought of how Diego and Emily would react than by the call itself.

"Photis?"

"Yeah, Photis." I tried to look simply annoyed, but I must have been pretty unconvincing. We were all thinking the same thing at that moment – how did Photis get this number? There were only a handful of people who knew I was living with Diego: my friends, some of Diego's friends, my colleagues, Axel... Shit, apart from that, not even my bank knew I lived here, they had my parents' address. Photis was eerily well-informed.

Emily walked over to the phone quickly and tapped at the keypad.

"What...?"

"Shh." She scribbled something on a scrap of paper and hung up. She then read out a phone number. "Mean anything to you?"

I told her it didn't. Diego was nodding his head.

"Good thinking Sherlock. Star 69, right? So we know where the guy was calling from. So now what?"

"Of course, if the guy is smart enough to track you down here, presumably he's smart enough to call from a payphone."

"Pete, my land line isn't even listed – who've you given this number to? It's not on the website or anything is it?" Diego was starting to look scared.

"Of course it isn't on the frigging website you shithead."

"Well how'd this psycho asshole get my phone number then? I can't believe..."

"Listen guys," Emily shouted, "listen, this isn't helping. The question is what do we do about it?"

"It's just Photis," I pointed out quickly. The last thing I wanted was for Emily and Diego to blow this out of proportion. "It's creepy, but it's nothing to panic about. If Photis were really after me he'd have done something already. It's just a stupid scare tactic."

"Shit man, he's doing a good job."

"Diego, listen, I'm sorry he got your number. I honestly don't know how."

"So now what?" Emily glanced back and forth between me and Diego.

"So you now trust me to deal with it, okay?" I think I must have sounded pretty convincing, because they dropped the subject while we finished our cake.

After a while Diego went into the kitchen to get us more drinks while I stepped out onto the balcony for some fresh air. Photis had unnerved me. I'd gotten used to him, but this was entering stalker territory. After a few minutes I heard footsteps and felt a gentle hand rest on the small of my back.

"You okay?" Emily's voice was hushed, as if the question contained some kind of secret. I brushed it off.

"Yeah, no problem."

"Pete, I'm scared."

This got my attention, more for the tone of her voice than for the words. The words were just melodrama, but the voice... there was more affection in that voice than I was used to. I turned to face her, but couldn't think of anything to say, so I did my best impression of a reassuring smile.

"It's just, I know I haven't been around much, but I've still been following what you've been doing. And I guess now that I've lost Daniel, I've had to do a lot of thinking, and I'm seeing things a little differently."

"What is it Em?"

"I just don't want you to get hurt. Maybe I've just kind of missed you." She forced a smile, which lasted only a second or two before fading, but her eyes stayed fixed on mine. We were close, alone, her face only inches from mine, and like a character in a science fiction movie I seemed to find myself in some parallel universe, one in which I was about to finally kiss the woman I'd dreamed of for years. Her hand reached up to touch my cheek, just as mine began to find the small of her back to pull her toward me. And, just like in the movies, in walked Diego.

"Hope you guys don't mind vodka martinis," he said with a forced cheerfulness in his voice. "I'm out of gin." I love Diego. But I will never ever forgive him.

"Um, yeah, great," I muttered, as Emily stepped back sheepishly and took a glass from Diego. The moment, whatever it was, was over.

We drank our martinis and talked and had a great dinner which Diego had prepared ahead of time, and then Emily got ready to go.

"Pete, you'll trace the number, won't you?" she asked one last time as she opened the door.

"Okay, okay. Tomorrow."

"Promise?" Emily had that schoolteacher thing about her sometimes – it drove me nuts.

"I promise. Now leave it alone, okay?" Emily frowned, then walked back over to the table and wrote down the number more clearly on the notepad Diego kept by the phone, scrawling "Photis" above it in big letters. She didn't trust me. And she was right not to. Days passed, and I still didn't trace the number.

The week that followed was a busy one. As it was, they were all busy, and getting busier. We had grown too fast, and I still wasn't very good at hiring people and delegating stuff to them. Jake had his assistant Carlos now, thankfully – there's no way I could have coped with covering his work while he was on vacation, even if I would have known how. As it was, I wasn't even coping with my own. I was slipping behind, and that Wednesday afternoon, with hours of work ahead of me, I found myself thinking that maybe success didn't suit me after all. Success was tiring. It was lonely. It meant working longer hours than my secretary, who waved goodbye cheerily at 5:00 and left me tapping away at my keyboard accompanied only by the hum of computer equipment and the occasional unexplained gurgle from the water cooler. A little solitude isn't such a bad thing, but the sheer dreariness of my office without any other sign of life was becoming distracting. I ate some cold pizza, looked at my watch, and decided I needed a coffee to keep me going for another hour or two before heading home.

I stood up to stretch my legs, yawned, and then froze. Something was wrong, a noise that shouldn't be there. It seemed to come from the front room, maybe the click of a door opening, or a tap at the window, it was hard to say. Hello? I called out, but there was no response. Slowly, quietly, I crept around my desk to the door and peered around it into the Vortex. Nothing but cold halogen lights, computers and a couple of potted plants. I shrugged to the imaginary audience we all keep in reserve for awkward moments alone and disappeared into the bathroom. The uncomfortable silence in that office made it easy for a tired mind to begin playing tricks, I told myself as I washed my face and returned to my office. I switched on the cappuccino maker, scooped some coffee into the filter and was just fitting it into the machine when a voice behind me made me jump. Coffee grounds scattered everywhere as I spun around, fists clenched, ready to fight for my life.

Susan stood in the doorway.

"Jesus Christ," I gasped, still feeling the tingling sensation at the back of my neck. "You scared the shit out of me." I couldn't keep the accusation out of my voice, however pointless.

"Sorry," she replied flatly, "I thought you heard me."

"It's alright," I said, catching my breath and brushing coffee grounds off my shirt.

"I called at home and Diego said you'd be here. I got your message the other day – I've been really busy."

I left the coffee for the cleaning staff to deal with and again filled the filter, making a cup for each of us. Susan sat down and looked around the office.

"It's been ages since I've been here," she said, her voice sounding distant and preoccupied. "Hasn't changed all that much."

I handed her a cup and sat down, unsure of where to begin. Susan chatted distractedly, telling me vaguely how work was going and the troubles she was having with a new associate who had started working with her a month ago. I listened politely, trying to gauge her mood. She seemed tired, stressed, but otherwise normal enough. I asked her if she'd had any word from Jake.

"No." She shook her head and looked out the window at pink sunset glow of the parking lot behind our building.

I went on as cheerfully as I could, wondering aloud whether Jake was enjoying Honduras and silently why Susan had chosen to drop by rather than call. My office was hardly on her way home.

"Did he tell you?" she asked, interrupting me mid-sentence.

"Hmm?"

She repeated, "Did he tell you?"

"I'm going to guess no."

"That we broke up?"

I shook my head, overwhelmed by the suddenness of it.

"Hmm." She didn't look at me, and spoke almost as if to an imaginary third person in the room. "I thought maybe he would have."

I would have thought so too, considering we had just been talking about her, but all I could say to Susan was "No. I'm really sorry." A pat on the shoulder and a commiserating hug followed. She looked sad, but still distant. Crying was not on the agenda.

"Me too," she said while fidgeting with a few paperclips on my desk. I realized that coffee was probably not the best thing to have offered her, but I didn't have any sedatives lying around. "It was a mutual thing. It just wasn't working. So that's not why you called, to talk about Jake?"

"No, I mean, yes in a way, but not about that. Mostly I just wanted to see how you're doing. I never see you anymore."

"Yes, well..." She seemed to change her mind about whatever she was going to say, and instead asked "What did you want to talk about Jake for if it wasn't about us breaking up?"

"Um..." It didn't really seem like the time to discuss it, not to mention the fact that it was now a little pointless. A recently ex'ed ex-girlfriend has about as much influence over someone as an out of state parking ticket. "It was nothing. Axel's just making a big deal out of nothing and I wanted to hear your reaction."

Her eyes shot up to meet mine. "Big deal about what?" There was an edge to her voice that had been absent a second earlier.

"He thinks Jake's sounding too Hare Krishna, that he's going off the deep end. He's trying to get me to rein Jake in a little."

"Good luck," she muttered. She sounded bitter.

"I'll just have to make the right noises and then brush it off."

"He's right Pete."

This wasn't the answer I'd expected, so I just looked at her stupidly. "I guess he does have a point, that if we're going to market this…"

"No, Pete, you don't understand. Axel's exactly right. Jake's taking it all way too seriously. It's getting…" She broke off, looking around the room with a strange, haunted look in her eye. She took a deep breath and continued. "Weird."

"I don't get it," I managed, all the time trying to evaluate Susan's degree of mental stability. "What's weird?"

She clenched her fists involuntarily, scattering paperclips onto the floor.

"Jake. Remember what I told you months ago, that I was worried about him? Well, it's worse than I thought. He's not normal, Pete. These discussion groups – these flunkies hanging around him all the time. His obsession with spirituality. It's not normal." I could see tears beginning to form in her eyes, but I wasn't in a position to comfort her from the other side of my desk.

"I can imagine it's hard. I'd really hoped things would work out for you two."

This was a little too much polite concern for her to bear.

"That's not the point," she yelled, slamming her open palms down onto my desk. She continued more quietly, but her words lost none of their anger or urgency. "He's becoming dangerous. They worship him. There are hundreds of them, all crawling around the canyon like ants, hanging on his every word. I think it must have started before Horokinetics. It's as if…" She sat there for the next few minutes and just cried, shaking her head but not trying to speak. I came around the desk and held her as her body shook with pain or fear or grief or whatever it was that had gripped her.

She wasn't the only one who was frightened. I had never seen Susan like this. She had always been stability itself, my benchmark for what was normal and boring and non-hysterical. To see her losing it here in my office unnerved me. I did what I could to calm her down – swayed her body from side to side a little, patted her back, muttered useful advice like "it's okay" – all those things you promise yourself you'll transcend when a friend needs you, but which you inevitably fall back on as soon as someone is sobbing in your arms. After several pointless minutes of my not knowing what else to say, Susan straightened up and wiped her eyes, a look of determination managing to fix itself on her wet, red puffy face.

"Sorry." Her voice was quavering and nasal. She sniffed hard. "It's just... you need to stop it." I just looked at her, watching her eyes as they fluttered and shifted, still oozing saline and avoiding my own. "Do you hear me? You've got to stop it."

"Susan, what is it exactly? What do I need to stop? Jake's discussion groups?"

"Not just that. Everything." She glanced up at me and then looked away again, growing increasingly incoherent. "All of it. Horokinetics. Jake. The discussion groups. All those freaks out there. It's..."

She was breaking down. I tried to hug her again, anything to get her to calm down, but it didn't work. She pushed my hands away and glared at me.

"Tell me you'll shut it down, Pete. Tell me you'll shut down the website. Stop the training program. End it."

"Listen," I answered, trying my best to sound reasonable, "you're upset, you're angry, you're worried about Jake. I understand. But I can't just close down the business. I've got employees, I've got a contract with Apatchi. Anyway, Apatchi would just continue Horokinetics without me. Why don't you take a few days off and rest, and then we can talk..."

"No, you don't understand. It's all because of Horokinetics. You've created this thing, and you have to stop it. They're using it. Jake can't do as much harm if you take Horokinetics away."

I tried not to let my concern or irritation show, but apparently they were both pretty obvious. Susan looked away angrily, standing up and peering out the window into the parking lot.

"Never mind," she said, keeping her face turned away from me. Her voice had grown cold and dead, as if a couple of wires had fused. She continued to talk, but no longer seemed to care what effect her words were having. "We can talk about it some other time. Are you staying here much later?"

It seemed a fairly pathetic change of subject, but I answered that I had a few more things to finish. "But listen," I added quickly, "do you want me to take you home? I can leave this stuff until tomorrow."

She shook her head, turning again to face me, eyes still remaining elsewhere. "Thanks, but I'm fine. Really. I just need a little sleep." I walked her to the door.

"Just keep an eye on him, okay?" she added, apparently forgetting that he was somewhere in a forest in Honduras.

"Sure. I will."

"He ..." She caught herself, breathed loudly, and managed a faint smile. "Just be careful, Pete. I'll talk to you later." She gave me a quick kiss on the cheek, the first truly Susan thing she'd done that evening, and walked down the cracked and weedy concrete path toward the parking lot.

I spent the next few minutes trying to get back to work, but all the while reshuffling pens and stationery and thinking about Susan. She wasn't the type to make things up. And some of what she said had clicked – Jake was weird, and the discussion group was a serious freak show. But then there is weird and there is weird. Jake was odd, but not evil. His friends were socially maladjusted, but they weren't quite the Manson clan. Susan, on the other hand, was tired and stressed and bitter, so it wasn't all that surprising that she was blowing things out of proportion. The question was, how to convince her to slow down a little, rest, maybe even talk to someone? I had long been a close friend, but usually she was the one counseling me, not vice versa. I wasn't any good at playing therapist.

Finally I accepted that I was too tired and too spooked to get anything more done. Shutting down my computer, I walked out into the front room, turned off the lights, and left, locking the door firmly behind me.

It was a cool evening, that wonderful coolness that always crept down out of the hills and into the valley the minute the sun started to disappear. The traffic noise was loud, but indistinct, thousands of cars somewhere in the distance, all rushing places that didn't require them to pass my office. I breathed deeply and exhaled as I left the path through the office complex and emerged into the parking lot.

The blow was sudden and fierce, knocking the wind out of me and doubling me over onto the pavement. I watched my car keys drop in front of me without hearing them hit the ground. The traffic noise had vanished, leaving me only the shuffling of tennis shoes on asphalt and the sickening sound of my own quickened pulse. I looked up to see what had happened but was knocked over again, onto my left side. The right side of my face went numb. The parking lot began to spin wildly. There was a tugging at my shoulders as a pair of hands tried to drag me to my feet. I made it half way up when a foot, seemingly unconnected to anything else, slammed into my stomach knocking my body against the cinderblock wall behind me.

I remember swinging my fists wildly, uncertain what I was aiming for, knowing only vaguely that I was being attacked. One of them made contact with something, something both fleshy and sharp, but the pain I felt in my stomach was now multiplying itself all over my body, stinging my face, pounding the air from my lungs and all coherent thought from my mind. After a few minutes I realized through the pain and panic that it had stopped.

My eyes opened, taking in my car in the distance, and between it and me, several pairs of feet, a fringed pair of black pants, a grey sock twisted awkwardly as it emerged from a Doc Martin. All seeming to sprout horizontally out of the oil stained asphalt.

Suddenly a handful of coins – nickels, I think – showered down on my face, bouncing and rolling on the ground in front of me with a strangely melodic tinkling sound. They were followed by a face: a malicious, evil face, a face I'd never seen before, framed by frizzy dark blond hair.

"Find another job, Judas," a voice croaked, but whether or not it came from the face in front of me I wasn't sure. "This one's killing you."

The face vanished, and with the sound of hurried footsteps blending themselves into the random buzz of distant traffic, the parking lot began to spin again. It seemed to move everywhere at once, following no pattern, just dipping and weaving however it chose. I could taste blood, feel it dripping down my face, but all that went through my battered and not quite functioning brain was a wave of concern for my watch. It was a nice watch, I thought. Was it still there? It had been on my left wrist, the left one, the one stretched up over my head pointing towards the car. I could look and see, it occurred to me, but as I tried to move my head the entire planet lost its sense of direction and spun into oblivion.

17

The fires came early that summer.

Usually they wait until August or September. By then southern California's brutal summer heat has had time to toast spring's grasses and wildflowers into acres of kindling, and there are always some stupid kids, frustrated that summer vacation is ending, who feel the need to climb into the hills and play with matches. They'll get their stash of illegal fireworks and head off to a quiet spot, thinking how clever they are to have evaded their parents on this hot, dry, windy day so that they could finally have some harmless fun with small explosives. You can just imagine the look on their faces as they are packing up to go and notice that the hillside behind them is beginning to emit clouds of black smoke. "Think one of our bottle rockets did that?" Someone will ask. "No, shut up and let's go," the oldest kid, the awkward 16-year-old with the car, will say. "No one says anything about this, alright." Of course, it's not always an accident. Sometimes it's pure malice: some spiteful bastard trying to burn down his friend's house, one of that sick tribe of attention seekers wanting to impress a girl, or maybe a land developer hoping to liberate a choice strip of property from the totalitarian grip of environmental protection laws. Sometimes, but I suspect that on the scorecard of destruction, stupidity beats malice, every time.

But that July we already had a bad one, with a huge blaze devouring acres and acres near Castaic, and another smaller one sweeping through Agoura. The smell of it was almost stifling out in the Valley, filling the already smoggy air with smoke and ash and the almost pleasant sense of impending doom. At least at Diego's the smell was faint. Santa Monica's sea air and distance from anything natural enough to be likely to burn kept most of the smoke away, and gave my lungs a welcome rest. They were the only part of my body that didn't ache.

I was lucky that nothing was broken, or at least so Emily and Diego kept telling me. I was also lucky that Susan had forgotten her bag and returned to find me sitting dazed and bloody in the middle of the parking lot. She'd taken me to the hospital and sat with me for hours until an overworked nurse took my blood pressure and vanished again. After they'd patched me up, she had dropped me at my parents' house for the night. Still, I didn't feel very lucky. I'd needed stitches over my left eye, and the livid bruise running down my cheek and cut on my lip left no question in anyone's mind as to who won the fight. The stares kept me inside as much as the pain did. "What the hell happened to you?" I could see everyone thinking when I dropped by the enormous shopping mall of a pharmacy in Calabasas to pick up my painkillers and assorted ointments for the stitches. Every face turned to look, and every face quickly looked away again in some sad attempt not to be rude. One smartass teenager with a skateboard under his arm shook his head and said "Damn, I hope you got the guy's license plate." It made me smile, but my lip split open again and the sight of fresh blood sent him hurrying off before I could come up with an answer. Good thing none of them could see the rest of me. My body was so bruised that naked I might have been mistaken for a Dalmatian.

Being rendered socially unacceptable by ugliness wasn't all bad. It got me a lot of parental sympathy that night, although by noon of the next day I'd had heard my mother sigh "oh honey" so many times and been offered so much chamomile tea – in a Horokinetics.com coffee mug, for Christ's sake – that I had to escape. It also rid me of Stacie quickly enough when she had dropped by to see Diego. It had been all I could do not to groan audibly when she walked in the door the evening after the attack. She had started to agree with the others in the global confraternity of psychos that I was cheapening Jake and Theogenes' message of hope to the world, and the thought of another night of disapproving looks and snide remarks was more than I could bear. But one look at my battered face inspired her to take Diego out to dinner rather than eat in as they had planned. "I hope you're taking lots of arnica," she muttered as she dragged Diego toward the door with a poorly concealed look of revulsion on her face. I didn't see her for another week.

For the next few days Diego and Emily stayed with me as much as their schedules allowed. As busy as he was working on his next project, Diego made a point of checking in on me whenever he could. Emily was doing some tutoring and job-hunting, but since the school year was over she was able to come by a lot. She did a good job of keeping me distracted, and she talked my ear off about just about everything, with two exceptions. We didn't talk about the attack, and we didn't talk about the other night on the balcony. I'd made very clear that I didn't want the attack even mentioned, and Diego and Emily backed off after a bit of well-intentioned urging to go to the police. As for the latter, neither of us was really sure that there was anything to discuss. If I'd been more of a man maybe I could have just come out with it and asked her if we were actually about to kiss when Diego interrupted, or if it was just some sweaty little fantasy of mine. But I couldn't do it. It had to have been my imagination, so I left it alone.

By Friday morning the shock was wearing off and I was starting to feel better. Diego and Emily noticed, apparently, because after a few minutes of talking quietly to each other on the balcony, they came in and started nagging me.

"Pete, we need to talk," Emily began, weariness and irritation already weighing her voice down so that it came out more as a sigh than speech. I glanced at Diego for moral support, but remembered that he was on her side for once. They were going to nag me again to go to the police.

"We've already had this conversation," I answered, trying to smile dismissively and splitting my lip open again in the process.

"Telling me that you don't want to talk doesn't qualify as a conversation."

"There's nothing to talk about. I got mugged. It happens every day."

"It wasn't a mugging, you dumb shit," she said, anger surging into her voice.

I snapped back "Well, it wasn't an invitation to tea and cookies. What the hell would you call it?"

"A deliberate attack. They didn't even take your wallet. You need to talk to the police."

I just shook my head. I couldn't explain to her why I didn't want to get the police involved, any more than I could explain it to myself. I guess it was plain old embarrassment. The beating had been painful, but far more than that, it had been humiliating. The thought of having it happen again scared the shit out of me, but the idea of having to tell the story to a group of strangers, probably over and over again, was even worse. To go crying for help, to admit that I couldn't take care of myself, was too degrading for words. And if I went to the police, the press would get hold of the story. There I'd be, the creator of Horokinetics, splashed all over the news as the archetypal computer geek roughed up by a few playground bullies and crying to the grownups for help. And for what? The police weren't going to find who did it, and they weren't going to be able to protect me if whoever they were decided to do it again. I just had to keep my head down, be careful, and hope that it was a one-off act of malice by some frustrated group of thugs looking for a little notoriety. And above all, pretend not to be afraid.

"There's no point Em," I answered, trying to sound unconcerned. "The police can't do anything about it. Anyway, I can take care of myself."

"Yeah, we've seen that," she muttered. I was about to sneer, but thought better of it. She continued "You at least need to confront Jake about it."

"Why Jake?"

"Because I think he knows something."

"Oh for God's sake, Emily, he's in Honduras. I know you don't really like him, but come on…"

"No, you come on. You know nothing about him. He just wanders into your life, takes over your business, and then as soon as he can't have his way with Horokinetics anymore, he vanishes into the jungle and you get beaten up. That seems to me to be enough to get you asking some questions, don't you think?"

"No, actually…"

"And besides," she went on, her cheeks beginning to turn red, "you said yourself that Susan had just warned you not to trust him, that he was up to something strange."

"Susan's been pretty strange herself lately. You've seen it as well as I have. She's totally overworked and now Jake's dumped her. She's cracking under the pressure and starting to see conspiracies everywhere. I feel bad for her, but I'm not going to sick the police on a good friend just because she's feeling stressed and becoming delusional."

Her voice grew quiet and grim. "You know, they've never heard of him at Boulder."

"Huh?"

"Jake. I called yesterday to check. The philosophy department at Boulder have never heard of him." The words winded me like a well-aimed fist. So he had been lying about his past. I guess I couldn't claim to be that surprised. Jake was strange and secretive by nature. It didn't really matter, I told myself quickly. He knew his stuff, whether he'd studied it in

Boulder or in Timbuktu. And he was a good friend. Emily was staring at me, waiting for a response.

"So what?" I said, glancing out the window in hope of hiding any look of doubt that might pass across my face. That seemed to shut her up, and we sat for a minute in obstinate silence.

"Listen, Pete," Diego intervened, "I don't know Jake, but for what it's worth – no offense, Emily – I think he's pretty low on your list of potential violent enemies. You know about the religious right-wingers and the tree-hugging left-wingers. We all know about your friend Photis. Shit, there may even be people within Apatchi who want you out for reasons of their own." I looked over at Emily as Diego spoke. Did that frown mean disapproval, I wondered, or did she have doubts of her own? "I guess my point is," Diego continued, his voice thinner and quicker than usual, "whoever you think might have been behind this, there are people out there who want to hurt you." Duh.

"Who want you to quit Horokinetics," Emily added quickly.

"Whoever they are, they're dangerous, and you can't just stick your head in the sand and hope that they'll go away."

"I'm not sticking my head in the sand," I protested, growing irritated more at being outnumbered than by all the obvious arguments they were making.

"Then what are you going to do?" Emily asked.

"I'm going to do exactly what Diego told me to do." A painful, almost spiteful smile must have crossed my face just then. "And Susan. And even Jake. "I'm going to keep my eyes open."

"And hope that someone doesn't knock them out of your head?" Emily was becoming furious, clenching her fists unconsciously as she spoke. It was a mannerism of hers I had always thought that was kind of cute, when it was directed as someone else. She let out a little puff of exasperation and looked away, as if for a moment she couldn't stand the sight of me, sitting there so smug and obstinate and refusing to agree with her. I took advantage of the pause in their attack to stand up and limp over to the coffee maker on the breakfast bar to refill my cup. It was late morning, and I could see that the beach and the street below were already writhing under the full weight of the sun. Too hot – it would be a good day to stay inside. If my friends would let me without driving me nuts.

"Fine" barked Emily so suddenly that it made Diego jump in his designer leather easy chair, a piece of furniture whose sole intention was to keep just such a thing from happening. She was on her feet and looking around for the sad little canvas bag she always had with her. She found it and was half way to the door before she stopped and whirled like a matador to face me again.

"No," she said, as if vocalizing an argument going on in her head. "No, it's not fine." If she noticed the little moan that popped out of my mouth before I could stop it, she showed no sign of it. "Pete, I have to say this.

"When you started this whole thing last summer I thought it was a bad idea, but I supported you anyway, because you needed something to get you back on your feet. And for a while I thought it had done that. You stopped whining and feeling sorry for yourself and started to take your life into your own hands. I felt like I was finally getting my old Pete back, the one I knew in college, the one with all that imagination and sense of humor, and a backbone. But I'm starting to think I was wrong. All Horokinetics seems to have done for you is make you lose touch with reality. You're not yourself anymore, Pete, and the person you've become isn't very likeable, or very smart."

"Listen, don't..." I began, but this was her moment.

"No, you listen. First you let some guy you met by the side of the road practically run your business for you, and then, not only do you sell it to a really disgusting company, but you actually help the creeps use it to manipulate people."

"What have we done that's so horrible? So we sell things. Big deal. That's what businesses do."

"What you sell people is lies that keep them from thinking for themselves. You're even ready to sell your own friends – you were pressuring Jake into going along with Axel's plans when you knew how strongly he felt about it, and you were even going to try to convince Susan to influence him. You're manipulating your own friends, and for what? Axel? It's like when you started Horokinetics you wandered into a tunnel, and you don't see anything outside of it anymore. You just follow Jake and appease Axel and nothing else seems to matter.

"I once asked you why you wanted to have a career designing monsters for movies. Do you remember what you said? You said it was because you could think of nothing better than to help people recapture that feeling of wonder you always had as a kid when you played at being a knight slaying dragons. You said you wanted to bring your childhood fairy tales to life. I thought that was an honest and beautiful thing to say."

She had started crying now, her hand clenching her bag as if it were a parachute and she was about to jump. I just stood there speechless. She took a breath and kept going.

"I liked the Pete who said that. He was someone I could really care about. I thought I'd found him again. The other night...." She took another step and reached the door. Opening it fiercely and turned her back to me as she walked through. But before closing it, she turned again to face me one last time.

"If he ever comes back, tell him to give me a call." She kept those big moist eyes fixed on me for a count of five and then abruptly spun and slammed the door behind her.

I stood there mutely as the door seemed to hum in its frame, but it didn't open again.

"Ouch." Diego had a way of stating the obvious that made me want to hit him. He remained seated in his easy chair, stranded there like a sea anemone at low tide.

"She'll be alright," I said, as if it was Diego who needed reassurance. He let out a nervous laugh, while I tried to look as if my intestines weren't slithering out across the floor.

"Pete, you're being a dumb-ass."

"Thanks, you want more coffee while I'm standing here like a fucking waiter?"

"Sure, thanks." I walked back over to where Diego was sitting and took his coffee cup out of his hand. I felt like a housewife with PMS, but I was glad to have something to do with my hands. Better making coffee than strangling Diego. Or myself. He continued: "Listen, she's right, you know. You need to take this seriously. You're not the only one involved in this, and you're not the only one who could get hurt."

"Fine," I answered petulantly. "What would you do, smartass?"

"Have you traced Photis' phone number yet?"

"Um."

"Do it, you moron. Takes five minutes on the internet. It's probably just a payphone number, but it's worth checking."

"Okay, I'll check."

"Good boy. Next thing, look at the people within Horokinetics. Think of who might want you out, and why. Like Axel – does he have any reason to scare you, hurt you, make you leave?"

"No."

"How about Jake?"

"Of course not."

"Really? He's not pissed off at how the business is going? Upset about being part of Apatchi? Nothing like that?"

"He's not that kind of guy."

"You sure? How much do you really know about him?"

"Well..."

"Find out more about Jake. Even if it's just so you can set the record straight for Emily. Maybe Susan knows who his other friends are, or what he does with his free time when he's not having philosophy orgies. It does no harm to ask a few questions."

I cupped my chin in my hands and thought. It felt wrong to go behind Jake's back. On the other hand, Diego was right. I owed it to Emily to at least do what I had promised and keep my eyes open. And if I found nothing, then we'd be back to Diego's original theory that I was being stalked by Christian fundamentalists who thought I was Satan's apprentice.

Diego went off to work and I obediently got behind the computer and found the address that went with Photis' phone number. It was a bookshop in Pasadena. Matthias' Books. I thought I'd heard of it. The chances of it having anything to do with the attack were slim – I was pretty sure that Photis was a harmless nutcase, and anyway, the fact that he borrowed the phone at a bookshop to call me didn't mean much. But it was at least a chance to show Diego and Em that I was taking things seriously.

So Saturday afternoon found me cruising up and down Colorado Boulevard in search of a parking space. A hot Saturday afternoon is a crazy time to try to park anywhere except in your own garage, but I wasn't helping matters much. I've got that LA parking thing – that deeply felt need to drive around in circles for half an hour rather than just accept that you may have to walk five minutes from your car to wherever you're heading. It's a particularly stupid thing to do in Pasadena, which is one of the few parts of LA where pedestrians aren't immediately looked on with pity or suspicion. Old Town Pasadena's a place where you could almost pretend to be in a real city, like on the east coast or in Europe, where people just walk around and browse in shops and stop at cafes. It didn't used to be – ten years ago it was still pretty scruffy, the kind of place people call "genuine," like where black people live but white people can still go and shop. It's not quite so genuine anymore, but it's cheerful and clean and as good a place to take a date as anywhere. I keep waiting for them to add the extra e's onto the name, to make it Olde Towne. They haven't yet, but it'll come.

Finally I gave up, parked in a lot a few blocks up on Fair Oaks and headed back down toward Colorado Blvd. Matthias' Books was in one of the little alleys just off the main drag, one of the few that hadn't yet been gentrified and lined with cafes and shops selling novelty stationery. You could tell that it had been there long before the rents had started going up – it was in what looked like an old warehouse, all dirty red brick and big windows with lots of little panes of glass and five layers of paint peeling off the frames. The kind of bookstore you expect to have a funny smell when you go in. It didn't.

It didn't seem to have any customers either. It was dead quiet, nothing but the distant traffic noise coming around the corner from Colorado Blvd. The only sign of life was the text on thousands of book covers, and even they said nothing, at least to me. They were speaking German. A sudden, uncomfortable feeling came over me that this all sounded familiar.

After a few seconds I heard something – the rustle of pages, maybe, or the scuffing of a chair on carpet tiles around the corner. I took a few steps forward to get a better look at the place. As far as I could tell it was U-shaped, with a tall bookcase dividing it right down the middle. The ceilings were high, and there was a sort of mezzanine reached by a wrought iron staircase that spiraled upwards from next to the large desk at the end of one branch of the U. Behind the desk was a door, and behind that, I realized, were voices just quiet enough to be all but lost in the hum of traffic outside. As I walked up to a large low table and started browsing among the English language "recommendations" lying there –

mostly political theory and philosophy books – the door in the back opened with a sharp click. In walked Daniel.

I froze before he did, but only because I saw him first. The Easter Bunny might just as well have walked in. The last time I'd seen him was at Jake's discussion group, and I'd been surprised then, but that was nothing like now. This time it wasn't just unexpected. It was sinister. Daniel, Photis, Jake, Theogenes. All sorts of things might have clicked into place, but they didn't have a coherent place into which to click. No place, at least, where I was willing to go.

"Be with you in a minute," he said curtly, picking up the phone. He paused for another second, a look of mixed alarm and disgust crossing his face as he examined all the cuts and bruises on my own and then, with a quick breath, looked down and started dialing. I faked interest in a biography of Goethe while Daniel spoke. He still had that overdone sense of authority in his voice, but now I could hear something else as well, as if that confidence, taken out of the context of the real world, placed in the context of this bookstore, was laced with doubt. He sounded nervous, like someone trusted with a little more than he thinks he can handle. This arrogant guy, with his Princeton diploma and high-paying job and his fucking subscription to the New Yorker, looked very small as he stood behind a counter of a book store in Pasadena.

"Yes, hello, this is Daniel from Matthias' Books. I'm calling to check on an order we sent in last week. If you could call me back, that would be great." He gave a phone number and a list of three or four ISBN numbers for the books in question, and then hung up the phone. Without looking at me, he scribbled on a piece of paper, and then walked over to where I was standing.

"Thanks for coming," he said quietly and, taking my arm, led me around the bookcase to the other side of the shop. It was larger here, and lighter; the windows looked out onto a busy street. One elderly man was flipping through a stack of books on a table in a corner, but otherwise we were alone.

Daniel led me down one of several aisles of chest-high bookcases and then stopped.

"So here he is, Pete McFadden, connoisseur of German literature. Surprising in someone who can hardly string together a sentence in English."

"Listen, dickhead, you know perfectly well why I'm here."

He stared venomously at me.

"To be honest, " he began, his voice strained, "I think we've all been pretty patient with you, but I also think it's time you called an end to this foolishness." It seemed well-rehearsed – no one uses a word like "foolishness" without having rehearsed it. But he couldn't possibly have known I was going to show up.

"Excuse me? *You've* been patient with *me*? Listen, pal, I don't know what you've cooked up in your head, and I don't really care."

Daniel rolled his eyes and pursed his lips in that prissy way he had, as if God should be apologizing to him for wasting his time with dumb bastards like me. He let out a nervous laugh.

"What I've cooked up in my head? This from the man who has the nerve to take credit for the centuries-old wisdom of Theogenes and then use it to sell sneakers and Caribbean cruises? You're a fraud, Pete. I don't know why Jake ever involved you with the Spiral Path."

I just stared at him a second, face frozen in contempt while I wondered if what he'd just said might actually be German for "Hey, sorry for the prank calls."

"The spiral path?"

His clean-cut features seemed to glow hatred. He glanced around before continuing.

"You know perfectly well what I'm talking about. The fact that Jake won't let you come to Group doesn't mean you don't still owe him a little loyalty. Your so-called business is starting to pose a real obstacle to what he's trying to do, and it's about time you put an end to it. I don't care how you do it, but you need to do it, and soon."

"What the hell are you talking about?"

"Loyalty. You want me to spell it?" He looked happy with himself for that one. It was all I could do not to hit him. "Jake made you, Pete. He's always defended you, even when you've been busy trying to ruin everything, but his patience is running out. All of our patience is running out."

"You got a gerbil up your ass? Who's we?"

"The Order of the Ammonite. You must have known I've been admitted. I was sworn in as a member of the First Chamber last month." He said it like a spiteful scientist might flaunt his Nobel Prize to a despised colleague. "And we don't like what you're up to," he added, trying his best to look menacing. It was like being threatened by a large squirrel. Speaking German. I had no idea what he was talking about.

"The order of the ...?"

He looked around again uncomfortably. The old man in the corner glanced up for a second, staring out the window, and then, shaking his head, returned to his books. Daniel's fingers started to twitch, whether out of frustration or nervousness I couldn't tell. His voice dropped even lower.

"The Order of the Ammonite. We seek truth along the spiral path of infinity, with the spirit of Theogenes as our guide. We embrace the one to enrich the many. We enrich the one to embrace the many." This too was a recital, but not one he'd prepared himself. He might as well have handed me a leaflet. "You even came to one of our meetings, asshole," he added as an afterthought.

"Look," he went on, seeing that I had nothing to say, "I don't expect you to see the beauty of it, and I don't expect you to have the brains to understand it, but what we are building is something extraordinary. It's more practical than philosophy, more honest than religion, more useful than politics. It's a creative, integrated approach to living, like nothing I've ever come across before. It's changed my life

Pete, and when you are ready, it could change yours. And Emily's – she's almost ready, and when she is, I'll welcome her back and teach her the path.

"But we can't help you if you keep allowing Apatchi to exploit our beliefs as some kind of pop cultural marketing tool. It's turning people off and tainting our message. Please." The edge in his voice softened, and he put a hand on my shoulder. "For Emily's sake, if not for mine, reconsider. You're doing far more damage than you realize. I know you have it in you to change." Why be a sinner, when you can be a winner? I couldn't believe he was saying this. Listening to this crap from Daniel was like getting off an elevator to find myself in a completely different building across town.

I was still trying to come up with a coherent question to ask him when his head jerked around, making me jump and reopening the scab on my lip. I hadn't heard a door open – I guess neither of us had – but suddenly there were voices approaching from behind the shelves that divide the shop in two, and shapes emerging around the corner. The faces, male and female, were both young, and both familiar. They were followed immediately by a third, an older man, smiling where the other two remained rigid with college kid self-importance. Then it all came together – Matthias. The others were Toby and ... Tammy, was it? Tina? No, Tara. One of the crowd I had met at Jake's, anyway, the serious one who had seemed to have a crush on Jake. Daniel. The Order of the Ammonite. Susan's words about the flunkies who hung around Jake came back to me in a dazed flash. "...they worship him... there are hundreds of them..." I suddenly felt very alone.

"Ah Daniel," said Matthias, as smooth as steel, "I see you've brought a friend. We have met before, no?" I did my best impression of a smile and we shook hands. "Welcome," he added amiably. "Daniel, I wonder if you and Toby could unpack those boxes in the back, the ones that arrived this morning? Please make sure the amount is correct – Markus will be dropping by for them this evening." Daniel gave me a nervous look and turned to go with Toby. Before going, Toby gave me an odd, leering smile, a smile made crooked by a large ugly cut on his lower lip. The gash along the knuckles of my right hand seemed to throb, and a watery feeling invaded my bowels. It was pure fear, and Toby lingered for a moment as if savoring its rank scent. He slowly drew his tongue across the livid scab and nodded grimly before turning to follow Daniel into the back room.

"Please have a look around, Mr. McFadden," Matthias continued, seemingly oblivious to the unspoken drama that had just unfolded before him. "I'm afraid our English language selection is limited, but we have many books on political philosophy that you won't find elsewhere. It is an educated citizen's first duty to understand the use of power and its consequences, don't you think?" he added, as if rounding off a familiar conversation between old friends, and turned to go. I forced myself to stay for another few minutes, browsing mindlessly among shelves of German grammar and dictionaries just so as not to give the impression of running away in terror. Finally I collected myself and walked towards the door, half expecting to see a gang of thugs blocking the way out. But there was only the girl, standing there silently, watching my every step with an intensity that made the hairs on my arms stand up on end. There was something in that look, it occurred to me as I escaped out the door and into the alleyway beyond, but it wasn't until I was half way down Colorado again, among the flashy restaurants and coffee bars and funky public art, that I realized what it was. She was as frightened as I was.

18

Not surprisingly I didn't hear from Emily that weekend, but I almost didn't mind. I wasn't ready to talk. There are times you want to communicate and share your fears, times you need your friends or family around so you can bounce ideas off them and bask in their support or encouragement or whatever. But there are also times you just want them all to shut up and go away so you can think. So I gave Emily her space and I didn't complain when Diego went off to spend Saturday night at Stacie's.

"You sure you're okay?" he'd asked, car keys already in hand. Everyone kept treating me like it was my psyche that had been kicked and beaten that night, like I was going to break down in tears any minute. I blame movies for that – whenever anyone gets hurt in a movie, they either suddenly become afraid of the dark and dredge up repressed memories of why Uncle Charlie's death was all their fault, or they pull out the heavy weaponry. So I promised Diego that I'd call him if I started feeling sensitive and shoved him out the door so I could spend the afternoon on my own.

By Monday morning I couldn't claim to understand any more than I had Saturday afternoon. It looked bad. Jake was some kind of Jim Jones, and Emily's bitter ex-boyfriend was spending his weekends working in a bookstore with one of my attackers helping mix the Kool-Aid. And just about everyone but Axel and my mother wanted to tear down the company I had built from nothing into a household name in less than a year. The large cross that had been burned onto the front door of our office over the weekend with "Sword

Arm of God" scrawled next to it didn't do much to clarify things.

"SAG are an extremist cult based out in Texas," the police officer told me that morning after calming my tearful secretary and taking a statement. "They've been conducting a wave of vandalism in the area over the past month, targeting abortion clinics, radio stations, that sort of thing. I wouldn't worry..." The look on his face as he spoke, his gaze constantly drawn to the purple ring around my eye, said otherwise, as did my own common sense. Toby seemed as likely to be a member of some Texan Christian cult as he was to be a cheerleader for the Raiders. But the cross, appearing so quickly after my attack, could hardly be a coincidence. Maybe Toby's fat lip had nothing to do with me after all. There were so many people who hated me these days... I suddenly felt back at square one.

Axel had patiently agreed to put off our meeting until 12:00 while I dealt with the police, but even over the phone I could feel the irritation in his voice. Join the crowd, asshole, I thought as I hung up and returned to dealing with what seemed like yet another nut hoping to do me harm. Another Monday meeting, something I needed like I needed a hole in the head. I had enough of those already. Axel hadn't even blinked, I noticed when I walked in to his office a couple of hours later, and I couldn't help but wonder what I was supposed to make of that. I didn't have time to wonder about much of anything, though, as he was eager to get through the items on his agenda.

We went through a handful of minor issues – stuff almost too stupid to be wasting our time on, but Axel seemed to be growing more and more meticulous as the weeks went by – and then he fell silent. He was wearing thin little wire frame glasses today, and he took them off carefully and rubbed his eyes as if trying to push them well back into his head. Finally he blinked, returned the glasses to the bridge of his nose, and let out a weary-sounding puff.

"Right, um, couple more things, and then I've got to get going. I've got a bitch of a meeting at 2:00... You talked to Jake's girlfriend?"

"Yeah, I did," I answered nervously. I hated to be the bearer of news that would make things between Axel and Jake even worse than they were, and I found myself scrambling for a way to present it, a way to make some excuse for Jake. "I don't think she'll be of much help..."

"Then fuck Jake." The words came brutal and swift, but casual, lacking any sense of surprise or real disappointment. "Actually, it works out great. The studio wants to shoot next week, and Jake's on vacation, isn't he? His loss."

"You don't want me doing it, do you? You know I'm just not good at this sort of stuff..."

"We'll get an actor to do it. The agency sent me a good one. Liz will email you his details, and you can brief him later this week, all right?"

"I guess so, but don't you think..."

"Just talk to the guy, you'll like him, trust me. He's real excited about it, and you need to keep the momentum going while you're hot. Now, the other thing I wanted to talk about before I go is our target audience." Even on the best of days Axel was hard to keep up with, his sharp clear voice racing ahead like scissors through paper, and today I had no chance at all. My mind was thick and slow with doubt, weighed down by the pain in my body. "Pete, you've done a great job helping to bring this thing mainstream – such a good job, in fact, that I think we need to cross the next frontier. You with me?"

"Um, what'd you have in mind?" It made me nervous when he talked like that – his speech hummed with the energy of decisions already made.

"Kids. You know three out of four kids have internet access in their homes? The US candy market alone is over $23 billion. Kids' clothing market is about as big. Kids spend over $4 billion a year of their own money – stuff they don't even ask their parents about but just buy when they see it. And the beauty of kids is that they're not only a ready market themselves, but also a future market that you can start grooming from early on. By the time they're teenagers you no longer even have to cater to what they want, you can just tell them what they want and they buy it. It's all about building trust from an early age." Axel had that look on his face like he was trying to sell a used car to a blind twelve-year-old.

"You want to try to get kids interested in Horokinetics?"

"You're sharp today. Yes, kids. Horokinetics. You're with me so far?" I hated it when he tried to be funny.

"I'm with you," I grumbled. "But I can't imagine kids finding Horokinetics very interesting."

"No, I agree, not as it is now. But imagine 'Horokinetics Jr.' I'm thinking more colors, simpler rationale, of course, educational science projects linked to fractals. And of course promotional tie-ins. Give it a little time we can have kids telling their parents that there's an evolutionary advantage to drinking soft drinks."

"But..." I croaked, but nothing else came out.

"I think the science link would be key here. Keep it fun but educational – we could even get Horokinetics in the Classroom with a little creative lobbying."

I didn't have the energy to even think about this. I did manage a meager protest, "But isn't that a little.... um, I don't know. A little immoral?"

Axel chuckled, unperturbed. "Pete, if you want moral, go join the guys putting crosses on your door. Listen, it's an idea. Something to work on. Of course it would have to be done tastefully, taking into account the developmental needs of our youth and all that. But I need you to start coming up with something solid so we can get rolling. I can put you in touch with our web design team. Colors," he said as he reached over to the phone and started dialing, "don't forget the importance of colors. Liz has the details for the talk show, okay?"

"Uh, yeah, okay," I stuttered, standing up and moving towards the door. "But Axel, seriously…" The smile vanished from Axel's face. He abruptly hung up the phone again and rested his elbows on the desk in front of him. His tightened jaw gave his face an almost cruel look to it. He suddenly reminded me of the German colonel in all those movies, the tall thin one who always had one of those small, long-barreled Mauser pistols at his side. The one who always smiled and said things like "I am afraid that the Gestapo might take a different view of that, Captain Biggles…"

"Pete, I've got two minutes, but I'll only use one of them. You're important to Horokinetics because you started the thing. You're important because you know the business and know how to deal with Jake Simms. And you're important because you know when to listen. That's where it stops. Now if it turns out that you are no longer able to control our spooky little mascot, and it turns out that you're no longer receptive to our needs, then we may need to start rethinking your role in all of this. I've given you a lot of leeway, I've continued to tolerate Simms against my better judgment, despite some of the things I've found out about him. But if you don't start towing the line a little more you may find yourself back where we found you, living off mommy and daddy and small-timing your way into bankruptcy. Got it?"

I just stood there speechless. Axel suddenly smiled, with just one half of his mouth, and then reached across the desk and patted my shoulder. "Listen, nothing personal, but you're going to have to shape up if you want to run with the big dogs."

I felt the hackles rise on the back of my neck. Axel saw it, and smiled.

"You just give it some thought, alright? I'll talk to you later. I've really got to make this call."

Shit shit shit. I headed back to the Valley for lunch, dropping into the El Happy Jalapeno around the corner from the office to pick up my usual burrito and a Coke. Jake and I came here a lot, and when he was busy or not around, I usually dropped in anyway and got takeout to eat back at my desk. I decided to eat inside to stay out of the heat and avoid the smoke and ash that still drifted across the Valley. As I slid into the plastic seat and wiped someone else's chicken grease from the table before setting my tray down, I found myself wishing Jake was there now. He would know what to do. He would be able to calm me down, at least. But then again, it was looking like Jake was somewhere at the center of what was happening. At the center of everything. He brought me here. It was his ideas that made Horokinetics so successful and so controversial. It was his encouragement that had kept me going. It was his sense of right and wrong that whispered at the back of my mind and was putting me on a collision course with Axel. And, for fuck's sake, it was his creepy bunch of acolytes who seemed to want me out of business, or dead, or both. Miserable son of a bitch, why couldn't he be here now?

I ate my food quickly, hardly tasting it, and then hurried back to the office. No Jake for another week meant another week of hell at work, and having missed a few days hadn't helped. I figured it would do me good to bury myself in my job; do what needed to be done and force myself to forget Axel and Jake and Daniel and the whole bastard world that seemed out to get me. When I got back I settled in behind my computer and went through my emails. There were dozens, including a handful of messages from spammers subtle enough to evade the spam filter by not putting 'teen,' 'pussy' or 'penis enlargement' in the subject line. There was one from Emily, brief and cold, yet promising by its mere existence. "Can we meet up? Emily." I wrote one about as affectionate back suggesting we get a coffee, and then continued to browse. Most were predictable: a handful of requests for website ad space that had collected over the past few days, something from the organizer of a big training seminar we were planning in Seattle next month. But it wasn't until mid afternoon that, scanning down the list, I came to an email from an unfamiliar web-based address. I stared at the address for a minute before opening it. Given all that had happened it was no surprise to find something vague and menacing.

"If you're looking for the truth, you'll find it at the Norton Simon, in front of Brancusi's bird. 3:00 tomorrow. Come alone, and tell no one." I double checked the date on the email, and found that it had been sent that morning, so tomorrow really was tomorrow. I deleted the email, along with a few old ones from Photis. If I was looking for the truth...I had already found more truth than I'd ever wanted. Truth was a boot in the stomach.

I have one strong childhood memory of the Norton Simon Museum of Art, one that significantly influenced my conception of 19th and early 20th century painting. It was the commercial. I couldn't recite the whole thing anymore, but the part that stuck with me was where they would start listing the famous artists exhibited there: Renoir, Degas, Goya, Picasso... There was something lyric, almost mantric about that list, as if by chanting it wise men could stave off society's accelerating descent into the barbarism of the late 1970's.

Renoir, Degas, Goya, Picasso. Brancusi definitely hadn't been on that list, and as I wound my way through the gardens towards the building itself, I wondered if I shouldn't take it as a sign that I should turn back. That's what common sense was screaming in my ear already. Given that I'd recently been beaten up and repeatedly threatened, you wouldn't think that I'd have been that eager to accept mysterious anonymous invitations to "come alone and tell no one." It was the classic girl in the basement scenario we've all ridiculed a thousand times. You're alone, it's late at night, the power's gone out, you're a young, pretty minor character in a B horror movie and you hear noises in the basement. Everything tells you not to go down there. But down you go. However slippery and undesirable a concept truth had become for me, I needed it. "What would Jim Rockford have done? I could hear Emily asking. I owed it to her, and to Rockford, and to myself, I suppose, to go. Besides, I figured, apart from rooms full of modern art, a museum couldn't be hiding anything that scary.

It took me a while to find the bird. It would have been easier if it had looked like a bird, rather than a large curved fountain pen. Bird in Space, "depicting the essence of flight in line with Brancusi's belief that what is real is not the external form, but the essence of things." A growing case of nerves kept me from pondering that for very long. I had done a quick scan of the room when I came in, looking for I'm not quite sure what: menacing looking men in trench coats, or maybe a solitary figure with a large scar running down one side of his face. Boris and Natasha from Bullwinkle. No luck, everyone in there looked like what they were: blank-faced tourists and a mass of summer-camp kids on a field trip.

I stood there stupidly for about five minutes, listening to the kids making all the jokes about modern art that kids make before being herded into the next room by their grumpy and morbidly obese teacher. The room grew quiet except for the hushed whispers of a handful of Japanese in the corner. The seconds dragged into minutes, but Brancusi's bird just stood there, essential, silent and utterly alone. And then, as I was about to cave in to fear and impatience, I saw a small figure peer into the room.

I recognized her immediately. Tara had made an impression on me at Jake's discussion group, mainly for the infinitely sad cow eyes she'd been making at Jake the whole evening, but I probably wouldn't have spotted the face had I not just seen it at the bookstore the other day. It looked now as it had looked then, fearful and sad.

She saw me, looked around as if to make sure we weren't being watched, and then walked briskly over.

"You came," she said quietly, clutching a ratty looking black shoulder bag and staring wide-eyed at me. "I didn't expect you to."

"I almost didn't," I answered cautiously. Tara seemed every bit as harmless as the Japanese tourists in the corner.

"I don't have long. There are some things you need to know. I suspect even you are smart enough to realize that Toby and his friends are the ones who attacked you." She examined my cuts and bruises for a second before returning her gaze to the less repulsive view of my chest. "You need to understand that they will do it again. They're more ruthless than you imagine."

"You're not one of them?" They, I assumed, was Daniel's Order. Tara had been as eager and earnest at Jake's discussion group as anyone else, and it had been her coming out of the back room of Matthias' bookstore with Toby just the other day. I'd seen enough movies not to believe in confessions.

"One of them? Yes, and no. Jake and I..." She broke off for a moment, visibly upset, almost shaking with the effort of telling her story. I stayed quiet and waited for her to pick up the thread again. "I never agreed to having you beaten up, if that's what you mean," she managed, almost contritely.

"But you're a member of this cult, the Ammonite Order, or something?"

She frowned, shaking her head slowly. "Have you talked to Jake about this?" I shook my head in response, and she looked even more confused. "That's not a name I've heard: typical Jake, though. Amon, king of the gods in the Egyptian pantheon. He never told me, but Jake keeps everyone in the dark." She spoke almost as if to herself, but then her eyes snapped up again to meet mine with a disturbed, urgent look. "You're right that it's a cult though. That's their plan, Jake and Jericho and the others. And you're helping them."

"What are you talking about? I've never had anything to do with any cult. I hardly..."

"You invented Horokinetics. You keep it going, you spread the word. That plants a seed in peoples' heads, and when they turn around and want more, Jake is there waiting for them. He's building a network of followers, all over the world. And you're helping him do it."

"Then why have me beaten up? Those guys were trying to get me to quit."

Tara spit out a short, bitter laugh.

"They were trying to scare you, that's all. That's how they work. They'll get you scared, and then Jake will ride to the rescue. Just wait for it. Then you'll be even more under his spell and he'll get you to do anything he wants."

"I'm not under anyone's spell. Anyway, why are you telling me this?" I asked defensively. I had gotten used to being attacked by evangelicals and fanatics, but having this earnest woman telling me that I was responsible for a bunch of lost souls was somehow a little too personal.

"Not for your sake, believe me." Her words were icy, even as a museum whisper. "I think you're as horrible as they are. But it can all get much worse, so much worse..." Her voice rose sharply and cracked, which started the Japanese tourists chattering in a muffled panic. "They seem so helpful, they make you feel so good about yourself, about them. You really begin to feel like they're right, that other people can't possibly understand you, that you have to break off your ties with the uninitiated... " She stood there for another minute or two, eyes closed, but then quickly regained control of herself. "You need to stop it," she said, spitting out each angry word as if each could stand alone as its own argument.

"How?"

"Stop Horokinetics."

My brief snort of laughter made one of the Japanese tourists jump. The essence of flight. It almost made me laugh again, except that the first time had sent enough pain throbbing through my stitches to dissuade me.

"Yeah, right. Listen, I couldn't stop it even if I wanted to. Apatchi owns the rights to Horokinetics, I only run the company that uses it. They'd just find someone else... Anyway, I've got a contract to honor."

"Peter, you started this. You may not have intended it this way, but Horokinetics has become something dangerous, and it's your responsibility to put a stop to it. Jake's becoming powerful, and he's using Apatchi and Horokinetics to make himself even more powerful. People are getting hurt. There's worse to come if you don't do something."

It was hard to tell whether or not to take this girl seriously. She certainly took it seriously. I brushed aside her attempt at melodrama, and said,

"Anyway, have you seen the website lately? It's cheesy. No one could turn that into a religion."

"They already have. Not your site itself, but the site and the training sessions give them the platform they need to collect followers from all over the world. You can't stop the Spiral Path, but you can at least pull the plug on Horokinetics. Cut off the flood of Apatchi money and publicity. Expose them for what they are."

"Like I said, even if I could, which I can't, that wouldn't stop them," I objected.

"No," she said sadly. "But you could slow it down. You have to try." Another handful of tourists entered the room, led by a docent giving them a brief history of 20th century art. Tara backed away from me slowly, a pleading look on her face.

"If not for the others, if not for me, then do it for yourself, while you still have the strength to resist."

"Resist what?" I asked. I shouldn't have. Never question people if they start to quote from Invasion of the Body Snatchers. Tara looked tired and let out a long, frustrated sigh.

"Peter, you said you're not under anyone's spell. Then tell me something. You know when Jake does his memory thing?

When he talks about the place within you where no one else can come?"

The hairs stood up on the back of my neck. "Yeah?"

"Take a good hard look into that place sometime. And ask yourself, if no one else can come there, what's *he* doing in there with you?"

Before I could answer, before I could even take in what she'd just said, Tara turned her back on me and was gone.

There were so many questions to ask, so much I needed to understand before I could bring myself to take her seriously. Was she one of them? She seemed so convinced, so frightened. And so unbalanced. It would have been helpful, it occurred to me as I slowly made my way back through the museum towards the exit, to have at least one person giving me advice who didn't seem like they had forgotten to take their medication that morning.

I hurried out of the building and through the gardens toward my car, eager to get back to the office. I still had enormous piles of work to dig my way through, and if I didn't get some of it taken care of soon I wouldn't have to expend any effort in letting Horokinetics go under. It would almost be a relief to bury myself in the relative sanity of my work. As I headed down the path I passed Rodin's gigantic Thinker, perched up on his rock, seeming to carry the weight of the world in that big bronze head of his. Rodin: he had been on that list as well. I paused for a second to watch as he tried to sort out the sticky web of fiction and reality that seemed to have spun itself in his disturbed, hard-working mind, and realized that he had about as much a chance of it as I did.

"Oh fuck off," I muttered, and walked away, barely registering the disapproving looks of a nearby couple wearing matching XXL bermudas and "Go Terps!" tee-shirts. Fuck off.

It was a long drive from Pasadena back to the office, a long time to sit there and squirm among the jagged edges of my fast-crumbling world. If I was feeling sorry for myself, this time I had every right. You're better off than you were a year ago, I tried telling myself as my car crept past dusty pepper trees, blue call boxes and a long line of idling SUVs stuck behind an accident in the far right lane. But I wasn't convinced. A year ago I was unemployed, but I was starting my own business, enjoying a good relationship and surrounded by friends. Emily was still speaking to me. Oh yes, and no one wanted to kill me.

The traffic had become annoying, so I got off at White Oak, sparing a glance at Tanya's apartment building before turning right and heading out onto the surface streets toward the north Valley. It wasn't much better there, but you can't do much of your own thinking on the surface streets with all the traffic lights, ticket-hungry cops and maniac drivers out there. It's a blinding snowstorm of potentially deadly distractions, and therefore requires focus. It pulls you out of yourself.

Turning into the parking lot behind my office pulled me right back in. The sick little puppy in the back of my head asked if the blood stains might still be there. I forced myself not to look too closely at the motley collection of oil patches and dog shit as I walked past the spot where it had happened, examining instead the new Taco Bell sign that loomed up over the pink cinderblock wall. Maybe it was fear for the future of El Happy Jalapeno that kept me from noticing that I was being followed. The voice, and the strong hand grasping my shoulder, got my attention quickly enough.

"Pete."

I spun, instinctively knocking the hand from my shoulder and balling my own into fists, and found myself face to face with Jake. Given that I had been about to hit him, you would think he would have looked at least a little startled. But no, he just stood there, a benevolent and pitying smile in his eyes as he saw the fear in my own.

"Easy, man, it's okay, it's just me," he said hoping, I suppose, to reassure me.

"You're supposed to be in Honduras," I sputtered, my fists remaining clenched. It was only after I said it that I realized that it was meant as an accusation rather than a statement. But he either didn't notice or chose to ignore the implication that he might have been lying.

"I hurried back when I heard what happened. How are you feeling?"

"You came back because of what happened to me?"

"Of course." He looked genuinely surprised at the question. "Wouldn't you have done the same?" I didn't answer that, either to him or to myself, but felt uneasily flattered by his obvious faith that I'd say yes. This is the creep who betrayed me, I had to keep telling myself.

"I feel okay," I said, as my fight or flight instincts started to fade. I didn't, though. For the first time ever, I felt afraid of Jake, and at the same time felt guilty for feeling afraid. "How did you find out?"

"Email's a wonderful thing," he answered with a grin, but then his face darkened. "I should have seen this coming, Pete. I'm... I'm really sorry. Take a walk with me?"

I followed him out of the parking lot onto Saticoy, and we slowly worked our way up the sidewalk towards the strip mall on the corner. We were the only people for two blocks who weren't sitting comfortably in their cars. Sidewalks in LA are one of the few public places where you're assured of being alone.

It was me who finally broke the silence.

"What's this all about, Jake?" I knew. God help me, I knew, but as I walked next to the man who had become one of my closest friends, who had helped me claw my way up from nothing, who had given me back years' worth of lost self esteem, I could only pray that I was mistaken. There had to be another explanation. But he wore his guilt like last season's hat.

"It was Toby," he said as quietly as possible without becoming inaudible under the traffic noise. "And if I'd been honest with myself, I would have realized that he was planning something like this." Sincerity and regret hummed through his normally clear voice. But when didn't Jake sound sincere? I decided that the only way to get to the bottom of this was to be bold and direct. Sadly out of character these days, but I gave it my best shot.

"You know, there's a nasty rumor out there that you planned it." For a moment Jake looked surprised, but he quickly regained his aura of omniscience.

With a rueful little smile, he said "You've been talking to Tara." I left it up to him to fill the hot, smoggy silence that welled up between us like car exhaust. "How'd she seem to you?" he asked.

"Messed up," I answered without thinking. Jake nodded.

"She grew... a little more attached to me than I ever intended," he muttered sheepishly. "I think when I broke up with Susan she'd hoped that she could, um, comfort me... Well, I tried to let her down gently but... you know how these things go."

Fighting off lovesick women had never been one of my more frequent problems, but I agreed knowingly anyway.

"Listen, Pete, Tara's a really good person, but she's going through a tough time, and it's coming from a lot more than just pining over me. She's been saying some weird things: conspiracy theories, persecution complex type stuff. I have been trying to convince her to get counseling but..." I stared down at the sidewalk, wanting desperately to tell him that I believed him, that of course I didn't think he was involved. But I owed it to myself to let him keep talking.

"Look," he continued, any sullenness in his voice vanishing, "it'll be different now that I'm back. I screwed up, going away like that without taking precautions, but you'll be safe now that I'm back. I can keep Toby under control – he won't dare touch you again, I promise."

"But he still wants to?" Jake nodded. "Why?"

Silence. He bit his lip, lost in thought, and then ventured, "It's complicated, Pete. People sometimes... sometimes what you tell people and what they hear are very different things. 'If you can bear to hear the words you've spoken twisted by knaves to make a trap for fools...' Well, I've tried to be a teacher to him, but..."

He was struggling. I interrupted during another patch of lost silence.

"Shit, you really have started a cult, haven't you? And you've used Horokinetics to do it."

His laugh – I've never known anyone else whose emotions were so external and whose thoughts so cryptic – wasn't the maniacal one we've come to expect from countless B movies. It was just a pure, genuine belly laugh, triggered by a sense of absurdity and, it seemed to me, a sense of relief. He looked at me without any embarrassment or remorse.

"No," he said, shaking his head and continuing to chuckle, "that's one thing at least that I'm not guilty of. You wouldn't be the first to ask me that, I have to admit, but no."

"People are saying you have. And having seen your discussion group... and why do they all hang around at Matthias' bookstore? You have to admit, it all looks a little Charlie Manson."

"I know it does. But think of it this way: I've assembled a group of people who are all interested in thinking about some of the same issues that interest me. It's a sort of thought experiment. We've spent months meeting together, helping each other form opinions about some of life's big questions. If we had all formed the same opinions, then yes, maybe you could call it a cult. But we haven't. You heard how much disagreement there was even over simple questions like free will. A cult teaches a specific worldview, a specific set of ideas or doctrines. Like religions, cults teach that there are answers out there and claim to know how to find them. But that's not what we're about.

"You know," he continued, pausing to search for just the right words, "what we've been exploring is what happens when you give people the tools to build their own lives. It's not much different from building a house. Mystics talk about expanding horizons, but building a house is the exact opposite: it's about limiting horizons, building barriers to give structure to an otherwise empty universe. Society offers us a few prefab model houses to choose from, like Christianity or communism or druidism, but if you give people the tools, teach them to value the idiosyncrasy of their own strengths and imperfections, then they'll each build something different. They stop searching for meaning and start creating it, weaving it from the world around them and the emotions within them. It's all about working on the process, everyone at his own pace. It's beautiful."

"Tara doesn't seem to think so."

Jake nodded slowly, as if weighed down by sadness. "One thing I've found is that freedom has its price. People look deep within themselves, into that place where no one else can come, and sometimes what they find there isn't pretty. You end up occasionally with people like Tara – you give them the tools and they build themselves prisons, and imagine you as the warden."

"And Toby?" I asked doubtfully.

"Toby wants to build armies. While the rest of us have been talking about the Book of Apeiron as a sort of intellectual point of reference, Toby's taken it as gospel. He's gotten out of hand, and I'm working on reeling him in. You have nothing to fear from him, Pete. Trust me."

I watched him closely as he spoke, looking for all those signs of nervousness that supposedly mark out all but the best of liars. But there were none. Jake may have been many things, but dishonest wasn't one of them.

"So no one's going to beat me up again?"

"No one."

"You sure?"

He smiled. "Positive. I hope someday you can forgive me for letting this happen. I wouldn't blame you if you didn't."

I returned his smile and his face lit up. He was once again optimism's poster child.

"Don't worry about it, man, I'll get over it." I smiled at him reassuringly, and wondered vaguely why I felt as if it was me who had just been forgiven.

19

A week went by, and another. Jake and I settled back into an almost normal routine again, not quite as if nothing had happened, but at least as if we were willing to pretend that it hadn't. We could still laugh together, still complain about Axel to each other, still have a beer now and then. But the shift could be felt, if either of us cared to feel it, in the things we no longer said. Jake stopped talking to me about deep memory, wanting, I suppose, to avoid saying anything that might make him sound like a cult leader. I avoided mentioning the attack, and we never discussed the phony live TV reading which had finally gone ahead and had been a huge success. The emails from Photis suddenly stopped, the emails and phone calls from other fringe lunatics slowed down, and it began to seem like the only real psycho who was still causing me any serious trouble was Axel.

More disturbing than any of this was the near total lack of communication with Emily.

She was waiting for me to say something, anything meaningful, about Horokinetics, about Jake, about us. But somehow I just wasn't up to it. Maybe it was because she'd been right, that there really was more behind the emails and phone calls and the attack than I had wanted to admit. That Jake really had been involved, even if it had been in a pretty innocent sort of way.

There are times when you see yourself from far away, like you're on TV, and you're just watching yourself knowing that you're messing things up, but you can't quite find a way to reach through the screen and give yourself a good slap. As I remember it, I saw myself being a dick towards Emily. Our friendship, and potentially more, seemed like it was quickly swirling down the drain, and I was the idiot holding the plug, but something was holding back my hand. Maybe it was one of those barriers that Jake kept talking about, the limitations we impose on ourselves to give life meaning. He seemed to think that the ability to construct our identities was a hard-won but ultimately good thing. I wasn't so sure. Jake had believed that by leading me on a path of self-examination he was setting me free to build my world anew. From what I could see, all I had managed to build was a self-obsessed asshole. And I was alienating the only person I knew who could help me tear it down again.

But one afternoon a couple of weeks after our fight, I finally plucked up the courage to call her.

"I was hoping we could meet up," I said, trying to be contrite without sounding pathetic. It's not easy when you know you've fucked up, but you don't really want to have to admit it. The idea was that I would ease gently into an "I'm sorry."

"Yeah, I think that'd be good." Her voice sounded tiny and thin. "Can I come over this week some time? I'll make you dinner. We've got a lot to talk about."

That sounded ominous, but we set a date for the next day. I was more and more realizing how much I'd missed her. And she had said something during our fight that I couldn't quite get out of my head. The part about caring about the old Pete. I guess it was more the way she'd said it, almost as if it was a confession. Combined with the near-kiss that I had suspected only took place in my own imagination, it was all starting to seem plausible. Wishful thinking, I told myself, but now that Daniel was out of the picture, who knew? Emily was worth groveling for.

I did the cooking, in spite of Emily's offer. Being considerate could do no harm, and as a byproduct I was able to fend off any serious conversation for a good half hour while I struggled with a pasta dish that was a little beyond my cooking abilities. But eventually I had to sit down, burned pine nuts and all, and face Emily. I had hoped that I would simply have been forgiven, but from the amount of time her eyes spent on her dish, her wine glass, and the wall behind me, I could tell it wasn't going to be that easy.

"So where's Diego," she asked, taking a bite of pasta and unconsciously wrinkling her nose. I tried mine, frowned, and handed her the salt.

"Doing damage control over at Stacie's. She's having another emotional crisis."

"What is it this time?"

"Dunno. Diego mentioned something about co-dependency and her personal psychic space being invaded. The girl's nuts. But I guess so is Diego. I think he thinks he can save her."

Emily managed a weak smile but didn't answer. We spent a little while longer painfully trying to make small talk. When we were together things had always been so natural, like flying on auto-pilot. I never had to think of something to say, or avoid saying something, or pretend anything. She was Emily, so conversation always just happened. But now clearly something had broken. It was as awkward as a first date, and as sad as a last one.

Finally it came.

"Pete, listen..." She took a deep breath and looked me straight in the eye. "I've told Ellen yes. I'm going to San Francisco."

She might just as well have taken the wine bottle and stuffed it down my throat. I thought for a second about the guys in the parking lot. This felt worse.

"But..." I spluttered helplessly.

"I need to go up there next week to find an apartment and settle in."

"Kind of sudden, isn't it?" I managed after a few seconds of shocked silence.

"Well, no, it isn't." Her mouth was tightening again in what any guy with half a brain would have recognized as anger. "I've been talking about this as a possibility for months now."

"Well, yeah, but ..."

"I don't remember you saying you thought it was a bad idea."

"No, but..."

"I don't remember any long helpful supportive conversations about what my options were. I don't remember you ever giving me a reason to stay."

"I guess I.. I don't know. But Em, San Francisco? It's kind of ... far."

"From what, Pete?"

Far from me, damn it. But it was too late for that. Emily had been trying for months to get me to start thinking about someone other than myself. Like the boy who cried wolf, when I finally really needed to be able to scream "what about me?", no one was willing to listen. That's what went through my head, anyway. That's what kept my mouth shut.

I guess Emily saw that I wasn't going to say what needed saying. She looked defeated, resigned, I don't know, whatever look a girl has when she realizes that her faith in someone was misplaced and that she's going to have to adjust her emotional landscape to work around that fact. At the time, all I understood was that it was a sad look, and that it was my fault.

"Anyway," she started again, as if waking up out of a daydream, "I need a fresh start after all that's happened. I have no job and no boyfriend – it's the first time since I left college that I'm totally unattached. A new city will be good for me. And think of it this way," she added, forcing a smile, "now you'll have a free place to stay in San Francisco. Five hour drive, give or take."

"But Em, listen, I'd started thinking... I just wish we had a little more time to, well, see if..."

"Stop." Shit, she looked like she was going to cry again. "Just stop, okay. This is what I have to do. Don't make it harder."

I stopped, and just stared at my plate in silence.

"I'm going in a few days. Just, if you want to do me a favor, let me go." She got up from the table and grabbed her bag. She was getting good at walking out on me. "Anyway, San Francisco's not that far. I'll email you my address when I'm settled in. Just take care of yourself, okay? When you find yourself again, when you're ready, you know where I am." I had risen to walk her out, and with that, she stepped forward and kissed me gently on the mouth.

"Bye," she whispered, and a second later she was gone.

The following weekend Diego and I went camping.

"C'mon, man, it'll do you good. There's a campsite right on the beach up by Big Sycamore Canyon. No hassle, we just pitch a tent, light a campfire, pop open a few beers and the world will seem like a much better place."

Diego was the only one of my friends who admitted openly that he knew of my infatuation with Emily, so at least he understood why I was so down. And while his assertion that there were no straight men in San Francisco for Emily to hook up with wasn't the greatest comfort in the world, I have to admit that we had a good time. As it turned out, he was as eager to get away as I was. Stacie's paranoia and bouts of depression were becoming more than Diego could bear, and he was happy to spend the weekend with someone who, however momentarily fucked up, didn't randomly burst into sobs, or badger him about the meaning of the universe, or tell him that he didn't understand her and that she was going to leave him to save her own soul. So we drank beer, roasted hotdogs and marshmallows over our state-park-approved fire-pit campfire, and pretended that we weren't both entering our thirties with a lot less confidence and certainty about the future than we'd had when entering our twenties.

Sunday after lunch we packed up and headed back to Diego's. Stacie had stayed there for the weekend – to feel the safety of Diego's energy even in his absence, she'd explained.

"Ten bucks says she's in bed," Diego said, smiling, as he dug out his keys. "Or she's on the balcony staring into space. Those are the only two choices these days – bed or space."

This time it was bed. We did our best to be quiet, but after a few hours had passed and it was almost dinner time, Diego decided to go in and wake her up. I could hear him whispering her name, at first softly, then a little louder, then urgently, a panicked cry in which her name became barely intelligible. Somehow I realized it without having seen her yet. Stacie was dead.

My first reaction was sheer panic. Not over the fact that she was dead, or that my friend was suffering, or that, for all I knew, we could still be in danger from whatever, or whoever, had killed her. It was panic at the simple queasy fact of being there. If there was a script for this sort of thing, I knew what my next stage directions were supposed to be. I was supposed to run into that bedroom. I was supposed to comfort Diego. I was supposed to call the police, call the ambulance, perform CPR. Do something constructive. But whatever I had to do, I first had to go into that room, when what I really wanted to do was run. Even with all that's happened to me, with everything I've done, the most paralyzing moment of my life was in that living room when I heard Diego cry out. But, fighting down the acrid taste rising in my throat, I took one step, then another, then broke into a run and flung myself through the door to Diego's bedroom.

It wasn't my first corpse. My grandfather died when I was in college, and he had an open casket funeral. I thought I had found that shocking, the sight of that placid, dead old patriarch lying so clean and waxy and cold in his creamy satin casket. But the dead are generally well-tended by the time we get to them, their open eyes and garish smiles carefully dealt with to give the impression that death is really just an unusually quiet and formal cocktail party. But Stacie's body showed me death in its natural habitat. She was young, aggressive and raw in death, her face twisted in a rigid rage at the world that had done this to her. It turned out to be one of those playful tricks of rigor mortis – the coroner later reaffirmed what the empty bottle of sleeping pills had already told us, that Stacie had been deeply unaware of the last moments of her life – but when I first saw that angry corpse I could have sworn that she was ready to wrap her cold hands around my throat. This was a silent, sad death, but there was nothing polite about it. Those dead eyes and bared teeth were more accusing than her leers and snide comments in life had ever been. How could Diego have been so oblivious to have bothered whispering at this?

"Diego." I spoke quietly, as if not to wake the dead girl. Clutching his shoulder, I tried to draw him out of the room, pulling him away from the thing that until at most a day ago had been his girlfriend. It took a second for him to notice my tugging at him, then he turned to look at me. Tears rolled down his face, and his whole body shook.

"This isn't happening," he muttered, his voice hoarse and unsteady. I had nothing to say, so I led him out to the living room, sat him down on the sofa and dialed 911.

The next few days were a blur of police, grief and grinding silence. Stacie's family wanted her body brought back to Minneapolis to be buried, and that Friday I found myself boarding a plane with him to go to the funeral. He didn't ask me to go, and I didn't ask him if he wanted me to. It was just one of those obvious things that you don't know that you'll do until you do them.

The funeral itself took ages as family and friends lined up to say all the things they'd meant to say while she was still alive. She was out of our hands now, and we both felt about as welcome as the backhoe driver waiting at a not quite discreet distance for the ceremony to end so that he could finish up and go home. It's not her lying there, we told ourselves, as you do, whether you believe it or not, and after paying our respects to her parents we got a taxi straight back to the hotel. I'd found us rooms at a soulless but clean airport hotel, the only real saving grace of which was the bar, which had a great view of the airplanes as they taxied by for takeoff. I got a couple of beers while Diego found a table by the window. His mind was already half way down the runway when I sat down across from him. He was turning what looked like a bottlecap over and over in his hand, staring into emptiness.

"You know, he said finally, once I was half way down my glass of beer, "she kept telling me that she was on this difficult spiritual journey. She was always going on like that. I just tuned out."

"It's not your fault, Diego." Slowly, very slowly, I was getting better at being supportive. It was hard work, trying to comfort a grieving friend without sounding like someone who has just read a self-help book on how to do it.

"Well," he said softly, staring into the distance, the fingers of his right hand working ceaselessly at keeping that bottlecap turning. It looked like he also had a piece of string in his hand, but I couldn't tell. Some memento, I figured. "You know, she told me not too long ago that my movies were contributing to the death of the human spirit. Said I was just, like, part of the machine that was strangling all hope of individuality. Man, she really believed in that kind of stuff." He smiled weakly and drank. I said nothing. We hadn't really discussed her death yet, not deeply anyway, and I figured that my job was to let him talk.

"She left me this in an envelope," he continued, and held out the object he'd been fondling. "Even her stupid suicide note had to be cryptic. 'Follow the spiral path and you will find me, always.' Shit, man couldn't she have just said why, like everybody else?"

"What is this?" I asked, trying to keep my voice steady.

"Hmm? Oh, just something she wore," came his distracted reply. "Fossil ammonite. Got it from a friend last Christmas and never took it off since. Not even in bed. She used to play with it through her shirt when she got nervous, didn't you ever notice? You know, it's stupid, but for a while it made me suspect her of cheating on me. All she'd say was that it was something deeply personal."

He laughed, a remorseful, strained laugh. I just stared with my mouth open at a nearly exact copy of the necklace I still wore hidden under my own shirt. The Order of the Ammonite. The spiral path. I immediately thought of Tara – strange, sad, paranoid Tara – and wondered if she also wore a little present from Jake on a thin leather cord, and how long it would take before the weight of emotional baggage that hung there would become too great, as it had for Stacie. And how many others had been driven to despair by their faith in Jake, faith inspired by the language of Horokinetics that I had given him?

Panic brings either paralysis or clarity. You don't get to choose, I don't care what anyone says. You just have to wait and hope the coin lands heads up. And if it does, if you are seized by clarity of purpose and find it within yourself to act, then you just have to hope that it's not too late to matter.

I knew what I had to do, but I needed to have my facts straight in order to do it. There were too many stories flying around, too many lies and plausible lies and half truths cluttering up my world. Jake had been my friend, after all, and whatever he'd done I owed it to him, and to myself, to be certain of the truth before I brought the bastard down.

When we got back to LA, my first stop was the internet. Big surprise: it seemed like every time I was in need of the truth about something out there in the real world I ended up looking for it in that box of radiation on my desk. I knew damn little about Jake, except that he didn't study philosophy at Boulder, that he claimed to have worked for some aid agency I couldn't remember the name of, and that he lived in a very large house which he said was owned by a family friend. That family friend was the only human link with Jake's past that I could find, so my first thought was to track him down. Easy enough, I figured. I sent in a request to search the public records for the owner of 3711 Old Blackrock Canyon Road, and by late afternoon I had received an answer. The owner was one Jacob L. Simms. No record of a mortgage.

So much for Jake's supposed poverty. Tara had said he was growing rich. As Horokinetics prospered I had raised his salary a lot, but not enough to buy him a house outright. So now what? What would Rockford have done? He would have had the balls to confront Jake again, for a start. He would have started to put things right.

So the next day when Jake arrived at work I asked him to come into my office and sit down. And just like that, the man who for months had been at once colleague, teacher and friend obediently sat down and waited to hear what I had to say. For a minute, I just stared at him in confusion. So I took a deep breath, braced myself, and charged forward.

"Right, I'm glad you're here. I'm not happy having to do this, and I don't want to waste a lot of time on it." What a shitty world, I thought as Jake shot me a bemused look, where the minute I decide to be my own man I end up sounding just like my brother. But there was no other choice. I took another deep breath, blew it out slowly, and looked Jake in the eye. It was like staring into the mouth of hell.

"Jake," I began, my voice nearly cracking, my hands slowly wringing the life out of a hapless ball point pen, "This isn't easy for me. You've done a lot to make this company a success. I'm grateful for what you've done, and for all the hard work you've put in." The bastard smiled at me. Did he really not know what was coming? The thought of it almost made me question what I was doing. But the time for questions was long past. "What I didn't realize was that you were doing it for yourself, not for me or for anyone else. You've been using me, and using our company, to build yourself an empire. All your talk about helping people was a lie, Jake. You're not about helping people, you're about controlling them, and using them for your own ends. That's your business, but I'm not going to stand by and watch you do it any more. I want your desk cleared out by lunchtime. You no longer work here."

Jake didn't try to interrupt. He didn't object or argue or even look surprised. He just remained seated, fixing his stare on the wall behind me and clasping his two hands together under his chin as if deep in thought. I couldn't look at him. My office had become one big blur of resentfulness and regret and testosterone, all of it mine. I could see my brother looking uncomfortable but impressed, my parents surprised and almost intimidated. I could see Diego smile with whimsical approval. I could see Susan take notes. And I could see Emily, above all of them Emily, slowly and sadly nodding her head at the belated recovery of my self-respect. And beyond her, gray and uncertain in the shadows of consciousness, my office, filled with the silent and unmoving form of Jake.

"What part of all that didn't you understand?" I asked, my voice trembling. Just go, I begged him silently. Just go, this is already too hard. On the wall behind him my UCLA diploma stared back at me stupidly, offering no consolation and even less advice. They just don't prepare you for this kind of shit.

And then Jake spoke. His voice was quiet and forgiving, a smooth flowing stream of compassion and regret.

"Pete, why don't you tell me what this is all about." At that moment I wanted desperately to kick him. I contented myself with screaming.

"I just told you what this is all about, you asshole. You've started a cult using Horokinetics. You're trying to turn yourself into some kind of fucking Messiah and you're using me to do it." My secretary, a jittery Korean woman in her

245

forties who had little tolerance for bad language, nervously poked her head in the door to make sure we weren't killing each other. What she would have done if we had been I have no idea. I glared fiercely at her, and she vanished.

"Are you sure that's all it is?"

"What?" I barked back at him. I was losing it. I had promised myself I would stay composed, but this was too much. "Is that all it is? Shit man, you lied to me. You lied to me about studying at Boulder, you lied to me about not owning that big house of yours, and you lied to me about the stupid shell necklace. And you know what? I don't really give a fuck. It doesn't matter what you tell me, but there are people out there who are killing themselves because of whatever messed up bullshit you're telling them. That's got to stop, and I know now that I can't trust you to stop it."

Jake nodded, clasping his fingers together as if in prayer. "Of course. You feel betrayed. I'm sorry about that, Pete, I'm sorry I had to mislead you. I just didn't want you to get drawn into all this."

I turned away from him to stare out the window, through the cheap Venetian blinds, into the parking lot. A couple of cars, some pepper trees, and that pink cinderblock wall separating me from the busy, mean streets beyond. I let the opaque silence linger between us for a minute, and then muttered "Damn it, Jake, what were you thinking?" I kept my eyes directed out the window, not fixing them on anything but just letting them float somewhere above the tail end of my car. "She's dead, man. Stacie's dead, and God knows who else. What were you thinking?"

"I was thinking that I had stumbled across a way that I could finally help people, really help them to take control of their lives. And I was right. You, Peter McFadden, showed me the way. You gave me the language I needed. Look, I spent years out in the southern Sahara, in some of the bleakest places on the planet, and you know what? Those people were happy. They had nothing but family, religion and sand, and they suffered more than most people here can imagine, but they were happy. And then I got back to the supposedly civilized world and realized that everyone here is miserable. We have more than we can ever need, and we're unhappy. Christianity, patriotism, Zen and the art of buying shoes, all the unsatisfying garbage that's pushed on us as a substitute for building meaningful lives is failing us. The psychologists we pay to fix what was never built right in the first place are failing us. Our culture is letting us down."

Jake stood up, looking around him for room to pace while he talked. There was none, so he had to settle for waving his hands and letting his enthusiasm shine from his eyes.

"And then with Horokinetics I saw what it was. Those people out there in the desert had built themselves a garden in their minds. Every rock and alley and camel, every taste of bread, every miserable little hut they came in contact with had meaning for them, deep personal meaning carved from the emptiness by experience and emotion. That is power. They can't buy computers, they can't surf the net or get credit cards or drive BMWs, but they are powerful because they have created their own world. That makes them gods.

"And now Horokinetics is helping me to teach people here to be their own gods. My students are learning to reconstruct their lives. It's beautiful. You know it is, you've seen it. I'm bringing them power."

I had turned to watch him, and I couldn't help admiring his passion and courage of conviction. He was everything I had never been and always wanted to be: strong, confident, and unquestioningly aware of where he wanted to go and how to get there. But the image of Stacie's body lying in that bed – no, the image of Diego crumpled and helpless at her side like the remains of a bombed house – laced my admiration with anger. I rubbed my eyes hard, but the image stuck.

"Bullshit, you're just giving yourself power over them. You and Toby and that bitch Jericho – I'm right, aren't I? – you're building an empire by fucking with people's heads. The only person you're trying to turn into a god is yourself."

Jake looked deeply hurt.

"I can't believe you'd think that Pete. Toby is nothing, simply an enthusiast who has lost perspective. And yes, Jericho is my partner in this, and it's true that she has some different ideas about how best to help people. I believe in working with people. I think people can only make the journey if they really want to and are really ready. Jericho thinks they need us to carry them down the path. But either way we're setting people free."

"Only death sets people free," I growled, feeling ridiculous but slightly pleased to sound almost as apostolic as Jake, "so I guess you're doing a good job." He sighed.

"Yes, there have been one or two... unfortunate cases. But they were already heading in that direction when we found them, you have to believe me. I would never take my teaching forward with anyone if I felt that it would do them more harm than good."

"What about Jericho? You think she cares?"

"Jericho isn't in charge. I am, and she respects that."

I thought back to the arrogant look on Jericho's face when we glared at each other on horseback. It seemed like ages ago.

"Does she know that?" I snapped with as much contempt as I could manage. Every harsh word spoken to Jake cost me, and I wasn't sure how much longer I could keep up my anger and avoid accepting his innocent and perfectly reasonable explanations. Of course he could keep her under control, how could Jake fail to keep anyone under control if he really wanted to?

He suddenly sat down again, looking wild and urgent. I wished to hell he would just stay still for once, but that was no more in his character than admitting defeat was.

"You have to trust me, Pete. The Order is my creation. I am Theogenes of Athos," he added with a mischievous smile, "and I won't let my words be used to entrap people. I can keep it under control. Trust me. The only harm it can do is if you keeping bowing to what Apatchi wants."

There was perfect confidence radiating from his strangely pleading face. It was his creation, he could control it. I let this soak in for a minute, and I could see Jake's confidence grow. A wave of relief began to spread across his face, infecting his entire body as he almost imperceptibly squared his shoulders and straightened his back. And then I started to laugh.

I probably sounded a little hysterical, and the alarmed tremor in his voice when he asked me why I was laughing only set me off even more. Finally I regained my composure after managing several deep breaths.

"Jake," I said, looking him square in the eyes for the first time in ages, "listen, thank you for everything you've done for me. You gave me the tools to rebuild myself, just like you always said. But I don't really like what I've done with them. It's time for me to start building something better.

"And it's time for you to go home. I don't want to see you here again. It's over."

"I don't understand," he answered helplessly.

"Go do what you have to do. You have your work, and I have mine. Goodbye Jake."

"Axel's forcing you to do this, isn't he?"

"I haven't told him. He'll probably kill me, but I don't care."

"Maybe we should…"

"Don't make this harder." It was everything I could do to keep my voice steady. "Please. Just go."

His look grew cold and formal, calmer but more intense than the one he'd given Toby that night in June. "Firing me will only make them stronger, Pete, you know that," he said, almost as if trying to be helpful for old times sake. "It's too late to undo it all now."

I leaned forward, crossing my arms and resting my elbows heavily on my desk. "Watch me."

And with a sad little shaking of his head, Jake stood up, towering above me for a moment, and then walked out. I could feel my throat constricting as I reached up mechanically to fondle the fossil ammonite that still hung around my neck. I heard his motorcycle engine rev angrily in the parking lot and the scraping of loose asphalt as he drove off. "Christ," I muttered. Now I was really alone.

20

I knew that firing Jake was going to be an unpopular thing to do. Everyone loved Jake, or damn near everyone. He was the face of Horokinetics and, more importantly, its soul. So when the news broke that Jake Simms had been fired "for reasons unknown," I became overnight the Saddam Hussein of cyberspace.

Expecting something and enduring it are two different things. It's easy to pretend that you don't care how you are portrayed in the media, but seeing your name vilified in newspapers and on websites, in magazines, in blogs, even on TV can really get you down. It's hard not to take it personally when everyone calls you a greedy, disloyal backstabber. Even the people who hated Horokinetics read my dismissal of Jake as something sinister and underhanded. Newspaper after newspaper came out with articles speculating as to why I might have done it, and none of the speculation was in my favor. The possibility that he had deserved to be fired never entered anyone's head. Jake kept his comments to the press brief, stating only that he considered the rift between us "unfortunate and unnecessary," and hoping aloud that the company would eventually resume espousing the ancient and profound principles of Horokinetics rather than continue its downward spiral into the abyss of corporate greed and corruption. And from Apatchi itself, nothing but an eerie silence. Axel was "away from his desk" every time I called, and he never called me back. Clearly I was on my own.

I defended myself as best I could. I replaced that Friday's "Our Nation's Fractal" with what I thought was a calm, well-reasoned statement, explaining that Jake Simms had been misusing the website to promote the interests of a dangerous cult known, among other things, as the Order of the Ammonite, and that that was why he had been fired. I insisted that Horokinetics was in no way formally connected with that group and that we neither encouraged nor supported their activities. That, I had hoped, would be the end of it. I really believed that it would be.

By Monday the Order of the Ammonite had already responded with a press release. The Order, explained ads in the LA Times, the New York Times, and USA Today, was a charitable organization set up in Omaha, Nebraska in 1977 by entrepreneur and philanthropist Elijah Tomkins for the support and rehabilitation of victims of child abuse and domestic violence. It had no connection to Horokinetics or Jake Simms, and demanded a full and public apology for my falsely accusing them of being a cult. They had not, the ad noted grimly, ruled out taking legal action. Several newscasters and editorials mused soberly over what I could possibly have against assisting abused children. I issued an immediate apology for the confusion, but no one noticed. That, apparently, wasn't news enough to make the papers.

And then things got bad. A few days later Enrique Guttierez, investigative journalist for the Chicago Register, published an article in which he claimed that, according to "reliable sources" within Apatchi, I had insisted on firing Jake in order to cover up my involvement in a wide range of criminal activities in which Jake had refused to take part. I had been, among other things, selling customers' credit card details, embezzling money, and using the company for money laundering. Guttierez claimed that Jake Simms had begun to suspect me of misconduct when I began to host lavish sex parties involving underage girls and seemingly limitless supplies of cocaine and ecstasy. Well that really got people talking. Newspapers, radio and TV stations all over the country immediately picked up the story and ran with it. By the end of the week half the female heroin addicts in LA had come out with lurid stories of how I had paid them for sex. The papers noted with smug satisfaction that the police had opened an investigation. It wasn't true, but that inconvenient fact wasn't considered newsworthy.

There was only one place this could all be coming from. I didn't want to believe it, but it was a conclusion that was growing harder and harder to avoid. Jake was striking back. And he was doing a damn good job of it. During the days that followed the first accusations, Jake steadfastly refused to comment, and his silence seemed to elevate him to sainthood as quickly as it elevated the speculation into gospel. I tried calling him, but he didn't answer. I even dropped by his house so I could confront him, but I was met in the driveway by Toby and three of his friends whose lumbering, thick-necked presence silently persuaded me to turn around and go home. It was all too clear that I was outgunned. I needed help, and that was in pretty short supply. I didn't want to bother Diego with my own problems – I figured dead girlfriends trump bad press any day – and quite frankly who else was there? I'd been so out of touch with all but my closest friends that there weren't very many people I could confide in. Dave and Alana were good for a little bullshitting over a beer, but they weren't too well equipped to deal with real life problems. My parents were very upset and very concerned, but familial puffing and sighing, as comforting as it might be, can't quite replace good advice. I could have called Emily, I suppose. She had sent me an email when I started making the headlines: "Don't back down. Call if you need me. SF's a stone's throw away. Em." It was the first thing to make me smile in days, but I couldn't make the call. Not yet. This was a situation that I couldn't face alone, but it was one that I had to face without her. Anyway, her advice was already with me. What would Rockford do? I'd need to puzzle through that one a while. In the meantime, something a little more concrete would have been useful.

So on Friday night when, after watching a movie on TV and downing a few beers, I stumbled across Diego's note that Susan had called, I raced to the phone. I had felt awkward about Susan for weeks. I had written her off as mentally unbalanced and more than a little self-obsessed, but she had been right all along. She had said it herself, Jake was becoming scary, and I had been dismissive. We hadn't talked since. I didn't care if she was calling up to say I told you so; she had told me so, and I was happy to admit it. Just to hear a friendly voice, a little commiseration, and maybe, dear God maybe a little advice as to how I could dig my way out of this crap heap I had pulled down on my own stupid head. I dialed her back, holding my breath, and on the fourth ring she picked up, sounding groggy. Only then did I realize that it was nearly 1:00 am.

"Hey Susan, sorry, did I wake you?" She mumbled almost incoherently that yes, I had.

"Listen, I'm really sorry, but I just got your message to call you. It's good to hear your voice." I could hear her take a sip of water and clear her throat, then mumble something inaudibly. She wasn't alone.

"Um, should I call tomorrow?" I asked, awkwardness running up the phone line and through my body like an electric current.

"No, no Pete, this is as good a time as any. You've got nerve calling me back, I'll grant you that."

"Look, I'm sorry I haven't been in touch, but..."

"Just what the hell do you think you're doing? I mean, how could you?"

"Oh come on, you don't believe that stuff in the papers, do you?" She couldn't believe it – she'd known me too long to believe it.

"Quite frankly I don't know what to think anymore, and to be honest, I don't really care what sordid things you've been up to. I just can't believe that you'd betray Jake like that." It took me a few moments of silence to take it in. Again she mumbled to the unidentified presence that was presumably lying in bed next to her.

"Wait a second," I stammered, "I was getting myself geared up to apologize for not having taken you seriously when..."

"You've done some shitty things over the years, you know. You're lazy, uninspired, flaky, insensitive and totally self-obsessed. But I have to admit, I never thought you were capable of being treacherous. That's the one reason I've stayed your friend for so long; whatever your weak points, you were always loyal, and I guess I thought that counted for something. And now this. Jake made you. He did everything for you, and you just turned around and stuck a knife in his back."

"How can you say this to me Susan? You of all people. You're the one who told me he was dangerous."

"I was extremely vulnerable Pete. I thought you were intelligent enough to understand that. I guess that's just one more thing I was wrong about with you." There was anger in her voice that seemed to border on hysteria, but it was a strangely controlled anger, too smooth and focused to be entirely unrehearsed.

"What, so it was all bullshit then?"

"No, it wasn't all bullshit," she snapped with mock-patience. "I didn't say that Jake was dangerous, I said that I thought the people around him were. I was in a bad place then, and I was afraid, and I didn't give Jake enough credit. It's different now."

"How?"

"Because unlike you, he has a backbone, and he can keep his people under control. He's strong enough to take responsibility."

"What the hell do you think I'm doing?" I screamed down the receiver, enraged less by her words than by the smug, prissy tone that rang through them like the chime of a cheap bicycle bell. My brain, buzzing with anger, fumbled when it went looking for words to describe what I was doing, how I was finally standing up and doing what I knew was right, consequences be damned. But the moment was lost.

"It's pretty obvious. You're lashing out in fear," she answered, her attempt to sound matter-of-fact undermined by the tremble in her voice. "Power has corrupted you, and you decided you had to get rid of Jake before he found you out. I guess you didn't cover your tracks well enough, did you? Someone did find you out."

"Susan! I didn't..."

"I'm really not interested, Pete." She abruptly dropped her voice, mumbling "Oh, no, honey, really, it's fine," but not to me.

"He's there, isn't he? You're back with Jake again."

"You're a criminal, Pete," she continued, ignoring my question, "and a pervert, and I suggest that you seek professional help. But not from me. And don't call me anymore. I look for better in my friends."

"But Susan, listen..."

"Goodbye." The phone clicked, and it was done. First Emily, then Jake, and now Susan. I'd just scored a hat trick.

I woke up late on Saturday morning and found Diego on the balcony, sipping what turned out to be his fourth cup of coffee. I poured out the last of the pot, sniffed it, and decided that it wasn't quite stale enough to put me off. The heat outside felt good; the pounding triple digits of August were starting to give way to that comfortable back-to-school temperature, somewhere in the low 80's, calculated just right to heighten the misery of students returning to the classroom. The horrible feeling that would pass over me as I packed my new Trapper Keeper into my backpack and headed off to the first day of class came back to me in a rush, and I shivered, almost appreciatively. I had really thought back then that I was tasting despair.

Diego glanced up and grunted, his eyes drifting away from me again to fix themselves on a wisp of cloud floating out somewhere over Catalina. I sipped my coffee in silence for a few minutes, and then he asked me,

"So, I guess you talked to Susan?"

"Mmm. Sorry if I woke you up."

"No worries, man, I was awake. Her message sounded pretty pissy."

"You should have heard her live." I gave him a quick summary of what she had said. "I guess if every news program in the country is already convinced I'm guilty, I can't blame her for thinking they're right. Especially if she's got Jake whispering in her ear."

"Damn," he said quietly. "So, what does Axel think of it all? He must be pissed off."

"Dunno. I haven't had a chance to talk to him about it since I fired Jake. He cancelled our last meeting, and he won't return my calls. I guess that's not a good sign."

Diego stayed quiet for a minute, staring into his empty cup as if he'd just found a dead frog at the bottom.

"So you think Jake was really the source of those articles?" he asked, putting down his cup as if to be able to concentrate better. I shrugged.

"Who else?" I asked, already suspecting what he was driving at. He arched his eyebrows knowingly.

"No, no way. Axel's a freak, but he has nothing against me. He's the one who was always egging me on to come down harder on Jake."

"Which is interesting in itself. But listen, who's been attacking you?" He sat up straight, the thrill of conspiracy obviously starting to pump energy through him. This was the kind of thing he lived for.

"The media," I answered.

"Yeah, fine, but who exactly. Which channels? Which radio stations? Which newspapers?"

"Shit, I don't know, all of them by now."

"Which ones broke the story? Which ones are the most persistent? Come on, man, just play along with me." So I rattled off the few newspapers and TV news shows that seemed to have it in for me more than the others. Diego took it very seriously, even wrote it all down, which struck me as a little silly. He was obviously off on another of his conspiracy theories, but I didn't have the heart to laugh at him. At least he was on my side.

He took his list and sat down at the desk in the corner where he had his laptop set up. He was quiet for a while, filling the air only with the nervous and arrhythmic clacking of bad typing, but soon his lips joined his fingers, muttering softly to himself at first, and then aloud, offering up the occasional "uh huh," "yep," or "thought so." I sat on the couch flipping through a magazine, but after about five minutes of tuning in and out in the expectation that he would actually string some of these words together into a coherent thought, I got up and stood behind him in order to peer over his shoulder.

"Okay, dumbshit, look at this." Diego's face had come alive as I hadn't seen it do for weeks. For a few brief minutes, he forgot everything and reveled in a sort of persnickety satisfaction like a car freak who had just finished waxing his 67 Mustang. He had found what he had most wanted to find: order in a chaotic universe. Little facts that lined up to form sinister shapes on his computer screen.

"The Chicago Register," he enunciated in a crisp, professional tone as his fingers found the website back. "Owner: Clearwater Communications. Next," pause for effect while the fingers clicked again, "the LA Chronicle. Owner: Clearwater Communications. Now, for the TV stations, Ferret News Network, owned by Clearwater. KCON Los Angeles, owned by Clearwater. And then, WBUL Radio New York. Want to guess?"

It was spooky, I had to admit. I'd heard of Clearwater – they owned a lot of Christian broadcasting groups and periodicals that had been attacking Horokinetics months ago when Jake and I were being billed as the antichrist brothers.

Now that it was just me, and I was a pervert and a thief, they were back in action. No surprise there. Diego could see that I wasn't all that impressed. But he had saved his trump card.

"Okay, now here's the good part. Who owns Clearwater?" I shrugged. Everyone was owned by someone, so I guessed Clearwater, gigantic as they were, had to be owned by someone too. Didn't Time-Warner-AOL-Microsoft-GM-Procter & Gamble-Boeing-Monsanto-Coca Cola-Disney own everything? "It's not that easy to find, he continued smugly. "They're owned by Clearwater Productions, a subsidiary of Karazian Kline Entertainment. But then you find that KKE is owned by Tomlinson Media. Whose majority shareholder is ... Drum roll, please. Apatchi International.

"There you go, my friend. You are being toasted by your friendly business partner."

I just stared at the computer screen for a minute, as if it had anything to add. The home page of the Ferret News Network website smiled back at me, "Bringing Honesty to the News, Honesty to the Nation." Damn. I just continued to stare.

"That son of a bitch," I muttered, too dazed to bother clarifying whom I meant. It didn't seem to matter to Diego.

"Look, Pete," he said briskly, standing up and grabbing my shoulders as if to keep me from escaping, "this is your thing, man. I don't know all the ins and outs. But these people are too big for you. If I were you, I'd go straight to your guy Axel. Tell him you're sorry."

"What for?" I burst out, feeling like I'd just been slapped.

"For whatever, man. How do I know? Whatever you've done to piss them off. At least sound him out on why this is happening. Listen, you need to cut your losses before they grind you into dust. Cut a deal. There must be something you can do to help ward off the worst of what they have planned for you. So offer a truce, tell them you want to be as cooperative as possible for the good of the company."

"But I haven't done anything!" I protested to the world in general. "There's no way I'm going to grovel to them. If they want to drag my name through the mud, then fine, there's not much more they can say that they haven't already said."

"It's a shitty world, Pete. Go talk to your guy Axel. See what he says. Just don't wait around for the good guys to win, okay?"

Anything I heard from Diego I had learned to treat with suspicion. So, while I didn't have any better explanation for the improbable coincidence of so many Apatchi-owned media companies being out to get me, I still wasn't totally convinced that Axel was behind it all. There were so many people out there ready to go for my jugular that it seemed almost uncharitable to write it all down to a single person or company. The evidence was compelling enough, but I needed more. I needed proof.

So early Monday morning I dragged myself out of bed, showered, and started to get ready. This had to be done carefully. First the shirt, professional white, starched and ironed as crisp as a clean page of printer paper. Then I slid on the pants of my serious charcoal gray suit and strapped on a heavy, stiff black belt. One, two, three notches, and the chunky buckle clicked into place. Dark, no-nonsense socks and sturdy, competent black brogues. Then the tie: red with a conservative pattern on it. No, I looked like a college kid going to his first job interview. The tie came off, and in its place went bright blue, a fierce contemptuous peacock blue, the kind of blue that tells the world that you don't care what they think about you. Peter McFadden, King of Horokinetics, ready for battle. I took one last look in the mirror, shook my head at the overgrown teenager I saw staring back at me, and headed for my car.

I had realized that Diego was right, I needed to confront Axel in person, face to face. The decision was bold, decisive, totally out of character, but something strange had begun to happen to me over the past few weeks and months. Most of my adult life had been spent behind a computer or at the end of a telephone, successfully pretending to engage with the outside world while avoiding all but the bare minimum of contact with other hominids. And by and large that's how I preferred it. But lately I had developed a perverse, possibly irrational faith in doing things in person. There was something about getting up and actually going places – to being able to feel the sun, smell the outside air and see in three dimensions the people you were dealing with – that seemed to work a certain magic when it came to getting stuff done. So, filled with the thrill of meeting the world head on, one to one in battle like some ancient warrior stepping out onto the dusty plains of Troy, I took one last look in the mirror, climbed into my car, cranked up the A/C, and set out for Apatchi.

"No, I don't have an appointment" I stated confidently to the receptionist as she glanced doubtfully at my tie. "Just tell him Pete McFadden's here, and that it's urgent." The look of doubt shifted from my tie to my face as she asked me to have a seat and dialed his extension. After a brief muffled exchange she announced that someone would be out to get me in a few minutes. I settled into a large black leather sofa, surrounded by crisp and menacing copies of the *Wall Street Journal, Business Week*, and the peculiar pink pages of the *Financial Times*. Even after a whole year as a CEO, I felt about as comfortable as a pork sausage at a Seder. It didn't help that the receptionist and several other people who passed by shot disapproving glances in my direction. They all clearly knew who I was, if not from my weekly visits to Axel, then from the recent news stories. No one offered me coffee.

It was a good half hour or so before Axel's emaciated secretary emerged from a door behind the receptionist's desk and led me to his office. Axel was behind his desk, tapping at his keyboard and seemingly lost in thought.

"Sit down" he muttered, eyes still fixed on the screen. "I'll be with you in a minute." His secretary flashed me a nervous smile and then scurried back to her open-plan cubbyhole. I stayed where I was.

Axel abruptly stopped typing and looked up.

"Good to see you, Pete. What can I do for you?" His right hand reached out and found a ballpoint pen, which it started to twirl nervously like some miniature drum majorette in a high school band.

"You can't honestly be wondering what I'm doing here, can you?" I asked, not concealing the tone of challenge in my voice. He nodded, as if answering some question echoing in his own mind.

"You're getting some bad publicity, sport." He said it with all the sense of gravity and concern of a friend who had just seen someone beat my high score at Mario Brothers.

"You could say that. And don't call me sport." He held his hands up in mock apology.

"Consider it retracted. So, you're getting slammed in the press. And, let me guess, you're wondering what you should do about it, right? Wondering if uncle Axel can make it all go away? Hmm, not much chance, I'm afraid. Freedom of the press, first amendment and all that." Diego's hypothesis was looking stronger by the word, but I wanted to keep testing him.

"I was hoping for help," I said, trying to sound confident that I had the moral high ground, "but if you don't have anything more helpful to say than that, then I'll simply ask you for information. Apatchi seems to own at least one of everything, so how about a law firm? One who might be willing to represent a poor unworthy colleague in a libel suit?"

"Libel?" Axel laughed. The bastard actually sat there and laughed like some Bond villain. I wanted to dump his pretentious little inkwell in his lap, but I kept my cool.

"Yes, libel. You know, where people print lies about you and you take them to court for it? I want to sue some of these journalists. Unless maybe you have some reason why you wouldn't want me doing that."

Axel took a deep breath, as if he had decided at last to get down to business and confess his sins.

"Pete," he said, his eyes darting from object to object on his desk, "it looks like you've got yourself into some trouble. I sympathize, I really do. I have some good friends who've been raked over the coals by the press, and I know it's no picnic. But there's just not much I can do about it."

"You mean there's not much that you will do about it."

"Look, this is no fun for Apatchi either. Guilt by association. And you know I have a very soft spot for Horokinetics. I've spent a lot of time on it with you because your management of Horokinetics had seemed to add value. So please, don't sit there and think I don't care, because I care very deeply." He looked as if he was having a hard time not laughing at his own transparent insincerity. But it seemed to me that he did have one point – what was bad for Horokinetics was bad for Apatchi.

"Good, then lets figure out how to solve it," I proposed.

Axel glanced at his watch. "I've got a conference call in 15 minutes, and I don't know if a quick brainstorming session is really what we..."

"It's simple, Axel. Most of the stories are coming out of a group of maybe a dozen newspapers and TV stations. They are the ones playing it up, and the rest of the media are just following along. Apatchi owns most if not all of them. So tell them to stop."

Axel suddenly grew half a foot taller in his chair. "I'm very sorry, but our media operations aren't just businesses. Owning a TV station or a newspaper is a sacred trust, and that's something we take very seriously. It would be totally unethical to tell them what news they can and can't print, and to be honest Pete, I'm a little disappointed that you would suggest it." Funny thing was, he looked genuinely shocked, like some sanctimonious drug dealer being accused of selling adulterated ecstasy.

"Fine, well, we wouldn't want to do anything unethical," I sneered.

He answered, deadly serious, "No, we wouldn't."

"So, okay, at least Apatchi could stand up for me." That inspired nothing but a blank look, so I explained. "Issue a press release. You do that kind of stuff all the time right? Issue a press release saying that DTITech Innovations and its parent company Apatchi International have confidence in me and... whatever. Deplore, that's it. Say that they deplore the totally unfounded allegations blah blah blah. Tell the world that you don't believe this bullshit."

Axel's tongue flicked nervously along his thin, hard lips and he put the pen down on his desk. He leaned back, linking his fingers together thoughtfully in front of him and, letting out a brief, frustrated puff of air, he said

"It's not that simple."

"Why?" Another puff, and another few seconds of silence.

"Pete, you know what I really liked about you when we first started working together?" He paused, waiting for me to ask him what, so I obliged him.

"That you were a team player." Christ, I thought to myself. In a flash I could see my brother Michael in this chair, having this same conversation with some other poor asshole in some other unfair parallel universe. They were all my brother: Axel, Vas Papayannis, my old boss at Alcantrix, even goddamned Phil the bank manager and his fucking bald head. They were all Michael, all cut from the same bastard-shaped cookie cutter and frosted with cold whipped bullshit. I rolled my eyes in disgust, but he continued before I had the chance to say anything snide.

"No, listen to me. I mean that. You were a team player. Horokinetics had all sorts of problems when Apatchi stepped in, but we worked together to sort them out. It was all about consultation, compromise, give and take. But now... well, you've changed. That little talk show gimmick we'd agreed on ... suddenly it became an issue and you wanted to back out." I tried to protest, but Axel just kept talking. " And then there was that discussion we had about market expansion. I thought we were making progress, but you just switched off."

Axel started shaking his head to express some deep regret or confusion, or maybe just falling prey to some nervous tic. "You've grown erratic," he continued sadly. "When I would make even the tiniest criticism of Jake, you would act like he could do no wrong. Then out of the blue you get rid of him without so much as warning me, when you how important he is to both Horokinetics and Apatchi. And now, well... all these allegations. And you want Apatchi to jump to your defense without the slightest investigation of whether or not the allegations might be true." He shook his head again maddeningly, and I exploded.

"God damn it Axel, you mean to tell me that you believe this shit?"

"I just don't know what to believe any more, Pete," intoned St. Axel, shaking his head with a deeply weary sense of sorrow for the sins of this imperfect world.

"Why are you doing this to me?" I was losing it, becoming desperate both with anger and with the bowel-emptying realization that I was helpless and alone.

"Drop the persecution complex, we're not doing anything to you," he said, the struggle to remain patient making itself evident by a renewed flurry of pen-twirling. "What you've done, you've done to yourself. You decided to enter into some kind of weird power struggle with Jake, and it looks like you're losing. It's a pity."

"I was just doing what you said, getting him to go along with what you wanted..." I could hardly get the words out anymore. I sounded stupid and childish, I knew, but I could hardly believe what I was hearing.

Axel smiled, as if at his own joke.

"There's just not much I can do for you. I can't defend you, Pete. I want to, but I can't. All I can do..." He hesitated.

"What?"

"Look." His voice became laced with the sort of overdone concern you see on soap operas. "These kind of allegations can get really ugly. For all of us. You realize what it looks like, don't you? First you fire Jake, the heart and soul of the company, for no obvious reason. Then rumors fly around about corruption and theft and sexual deviance. It won't be long before the press put it all together. You and Jake running an empire of greed and perversion, not satisfied with exploiting the weak minded but even finding it necessary to dig into the corporate cashbox. And then you fall out over dividing the spoils, or maybe you fight over some poor underage girl you've been abusing, I don't know. You try to get rid of Jake, so he leaks the story to the press in revenge." He clicked his tongue and renewed the head shaking. "Not good for any of us."

"That's bullshit and you know it Axel. I don't even think that these stories are coming from Jake. I think they're coming from you," I lashed out.

"They're coming from the press Pete," he said grimly. "Who knows where they get this stuff. All I'm saying is that it can all get a whole lot worse if we don't come to an understanding."

So here it came at last. The bottom line. I waited for Axel to continue.

"I want to help you, Pete. Apatchi would be willing to continue its business relationship with your company and we would do everything within our power and our sense of propriety, behind the scenes, to mitigate the negative publicity."

"Would be willing, if...?"

"If you apologize. Jake gets rehired, you admit to having behaved erratically because of a drug problem, and go into rehab. And when you're out of rehab, you shut up and do what we tell you."

I swallowed hard. "And if I won't?"

Axel stared into space for a moment, then checked his watch again.

"Then it's simple. We toast your gonads for you. We terminate our contract with you, take credit for having rescued Horokinetics from your evil clutches, and go on our merry way. People love and trust Horokinetics, and they'll love and trust the company that has the courage to rescue it. We set up a new company to do what you do. That company would rehire poor misunderstood Jake – the press would lap that up.

"It's all very easy," he said, holding out his open palms as if for me to inspect them.

"But he's started a cult – he's dangerous. You can't... You couldn't..."

Of course he could. Axel couldn't help grinning at me.

"So our product is becoming a spiritual and religious need to a small but growing group of fans? Gee wiz, that's terrible. Pete, do you have any idea how hard it is to convince people to spend money? It looks easy, but only because so much effort goes into it. Marketing is everything, and I don't mean just telling people about products. I mean creating the psychological and social environment in which people feel a need to give you their money, in which it actually brings them happiness and fulfillment and all that crap. Where meaning itself has a price tag. That's not that easy – especially when people are always trying to reject what is mainstream and corporate and commercial. So you have to find new ways of co-opting people's beliefs. If they're all becoming hippies, you make sure that to be a hippie means wearing certain clothing, and you sell that clothing. You make it your brand. We're already good at selling products – what matters today is not selling stuff, but driving taste.

"So now you're telling me that we're at risk of selling people religious beliefs? That we might accidentally be manipulating people at the deepest level imaginable, even to the point that we become one with what they see as a brave countercultural anti-commercial ethos embodied in the spiritual teachings of some medieval heretic poet? That we are learning how to make ourselves a part of the deep memory of our customers? That we hold the keys to the spiral path without which their emotional and spiritual lives are barren? To earn a living by satisfying people's deepest needs isn't such a bad thing, is it?"

I would have loved to smack the snide little shit in the face, but I was too stunned. This was beyond any conspiracy theory of Diego's. My friend was not only a cult leader, but his cult was some kind of elaborate experiment in corporate mind control. He was a fucking Bond villain. They both were.

I bit my lip and then stood up quickly. Brushing off the front of my suit and straightening my tie – a pointless gesture, but it seemed all I could do to look dignified – I turned and walked to the door.

"So what do you say Pete?" Axel's voiced chased me as I grasped the handle and turned it. I paused, then opened the door and turned to face him. The gentle hum of tapping keyboards and hushed voices from the secretarial pool outside drifted into the office. It was like letting oxygen rush back into that poisoned little airlock of an office. I did my best to smile bravely.

"What do I say..." My smile broadened, and Axel looked almost hopeful. "I say fuck off." Without waiting for an answer, I turned to slam the door behind me. It was dead silent, and the eyes of a dozen secretaries fixed upon me as I walked down the hallway back towards reception. I smiled. Victory, however pyrrhic, wouldn't be the same without an audience.

21

I knew what I had to do, but I was paralyzed. None of this made sense. I mean, it did, in the abstract, but somehow I couldn't accept that Jake was working with Axel to do marketing for Apatchi. Jake may have lied to me about a lot of things, but I'd gotten to know the guy. This was not Jake. But Axel's words were pretty unmistakable. He mentioned deep memory, the spiral path – that wasn't official Horokinetics, it was pure Jake.

But I had to know for certain. I needed to talk to Jake.

That was easier said than done. Jake didn't answer the phone, and I wasn't exactly welcome at his place anymore – I dropped by three times over the next day and a half, and every time I saw a few cars in the driveway and at least one guy with big arms and no neck, presumably a cult member, hanging around outside. My scabs and bruises had almost disappeared, and I had no real urge to acquire any new ones. This was getting me nowhere. So when I headed north, up the coast and up the canyon, straight into the heart of neverland for the fourth time, I had something else in mind. I thought about the Rockford Files. I knew what Jim would do.

I drove past the house and left my car a half mile further along where the road widened just enough for me to park. The road more or less followed the creek bed that Jake's house was perched over, so when I recovered about half the distance back along the road I climbed down through the trees and brush and made my way carefully up among rocks and boulders and the occasional pile of beer cans. I'm not sure what I hoped to find but my plan was to work my way up the slope opposite the back of the house and see what I could see through the windows. I expected to see a dozen or so cult members, hanging out and casting fractals or planning Armageddon or doing whatever the fuck else these people do. But if I could locate Jake, get his attention from outside, or maybe find my way in unnoticed... I had to try.

After about ten minutes of struggling through the undergrowth, scraping my hand on a rock and narrowly avoiding a patch of poison oak, I reached a point in the gully just underneath the house. It was already hot in spite of the shade from the trees that clung to either bank above me, and the pathetic trickle of slimy water that still remained in the creek bed made the air close and humid. With branches scratching at my face and gnats circling my head, I began to feel like an extra trudging up the Mekong River in some budget remake of Apocalypse Now. An image passed through my mind of Kurtz's camp, with all those heads on stakes, and I began to wonder what I was doing here.

I started to climb, and after a minute or so I could see that there was at least one motorcycle in the driveway, and what looked, from behind a tree, to be the bumper of a car. My cautiousness had turned out to be well-founded – I was not alone. A twig snapped loudly under my feet, and I froze, listening intensely for voices. There was nothing, and slowly I continued picking my way behind bushes and under trees until I was level with the bottom floor of the house, where I stopped again to watch and listen. Behind the silence, the faint sound of a radio or a TV seemed to whisper through the gully, but the acoustics were funny and I couldn't be sure that it came from the house.

The curtains of the bottom floor window were closed, so I scrambled up a little higher until I was just opposite the next level. From there I could look straight into two windows, behind each of which I could dimly see what appeared to be bedrooms. One contained a chest of drawers and a large bed, and the other seemed empty except for a mirror on the far wall and a table with some clothing piled on top. I was about to continue climbing when I caught sight of movement in the doorway of one of the rooms. I froze, keeping my eyes fixed for a few more minutes, and then saw a shape pass across the door and continue down what I assumed was a hallway connecting the two rooms. From the long brown hair I guessed female, but whoever it was didn't appear at the next doorway so I couldn't get a better look. A few more minutes of nothing. I began once again to climb.

It was then that I heard the voices. Quiet at first, muffled, but growing louder and nearer, and accompanied by a sound like distant hammering or chopping wood. I stayed where I was, crouched low behind a bush, and listened intently, but the acoustics made it seem as if the sound was coming from somewhere on the slope above me. Horses, I realized as the clip clop of their hooves sounded almost next to my head. Two or three people on horses. I looked around but didn't see anyone, and in a minute or two the sound had faded. It took a little while longer for my pulse to return to normal.

This is crazy, I thought, as I worked my way up to the level of Jake's large balcony where we had had dinner that strange evening in November. Here I was, nine months later, hiding in the bushes, probably trespassing, almost certain to be caught and accused of being a burglar or a pervert or God knows what. And for what? There was nothing to see. The balcony and its long dining table were empty. I realized then that what I was really hoping to see was some kind of gathering out there, some group of obvious lunatics chanting hymns, maybe setting the Book of Apeiron to music. But if I'd hoped to catch Jake's followers in the act of sacrificing a goat to the great infinity of the cosmos, I was clearly going to be disappointed. A person or two staying at his house proved nothing.

"He's not there." The low creamy hum of a voice just behind me nearly sent me tumbling down the hill and onto the rocks below. I turned, wishing I had brought a knife, or a bodyguard, or had at least not quit karate classes after only one week. There, standing behind me and a few feet uphill, was Jericho. If she had wanted to, she could easily have kicked me into the gully.

Instead she sat down where she was, putting my head level with the tight crotch of her faded jeans. It was hard not to stare. She was sexier than I'd remembered. I tried to come up with some excuse for being here, but nothing came to mind, so I just stammered like an idiot. She gave me a cool, almost pitying smile, as if suddenly aware of the effect her own body could have.

"Toby, I mean. He's not there, you don't have to worry. Did you want to have a look around?" I turned to look, but she didn't wait for me to answer. "It's not that interesting, actually. You've seen most of it."

"I was just..." I tried to answer, but nothing else came out.

"Hoping to find out what Jake's really up to?" She shook her head and laughed. "Boys. You're all the same. You all want to be James Bond." Rockford, you bitch. But I just stared defiantly. "So you want to know the truth? Little Tara whet your appetite, did she?"

"I don't know what you're talking about," I said, I suppose thinking that in some way I could protect Tara. Sweat was beading on my forehead, but Jericho's skin looked cool and papery dry. "I came by to drop something off for Jake, but I saw that there was someone else in the house, so I wanted to see if maybe he was being robbed. I..."

"You're pretty bad at lying for someone who makes his living at it. Tell you what, I'll give you ten minutes. Ask me whatever you like."

I stared at her a minute, trying to gauge whether or not she was serious. She was.

"Why would you tell me anything?" I asked, shifting forward a little to try to keep my footing on the steep, crumbling hillside.

"Why not? There's nothing you can do to harm us, so why shouldn't you know what we've made of your little invention. Now that you've stumbled into the heart of darkness you might as well get some satisfaction before you go. Nine minutes. Ask."

"So has Jake really turned Horokinetics into a cult?"

"Yes and no. Better to say he's used Horokinetics as a tool to help promote and develop a cult, if that's what you want to call it."

"What would you call it?"

"A way of life. Next question."

"And..." It was crazy. Here I had found a genie who had come out of her bottle to answer all my questions, and I suddenly couldn't think of what to ask. "And it's called the Order of the Ammonite?" She unexpectedly burst out laughing. I nearly lost my balance.

"So Daniel's been talking to you too? Good to know. It's sometimes called that. People join us for different reasons. For some it's spiritual, for some it's intellectual. For some it's political. For the weaker ones, it's a sense of belonging, a need to feel special. We give people what they're looking for. Daniel was looking to be a member of something that sounded big. We gave him that."

"But it has something to do with ammonites," I objected, pulling Jake's necklace from my pocket.

"A symbol, that's all. For the Maori the spiral is a symbol of infinity. We adopted it, but as a fossil." She pulled a similar necklace out from under her own baggy western style shirt, and ran her finger slowly in circles across the front of it. "We're all like that, do you see it? Chamber after chamber of frozen memories, little moments in time unique to each of us, clinging together in an endless spiral into the infinity of our being. That's what makes us what we are, unique and beautiful. That's what makes us generous or wise or petty or terrible, the endless chain of thoughts and feelings and associations that go into making up a human soul. And as the chambers wrap around each other, you can never quite predict which ones will end up next to each other, can you? You go to the park one day as a child, and you play with your mother in the grass, and twenty years later you come to find out that the smell of freshly cut grass means love and safety to you. All from some silly trip to the park." She paused, as if savoring some such memory.

"And then," she continued, an almost dreamy look in her eye, "you run across someone who understands this, and he makes himself become the smell of grass, and next thing you know he *is* love and safety to you, and you'll do anything for him. Like he's inserted himself into your own childhood. Suddenly you can't do without him. You need him as deeply as you need your own selfhood, because now he is your selfhood, and without him you're nothing."

My mind raced back to everything Jake had told me over the past year, to all the childhood memories and feelings he'd helped me to resurrect from the junkyard of TV ads and breakfast cereal jingles that had cluttered up my mind. He had given me myself, but with himself attached to it, like one of those electronic tagging devices they used in clothing stores. "The place within you where no one else can come." Except the one who opened the door for you. Son of a bitch.

"Jake controls people by making them emotionally dependent on him," I said, shaking with resentment. She nodded casually.

"If it makes you feel any better, that wasn't Jake's intention. He dreams of allowing people to explore and discover themselves, to free themselves from the chains with which mass culture attempts to capture our souls and stifle our freedom of thought. But every experiment has its unintended consequences, and emotional dependency was one of them. At least for some people. I think he regrets that part of it. He takes it so personally when someone breaks down or commits suicide. But some people just aren't ready to be liberated."

"That's sick. I can't believe he would do that."

"Of course you can't. You're programmed not to." I blushed, but Jericho just grinned. "No, that's an exaggeration. Really Pete, we need to find you a sense of humor," she said amiably, pausing to chew on a fingernail. "Jake changed my life. He's changed all our lives. He really does want to help people, but you can't just set people free. The first obligation of anyone wanting to help the world is to acquire power." Her smile broadened. Then she added with a look of satisfaction, "I taught him that. I've taught him all sorts of things, although sometimes he's a little slow to realize it. And of course I gave him Apatchi."

"What? Apatchi came to us."

"Yes, sweetheart, of course they did. Axel was very happy to find you. And Jake was very happy to find Axel. Such a good team – it's a pity they hate each other. They both love you, though."

"Bullshit, they both betrayed me."

"Of course they did. That's what you're there for. Axel needed Horokinetics to perform his little experiment in psychological marketing to the anti-globalization left. He needed Jake to make it work, of course. And he needed you to keep Jake in line, and to be able to blame you for having kept Jake in line when the great unwashed started to object. He's very good at all that, you know."

"And what does Jake get out of it all?"

She rolled her eyes and smiled.

"Jake's an idealist. He needed a platform for his ideas, and he needed cash to spread the word. He's very grateful to you. That made it much harder for Axel to drive a wedge between you. But Axel gets what Axel wants."

"And so does Jericho."

"So what does Jericho want?" I asked, trying my best to maintain a tone of sarcasm in my voice. It's not that easy to do when you're frightened and confused.

"All I want is to spread the word. Axel thinks that the spiral path is a corporate tool. Let him. It all goes so much deeper than he can understand. Jake is a genius, a prophet. He just doesn't want to admit it or to accept the consequences of it. Which is fine – that's what he's got me for."

A surreal blur of thoughts crowded my mind. I wanted to kill her. I wanted to jump. I wanted to run off and find Jake and squeeze his throat until he convinced me that none of this was true. But it all made sense. Emily had been right after all – I was in over my head. I had been playing someone else's game all along.

"It's ugly, isn't it?" Jericho said suddenly, looking over my shoulder. I turned to follow her gaze. "The house, I mean. Jake thinks so too. He told me when he bought it that it was an architectural nightmare on the outside, but he didn't care. He said he didn't mind what it looked like from here, as long as it was a beautiful place on the inside, where it mattered. That's what our little family is like, Pete, whether you believe it or not. It's a good place to be, a really beautiful place to look out from, even if it looks ugly from out here."

Jericho allowed herself to slide on her butt a few feet down the hillside towards me so that she was sitting almost at my feet. Slowly she stood up, and as she rose her right hand slid up the inside of my left thigh until it came to rest between my legs.

"You, on the other hand, are not bad looking at all on the outside." Her left hand grabbed me firmly at the back of my neck, and before I knew what was happening, her tongue was in my mouth. The kiss lasted for a few mind-numbing seconds during which I was only aware of being intensely aroused and hopelessly confused. Then, just as suddenly, her mouth pulled away from mine and frowned.

"But on the inside you're a weak and worthless piece of shit," she whispered hoarsely, her lips still lightly brushing against mine. Contempt poured off her like pheromones.

Then, her face betraying nothing, her surprisingly strong hands gave me a short quick push backwards. A strangled gasp seemed to congeal into jelly in my lungs as I felt the emptiness of the gully behind me draw me backwards, like a drain sucking water down its metal throat. My arms flailed uselessly for a split second, already imagining themselves being shattered on the rocks below. And then it stopped. Jericho's hands still held me up, and gently she pulled me back to vertical and I regained my balance.

"Don't get yourself hurt, pretty boy," she muttered, giving my testicles a painful squeeze before letting go of me. Without the slightest fear that I might lash out, she turned her back on me and climbed back up the slope towards the riding trail I hadn't noticed, just a couple dozen feet above where I had been hiding.

I watched her until she disappeared over the edge, and then waited another few minutes to be sure she was really gone before I slowly made my way back to the car.

22

Everyone has his own way of getting motivated. Some people swear by yoga. Others suggest going for a run in the morning before work. Me? I find there's nothing like dangling off a cliff with a maniac holding me up by my balls to spur me into action.

My first action was extremely practical. I went home, made myself a martini, and sat on Diego's balcony. Martinis bring as much clarity to life as anything else does, and as a guide to seeing the way forward are at least as valuable as astrology. So I sat, and drank, and thought, perched five floors up above the hum of traffic and the crashing of waves.

What I began to realize that evening, watching the tiny boats bob their way across the vast rolling sludge of Santa Monica Bay, was that even as its inventor, even as CEO of the company licensed to exploit it, I couldn't have stopped Horokinetics from being misused. I had blocked the occasional proposal from Axel, maybe, but in the end there was nothing I could do to keep it from being used to exploit people. I was hopelessly outgunned. I suppose we all are, but I had a hard time not taking it personally. Growing up with Michael had made me a little bitter about feeling helpless in the face of overwhelming force. But then, it occurred to me as I ate the olive at the bottom of my glass, Michael had prepared me for just this moment. I smiled at the thought, remembering all those stupid pointless games of Stratego we played as kids. It didn't matter what I did, I couldn't win. He was better than I was, for a start, but even if I got ahead, he'd find some way to knock me back. Suddenly the rules would change on me – didn't I know that bombs can't kill generals? That colonels can move diagonally? And if he had forgotten to hide the rule book and I dared to check it, I'd be informed that the book was wrong, that the rules had been revised, or that I just wasn't reading it right.

And that's when it hit me. Stupid bastard, I thought, standing up suddenly and feeling the gin-induced numbness grip my legs. I wasn't entirely helpless after all. I had one chance, one move left, but I would have to play it quickly. I looked around pointlessly, and then sat myself down again and smiled, realizing even in my half-drunken state that I would need to wait until morning. Stupid Michael, finally he had given me something. He was a shit, would always be a shit, but there had been a valuable lesson to be learned at the receiving end of his relentless and unavoidable abuse, a lesson that had given me the simple, liberating answer I needed.

If you can't win anyway, you might as well kick the board and send the pieces flying.

So I called the LA Times. If Axel wanted headlines, I'd give him headlines. The world, or at least that part of it that cared about Horokinetics, was waiting to see what would happen to me. I'd been accused of being a pervert and a thief. They would expect me to protest my innocence – an exclusive interview in this kind of situation would usually mean a carefully scripted conversation in which I would dismiss the allegations against me as nonsense and defend the moral integrity of my company. That was pretty clearly what the reporter expected when she rushed over to the apartment in a parasitic frenzy, like some half-starved mosquito that smelled blood. She was short of breath when I opened the door and let her in, as if she'd run all the way.

"Right," she said, her voice cool and professional once we had settled down at the dining table and she had started her tape recorder, "let's not waste any time. Mr. McFadden, thus far you've been silent about the incriminating stories that have arisen over the past couple of weeks. Are you now prepared to comment?"

Public denial was supposed to be my last move before my General was captured and the game was over. So I played my move, denied everything. And then I did the unexpected. As the reporter listened in disbelief, I exposed the ancient and profound system of Horokinetic divination as a cheap fraud. Foot hit board.

I held nothing back. I explained everything, right from the beginning: the good, the bad, and even the embarrassing parts of how a broke, unemployed middle class 20-something pulled a religion fully formed out of his ass and fooled millions. I described in detail how I, with a couple of friends, had hatched Horokinetics from scratch one night at a cocktail party. I explained that the science was nonsense, Theogenes of Athos a fabrication, the philosophy simply the product of Jake's desire to control people, and the psychological profiling a transparent adaptation of pop-psychology, broad generalizations and cheap flattery in order to separate people from their money. I accused Apatchi of exploiting this already ethically dodgy attempt at spiritual pick-pocketing as a wide-scale marketing gimmick. No attempt at hiding the fact that my motives were cynical and deceitful. No attempt at making excuses. No attempt to exonerate myself at all. Just pure confession. It was ugly.

Of course, if you drop 15 megatons of truth into a sea of bullshit, you have to be prepared for a little mess. That was the idea. With Axel it was a simple solution. Destroy Horokinetics, and I would destroy his new toy. He could target children all he wanted, but if Horokinetics was turned into a transparent, laughable flop overnight it wasn't going to be of much use to him. It might not change much – Axel and the whole army of Axels who worked for Apatchi had plenty of other weapons in their arsenal for the corruption of innocence and all that – but at least it wouldn't be my invention doing the damage. Somehow that mattered to me now.

Jake and Jericho were my bigger concern, and a tougher challenge. Horokinetics was useful to them, I knew, but it was no longer crucial. Jake would continue to attract followers with or without my help, and maybe would even do better without the embarrassment of it. But if the ending of Horokinetics couldn't stop him, the beginnings of it still might. Horokinetics was a fraud, designed for the sole purpose of exploiting the kind of people who swam in the murky waters of the occult and metaphysics in search of improbable but inspiring answers to life's questions. In other words, it had been invented as a mockery of just the sort of people who were inclined to join Jake's cult. I figured if I could expose Jake as the sort of guy who would take part in such a cold-hearted fraud, then I would have gone a long way in ending his influence over people. The shock for his followers would be brutal, I knew, and the possible consequences for the more disturbed ones frightened me, but in the long run it had to be done. He would rise again, but not through me. My days as Godmaker were over.

I had devoted a year of my life to building a company, and now, for my all my trouble, I had nothing. No, not quite nothing. I'd earned a very good salary, and a decent chunk of money from the sale, which in itself was enough to live on comfortably for a while. But the big money, the career, the glow of success were gone. I was back where I started: an unemployed computer geek fallen prey to the very real hostility of a virtual world.

At least, I figured, I'd have the satisfaction of putting things right. Of bringing those bastards down with me, watching the pieces fly. So I sat back and watched. My shocking revelations in the LA Times took everyone by surprise, and it managed to piss off people from all walks of life. But not exactly in the way I had hoped.

Our clients were outraged, not at Jake or Apatchi, but at me. The New Age and astrology community were furious at my insinuation that someone could just invent a system of divination from scratch and convince so many people – people accustomed to the vagaries of the spiritual realm – that it worked. "Does Mr. McFadden really want to suggest," mused one letter to the editor of a prominent New Age magazine, "that the high success rate enjoyed by his former colleagues in the field of fractal horokinetics is just some kind of coincidence? If so, his claim to being a fraud is perfectly valid, at least in this instance. And a bad fraud at that." Others seemed to agree, as letters and articles poured into newspapers pointing out all the logical and illogical flaws in my claim. My assertion that Jake had invented the Book of Apeiron was laughed off as almost unworthy of comment. You can't invent history, one editorial asserted. Another paper printed a contemptuous letter from a German philologist who found it "amusing" that I thought I could wish out of existence the entire body of work of one of the greatest thinkers of the late Byzantine period.

It took about a week for a common consensus to develop that I was nothing more than a vindictive parasite. I had contributed the technology as Jake's helper and apostle but, corrupted by greed, I had turned Judas, and had tried to destroy by lies what I could not possess by betrayal. Horokinetics was real, it was just me who was fake.

You did it too well, Pete, I could hear Jake saying at the back of my mind. We did it too well. They believe, and they won't turn back. Why should they accept your invitation to eat gruel when they've tasted cake? Remember, I once told you that beauty is truth, truth beauty. We have created something that is beautiful, that makes sense to people, that they want to believe. You can't just say "oops, never mind." It's grown beyond you. Ideas are children. They grow up and leave home, and you can't stop them.

I had created Horokinetics based on my belief that given the choice between the comfort of faith and the indifferent cruelty of fact, people will discard fact. And in the end, I was right. The site was more popular than ever. For a about a week the commentary continued to flow. My story was treated with universal contempt.

Not long afterwards Apatchi International held a press conference about the future of Horokinetics. Their contract with me had been terminated, and the rights to Horokinetics were to be leased for a nominal amount to an organization called The Theogenes Trust.

"We feel that Peter McFadden has misused Horokinetics, and as a family of companies, committed to family values, we are acting to maintain the integrity of this important piece of our intellectual and spiritual heritage," announced the company spokeswoman, without the slightest touch of irony. "We hope that under new direction Horokinetics can flourish and continue to provide inspiration and guidance without the interference of crass commercialism."

So Apatchi was riding in to save Horokinetics from the evil clutches of nasty old Pete McFadden. It was a ridiculous but disturbingly convincing story. Apatchi, as such a family-oriented company concerned about protecting the legacy of Theogenes from the likes of me, would not entrust Horokinetics to just anyone. The Apatchi group had its beginnings as a merger of two very successful family companies, the spokeswoman explained. Allied Agricultural merged with PT&C over 30 years ago, but the family empires behind those two businesses had stayed very much involved with the new corporation. And Horokinetics would now be entrusted to the granddaughter of the founder of PT&C, a woman who had earned a glowing reputation in her philanthropic work and in her funding of The Paulson Institute for Higher Sciences, a well-respected think tank for all things spiritual.

"We are confident that Horokinetics will thrive," the spokeswoman concluded, "under the wise and trustworthy guidance of Jericho Paulson."

23

Can anything be truly unexpected in a fractal universe? That's a question for Jake, not me, but I imagine he'd say yes. "Just as there's a pattern to the chaos, so there is chaos to the pattern," as Theogenes of Athos was reportedly fond of saying. Expect the worst, I'd say. It's not very deep, maybe, but at least it prepares you for trouble.

I saw Jake about a month later.

It was an afternoon in late October. By then the Santa Ana winds have filled the canyons with the heat, dust and higher suicide rates they bring every year, and the first rains have washed them clean again. The sun is still warm, but no longer brutal, and the cooler air seems to open a hole in the inversion layer so the smog can drain out of Southern California and sneak across the border into Mexico.

Once I had plucked up the courage to start leaving the apartment again, I'd begun to spend a lot of time in the canyons. Driving, of course, but I started walking more as well. Often I'd drive up Stunt Road, and on the way I'd pass the clump of oaks where the dragons lived. It made me smile. They were back, those dragons, after a long absence, nesting in the rich warm stream of memory that still flowed through that valley, and whenever I'd start to get depressed I'd pay them a little visit. And then, with plenty of time to kill, I'd park up at the top, walk around a little and watch the sun set into the Pacific. It was a good way to spend an evening.

That particular day I was throwing rocks down into the ravine, watching the sun as it slowly gathered its army of reds and oranges for the final march across the blue black horizon. It was a pleasant, cool evening, and my thoughts slid carelessly across the landscape, taking in colors and smells and converting them into nothing more and nothing less than a vague sense of time and place, a mood and a memory that would stay with me once it grew dark and I returned to Santa Monica. I picked up a good flat stone, smooth with rounded edges: a perfect thrower, the kind you rarely find except in creek beds. Good luck – this one would fly.

And then I heard it – a faint and rhythmic clicking off in the distance, steadily growing louder and clearer to become identifiable as horses. After a few minutes they came into view, approaching at a good clip along a dirt track that joined up with the road not far from where I stood. Was it the shyness that comes with being a notorious villain that made me move a little ways down the hill to avoid being seen, or was it some kind of prescience? There were four people on horseback, and as they neared the road I recognized Jericho at the head of them. And just behind her, the unmistakable form of Jake, tall and proud on his horse, blond hair shaking carelessly behind him as he came within thirty yards of where I sat behind an Indian tobacco bush. I could see his face clearly – if he felt any guilt or regret for what had happened, he showed no sign of it now. He looked peaceful, happy, unaffected by the tragedy of the world around him. He looked in control.

As the group turned their backs to me and began their descent down the road to my left, heading deep into the canyon towards the ocean, I began turning the rock over and over in my hand. I looked at it closely, half-expecting to find a fossil in it. An ammonite, maybe, a symbol that would suggest some cosmic significance for everything that had happened, everything I'd done or had done to me, I still wasn't quite sure. But there was nothing. Just a decent sized rock, waiting for me to choose it a target. I looked again at the receding backs of the riders.

It was then that Jake looked back. Maybe it was a coincidence, or maybe he'd seen me when they went by and only now had decided to acknowledge my presence. Either way, he turned his head and saw me there, with God knows what sort of twisted expression on my face, glaring at him and holding a rock. Our eyes met for maybe a count of three. He didn't seem angry or hopeful or sad, didn't seem at all worried that I might hurl the rock at him. He just gave me this blank look, as if inviting me to fill it with whatever meaning I wanted, and then turned back and went on his way.

I stayed there up at the top of Stunt Road a while longer, turning that stone over and over in my hand long after Jake and the others had vanished. The air slowly grew colder. The sky started turning red over the long stretch of Pacific coastline that curved past LA on its northward sweep towards San Francisco. Once Stunt Road hits coast there are only two ways to go. Left would take me back to Los Angeles. Right would take me to Emily. Finally, with all my strength, in one fluid, sweeping motion I pitched the stone as far out into empty space as I could, and turned to walk back to the car. Starting the engine, I put her into drive, and coasted slowly down towards the lights now appearing in the gathering haze below.

Acknowledgements

No writer is the author of his own book. Writing may be by nature a solitary vocation, but producing a book is a highly social process. Over nearly a decade I have worked on this in the company and with the collaboration of many others. My indifferent fellow passengers on the London Underground, my alternately bemused and irritated colleagues at Freshfields Bruckhaus Deringer, supportive mothers in the Queen's Park playground... they all left their mark in one way or another. If nothing else, their constant presence reminded me that the people who read a novel are as much a part of it as the characters who populate it.

I cannot list everyone who directly contributed to this book, but I would like to particularly thank my wife Sophia, who has read and helped me refine *Stunt Road* over and over again for the best part of a decade. I also owe an enormous debt of gratitude to family and friends who took time out of their busy schedules to proof-read the manuscript, and who had the frankness and courage to point out nonsense and call it by name. Your willingness to criticize is the greatest proof of friendship I could ever hope for. This book is the product of and a testament to your generosity.